SILENCING EVE

ALSO BY IRIS JOHANSEN

SILENCING EVE

IRIS JOHANSEN

**Doubleday Large Print
Home Library Edition**

ST. MARTIN'S PRESS ✖ NEW YORK

This Large Print Edition, prepared especially for Double-day Large Print Home Library, contains the complete, unabridged text of the original Publisher's Edition.

This is a work of fiction. All of the characters, organizations, and events portrayed in this novel are either products of the author's imagination or are used fictitiously.

SILENCING EVE. Copyright © 2013 by Johansen Publishing LLLP. All rights reserved. Printed in the United States of America. For information, address St. Martin's Press, 175 Fifth Avenue, New York, N.Y. 10010.

ISBN 978-1-62490-781-4

**This Large Print Book carries the
Seal of Approval of N.A.V.H.**

My daughter, Tamara, is always saying
life is good no matter how tough it gets.
But it is her strength and resilience and ability
to find joy in every moment that makes life
good for all of us close to her. She lights
our lives in a very special way.

ACKNOWLEDGMENTS

My son, Roy, is a constant help and inspiration to me even when we're not collaborating on a book. Whenever you see that Kendra has done something particularly clever, you can bet Roy has had something to do with it.

SILENCING EVE

come together, they had found a closeness that had saved them both. "And he
loves Luke. He wouldn't hurt him," said Jin.
Chang didn't always have the same opinion of right and wrong as others. "He knows
that it would break our friendship if he did
something he knew I wouldn't forgive. Luke
is valuable to the friendship and to Jin Chang."

"You sound as if you're trying to talk
yourself into something."

"Nonsense. Jin Chang is brilliant, and
Luke is learning more from him than he'd
ever learn in school. These last months in
Hong Kong have been wonderful for him."
She added. "But thank you for calling Jin
Chang and telling him what happened. I'll
call Luke again tonight and explain."

"You're welcome. I was just clearing the
decks for you. I knew you'd be on the hunt
as soon as Quinn told you that you had a
chance at Hadley Eve. Remember to tap
Venable for any information you can
squeeze out of him." He hung up.

She pressed the disconnect and slipped
the phone in her pocket. She felt a sudden
rush of hope as well as excitement. John
Gallo was on the move.

Time for her to move, too.

CHAPTER

1

Atlanta Airport

Dead.

Eve was dead.

The words kept drumming in Catherine Ling's mind as she walked up the gateway to the terminal. No matter how many times she told herself it was true, she still couldn't believe it. Not Eve Duncan. Not her friend, the woman who had helped to save her son.

"Agent Ling?" A sandy-haired young man was running after Catherine as she headed for baggage. "I'm Brad Linden." He showed her his CIA credentials. "Agent Venable sent me to pick you up and take you to the memorial service."

"Then go get your car while I pick up my bag." Catherine Ling didn't stop as she strode ahead of him. "And why the hell didn't Venable come and get me himself? I need to have a few choice words with him."

"He's at the service. It's going on right now. He didn't want to show disrespect. I'm afraid you're a little late."

"Because no one told me that Eve—" She broke off. He was gazing at her warily, and she knew she must be radiating all the ferocity and sadness she was feeling. There was no use ripping at Venable's errand boy because Venable had left her in ignorance of Eve's death or the search when she was kidnapped several days ago. He would only try to make excuses for the inexcusable. Yes, she had been undercover in the jungles of Colombia, but that didn't mean that she wouldn't have somehow extricated herself and come home to help find Eve. Venable should have gotten word to her. No, she'd had to find out in Miami when she'd retrieved her own computer and been hit in the gut with the news story in **USA Today.** "Just have that car out front and get me to that memorial service ASAP, Linden."

While she was waiting for her bag, she scanned the story in **USA Today** again. What did she expect to find? She had practically memorized the damn story on the flight from Miami. She supposed that she was trying to find an answer when there was no answer. The actual story of Eve's kidnapping and murder was fairly cut-and-dried. The murderer had obviously been unbalanced and ignited explosives at a ghost town in Colorado, where he had been holding Eve captive. Since the details were sparse, they had concentrated on Eve Duncan herself. Her background, her accomplishments, quotes from famous law-enforcement officials who had used her services. All were very worth reading, Catherine thought bitterly. It wasn't often that the media got a chance to spotlight a genuinely good person. Eve had been an illegitimate child born in the slums who had given birth herself at sixteen to a little girl, Bonnie. The child had changed her life. Eve had finished her education and straightened out her mother, who was on drugs. Then the world had come crashing down when her Bonnie, seven years old, had been kidnapped and killed. Yet Eve hadn't let it destroy her. She had gone back to school and studied forensic sculpting. Since then, she had become perhaps the most skilled forensic sculptor in the world. She had brought closure to thousands of families whose children would never have been identified without her help.

Never let a good deed go unpunished, Catherine thought. That old adage was too true in Eve's case.

And, dammit, she was misting up again. She closed her computer and jammed it in her carry-on bag. She grabbed her phone and tried Joe Quinn again. Voice mail. She'd called him from the Miami Airport as soon as she'd read the story about Eve's memorial service being held today. It had gone to voice mail then, too. She'd left a message, but he hadn't called back. Maybe he didn't want to talk to her, she thought. Why should he? He had loved Eve with every ounce of his being, and he thought Catherine hadn't even cared enough to try to find her when that monster, Doane, had kidnapped her.

I cared, Joe. God, how I care. I would have come.

She wanted to kill Venable.

She might do it if he didn't have an explanation that she could tolerate.

And she wanted to release the tears that she had been forcing back since she'd read that damn news story. Her friend was dead, and, somehow, she felt as if it was her fault, that if she'd known, she might have been able to stop it. Lord, her eyes were stinging.

Not here. Not now.

When she was alone with her thoughts and memories of Eve and had gotten through this memorial service.

Not even a funeral because that crazy bastard had blown them both to bits.

She wished with all her heart that Doane was still alive and here, so that she could personally send him straight to hell.

But Venable had cheated her out of that pleasure, too, by not bringing her into the picture when Eve needed her most.

Damn him.

She grabbed her bag as it went around the carousel and headed for the door.

God, Ling was gorgeous, Bradford thought as he pulled his car close to the curb where Catherine Ling was waiting impatiently. She was sleek and sexy, with shoulder-length dark hair and eyes tilted slightly, increasing the exotic magnetism she radiated. He knew she was the illegitimate daughter of an American soldier and a Korean whore who was half-Russian. She'd been born in Saigon but had grown up on the streets of Hong Kong. He'd heard stories about her from other agents, but he'd never met her. The stories had been interesting but very, very lethal. She was sharp and independent and likely to run her own show when she was on a mission. Something Venable definitely didn't like but evidently tolerated because she got the job done. She'd been CIA since Venable had picked her up in Hong Kong when she was only fourteen. What was she now? Late twenties?

"Got everything?" He leaned over and opened the passenger door for her. "I'll have you at Quinn's lake cottage in thirty minutes. I just called Venable, and he said the service had just ended."

"Dammit, I missed it? I'm surprised you got through to him," she said sarcastically. "How nice. He's not been answering my calls."

Oops. "I'm sure that's just a technical error. He was very concerned about you." He hurriedly handed her his computer. "I've pulled up the files on Doane and the catastrophe at the ghost town. Venable was sure you'd want to look them over."

"I would have liked to look them over before the son of a bitch blew her up." She gazed blindly down at the computer. "You've read it. Fill me in."

"Eve Duncan was kidnapped from her lake cottage home in north Atlanta several days ago. Because she's one of the foremost forensic sculptors in the world, it was assumed at the time that the kidnapper might be one of the nuts or serial killers she'd targeted by her work."

"But if Venable is involved, then that's not why she was killed," Catherine said grimly. "I'm surprised Eve let him pull her into a CIA mission."

"She didn't. James Doane had been in a safe house in Goldfork, Colorado, and slipped away from the agent guarding him. When Venable realized he was gone, he thought there might be a possibility of his heading toward Eve Duncan, but he couldn't be sure that—"

"Why? Why would he go after Eve?"

"That's not in the report. You'll have to ask Venable."

"You can bet I will. Venable fouled up and didn't protect Eve. Is that the truth?"

"I'm sure there is an explanation. As I said, he wasn't sure Eve Duncan would be a target."

She drew a deep breath. "Let's go down another path. Why was Jim Doane in that safe house? Was he a foreign agent? A witness?"

He shook his head. "He was the father of Kevin Relling, who was assassinated five years ago. His son was in Special Forces in the Army and turned very dirty. He was working with al-Qaeda in Pakistan and blocking the hunt for Bin Laden. He also indulged his penchant for raping and killing little girls in whatever city he found himself. He killed the five-year-old daughter of General Tarther in Marseilles because the general was trying to zero in on the al-Qaeda group."

"Very dirty. Scum."

"The general went crazy and eventually hired a hit man, Lee Zander, to find and go after Doane's son. Zander killed him and hired a funeral director to cremate the remains. Doane arrived too late to grab anything but his son's skull from the furnace."

"Okay, then that would be a reason for his kidnapping Eve. Doane wanted Eve to do a reconstruction on the son's skull. Right?"

"I understand that she was doing just that while she was his captive."

"Then why would the crazy bastard kill her? She was smart. If that job was the ransom he wanted, she wouldn't risk her life by refusing to do a reconstruction."

"You'll have to ask Venable," he said again. "All I know is that Doane took her to a ghost town in the Rio Grande Forest in Colorado. We traced him to an abandoned saloon there. When our units, Quinn, and Jane MacGuire were closing in on him, he set off a charge that blew up the saloon and half the town." He glanced at her. "You look— Are you okay?"

"No, I'm not okay. It shouldn't have happened. Someone should have stopped it. Venable should have stopped it." Her voice fell to a whisper. "I should have stopped it."

"Venable said that you were on a very important mission and that you—"

"Screw Venable." Her gaze shifted to the

passing scene out the window. "Anything else? Are they sure she was in that damn saloon?"

"Yes. Everyone saw Doane take her into the place, and, a few minutes later, our infrared scopes confirmed two people inside. They were still on the scopes when the place blew."

"DNA?"

"We're working on it, but it may take a long while. There wasn't much left. As I said, the blast practically leveled the town. She was in—"

"I don't want the details. Not now."

It appeared that Ling was not as tough as he had heard, Bradford thought. Or maybe she's just human, like the rest of us. "I hear Eve Duncan was quite a woman. It's a great loss. Everyone from senators to a dozen police chiefs are at that memorial service."

"They don't know how great a loss," Catherine said. "They know the work, not the woman, not the friend." She was silent for a while, forcing herself to read the file. Then she looked up, and asked, "How close are we?"

"Five minutes. The service was held outside by the lake at the cottage where she lived with Joe Quinn. He thought she'd like it to be at her home. Pretty place."

She didn't speak for a moment. "I know. That's where I first met Eve. I stayed with her while she worked on a computer age progression on photos of my son."

That was one of the stories about Ling, too. Her son had been held prisoner by a Russian criminal for nine years, and she had never ceased trying to find him. It was only after Eve Duncan had helped her that she had been able to locate him. "I'm sure you were very grateful."

"Are you?" She looked at him. "You have no idea."

He pulled his gaze away with some difficulty. Catherine Ling might be as lethal as a striking panther, but he was suddenly finding himself having visions of ladies in distress and knights in shining armor and himself somewhere in the mix. Crazy. It just went to show how right the stories were about the fascination she effortlessly exerted. "I know you're upset. If I can help, just call me." He almost bit his tongue. Venable would not like the idea of his moving into Ling's camp when she was definitely at odds with him. "Though I'm sure Venable will straighten everything out."

He swung into the grove that Quinn had designated as a parking area. "Here we are. I'd drive you closer, but there are people milling all over the place." He quickly got out, ran around, and opened the door for her. "Everyone is around the cottage down toward the lake. Would you like me to go with you?"

"No." She strode toward the cottage. "I'd advise you to stay clear. You wouldn't like dodging the flak."

He watched her disappear from view, then reluctantly turned away. Catherine Ling might be wrong. He found himself experiencing a strange blankness as if he'd been witnessing a fireworks display, and now there was only dark sky.

It might be worth dodging a little flak to see her in action.

Catherine spotted Venable in the crowd two minutes after she turned the corner of the cottage.

He was wearing a dark suit and looked surprisingly formal. He was talking to a man in an NYPD uniform. Then he lifted his gaze and saw her at the edge of the crowd.

Wariness.

Then he lifted the wineglass in his hand and nodded.

Catherine drew a deep breath and tried to smother the anger. If she confronted Venable now, she would make a scene, and that was the last thing she wanted to do at this service honoring Eve. She'd deal with him later. She nodded curtly and turned to look for Joe Quinn.

He was standing talking to a tall, white-haired man she vaguely recognized as a congressman. Joe looked pale and unsmiling, but he could obviously still function. She started to make her way toward him.

He looked up and saw her. Then, with a word to the congressman, he left him and was walking quickly toward her. "Catherine."

"Joe, I tried to call you." She took a step closer. "I didn't know. Believe me, I didn't know anything, or I would have come to—"

"I saw that you'd called, but I couldn't talk." He took her elbow and was propelling her toward the corner of the house. "I've been surrounded all day." He stopped as he reached an unoccupied stretch of lawn on the side of the cottage. He took a minute to look around and make sure there was no one near. "I can't really talk now either, but you have to know, dammit."

"What are you talking about? I do know. I just found out today in Miami. I can't tell you how—"

"Listen." His hands grasped her shoulders. "It's not what you think." His voice lowered. "Go into the cottage and talk to Kendra Michaels. I told her earlier that you were coming. I knew I couldn't get away from this hullabaloo."

"Joe, what the hell are you saying?"

"I'm saying that though you look terrific in black, you shouldn't go into mourning." He turned away. "I'll see you later. Go talk to Kendra."

She stared in shock as he walked away. For a moment, she couldn't get her breath. He couldn't mean what she thought he meant.

She closed her eyes. Oh, God. Let it be true. Let it all be a nightmarish mistake.

Let Eve still be alive.

• • •

Catherine entered the cottage and slammed the door behind her. "Kendra Michaels?"

"Yes." Kendra was standing at the window, staring down at the mourners moving from group to group on the lawn bordering the lake. "That's me. And you are?"

"Catherine Ling." She crossed the room and showed her ID. "Joe told me to come to see you. Apparently it's your job to tell me what the hell is going on here."

Kendra nodded. "Joe called me and told me you were coming up to ask questions. I just had to verify your ID. There are too many reporters drifting around here at the memorial service. Eve was very well-known." She smiled faintly. "Very private, but everyone knew she was phenomenal."

"You're damn right she was." Her lips tightened. "We're both talking past tense. Yet from what Joe said, I'm guessing she's probably very much alive." Her voice was uneven. "Don't tell me that he's wrong. I won't have it."

"Sorry. Joe didn't steer you wrong. I've just gotten used to playing the sorrowful, regretful friend in the last week," Kendra said. "I believe the chances are excellent that Eve is alive."

Catherine felt a wave of relief surge through her. "Thank God."

"I can't be absolutely sure, but I'd bet every particle of my experience and judgment that she lived through the explosion at that ghost town in Colorado."

"And why should I trust your judgment?"

"Maybe you shouldn't." Kendra tilted her head. "I don't believe you have much to do with trust."

Catherine's eyes narrowed on her face. "Why? Did Eve or Joe tell you about me?"

"No. Just an observation. Did Eve mention me?"

"Yes, Eve told me about you a few months ago. You were born blind, but a surgical procedure gave you your sight just a few years ago, is that right?"

Kendra nodded.

"But while you were blind, you developed your other senses to such a degree that you've become quite the detective."

Kendra shrugged. "Make that a reluctant detective. My profession is music therapy. I've helped out on a few cases."

"You weren't reluctant as far as Eve was concerned."

"No, we became friends. You help your friends. Then, when I heard she was abducted, I dropped everything and came right down." Kendra studied her. "Joe said you were close to Eve, but she never mentioned you to me."

"Why should she? Our relationship was . . . confidential."

"Confidential? That's an interesting designation for a close—" Kendra stopped. "Oh, you're CIA, aren't you?"

Catherine's eyes widened. "Where did that come from?"

"I don't expect you to confirm it. I was watching out the window, and I saw you and that CIA guy, Venable, exchange a look when you arrived. He was tense, you were angry. Oh, yes, you know each other. Do you work for him?"

Catherine looked away.

"I don't expect you to answer that either." She smiled faintly. "Oh, and you quite often wear a shoulder holster under that black jacket, but not today."

Catherine nodded. "Out of respect." She

looked under her left arm. "It's that obvious?"

"It's a little baggy there. Nothing anyone would notice."

"Except you?"

"Except me."

"Or maybe a North Korean assassin. It might be time to invest in a more discreet shoulder holster."

"I'm sure you're equipped with other weapons." Kendra tilted her head. "I'm good with dialects, but I'm having a tough time with yours. You're clipping your consonants and slightly flattening your vowel sounds. Did the linguistic people at Langley teach you to do that?"

"They may have."

"It's very effective. I have no idea where you're from."

"Good. I've made a few enemies over the years, and the last thing I want is for them to be able to find out anything about me."

"Then you've done a good job."

Catherine gave her a cool glance. "You're doing quite an efficient job yourself. You're laying out your credentials on display to show me just how good that judgment I challenged is."

Kendra smiled. "I thought it would save time in the long run. I don't need your trust, but I need an open mind."

Catherine took a step closer. "So are you going to tell me what happened in Colorado?"

"How much do you know already?"

"Just what I read in the newspaper and the CIA records. Plus Joe's rather cryptic reassurance that Eve is probably still alive, which makes this entire day rather surreal."

"That it is."

"Then talk to me," Catherine said fiercely. "I don't have many friends, and I don't like the idea of losing one. I don't like it so much that I'm on the edge of violence. I've got to know something."

"I'll tell you everything I know. When the saloon exploded in that ghost town, the infrared scanners showed two people inside."

"Those recordings are always very accurate. The explosion was so powerful, it rocked the whole town. There's no way anyone could have survived that."

"They didn't. And we found the skeletal fragments and burned flesh."

"Am I missing something?"

"Those two people were possibly dead already. But they weren't Eve and Doane."

Catherine was silent. Let it be true, she prayed. "Are you sure?"

"We're still waiting on DNA, but I'm sure. I think each of those bodies was wrapped in thermal-reflective sleeping-bag liners to hold their body heat for the infrared scopes. I went down with the forensic team after they extinguished the fire and found traces of the reflective material at the site."

"But there were a dozen witnesses who saw Eve and Doane go into that saloon just a few minutes before that blast. How could they have gotten away without someone's seeing them?"

"Doane obviously knew the area very well. They were in a ghost town in the bottom of a small, bowl-shaped valley. Locals call it the punch bowl. It had been raining heavily, and the street was muddy. The strange thing was that it wasn't flooded."

"Why was that strange?"

"With water coming down from every side of the valley, it had no place to go. It should have flooded, unless . . . it was draining to someplace."

Catherine thought about it. "Like a cavern?"

"Very good. There were fissures that ran behind the buildings. Water drained through them to a stream in an underground cavern. It feeds an even larger stream that runs down the mountain. We didn't know about the cavern and the underground stream, but we used the water from that bigger stream to help put out the fire."

Catherine could feel the excitement surging within her. "You think Doane took Eve out the back and down into this cavern?"

"It's a twenty-foot drop, but the water is deep enough that it wouldn't have been a problem. The fissure was so narrow that when Doane first got to the ghost town, it was easy for him to cover it with brush to hide the cavern. And the explosion completely covered up the fissures with debris, so we didn't even know they were there until I looked for them later. Doane did a good job of covering his tracks."

"Do we know whose bodies were in there?"

"Not yet. There wasn't much left of them. We were lucky they weren't vaporized. But the fact that it was so muddy gave me some interesting tracks outside in front of the saloon. An off-road vehicle arrived, and Terence Blick, a partner of Doane's, stepped out of it. Then Blick walked around to the back, unloaded something heavy, and walked into the saloon with it."

"You got all that from footprints?"

"I had a run-in with Blick a couple days before. I stopped to see if I could help a policeman he'd shot down, and I saw Blick's footprints then. He was wearing different boots, but the stride was unmistakable. He swung his legs in such a way that the right and left prints were directly in front of each other, almost single file. Fairly unique. And the footsteps sunk about three inches deeper after he walked around to the back of the truck."

"You think he took a body into that saloon. But there were two bodies in there."

"I believe the second corpse could be Blick himself."

Catherine slowly nodded. "Doane killed his own partner?"

"Blick's footprints went in, but never came out. But the off-road vehicle was driven out of the town. I'd bet Doane charged Blick with securing a woman's corpse, but he needed a second one, a male. So he killed him. He went outside in the street with Eve and showed us all that she was there, then went back inside. He slipped out the back and jumped, either dragging or carrying Eve with him, into the cavern before Venable's team arrived with their infrared gear. He had a raft down there and rode the stream about three miles away, where he had Blick's vehicle parked. I saw the prints on the bank. The tire tread belonged to a set of Super Swamper TSL. That meant it was almost certainly the same 4×4 off-road vehicle that Blick drove into the ghost town. Doane took Eve away while the town was still burning." She smiled bitterly. "Quite a distraction."

"How long did it take you to piece this together?"

"Too long. Hours. Doane could have taken Eve anywhere by the time we figured out that they were still alive. It might have taken me even longer if Margaret hadn't—" She broke off and leaned back against Eve's workbench. "I should have seen it all sooner. But I couldn't see anything clearly that night. All I could think about was that moment when the saloon blew only minutes after I'd seen Eve dragged through that door. We were all in shock."

"I can understand that."

"Well, I don't understand. I should have been thinking, acting, not feeling."

"It's amazing that you figured it out at all. Eve was right to be so impressed with you."

"Fat lot of good it's done. She's still out there . . . with him."

Catherine glanced at the funeral guests outside. "Why this charade? Why not let on that you know they're still alive?"

"Venable supposedly has an army of agents searching for Doane and Eve as we speak. We thought we might have better luck if Doane didn't know we were still looking for him. He was evidently counting on the fact that DNA on those skeletal fragments could take weeks to come back and allow him to proceed with his plans." Her lips twisted. "According to Venable, Doane is very proud of his ability to concoct his nasty little plans. This particular plan was very intricate, and he clearly wanted us to think they were both dead, so that he'd be free to go forward."

"And do what?"

"He has a target. Lee Zander, the man

who killed his dirtbag of a son, Kevin. Not an easy target. Zander is probably one of the foremost assassins in the world."

"And what does Eve have to do with his damn target? I thought that she'd been taken to do a reconstruction on the son."

"That's what we all thought. But it appears that wasn't Doane's primary motive. Doane thinks Zander is Eve's father. Since Zander killed his son, he wants to see him bleed as he kills his daughter in front of him."

Catherine went still. "Father? And is he?"

"I don't know. Venable seems to think that he is." She shook her head. "But what does matter is that Doane thinks it's true."

Frustrated, Catherine said, "There are too many unknowns. What the hell is happening here?"

"I don't know. Ask Venable. Though I'm not sure he'll tell you."

"What do you mean?"

"I don't like the way he was trying to run the show at the ghost town." She paused. "I thought he was being stupid by bringing in an attack team to go after Doane in that saloon. But now I'm not sure if he was stupid or a little too smart."

"What are you saying? You think Venable's crooked?"

"I think he has an agenda, and Eve's not at the top of it." She met Catherine's eyes. "And why didn't he let you know about what was happening to Eve? You're her friend, and I'd judge you're fairly lethal. Why not bring you into this chaos of a situation?"

"That's what I asked him."

"Were you satisfied with the answer?"

"No. He's been dodging it."

"Good. Then you'll not trust him any more than you do me."

She smiled faintly. "But I believe I'm beginning to trust you, Kendra." Her smile faded. "I've got to get this clear in my mind, but I don't want to blow your little scenario. Who knows that Eve is alive?"

"Joe, Zander, Jane MacGuire, Margaret Douglas, and the people who have been concerned with the hunt for Eve from the beginning."

"Not Eve's mother, Sandra?"

"No, it was Joe Quinn's call. He decided that she was too erratic to trust with that information." She made a face. "Actually, Joe was being diplomatic. Replace erratic with selfish. You'll notice she didn't come today—too devastated. But not too devastated to give one TV and three print interviews this morning." She shrugged. "I don't know what their relationship was, but it was definitely complex."

Catherine was mentally going over the other names Kendra had given her. "Margaret Douglas . . ." she repeated. "You broke off in the middle of telling me something about a Margaret. Why?"

"Margaret is . . . difficult."

"You don't want to talk about her." Catherine's eyes narrowed on her face as she tried to remember the exact words Kendra had spoken. She had been so upset and intent on digging for the truth that she had dismissed it at the time. "You said something about your not being able to put the entire scenario together sooner except for her."

"No, just not as soon." She turned back to the window. "Look, I'm not going to try to explain Margaret to you. She has to be experienced. All I'm telling you is that she's a good kid and no phony. I'd trust her in the trenches."

"But I'm not you. I'll make up my own

mind," Catherine said. Her gaze followed Kendra's to the crowd below. "Which one is Margaret?"

"The girl standing next to Jane Mac-Guire. She tends to stay close to her when she can. She's a bit protective."

"Of Jane MacGuire?" She had met Jane, and no one appeared to be less in need of protection. Strong. Very strong. And Kendra had been referring to Margaret as a girl, even a kid. She gazed curiously at Jane and Margaret standing beside her.

Golden. Margaret seemed bathed in sunlight, tanned, sun-streaked hair, slim in her simple black dress. She did look young, nineteen or twenty at the oldest. She was appropriately solemn for the occasion but there was an aura of vitality, a barely re-strained exuberance, held in check. "Why protective?"

"Jane saved her life. She took a bullet for her from Doane's cohort, Blick, when all of this madness first started. Margaret believes in payback."

"Interesting. I believe I have to talk to this Margaret Douglas." She turned toward the door. "Would you like to come along and introduce me?"

"No, I have some thinking to do. You're on your own."

"Thinking?"

"Things are changing," Kendra said soberly. "I have some decisions to make."

"Don't we all," Catherine said. She opened the door. "Thank you, Kendra. And thank God you found out that we might still have a chance of freeing her."

"I should have found out sooner. It's to do all over again."

"Maybe not. It appears a trap is in the offing."

"He's managed to sidestep traps so far." She paused. "Good luck, Catherine."

The words sounded curiously final, Catherine thought, as she left the house and ran down the porch steps. Imagination? Maybe. Everything was looking dark to her right now.

Dismiss it.

She had to probe, to find which way to go. She had not been pleased that Kendra Michaels had been suspicious about Venable's motives and response to that disaster in the ghost town. Kendra had impressed her as being very sharp. Catherine had worked with Venable since she was a girl of fourteen and knew him as well as anyone. He was always an enigma, but he was a professional. Yet his priorities were always to the job, and she could see that if he had been torn, Eve might have been downgraded in importance.

So walk carefully and discreetly around Venable.

And don't trust him any more than she could throw him.

She started to make her way through the crowd toward Jane and Margaret.

But she'd only gone a few steps when Margaret Douglas said something to Jane and was walking briskly toward Catherine.

Catherine stopped and watched her move. Margaret was worth watching—confidence, grace, vitality. Smiling at the people in the crowd as she brushed by them. She couldn't decide whether Margaret was beautiful or just attractive because that inner glow was so strong it dominated everything about her.

"You're Catherine Ling," she said as she reached her. She reached out to shake her hand. "I'm Margaret. You'll want to talk to me."

"I will? How do you know?"

"I saw you going up to the cottage to talk to Kendra, and I asked Jane who you were." A smile lit her face. "I'm glad you came, Catherine. Jane said you're very tough, very clever, and that you owe Eve a debt for helping to save your son. A debt like that is great motivation." She looked around her. "Want to go for a walk with me in the woods? There are too many people around."

Catherine fell into step with her. "How did you know that I'd come looking for you after I talked to Kendra?" she asked again. "What do you know that she doesn't?"

"Nothing. But she doesn't like to talk about me." She chuckled. "It's part loyalty because she likes me. And it's part discomfort because I'm kinda hard to explain."

"That's what she told me." They were deep in the woods now, and Catherine stopped and turned to face her. "I don't give a damn about discomfort, but I don't like lies. She said something about your not being a phony. What was that supposed to mean?"

"Did she say that? That was nice. It's particularly hard for her to defend me when

I offend her sense of logic. That's a primary sin for Kendra." She reached down and took off one of her high heels. "I have to get these off for a minute. I'm not used to anything but my flip-flops or tennis shoes." She flexed her bare feet. "That's better. I knew I had to look somber and dressed up, but I can't stand these heels. I bought them at Payless at the mall, but they don't—" She broke off. "You're looking impatient. Sorry. You're worried about Eve like the rest of us, and you're in the dark. How can I help?"

"By shining some light," she said curtly. "You're right, I'm worried about Eve, and I'm not going to let that bastard kill her if there's a chance of saving her. I have to know everything, dammit. Kendra said that you were the trigger that made her realize that perhaps Eve hadn't been killed. How did you know that was possible?"

"Oh, it was more than possible," Margaret said. "It was fact. I told Jane and Kendra that the night of the explosion, but they're both cautious. They wanted to believe me, but they couldn't bring themselves to raise their hopes until they had proof." She beamed. "So I sent Kendra to use all that logic and deductive reasoning that she does so well to gather their proof. Didn't she do a fine job?"

"Excellent. Now tell me how you knew that Eve's being alive was a fact."

She sighed. "Okay, here it comes." She made a face. "There's a wolf pack in those mountains, and wolves are usually easy for me to deal with. Not like a dog, but close enough."

"What?"

"The pack is always on the hunt for food. Naturally, since they're in the wild, they would have to be. When the wolves noticed Doane and Eve in the mountains, they were considering them for their next meal."

"Where is this going?" Catherine was frowning. "I don't want a nature lesson, Margaret."

"But you want an answer from me. That's what I'm giving you. For some reason, the wolves became intrigued by Doane." Margaret tilted her head. "Peculiar. But you can never tell what a wolf will do. Anyway, they started tracking, shadowing him . . . and Eve. I asked if it was because of the food factor. But that wasn't the reason, it was something else. Doane had to go away. It was important for him to go away."

"Go away?"

"Die. Doane had to die. It was important to the wolves that he die."

Catherine couldn't take any more of this. "Stop spinning fairy tales. I want answers, Margaret."

"You're getting them." She added simply, "The wolves didn't like Doane, but there was something else. They felt he had to die. It was something to do with the natural order. I couldn't get it clear. It had some connection with death and silence and a little red-haired kid."

"Margaret."

"You want to know how I know."

"I want to know why you're bullshitting me."

"I know because the night of the fire, I tracked down one of the males who was staking out the ghost town. I heard him howling, and I thought maybe . . ." She smiled. "And I struck it rich, like they say in the gold towns. Pure gold, Catherine. Karak was pure gold."

"Karak?"

"The wolf. That's the closest I can translate his name."

"Wolves have names?"

"Yes, not all animals identify themselves in that way even mentally, of course. But wolves are on a higher plane." She drew a deep breath. "I'd better get this over with quickly. You're getting impatient and angry and ready to call the local booby hatch. Look, I have a certain ability to communicate with animals. I've had it since I was a kid. No, I'm not some kind of Dr. Doolittle. I just get impressions and can sometimes tap into memories. It can help on occasion. I was working as a tech at a canine experimental facility down in the Caribbean on Summer Island when I was drawn into all this. They thought I was damn valuable." She grimaced. "Weird, but valuable. And they eventually got used to me. Does it make you feel better to know that those vets actually believed in me?"

"No, I make my own opinions."

"Then make it now."

Catherine looked her directly in the eye. Margaret never flinched but held her gaze with boldness and shining clarity.

Truth. Catherine couldn't know whatever else comprised the person who was Margaret Douglas, but she recognized honesty.

Catherine shrugged. "Kendra says you're not a phony. That's all that's really important. As for the rest, I've run into stranger things. Voodoo, snake charmers . . . ghosts. I grew up on the streets of Hong Kong, and I've traveled all over the world. It's hard to cling strictly to reality when you've gone face-to-face with some of the things I have." She added, "So bring on your wolf if he can help me find out anything about Eve."

"I didn't expect that." Margaret's face glowed with delight. "It's not often I run into someone who is easy. Joe was a little skeptical, but he gave me a chance. Kendra was very difficult. It's hard for her to accept anything that's not black-and-white, and I'm definitely on the gray side."

"So are wolves. Can we get back to your story now?"

"Oh, yes. Karak. After I tracked him down, it took hours before I was able to find out anything other than that it was necessary that Doane die or go away as he termed it. But when he began to trust me, he let me see more." She paused. "It was the stream. He saw Doane and Eve go down the stream in a raft and go ashore miles away from the town. Eve didn't move, probably unconscious. Doane deflated the raft and tossed it in a vehicle and took off."

"Where?"

"Out of the forest, headed south. They lost his scent after that and came back to the mountains."

"Damn."

Margaret chuckled. "You can't expect anything more. They did the best they could. Anyway, Kendra believed me when I showed her where the vehicle had been parked, and she found the tire prints. After that, she started investigating on her own. She didn't tell anyone what she was doing until she'd gathered all the information, then she went to Joe and Jane to decide what to do."

"And they decided on this charade."

"Yes, a chance to take Doane off guard." Margaret nodded. "It might or might not work, but if he doesn't expect anyone to know he's alive, it gives us a little edge. At this point, we'll take any advantage we can get." She added soberly, "We have to find her, Catherine. In those hours after we thought she was dead, it almost broke Jane . . . and Joe. Eve is too important to too many people to let her go. All of those people who came to this memorial service . . . The stories I've heard today. Every life is important, but Eve is special."

"Yes, she is," Catherine said. For an instant, memories flooded back to her of moments in her own life when Eve had stepped in and given her time and risked her life to help bring her boy home to her. She cleared her throat. "Of course we'll get her back. Do you know anything else that could help me?"

Margaret shook her head. "Nothing but that those wolves really wanted to bring down Doane for some reason."

"That's interesting but not pertinent." She smiled. "Now I suggest that you put on your shoes, and we go back to that crowd. I want to talk to Joe again if I can get him away from all those mourners who have him cornered."

"He's hating it. He's particularly angry about all those reporters and media people he had to let come to make sure Doane would know about Eve's service. He said

Eve would hate this kind of show if she were really dead."

"If she were really dead, she wouldn't care either way."

Margaret gestured. "You know what I mean."

"Yes, I do. She'd just want to fade away and live on as a memory. That's what I'd want, too." They had reached the edge of the trees, and she saw that Joe was still surrounded. She'd have to wait until he was free, she realized impatiently.

She had a sudden thought. "Zander. Is Lee Zander here? I need to talk to him. He seems to be the center of this equation."

"Zander didn't come. He disappeared shortly after the fire was put out." Margaret shook her head. "Don't count on talking to him. I'm not even sure he cares whether Eve is alive or not. Though the idea that Doane is still a threat to him might spur him."

"To hell with what he cares about. I'm going to talk to him."

"Whatever." Margaret was strolling toward Jane. "I warned you. Everyone has to march to their own drummer."

Catherine stayed where she was at the edge of the crowd, waiting for Joe.

She could see why Joe was on edge about the media. A TV cameraman was drifting around setting up shots of different dignitaries. There was no bank of microphones, but there were two reporters who had hand mikes.

She instinctively tried to fade back into the shadows. Was it worth it? All this media attention that Joe Quinn hated so much and was enduring on the chance that it might help Eve in some way.

Are you out there watching, Doane?

CHAPTER

2

Starlite Motel
Casper, Wyoming

"You're not watching, Eve," Doane said. "I've made you a star, and you're not paying any attention." He turned the sound down on the TV. "Though those fools thought you were a star anyway, didn't they? But people always look kindly at victims after they're dead."

"Turn off the TV." Eve looked straight at the reconstruction of Kevin she was repairing. It had been damaged during the time they were in the stream flowing out of the cavern. "I can't concentrate with it on."

"Of course you can." He leaned back in the chair. "You're so talented. Listen to all those people being interviewed who are raving about you. I've counted four police chiefs so far who have sung your praises."

"You listen to them. I don't give a damn. It was always the work, not what anyone thought of me." She didn't look at him. He was trying to disturb her, and he was succeeding, but she couldn't let him know. It would be a victory, and he'd had too many victories lately. "I thought you wanted this reconstruction of your monster son finished. It wasn't me who did all the damage this time. You can't take a skull reconstruction down into an underground stream without water damage. You almost ruined him beyond repair." She smiled maliciously. "Kevin wouldn't be pleased, would he?"

Doane's smile vanished. "He knows I'm only doing what I have to do. It was all your fault that I had to find a way to get us out fast when all your people were closing in on me." He added with satisfaction, "But I'd prepared a way to do it. It was a good plan. Just like the plans I always made when Kevin was alive and with me. He was always proud of me."

"Yes, luring little girls into your son's web

was something for which he'd praise and stroke you, wasn't it?" And those many children had been raped and murdered by Kevin, Doane's son. In the end, which one, Kevin or Doane, had been the most evil? "He was your son. You could have stopped him. You could have saved the lives of those little girls. That would have given you a little reason for pride."

"You don't understand. I've told you, Kevin was special. He could have ruled everything and everyone around him if he'd been given a little more time. The little girls weren't important." He shrugged. "Great men need a release. Kevin chose the children."

She felt sick. She should be accustomed to Doane's horrible justifications after these days of being with him. But the words were new and painful every time he spoke them. "And he'll burn in hell for it. So will you, Doane."

"He's not in hell," he said softly. "We both know that, Eve. He's right there, waiting. Death can't hold him." His eyes were glittering. "But I'm sure he's enjoying being so close to your Bonnie. You know how he needs little girls. They're together, you know. Only a little more power, and he'll be able to scoop her up."

"You're crazy." She tried to smother the panic. Keep calm. Doane's hallucinations regarding his son were infectious. While working on Kevin's reconstruction, she had actually wondered if that demon spirit was reaching out, trying to merge with his father to take back the life that Zander had stolen. Not only reaching out to Doane but to her . . . and, maybe, Bonnie. "I don't know anything about what happens in the afterlife. But my Bonnie would never be anywhere near that monster. She's light to his darkness."

"A light to warm his hands when he stretches out to—"

"Shut up!" Get control. He often taunted her, but she didn't usually let him get to her like this. It was the strain of working on this damn reconstruction that she only wanted to crush and destroy. They had been holed up in this tiny motel since Doane had brought her here the night of the fire. He had given her an injection, and she had not regained consciousness until just a little while before they had reached this seedy motel. It was the smallness of their quarters that she found nerve-wracking. Their motel room had two full-size beds and one bathroom; he'd converted the round dining table to use as her work-bench, and the proximity with Doane was suffocating. He'd watched her like a hawk, handcuffing her whenever he left the room, sniping, trying to hurt her at every oppor-tunity. Usually, she could handle it, but not when he talked about Bonnie. She whirled and headed for the bathroom. "I can't lis-ten to you right now."

"I didn't say you could stop working and leave."

"I need to go to the bathroom and wash my face. I haven't had a break in hours, and my eyes are getting blurry. You wouldn't want me to make a mistake with your Kevin." She slammed the door behind her and leaned back against it.

She had been telling the truth about her stinging eyes, and she closed them for a moment. She'd shown weakness to Do-ane, and she mustn't do that again. He knew that to strike at Bonnie was to strike at Eve's heart. Her little seven-year-old daughter, who had been killed and taken from Eve so many years ago.

No, not really taken. Eve had not found Bonnie's body until recently, but she had been aware that Bonnie's spirit was still with her from about a year after Bonnie's death. She had first been conscious of her in what she had thought were dreams but had gradually begun to believe the wonderful truth. Bonnie was being permitted to come back to her from that place beyond. The knowledge had kept Eve alive when she'd only wanted to die and join her Bonnie.

Where are you, Bonnie? My God, how I need you.

But Bonnie couldn't come to her. She had managed to reach Eve only once since this nightmare had begun. That had been at the Colorado house to which Doane first brought her after he had kidnapped her. But then she had been in a deep-coma state, and Bonnie had told her that was the only reason she had been able to reach her, that Kevin was keeping her back.

Why was it so difficult for Eve to believe

in a demon of supreme evil like Kevin trying to breach the border between life and death? She knew that her Bonnie had done it.

Because evil should be contained and destroyed, and goodness should live forever.

"I don't mean to complain, Bonnie," she whispered. "I know you're doing your best. But I'd really like to just have you come once, so I know that you're all right, and all of Doane's poison are just lies."

She straightened and opened her eyes. Just this tiny box of a bathroom. No endearing little figure in her Bugs Bunny T-shirt.

Of course not. So stop whining and go back and face Doane again.

No, she'd rest for just a little while before she had to go back to face Doane . . . and Kevin. She took a few minutes, then went to the sink and started to run the water.

The volume of the television in the other room was suddenly turned down.

She stiffened. Another telephone call? The walls in this fleabag of a motel were paper-thin. Twice before when she'd gone into the bathroom, she'd heard Doane talking on the phone. The first call had been barely audible, but she'd caught a name.

Cartland. The second call had been to the same man, but she'd heard a little more. They were talking about a city, Seattle. The second in the chain, Doane had called it.

What chain? she thought with exasperation. And what did this Cartland have to do with Doane's so-called master plan? Whatever it was must have been important to him. He was very careful about going out, or he would probably have made the calls outside the motel room.

What did she care about all of Doane's crazy plans and telephone calls? Lord, she was tired of dealing with him.

She gazed at herself in the mirror over the sink. She looked as tired as she felt. And she looked . . . different.

Her face was thinner, the eyes sunk deeper, her lips more defined. She looked tougher, ready to face down the world. She had changed in these days with James Doane. She resented the fact that he'd had the power to carve out all the softness and left only the lean, sharp essence. But her greatest fear was that the hardness had scored deep beneath the surface. She desperately wanted to keep the humanity that made her what she was. She wouldn't let him steal that from her.

And she wouldn't give up fighting because of the exhaustion. The phone calls Doane was making were signs of need, signs of weakness. Things weren't going entirely the way he'd planned. Find out the weakness. Find a way to strike out at it.

She moved quietly closer to the door. She'd missed most of the conversation but heard the last scrap.

"I'm not going to argue with you, Cartland. You'll get the location when you give me the money and the manpower to do the job. When Zander is dead, you'll have what you need. Of course I'm not bullshitting you. You know you can trust Kevin. Has he ever disappointed you?" He hung up.

The TV volume was turned up again.

Trust Kevin? Kevin was dead. What the hell could Kevin give to this Cartland?

Think about it. Listen. Watch.

She turned the water on full and splashed her face. She wiped it on the hand towel and turned and opened the door.

Doane was smiling at her. "You look much more refreshed. But you shouldn't have run away. Did I disturb you by telling you Kevin's plans for your Bonnie? It was true, you know. She may be dead, but she's not safe. No one is safe from Kevin."

She felt herself tense, and she wanted to run away again. Okay, try to distract him and get him away from verbally attacking Bonnie. "You didn't make me run away. I'd just had enough of you. And turn off that damn TV. Do you think it hurts me to see all those people I love at the cottage mourning me? Well, you're right. It does. It also makes me less able to work on Kevin. You said you wanted him ready by tomorrow."

"I do." He tilted his head. "But this is too enjoyable to miss entirely. I've been looking forward to this memorial service since it was announced on CNN. I can't get enough of it. I've recorded it, and I'll try to catch it on another cable station later."

"It will probably not be shown. I'm surprised they're giving it any airtime at all. I'm not that important, Doane."

"You're too modest. You notice that your mother didn't show up for the service? But, then, she doesn't care anything for you, does she?"

"She cares. In her own way."

"And I don't see Zander in the crowd."

"Why should he be there? You say he's my father, but I don't accept it. He's only a hired assassin who doesn't care anything about me."

"He cares. A father always cares about his child. That's what this is all about. It would be dangerous for him to show up at your memorial service, but he'll be mourning you in his own place and way." He smiled. "And after you finish Kevin tomorrow, we'll go join him."

"It's all a stupid—"

"Shh." He help up his hand. "Now pay attention. They're filming your Joe Quinn. He looks totally devastated, doesn't he?"

Joe. Beloved. Friend. Protector. She studied his face. His expression was tense, the jaw clenched, his brown eyes glittering.

Devastated?

She stiffened. Careful. She tried to keep her own face expressionless as she gazed at Joe. She knew that face. She could read every expression, every hint of feeling.

Joe was **not** devastated at losing her. He was impatient. He wanted this media circus over.

Why? If he had set it up to honor her?

Then it sank home. She had been so numb in these last days, fighting to recover physically and mentally, that she had just accepted what Doane had said to her about the memorial service. Joe would never have thrown a huge media party like this because he would have known she'd hate it.

Which meant he had set it up for someone else. Doane?

Doane had been so certain that everyone had been fooled by his grand plan. He had been smug and completely obnoxious about it.

"And there's Jane MacGuire," Doane said. "She's very beautiful, and it's no wonder the cameras focus more on her than anyone else. Poor Jane, she has to be heartbroken that there was nothing she could do to save you."

"Heartbroken," Eve repeated, intently studying Jane's face.

Jane had been more close friend than daughter to her since she'd adopted her when she was ten years old, but the love was strong between them. She knew exactly how Jane would react.

Jane was pale and unsmiling.

No agony. Only tension. And the same impatience Eve had seen in Joe's face. They wanted this show over.

Eve felt the joy and hope surge through her.

Oh, Doane, you've underestimated them again.

They've found out about your little escape plan.

They know I'm alive.

"You need to get out of here," Margaret whispered to Jane when she reached her. "Your nerves are shredded from all this crap. Why don't you go up in the house with Kendra?"

That sounded wonderful to Jane. Peace. Quiet. No pretense. She reluctantly shook her head. "Kendra isn't family. I am. I'm expected to be at this circus. I can do this."

"You can do it," Seth Caleb said roughly as he suddenly appeared behind her. "But why should you? You've only been out of the hospital a week, and you've been under stress all that time. You've done your job. The cameras love you, and the TV crews focused on you during most of the service. Now let someone else have a photo op." He took her elbow and firmly swept her away from Margaret and started propelling her toward the steps leading to the porch of the cottage. "You need a break."

"You don't know what I need. Let me go, Caleb." Jane carefully kept her voice low to keep anyone around them from hearing as she tried to pull away from him. "What do you think you're doing?"

"I'm being kind and concerned and sympathetic. Can't you tell?" He glanced across the crowd at Mark Trevor, who was nodding with agreement at something a guest was telling him. "Since Trevor is involved with doing all the right things like you are, I figured someone had to be the bad guy." He smiled faintly, as he murmured, "And who does it better than I do?"

"No one." She glanced up at him. Dark eyes glittered recklessly from that strong, fascinating face. She was immediately aware of the animal magnetism and powerful sensuality that were parts of his basic personality. She always tried to ignore and block them out, but she seldom succeeded. Even now, his grip on her elbow was sending a tingling through her arm.

"I've been surprised how tame you've been during the last week."

"Oh, I'm an excellent actor when I need to be. In this case, the need was yours, and I always try to meet your every desire." His smile was fading. "Though I haven't had an opportunity lately. Trevor has been covering you with that cloak of golden charm he drapes over you whenever he's near. It's hard to compete when I have no golden cloak, and you're so wary of me."

"Golden cloak? That sounds like something from Disney. Bullshit." She didn't try to deny the last part of his sentence. They both knew she was wary of Caleb. She not only had an erotic response whenever she was around him, he was not like anyone she had ever known. Hell, he was probably not like anyone the majority of the population had ever known, she thought ruefully. That weird talent he possessed that allowed him to affect the flow of blood in those around him was bizarre and a little frightening. Eve had told her she had seen him kill a murderer with that talent a couple years ago. And Jane, herself, had experienced the hypnotic sexual aspect to that control of the blood.

Yes, "wariness" was definitely the word for what she felt for Caleb. Among other more confused emotions. It was Caleb who had been there for her, flown her here from London, when she'd first become drawn into the nightmare of Eve's kidnapping. He'd stayed with her after she'd been shot by Doane's accomplice, and no one could have been more supportive during the hunt for Eve. He'd been very clear he wanted and intended to go to bed with her, but for the most part, he'd set lust aside and concentrated on helping her find Eve. "Trevor is just doing what I asked him to do. He's making himself visible and adding to the authenticity. Which you are **not** doing, Caleb."

"I did my best. Making myself visible at occasions like this usually adds more of an air of disturbance rather than authenticity. People seem to sense that I'm out of place." He shrugged. "As I said, your lover has the advantage of being able to charm birds off the trees."

"Trevor's not my lover."

"Thank God. But he was your lover a few years ago, and he wants to be again."

He met her eyes. "But he's missed his chance. He shouldn't have let you go."

"He wouldn't try to hold me if I didn't want to be there. I go my own way, and we realized that it wasn't working out." They had reached the steps, and she stopped and looked up at him. "Not that it's any of your business. I've warned you about that, Caleb."

"Just chitchat." He tilted his head. "Now run up those steps and go take a rest. I'll tell Joe where you are."

She gazed at him in astonishment. "I have no intention of leaving this memorial service. I only let you bring me here to avoid a scene." She jerked her elbow away from him. She repeated the words she'd said before, "I go my own way. Step aside, Caleb."

He didn't move.

"I mean it."

"If I do, you'll collapse within ten minutes."

"What?"

"I warned you," he said softly. "I can see it coming. You've been going at a frantic pace, helping Joe with all the preparations for this media circus. I'll bet you haven't slept at night."

"I've slept."

"But not much. I told you when you asked me to try to heal you enough for you to be released from that hospital that the effect wouldn't last if you overdid it."

"I feel fine," she said quickly. It wasn't true. She felt exhausted, but she'd hoped it had nothing to do with the wound and infection that had put her in the hospital and out of the hunt for Eve. "I'm just tired."

"And you might last a little while longer if you rest now." He smiled. "And I told you I was at your service if this happened."

"Screw you."

He laughed. "I wish. Now admit it, there was nothing about the experience that was unpleasant. As I told you, there are all kinds of medical studies being done on the value of laser therapy stirring the blood around wounds to induce healing. I just stirred the blood in a wider area throughout your body and used my own method. Much more efficient than any laser."

Unpleasant? Bare flesh to bare flesh. His mouth on the wound in her shoulder. His hands stroking her body, his tongue on her nipples.

Heat.

Intense need.

Swirling darkness.

Fiery tingling.

"You're remembering." His gaze was on her face. "Pleasure, Jane. Not complete. But you didn't want it to stop. I'm the one who backed away."

It was the truth. She had been completely helpless against that powerful wave of feeling. "You didn't tell me that what you were doing would have a sexual effect."

"You would have done it anyway. You were still weak and ill, and the doctors at the hospital wouldn't release you. You were desperate to get out of that hospital and on the hunt for Eve." He chuckled. "And I wasn't sure that it would be quite that explosive. It could be because you had my blood in your veins, which I donated to you after you were shot. Though it might not have mattered anyway. You might not trust me, but you can't deny the chemistry between us."

"I trust you . . . sometimes." She stared him in the eye. "I'll trust you now if you tell me that you were telling the truth about my being on the verge of collapse. Were you lying to me, Caleb?"

His smile faded. "No, it may take a little longer, but you're on the way. I told you that I'm no healer. I can manipulate the blood and give you a constant rush of energy and a temporary masking of symptoms. That's what I did in the hospital, so that the doctors would release you. If you'd rest, you'd even heal yourself. But we both know you're not going to do that. Not until you find Eve."

"Damn."

"But maybe you can stave it off if you'll take periodic rests. There's a possibility that you can do without undergoing the same bonding we did last time." His brows rose. "You see, I'm not giving you the answer I'd like to give you. Maybe because I don't like being a drug you can't do without even on a temporary basis. Well, actually I would, but I don't want it to be based on a physical weakness. When I touch your body again, I want you strong and wanting it."

She forced her gaze away from him. "I believe you're being honest with me. Though I don't want to believe it." She started up the steps toward the porch. "I can't afford to be stupid about this. I'll see that I rest more."

"And I'll be close by in case you need me," he said softly. "All you have to do is call."

She ignored those words. "Tell Joe I'm fine, that I'm only going up to see Kendra. Do **not** tell him I'm tired."

He nodded. "Whatever you say." He stood watching her from the bottom of the stairs. "But Quinn never trusts me entirely. He's too protective of you, and he's seen me do a few things that are both violent and unorthodox. It might be better if you give him a text from your cell."

Yes, she'd say that Caleb's causing a killer's heart to explode from a rush of blood could be termed both violent and unorthodox. She opened the cottage door. "Perhaps you're right. I'll tell him myself."

CHAPTER

3

Caleb watched the door close behind Jane before he started to turn away. She had looked fragile and almost breakable during those last moments. That would not last long, and the strength would be back. It was Jane's strength that had first drawn him to her when he'd met her all those years ago. Yet now this breakable quality filled him with an almost primitive desire to reach out and touch, hold. Hell, he wanted to touch, stroke, hold, whenever he looked at her, no matter what the circumstance.

He should have lied to her, he thought recklessly. He had never wanted to have sex with anyone as much as he did Jane, and that lust was growing in intensity. Yet for some reason he couldn't reach out and take what he wanted. Most of the time lies were counterproductive, but to increase Jane's physical need for him could have been—

"Is she okay?"

He turned to see Margaret standing behind him. "Hello, Margaret. I'm afraid I was a little rude when I whisked Jane away from you." He added mockingly, "Did you trail along behind us to make sure I wasn't going to harm her?"

"Yes," she said bluntly. "I knew she'd slap you down if you annoyed her too much, but I'm never sure what you're going to do. You're one of the wild ones. I thought that it wouldn't hurt to tag along."

"I'd hardly cause a furor at this sad occasion."

"Yes, you would. If it suited you. But you know that Jane would never forgive you." Her gaze went back to the door at the head of the steps. "She did look tired. Is she okay?"

"If she rests."

She turned to look at him with narrowed

eyes. "You know that's true. Why? Is it that blood thing that Jane told me about you?"

He said warily, "It depends what she told you."

"Only that you have this kind of blood gift that was passed down through your family since ancient times." She giggled. "And that you're not a vampire."

"How kind of her to specify."

"I was disappointed. I was sort of sensing that blood thing whenever I was around you. That's why Jane finally broke down and told me about your family. She didn't want me asking you about it. I think she didn't know how you'd react."

"You wanted me to be a vampire?"

"No, but I've always been interested in vampire bats because I can never read any of their impressions. I thought I might be able to get a clue from you how to do it." She made a face. "Not that I can read minds or anything. I just get occasional impressions, particularly from the wild ones."

"And I'm a wild one?" He smiled. "Let me see. Primitive, barbaric, possibly violent?"

She nodded. "All of those things. Along with intelligence and cynicism and . . ." She shrugged. "Who knows? Every person has their own soul." She beamed at him. "But I've always liked you, Caleb. You're very interesting. I just have to watch and be careful that you don't hurt Jane while you're trying to have sex with her."

"Indeed? May I say that it's none of your business, Margaret?"

"Of course you may. But you'd be wrong. Jane saved my life and I can't have her hurt." Earnestly she said, "I know you've been stalking Jane since I met you, and it's perfectly natural behavior for you. She's probably very receptive to you on a basic level, but you mustn't hurt her. You're disturbing. I think she's very vulnerable at the moment." Her gaze left him and went across the crowd to Mark Trevor. "If she wants sex, Trevor would be better for her right now."

"No!" He smothered the violence. "Margaret, I'm becoming a little annoyed with you."

She nodded. "It happens. I just wanted to get everything straight between us." She looked at her watch. "It's getting late. Some of the media people are packing up to go. This should be over with soon." She looked up the steps again. "I don't want to hover. Does she need me?"

"No."

"Then I'll go see if I can help Joe." She turned. "You're probably going to hover around here anyway. Only in you it doesn't look protective, it looks slightly sinister." She drifted away. "See you . . ."

Hover? He did **not** hover.

And he would not go away from the cottage just because Margaret accused him of doing so. Those media people would love to corner Jane while she was in the cottage and bombard her with questions. It would do no harm to grab a drink from a passing waiter and stick around until the cameras and reporters were gone.

Dammit, that was not hovering.

"Hi." Jane closed the door behind her. "It's crazy down there. Do you mind if I hide out for a while and join you?"

"It's your home. I'm the one who should ask you that. I just had some thinking to do and didn't want to interfere." Kendra got up from the couch and went to the kitchen. "Sit down. I'll get you a cup of coffee. You look like you could use it."

"Don't say that." Jane grimaced. "I'm fine. If I remember, it was you who told Joe I had an infection from that gunshot wound, and he should take me to that damn hospital. If you weren't so observant, I'd have—"

"You'd have gone on until you were so ill that Quinn would have been frantic about you as well as Eve." She handed her a mug filled with steaming coffee. "No apologies." Her gaze raked Jane's face. "And you're looking a little fragile at the moment. Should I be calling Quinn?"

"You do, and I'll break your neck," Jane said. "I'm grateful for everything you did to track Eve down to that ghost town, but you worry about Eve and not me. I'll be fine."

"Maybe." Kendra's tone was skeptical. "But I'll let it go. You're right. Everyone and everything has to be concentrated on Eve." Her jaw tightened. "We were so close. We almost had that bastard. Then everything went wrong. We can't let it happen again. Everything has to go right this time." She took a sip of her own coffee. "Zander. Doane will be targeting Zander. We have to target him, too. Where the hell is he? He left Colorado the day that Venable told him that Doane and Eve were still alive, and Venable says he's not answering his phone."

"Joe will find Zander," Jane said grimly.

"We just can't be obvious if we want to keep the surprise factor. It's the only weapon we have against Doane. That's what this idiotic show is all about." Her lips twisted. "I try to tell myself it's all a farce, but it hurts me. I keep thinking, what if it was real? What if we're wrong about Doane's wanting to keep Eve alive so that he can kill her in front of Zander." She shook her head. "But we're not wrong. He wouldn't have gone to all that trouble to stage that fake death if he hadn't wanted to keep her alive a little while longer. I have to keep thinking that's true, or I'd go crazy."

"Me, too," Kendra said. "I feel guilty as hell I didn't figure it all out sooner." She paused. "And I agree that Doane mustn't have any idea that we know he's alive. I'm scared to death he might decide to change his precious plans in midstream."

"And kill Eve?" Jane whispered.

"I'm not projecting that kind of scenario, any kind of scenario. I just don't want to set Doane on a different path than the one we know he wants to travel." She moistened her lips. "So our actions must seem absolutely logical and normal to him. Before he disposed of his buddy, Terence

Blick, we know he probably had him doing surveillance on us. Venable said a man of his description had been sighted during the search on the other side of the lake by one of his agents. That means we have to assume Doane knows who was here at the cottage." She tapped her chest. "I was brought here to investigate Eve's disappearance. No one tried to hide it. It couldn't have been more clear. Blick knew I was at Goldfork. Again, it was very clear why I was there."

"What are you trying to say?"

"I'm not trying to say anything. I'm saying it. I think I'm being exceptionally lucid," Kendra said. "That's why I've been sitting up here trying to talk myself out of being so damn logical. I don't want to be right this time." She paused. "But I am right, Jane." She put her cup down on the coffee table. "And that means I'm no longer an asset to the hunt, I'm a liability." She got to her feet. "If we believe Doane and Eve are dead, then there would be no use for me to still be here. The fact that I remain after the memorial service would automatically set off alarm bells if we're still being watched."

"But Blick is dead, and he was the one

doing surveillance. We don't need to be quite as careful now."

"Don't we? I'm not so certain." She moved over to her duffel that was sitting by the front door. "There are too many unknowns in the equation. Doane may have been playing a different game than the one we were told by Venable. Different games have different board pieces. If Doane took out one piece, that might mean he made room for another." She unzipped her duffel and drew out a tattered journal. "And this might be the prize for winning the game."

Jane sat up straight on the couch. "What's that supposed to be?"

"It's Kevin's journal, which Margaret and I found in a hiding place in Doane's house in Goldfork, Colorado. We were trying to find some clue to where Doane might have taken Eve or, at least, anything to do with that disk that his son might have given him to use as blackmail to get the CIA to give him witness protection. No disk. Just this journal. I've gone through it several times, and I couldn't find anything that was more dangerous than the sick ravings of a mad pervert. But it was hidden, and that alone must mean that it has value to Doane." She paused. "And we were told that everyone was looking for the disk that had revealed names of embedded CIA agents in Pakistan. As I said, no one found that disk. Which makes me wonder if it actually existed."

"Venable said that it existed. He should know."

"Yes, he should." She moved back across the room. "Venable has been our source for most of Kevin's past history and what went on during that period in Pakistan."

Jane's gaze was focused on the journal in Kendra's hand. "You haven't told Venable about this, have you? You told me before that you have some doubts about him."

"Do I think that he's one of the bad guys in this scenario? No, I'd never have let Quinn tell him that Eve and Doane were still alive if I'd thought that was a possibility. It was safe to turn him loose to try to locate Eve and Doane. We needed someone with his power and connections who could move discreetly behind the scenes. But I think that Venable's one of those people who balance what he considers the good of many against the good of one. I've run into agents like him before."

"I've always trusted Venable. But it scared me when I saw Venable's attack team swarming down the mountain and firing on that saloon. He swears none of his team's bullets caused that explosion."

"I believe him. I think that Doane staged it and blew it himself. But that doesn't mean that Venable couldn't have been responsible. He took a risk." She added deliberately, "And I don't think he did it for Eve's sake. He wanted to get Doane. It would be interesting to know what orders he gave his men. Kill or capture?"

"So are you going to confront him with that question?"

"No, he'd only sidestep." She shrugged. "Besides, I'm out of it." She thrust the journal at Jane. "It's your decision now."

Jane's eyes widened. "What?"

"You heard me. I'm a liability. I was deliberately brought in to find Eve. I can't stay here. I'm going home to San Diego. I'm going back to my teaching job."

"You're giving up trying to find—"

"No, dammit." She drew a deep breath.

"But it's got to look that way. I can't be on the scene. It has to look as if I gave up on the search because I thought Eve was dead. I'll still do what I can. I'll try to figure out what's going on with this journal, and you can send me anything that—" Her hands were clenched. "It's not enough. I hate it. It's going to drive me crazy. But this isn't about me. We may have only a small window of surprise with Doane, and I can't smash it because I want to be involved." She added fiercely, "But if there's something I can do that won't hurt the chances of keeping Eve alive, you call me, tell me."

Jane was recovering from the shock, and she felt a surge of sympathy for Kendra. "That goes without question." She smiled sadly. "I know how it feels to be forced out of the action and not being able to help. Those days in the hospital were terrible." She glanced down at the journal. "My decision, you said. Why are you giving it to me?"

"Because, other than Joe Quinn, you care the most for Eve. It's intensely personal with you, and you'll fight to the death to get her back. You don't have to strike a balance like Venable. There is no other answer for you."

"That's right, there isn't." She touched the cover. "You're not asking me to keep it from Venable."

"Your decision. I've made a copy of my own. I've told you my opinion, but you're going to be on the ground running, and I'm going to be in San Diego. I'm only asking you to think long and hard about it."

"I've already thought about it. I'll show it to Joe, and we'll discuss it, but Venable isn't going to get it until his motivations are a hell of a lot more clear."

"That's a relief. Look, Catherine Ling is here. If you need someone of CIA caliber, I think you can trust her to look out for Eve and nothing else." She made a face. "There I go again, trying to run the show. You don't know how hard it was for me to give up control."

"I think I do," she said quietly. "I've learned a lot about you since you came to search for Eve." She paused. "And all I've learned is good, Kendra."

"Naturally, at least, in my areas of expertise."

"That wasn't what I was talking about. You have a good heart. I trust you."

"And that's a true honor," Kendra said. "I've noticed that your trust is pretty well limited to Quinn and Eve."

Jane lifted her shoulders in a half shrug. "It comes from being a street kid. I was in a dozen foster homes before Eve took me into her life. Everything would seem to go well for a while, then suddenly I'd be sent back to DEFACS. Or maybe it wouldn't go so well, and I'd purposely do something that would make them kick me out. Either way, it wasn't a lifestyle to inspire trust."

"Even with Mark Trevor?" Kendra asked. "I've only gotten to know him during the days he's been here after Colorado, but I'd say that he's worth taking a chance on." She smiled. "Besides being fantastically good-looking and totally charming. Quinn told me that he was your lover but that you broke up a year or so ago." She held up her hand. "Forget I asked. It's none of my business. It's just my nature to probe into everything around me. Give me an inch, and I'll take a mile."

"I don't mind," Jane said. "Not from you. Trevor is all of those things. He was my first love, and he made me dizzy from the moment I met him."

"But you couldn't commit," Kendra guessed. "And you walked away."

"Something like that."

"Okay, I've pried enough. I've just always found you a fascinating blend of wariness and emotion and wanted to know what made you tick." She tilted her head. "You notice I didn't mention Seth Caleb."

Jane found herself unconsciously tensing.

"Because I knew you'd react like that," Kendra said softly. "He wasn't one who I'd want to bring into a discussion on trust. That's not part of your relationship. You try to keep from looking at him whenever he's in the room. I found that very odd until I noticed just how you connected. Very sensual. Very disturbing. Very complicated. No trust." She smiled. "Much too complicated for me to try to analyze. I believe you're having trouble with that yourself. You might try to resolve it as soon as possible. I had to bring it up since Caleb appears to be very much a factor in your life at the moment, and everything that affects the search for Eve is important."

"Not my personal life. I'd never let it interfere." But Jane was relieved that Kendra had slid away from talking about Caleb. She hadn't realized that their relationship was so transparent to outsiders. Perhaps it wasn't to anyone but Kendra. She changed the subject. "Margaret. If your presence here is a threat, wouldn't Margaret's presence fall into the same category? She came here at approximately the same time, and though she was obviously not an investigator of any kind, she was at the scenes of the crimes." She frowned. "And she was seen with you at the house in Goldfork."

"Very good," Kendra said. "But Margaret is your responsibility." She headed for the front door. "I'm going down to try to convince her she should opt out as I'm doing. But knowing Margaret, I don't think I'm going to get very far. She's stubborn as a mule and thinks it's her duty to take care of you." She paused to look back at Jane. "I repeat, she's your responsibility now. You take care of her, or I'll be coming after you."

"You're being very stern. You evidently became very close while you were on the hunt for Eve."

"As close as you can come to a character who's part Peter Pan and part Sheena, Queen of the Jungle." She nodded. "Yeah, I'm close to Margaret. And, if you're looking for someone to trust, you don't have to look any farther. But, unfortunately, she takes chances that she shouldn't."

"You don't have to tell me. I was there when we found her cuddling that wolf in the woods above the ghost town." She added, "Don't worry. I won't let her run any risks on my behalf. I'll find a way to keep her safe."

Kendra made a sound remarkably like a snort. "You can try." She opened the door. "And you might be busy keeping yourself safe. You stay here and rest for a while. You haven't convinced me that you're in the best of shape."

"I'm not in the best of shape. I won't lie to you. But I won't let it matter."

"I know you won't. Good luck, Jane. Don't you dare not call me if I can help." She shut the door behind her.

The house felt suddenly empty without that vital presence, Jane thought. She imagined that every room Kendra entered she effortlessly owned.

She looked down at the journal.

And since she was lacking Kendra's vitality at the moment, she might as well start reading this journal of Kevin's and hope that lightning might strike, and she could see something in it that Kendra had missed.

She shuddered as she reluctantly opened the cover and began reading the journal of a monster.

Penthouse
Drake Hotel
Denver, Colorado

"I've reached Weiner." Stang, Zander's personal assistant, entered Zander's suite after contacting Zander's information guru. "It was difficult. He got your message and said to tell you he'd already started the process. He said one of his contacts spotted an off-road vehicle with those special tires at the Wyoming border on the day of the explosion. It was a tan Toyota 4-Runner. He didn't want to call you until he had something concrete to offer you. He was afraid that you were targeting him because Joe

Quinn had found out that he'd done work for you."

"Thanks to you," Zander said dryly. "I don't appreciate your lack of discretion in giving away my contacts. I don't tolerate that lack of loyalty. Perhaps you should be the one afraid, Stang."

"Probably. But I'm done with that." He smiled. "You've been intimidating me so long that you've dulled the edge." He put the telephone number down on the desk in front of Zander. "Do you really think that Weiner can zero in on Doane?"

"It's possible he can help." Zander leaned back in his chair. "He's as close to an electronics genius as they come, and he thinks outside the box. He has the sophisticated equipment to make it happen. It depends on his motivation." His smile was tiger bright as he said softly, "And I don't wish to brag, but I'm quite good at providing motivation."

Stang was aware that Zander could persuade anyone to do anything if he chose. His physical presence was very powerful, and his reputation was chilling. Who should know better than Stang? He had worked for him for a number of years as his accountant and personal assistant, and most of that time, he'd been on the edge of fear. Zander was a brilliant assassin whose fees were in the millions, but he kept most compartments of his life strictly private. That was fine with Stang, he had no desire to know too much about Zander's dealings. It could prove dangerous, if not fatal. It was only lately that Zander had let Stang into his confidence. He had seemed to want him to know about the kidnapping of Eve Duncan by Doane. "What kind of electronics voodoo do you want Weiner to perform?"

"Something a little less than voodoo. Cameras are much more pedestrian."

"Cameras?"

"In the past, I've had Weiner track targets for me using public and private cameras. I give him an area, and he creates a huge wall-mounted map and uses a highlighter pen to track a designated vehicle."

"How?"

"Municipal traffic cams posted at major intersections. Most cities keep at least a few weeks' worth on their servers' hard drives. Live highway cameras feeds are available to anyone on the Internet these days, but Weiner takes it a step further by tapping into the Department of Transportation servers to review history. Then there are private-business security cameras. ATM cameras facing the roads. Toll-gate cameras . . ." He waved his hand. "It goes on and on."

"So much for privacy on the road."

"A few years ago, this kind of tracking would have been impossible. The camera feeds would have been recorded on videocassettes and stored at each place. Now the images are recorded on hard drives, usually networked, and thus vulnerable to remote hacking and snooping." His lips twisted. "And Weiner's network connections are truly impressive. Once he knows which road or direction Doane is traveling, he'll be able to follow his path using Google Street View, looking left and right at businesses, banks, etcetera, to see security cameras he can hack."

"Why tell him to focus on Colorado and Wyoming? For that matter, why are we holed up in this modernistic Taj Mahal instead of going back to Vancouver?"

"A hunch. That jump down into the cavern and the trip downstream was pretty rough. I'd think Doane would want to hole up and recuperate a little before he took to the road. First, he'd want to see if his little scam had worked; and then he'd start pulling a new plan out of his hat." He nodded at the memorial service broadcasting on the TV set across the room. "This should reassure him that he's safe to move." He smiled. "And it will also be the signal for Quinn to go after me and try to grab me as bait for Doane."

"It sounds like a good plan to me," Stang said.

"I'll make a decision on how to handle Doane when I make the approach."

"It seems to be the only way to keep Eve Duncan alive. Why not go along with Quinn?" He met Zander's eyes. "And don't tell me that you don't care whether or not Eve survives. I'm no expert about analyzing your reactions. God knows, you've had decades to grow that hard shell, and I've just accepted that it has become part of you. But I watched you after that saloon blew up, and everyone thought Eve and Doane were dead. If you're capable of caring about anything, you cared that night. You **cared,** Zander."

Zander gazed at him without expression.

"Maybe I was angry that I didn't get my chance at Doane."

"I don't think so. You let me read Eve Duncan's dossier. You talked to me about Doane and his son, Kevin. That was completely unlike you."

"Was it?"

"Yes, you wanted me to know about Eve Duncan. You wanted someone to be on her side, to try to convince you to go after her and try to save her."

"You think I'm that complicated?"

"I think that you're an unsolvable Rubik's cube."

"That you've solved?"

"No, but perhaps you've given me enough clues to see a way to do it." He grimaced. "Maybe. You're fighting so hard not to care about Eve. For God's sake, she's your daughter. It's pure instinct to care about her." He gestured to the TV. "And there are dozens of people at that damn memorial service who will testify that she's a life worth saving. She's a very special person, Zander."

"So eloquent. You must have been storing that dissertation up for a long time."

He was silent a moment. "It's what you want to hear from me, Zander. Now accept it and go save her."

"Is that an order?" he asked silkily.

Stang found himself tensing. He was on very shaky ground at that moment. "Yes, and a plea. She must have gone through hell. She deserves to have it end." He paused. "You had a meeting with her up in the mountains, didn't you? Before Doane captured her again. You must have some idea what kind of person she is after that."

Zander was silent. "Yes. She's extraordinary." His shoulder lifted in a half shrug. "And it has nothing to do with me. I could never have given her what her life experiences have done to shape her. It was good that I stayed away from her."

"No regrets? What about her daughter, Bonnie? If you'd been there, you might have saved her."

"Or brought a horde more of the scum of the earth down on her, who would only use her to destroy me. By the time I was twenty-five, I was on the enemies list of half a dozen countries and targeted by four criminal networks. The only way I could survive was to do it alone and with no encumbrances. Would you like to know how many people have died because I allowed them close to me? When I was a young man, I was arrogant enough to think I could keep it from happening because I wanted to reach out and pretend I was normal. That didn't last long. Revenge and greed are powerful motivations, and I attract the bastards who go after both." He gazed directly in Stang's eyes. "So don't try to lay any guilt trips on me, Stang. If I'd allowed myself to feel guilt, I would have put a bullet in my head a long time ago." He added impatiently, "And stop staring at me with that sickeningly maudlin look on your face. I didn't start being cautious with my associations because I wanted to spare anyone. I just realized that it wasn't safe for me either." He shrugged. "And it gets boring having to replace the people close to you. It's better to keep them at a distance."

"I see."

"And I know all the philosophies and psychological explanations you're probably stifling at the moment. Think what you like.

I've made my life what it is, and that's how it will remain."

"After you get Eve away from Doane."

"You're not listening."

"I'm listening very carefully. So carefully I'm hearing all the undertones and nuances." He pulled out his phone. "Should I call Weiner and tell him to speed up trying to find that Toyota? We need to locate Doane very quickly if you think he may be on the move after the memorial service."

Zander gazed at him for a moment. "No, I'll do it." He started to dial his phone. "You may have become bold as brass lately, but you lack a certain ability to inspire fear. Fear is our friend at the moment." As he waited for the phone to ring, he looked up at Stang. "And if you try to pressure me again, I'll broadcast to the four corners of the earth how much I value you. How I'd have a horrible time replacing you. I might even say I consider you as close as a brother." He smiled gently. "You'd be dead within two days.

"Weiner." He was speaking into the phone. "Zander. I hear you got my message, and you've started tracking. A Toyota

4-Runner? Where else was it seen? I need the results right away. I'll feed you as much additional information as I can, but pull every string on the Internet and that network that you've set up. Now give me every location that you have on hand . . ."

CHAPTER
4

Lake Cottage
Atlanta, Georgia

She should be able to talk to Joe soon, Catherine thought.

It was getting dark, and the guests were gradually saying their good-byes to Joe and drifting away. The last photographer had snapped a few mood shots of the darkening lake and taken off.

However, Venable was still here and socializing with various guests, which was completely out of character for him. If she didn't know him better, she'd think he was avoiding her. But Venable was never averse to facing anyone. He was probably just marshaling his thoughts and his arguments and would—

Her cell phone rang, and she glanced at the ID.

John Gallo.

Oh, shit.

She started talking as soon as she accessed. "I didn't know, Gallo. I would have told you about Eve, but I only found out this morning, when I got to Miami. I did call, but I got your voice mail. It's not my fault if you don't answer your phone. It seemed all I was getting was people who didn't want to talk to me. It was driving me—"

"Calm down," Gallo said curtly. "I didn't need you to tell me about Eve. I saw the story online three days ago. I was trying to get hold of you, but Venable blocked me at every turn."

"I know." She paused. "I thought you'd want to be here. If you knew three days ago, why didn't you come to the service?"

"At first, I was trying to be diplomatic and kind to Quinn and Jane MacGuire. I was Eve's past, and she had my child, Bonnie, when she was only a teenager. But Quinn was her present and future. I had no part in building that life, and I had no right to intrude."

"At first? What followed?"

"I talked to Joe Quinn. We had an interesting discussion."

"He told you."

"He thought I was qualified to be helpful, and he didn't mind using me or anyone else if it meant saving Eve. He's desperate."

Qualified? Yes, John Gallo was qualified in any enterprise that had to do with violence and mayhem. He had been a prisoner of war in a North Korean concentration camp, then had become an Army Special Forces agent whose specialty was infiltration and assassination. He was smart, experienced, and completely lethal. He had also had a few mental problems, fits of rage, due to torture while he was incarcerated in that hellhole of a prison. Catherine had met him when she had suspected he might have killed Eve's daughter, Bonnie, during one of those fits of rage. Their relationship from that moment had been as turbulent and volatile as a perfect storm that neither of them could fight.

No, that wasn't true. She was drawn sexually to Gallo, but there had definitely been a struggle to resist that magnetism. She had made her life what she wanted it to be. She was a CIA agent who was expert in her job. After she had found and rescued her son, Luke, he was tentatively coming to accept her. She did not need Gallo to disturb her and cause ripples in her life.

"You don't agree Quinn's desperate?" Gallo asked, when she didn't answer. "Those were the vibes I got, but you're on the scene."

"Oh, he's desperate." She tried to concentrate on the problem at hand. Gallo always managed to distract her. "He loves her. They've been through a lot together." She paused. "How are you feeling, Gallo?"

"Do you expect me to say I love her, too?" Gallo asked. He was silent a moment. "I do, you know. She was a big part of my life when we were young. We didn't know about love then. It was all about sex. But years later, when I came back, we had our memory of Bonnie and the realization that she would have wanted us to have some kind of bond. Neither one of us could walk away from that bond. Although God knows we wanted to be free from each other and go about our lives." He was silent again. "That bond still exists, will always exist, because of Bonnie. There are all kinds of love out there. She's my friend and the mother of my child. I will never be her lover in the conventional sense, that's Joe Quinn, but I'll be there for her if she needs me. Is that honest enough for you?"

"You don't have to answer to me, Gallo."

"Yes, I do. In spite of the fact that you're pushing me away."

"Why? I have nothing to do with your relationship with Eve."

"You know why. Though you're having trouble admitting it." He suddenly chuckled. "I'm in a fever to have sex with you. It's all I can think about. Well, almost. And I won't allow you to put any barriers between us because everything isn't clear to you about my relationship with our mutual friend, Eve."

She felt a surge of feeling that was hot and sweet and bewildering. She quickly changed the subject. "You never told me why you didn't come here for the service."

"I decided I'd get a head start. No one expected me to go to her memorial. I flew to Vancouver instead to try to track down Zander when I heard that he was the key to trapping Doane. That's where I am now."

"And did you find him?"

"No, I've been to Zander's place here, but it's deserted. I even did a little housebreaking to make sure. I'm going through some of his papers to see if I can find a clue to where he might have gone." He paused. "Zero in on Venable. If anyone knows anything about Zander, then he should."

"I'll do that. I'll let you know."

"I phoned Hu Chang in Hong Kong after I got your call and told him to tell Luke you'd been delayed."

"I called Luke myself the minute I got into Miami. He was down in Hu Chang's lab and was so excited he could only talk about their latest experiment. Luke trails behind Hu Chang night and day." She could hardly blame her son. Hu Chang was fascinating, and she had found herself trailing after him herself when she was just a few years older than Luke. "He probably won't even miss me."

"He'll miss you. Though I admit your friend Hu Chang is something of a spellbinder. How long are you going to leave Luke with him?"

"I'm bringing him back to Louisville to go to school in two weeks." She sighed. "At least, that's what I was going to do before I found out about Eve. I'll have to leave him a little longer now."

"I hate to admit it, but you couldn't ask for him to be in safer hands than Hu Chang's," Gallo said dryly. "As long as you get a promise from him not to teach the boy how to concoct any of his poisons."

"He wouldn't do that. He'd know that I'd kill him."

"Would you? I'm never sure how much leeway you'd give Hu Chang to do anything he wanted to do. Sometimes, I think he has you hypnotized."

"Don't be absurd. He's my friend." He had been her only friend for years after they had met in Hong Kong when she was only fourteen. An unlikely friendship. She had been a street kid who had found her niche in selling information to the highest bidder, he was a master poisoner who traveled the world and sold his wares to whoever could afford them. When they had

come together, they had found a closeness that had saved them both. "And he
loves Luke. He wouldn't hurt him." But Hu
Chang didn't always have the same opinion of right and wrong as others. "He knows
that it would break our friendship if he did
something that I felt was wrong for Luke.
He values that friendship as much as I do."

"You sound as if you're trying to talk
yourself into something."

"Nonsense. Hu Chang is brilliant, and
Luke is learning more from him than he'd
ever learn in school. These last months in
Hong Kong have been wonderful for him."
She added, "But thank you for calling Hu
Chang and telling him what happened. I'll
call Luke again tonight and explain."

"You're welcome. I was just clearing the
decks for you. I knew you'd be on the hunt
as soon as Quinn told you that you had a
chance of saving Eve. Remember to tap
Venable for any information you can
squeeze out of him." He hung up.

She pressed the disconnect and slipped
the phone in her pocket. She felt a sudden
rush of hope as well as excitement. John
Gallo was on the move.

Time for her to move, too.

Brush aside that sleek, gray-haired guest Venable was using to run interference against her. Make the bastard talk to her.

Venable looked up warily as she strode purposely across the bank toward him.

"I was worried about you." Mark Trevor watched Jane coming down the porch steps. "Particularly since I saw Caleb practically push you up those stairs. Are you okay?"

"Fine." She looked around the almost deserted grounds. "Better than fine now that I see everyone has gone home. I need to talk to Joe. I just needed a little stress-free rest."

"On Caleb's recommendation?" Trevor's lips twisted. "It's not like him to be a caregiver. You have to be careful of his motives."

"I'm always careful with Caleb."

"I know. And it makes me uneasy that you're so aware of him." He shrugged. "But that's the way things stand. I should never have left you for so long. I thought it was wise to give you space, but I'm not sure now. But now I'm back, and I'm closing that space down to inches." He reached out and took her hand. "And I'm an excellent caregiver. It's what I want to do. I want to be there to protect you in darkness and sunlight." He said softly, "Lately, I've been realizing that's maybe what I'm meant to do. I've even had a couple dreams about it. Crazy, huh? All the passion and the laughter was good, but in the end it comes down to what's really important. What role we're meant to play in each other's lives."

She didn't know what to say. This was completely unlike Trevor. He was sophisticated, sometimes dry, sometimes mischievous, never given to soul-searching. She searched his face for some hint of the Trevor she knew. No mockery. He meant what he said. She had known him since she was seventeen, but she had never seen him more sincere about anything. She laughed shakily. "Yes, pretty crazy. And I don't want anyone to take care of me. You should know that by now, Trevor."

"That doesn't seem to matter any longer." He added simply, "It's my role. I'll try not to let it get in our way." He linked his fingers with hers and pulled her toward Joe. "He's still talking to that police captain from Chicago. I'll distract him and get him out of your way while you talk to Quinn."

"How? You don't have any background in police—" She stopped and smiled. "Never mind. What am I thinking? You never have trouble with accomplishing distraction and sleight of hand. It's a product of your shady past. I forget occasionally what a checkered life you've led."

"Right." He smiled. "And it comes in handy to furnish you with what you need at any given time." He gestured as she opened her lips to speak. "And you'll take this little service from me because it could start the move toward helping Eve." They had reached Joe and the police captain, and Trevor's smile was suddenly brilliant, that powerful magnetism reaching out to envelop them. "Hello, Quinn, Captain Larimer, I just wanted to repeat my sincere condolences before I left." He turned to Larimer. "I know you must deal with this kind of tragedy on a daily basis, but you have to admit that this is far beyond—"

For the next five minutes, Jane watched Trevor with bemusement. In that time, he'd smoothly moved the police captain to the buffet and was pouring him a cup of coffee while he continued to ask him questions.

"Trevor's very good." Joe smiled faintly

as he watched the two men. "And I owe him. I tried twice to send Larimer on his way without being blatantly rude." He turned to Jane. "Margaret said you weren't feeling well. Should I be worried?"

"No, I was only tired." She grimaced. "Yet everyone immediately assumes I'm on death's door." She changed the subject as she turned and led him away from the cottage to the edge of the lake. "But I would have come down sooner except that I was talking to Kendra. And then, after she left, I was reading the journal."

He went still. "Journal?"

She quickly filled him in on her conversation with Kendra. "The stuff in the journal was sickening. Kevin was a monster. He was an egomaniac with a complete lack of conscience. The descriptions of what he did to those little girls were hideous."

"Anything else?"

"It's hard to get beyond the atrocities." She tried to think. "There were a few references to Pakistan, but no names that might have been valuable to al-Qaeda." She paused. "But there was a mention of his dealings with the CIA. Double dealings, according to him. A lot of money exchanging hands."

"That's not unusual. An embedded agent would pretend to be on the take."

"I don't believe he was talking about the embedded agents. He was talking about a specific CIA agent. And he was confident he'd persuaded the agent to go rogue. He was very happy about that. He said that he needed someone in a trusted position to pave the way to the project."

"Project? What project?"

"He never spelled it out. I assumed it had something to do with Bin Laden. That's who Venable told us was the target."

"Maybe." Joe frowned. "Maybe not."

Jane's gaze narrowed on his face. "Kendra didn't want me to give the journal to Venable. Now you have doubts about him?"

"I don't want to have doubts. I've worked with him a long time." He nodded curtly. "Hell, yes, I have doubts. He's not been listening to anything I've been telling him since this started. And I don't like the way he gave the okay for that attack team to tear down the mountain and start shooting up that saloon."

She could see his mind turning over, working through the facts and theories. "Anything else?"

"Venable was in the Middle East at the time. He knew what was happening in Pakistan. He was the connection to General Tarther and Kevin's assassination. But he was also the agent who offered Kevin's father sanctuary and provided him with a safe house and an income for five years." He paused. "And Venable told us that it was a disk that was the blackmail that Doane was holding over everyone's head."

"The disk may still be out there."

"But we have a journal mentioning CIA corruption." His lips tightened. "No, I don't believe we'll turn the journal over to Venable just yet."

"And there may be something in it that we can use. What if it's invisible ink or something?"

"Invisible ink? I doubt if even a madman would be quite that amateurish, Jane."

"You know what I mean. Things aren't always what they seem."

"No, they're not. But we don't have to rely on the labs at Langley. The labs at Quantico are just as sophisticated, and I have friends at the FBI."

"Then let's get it to them right away." She moistened her lips. "I feel as if we're spinning our wheels. We've been relying on Venable to keep up the search for Eve. If Venable is crooked, then what—It's been five days, Joe. Where is she?"

"I haven't totally relied on Venable. I've made him give me copies of every report from his guys in the field." Joe put his arm around her shoulders. "Could they be faked? Sure. I don't think they were. He's exploring every avenue that I would have ordered explored and done it with much less chance for leaks." He added, "And Venable's actions at that ghost town indicated he wanted Doane. Maybe too much for Eve's safety. But if we find Doane, we find Eve." He kissed her on the forehead. "After tonight, I'm going to go into seclusion, as would be natural in a grief-stricken man. I'll be in touch."

She had known this was coming. She had just hoped that they would have had something more to go on before the hunt began again. "Where are you going?"

"Vancouver. Venable is going to give me false papers and have me flown into a small airport north of the city. According to Venable, Zander's place appears to be deserted, but I'm hoping to contact Howard Stang, his assistant. He disappeared at the same time as Zander, but he may be the weak link." He shook his head. "Though I'm not sure how weak Stang will prove to be. He's something of an enigma."

"So is Zander," Jane said. "I can't forgive him for not saving Eve when he had the chance up in the mountains."

"Neither can I. He doesn't care about our forgiveness."

"He's her father, dammit."

"Neither one of them would say that had anything to do with their relationship. He never acknowledged her during her entire life. She doesn't want or need a father at this stage."

"Unless he can do something to save Doane from killing her. She needs him for that."

"And she'll have him as soon as I find the bastard," he said grimly. "Believe me, I'll serve Zander up to Doane on a silver platter if it will keep her alive."

She did believe him, and she was going to be as worried about Joe as she was about Eve. Zander was one of the most expert assassins on the planet. It wouldn't be easy even for a man as tough as Joe to overcome that skill. "I'm going to go with you."

He shook his head. "Not now. A mass exodus from here would definitely be suspicious. I'll call you as soon as I find Stang."

"You expect me to stay here and wait? It's not going to happen, Joe. I'm through with waiting."

"It would be suspicious," he repeated. "I'm not going to blow everything we've done to keep Doane off guard."

His jaw was set, and she knew he wasn't going to be persuaded. Frustration seared through her. "I won't blow anything, dammit. Do you think I'd do anything that might hurt Eve? Okay, I'll give you one day. Then I'm going to come after you. I'll ask Caleb to file a flight plan to London, and we'll leave Atlanta for Vancouver tomorrow afternoon instead. It will seem perfectly natural that I go back to London where I came from before this nightmare started."

"I'm not going to let Venable give you papers."

She smiled recklessly. "Screw Venable. I'm going, Joe. I won't risk Eve, but I won't sit here and do nothing. You go after Stang. I won't get in your way. I'll find my own way to Zander."

Joe muttered a curse.

"It's not the way I wanted it." Jane could feel the tears sting her eyes as she turned and started back toward the cottage. "I've put the journal in the last drawer of Eve's worktable. You'll want to get that up to Quantico before you leave. Keep safe, Joe."

Her eyes were so blurred, she almost ran into Margaret when she stepped out of the trees.

"Too bad that all the photographers have left," Margaret said quietly. "They'd get some wonderful shots. You're looking completely . . . lost." She gazed past her to Joe, still standing by the lake. "I was wondering if he'd try to keep you here." She shrugged. "When you're losing everything important to you, it's not unusual to try to salvage what you can."

"He's telling himself that he's being perfectly logical. I'm not needed; therefore, I should stay out of the way."

"And it hurts."

"I need to find her," she said. "I **have** to find her." She drew a long breath and tried to pull herself together. "Kendra left. Did she tell you she was leaving?"

"Yes, she tried to tell me that I should leave, too. That I wasn't needed and could be a liability." She smiled. "I told her that I was never a liability." She raised her hand as Jane started to speak. "But you're probably going to say the same things that Kendra said. That's fine, but it's not going to change anything. I'll just have to convince you how valuable I am and that you can't do without me." She tilted her head. "You read the journal, didn't you?"

"Yes." She shuddered. "It was terrible."

She nodded. "I read it, too. And I may have picked up some things that Kendra and you missed. We all look at life from different viewpoints, and with a man like Kevin, the horror of his actions sometimes blur the intent and the reason for what he did. That can be important."

"And it doesn't blur it for you?"

"Of course it does. But I virtually grew up in the forests. Nature is brimming with horror as well as joy. I learned to accept both and try to make them work to help me to survive." She cast another glance at Joe. "He's right about your not going immediately after Zander. But there may be other paths."

"What paths? Why didn't you say something before this?"

"It wasn't the time. I was going to speak to Kendra as soon as this brouhaha was over." She lifted her shoulders. "But now she's gone. Logical to the end."

"And probably right."

"I've never argued about that. It was a joy to watch her work." She chuckled. "And it was even more of a joy to watch her try to cope with the fact that I'm not at all logical and still manage not to screw things up."

"You're sorry she's gone."

She nodded. "You're always sorry when a friend leaves. But it's not as if it will be forever. I never let a friend be lost for long. They're too rare, particularly when I work so hard to get them to accept me as I am." She smiled. "Like you, Jane."

"It took a while," she said dryly. She had first met Margaret at an experimental animal clinic on an island in the Caribbean. Jane's dog, Toby, had been gravely ill, and no one could diagnose the cause. Until Margaret, a tech, had strode into the exam room full of love and empathy and that strange gift that allowed her to dive deep below the surface and decipher the dog's "impressions." Though it sounded to Jane that impressions meant memories. Anyway, she had diagnosed Toby's illness as poisoning and, to Jane's deep gratitude, had set him on the way to recovery. "And the circumstances aren't always in place to display that it's not the method but the result that matters."

"That's true. That's why I used the word 'rare.'" She changed the subject. "Kendra made several copies of that journal. Did she give you one?"

"Yes, and the original that I'm turning over to Joe."

Margaret's gaze narrowed on her face. "And judging by how upset you are at Joe, I don't think you're going to stick around the cottage for long."

She shook her head. "I'm packing up and leaving the cottage tonight. I'll check into an airport hotel. He's heading for Vancouver sometime after midnight anyway, but I don't want to be here to argue with him again." She paused, then said unsteadily, "It hurts too much."

"And you'll be traveling with Trevor and Caleb?"

"I don't know about Mark Trevor. I'll have to ask Caleb to fly me to Canada."

"I know about Trevor. He's crazy about you. He won't let you out of his sight." She tilted her head. "Caleb? I've never been able to read him. I don't know what he's thinking most of the time. But I keep trying because it could be either terrible or wonderful, and I wouldn't want to miss it." She turned away. "I'll go change and get my suitcase. Be sure to bring that extra copy of the journal. I need to go through it again. Do you want to take me to the hotel, or are you going to make me show up on my own?"

Jane stared at her with exasperation. "I never said you could come along with us, Margaret."

Margaret darted a mischievous glance over her shoulder as she strode away. "But I'm probably the only one who has an idea where we should be going. Therefore, it's you who are coming along with **me.**"

CHAPTER

5

Starlite Motel
Casper, Wyoming

The motel room was dark, and Eve could smell the musky scent of Doane's body in the next bed. He'd tied her wrists to the posts of the headboard, and she felt an overwhelming sense of helplessness.

Go to sleep, she told herself. It was easy to be ambushed by fear in the minutes before sleep came to rescue her.

Rescue. But she mustn't expect rescue. She had to save herself.

The telephone calls. Was there a way to find an out through this Cartland Doane had called?

"You're not sleeping," Doane said mockingly from the other bed. "What's wrong, Eve? Anxiety at last? It must have been terrible to watch your lover, Quinn, grieving for you. Did it make you feel lost? You are lost, you know. It's only going to be a few days more, and it will be over."

"I'm not lost. And the reason I can't sleep is that I can smell the stink of you in this tiny room. It makes me sick." She paused. There was a strange intimacy about talking to him in this darkness. Did he feel it, too? Would it help loosen his tongue? Test it. "Are we going to Vancouver after I finish repairing the reconstruction on your son? Do you really think that Zander is still going to be there? Not likely."

"Why not? He thinks we're both dead. There's no reason for him to close up his house and take off."

"Except that he'd be afraid that it wouldn't be safe since Venable and Joe would both know that Zander lived there. I imagine a hit man has to be careful of the number of people who have that information. You're probably not the only one who wants to get to him and cut his throat."

"But I'm the one who's going to do it," he

said. "And I'm not going to stumble into his lair without checking. That's not good planning."

"Oh, yes. Your great planning ability. How could I forget? So far, it doesn't seem to have panned out too well. Everything has gone wrong for you, hasn't it? And now you're stuck with me in this fleabag of a motel making more great plans. Who's going to check on Zander for you? You killed Blick. You're alone now."

"I'm not alone. I've just had to readjust my plans, and that takes a little time. Did you really think I was just going to burst into Zander's home and kill you the minute I saw him?"

"Yes."

"No, it has to be done with a certain subtlety." His tone hardened. "And now there's a price to be paid. I'm very angry with Venable. He was supposed to protect me, and I think he tried to kill me in that ghost town. I thought I had him under control, but I can't trust him any longer. So he has to be punished. They all have to be punished."

She stiffened. "All? Who else?"

"You're afraid I'm going to go after Quinn and your Jane. It might happen, but I can't waste my energy on them now that they're no longer a danger."

Thank heavens that it was dark and he couldn't see her relief. He'd pounce on any hint of weakness to hurt her. He was so volatile that he could change his mind in a heartbeat. "But you can target Venable." She paused, then asked again, "Who else?"

"All the sons of bitches who were responsible for that bullet that Zander shot into my boy. They could have saved him. They **should** have saved him. Kevin told them that if they let him go and gave him enough money, he'd give them the names of the other people in the sleeper cell."

"Cell?" She was confused. "You mean that disk that dealt with the embedded agents in Pakistan trying to find Bin Laden?"

"That had little importance. Kevin offered it to them in the beginning as an opening bid, but General Tarther made such a stink about the death of his daughter that Kevin knew he had to up the ante. He decided he might have to give him the sleeper cell."

"What sleeper cell?"

Doane was silent, and she was afraid that his brief loquacious period had come to an end. Then he spoke, "You think I'm going to tell you something that you can use against me and Kevin. You still think that you're going to get away from us." He chuckled. "You should be resigned by now, Eve. I've taken away every person you might have hoped could help you get free. I have total power. I could press a gun to your head right now and end it all."

"It wouldn't end. I'm not that important in the scheme of things. Someone would stop you and destroy all your dreams. Destroy you, Doane."

"You believe that your death would mean nothing. And that's one of my greatest regrets. You're not afraid to die. I can cause Zander to suffer when he sees you die, but you're going to cheat me of the same pleasure with you." He added speculatively, "So I might have to throw Quinn or Jane MacGuire into that mix when I kill Zander instead of attending to them later." He thought about it. "But I might be able to spark a response from you in a different way. Let me think . . . You have such a tender heart. Just the thought of needless death makes you sick, doesn't it? What if it was the deaths of thousands of children, thousands of innocent men and women? Yes, I believe that knowing you weren't able to stop that slaughter would cause your last moments to be a torment."

She stiffened. "Thousands of children?"

"You see, you focused on the children immediately." His tone was filled with delight. "I knew you would. Think about it, Eve, you've spent your entire adult life trying to bring children back to their grieving parents. How would you feel, if in the flash of a second, a greater number of children than the total you sent back to their parents were vaporized? No bodies to retrieve, no children for you to bring home to their parents. But, then, there might not be any parents grieving for their little ones. One has to consider that probability."

Probability, not possibility. The choice of words terrified Eve. "You're talking crazy, Doane. Vaporized? What the hell are you planning?"

"You know, I thought that the bodies of Blick and the whore he brought to the ghost town might be vaporized. Maybe I should have used more explosives. Kevin would know better than I what kind of effect a blast would have. I'm an amateur compared to him." He added, "But I believe the blasts that Kevin and his friends planned would cause vaporization. I hear that's what happened in Hiroshima. Come to think of it, the numbers might climb to millions."

She couldn't breathe. "Nuclear. You're talking nuclear."

"Of course. What else? Kevin wouldn't deal with anything that was penny-ante. I told you once how much he admired Hitler. If Hitler had gotten the atomic bomb first, he would have been a god. Naturally, Kevin would follow in his footsteps. Only his plans were much more brilliant than Hitler's, and he was right on track to bring them to completion."

"How?"

"Your voice is weak. I'm frightening you, aren't I?"

Don't deny it. She was frightened, and he was more likely to keep talking if he felt that heady sense of power. "How can I help it?" she asked shakily. "It's a horror story. He's a horror story."

"Kevin was magnificent. Horror is in the eye of the beholder. Horror can be power. It can twist the heart and bring a man to his knees." He added maliciously, "Or her knees. I think that you'll bow down before him before this is over, Eve."

"Those children . . ." she said hoarsely. "How?"

"It's really hurting you, isn't it?" He paused. "And I'm not afraid you'll ever be a threat. Kevin is getting stronger, and you're getting weaker."

"How?"

"And I'd really like you to be dreading it during the next few days. I'd enjoy that very much."

"How?"

"A very sophisticated device that can be triggered from a great distance. It was state-of-the-art five years ago, but nowadays it's a little behind the times. But it will work." He murmured. "Oh, my, how it will work. Boom! There go ten blocks of prime real estate in two American cities." He chuckled. "And the possibility of the rest of the city being unfit for habitation for the next three decades. It's a very dirty device. If Kevin does something, he does it right."

"Two cities."

"It was estimated that the destruction of two large cities would definitely destroy the

U.S. economy. What's left of it after the last years of recession. Of course, back when the plan went into place, the recession wasn't as rocky, and they were considering adding—"

"Who would do this? And don't say Kevin. He wouldn't have had the power to initiate a plot like that."

"Well, he didn't actually initiate it. It was funded by Iran. They were having trouble getting their nuclear program off the ground, but a small device is much simpler. There were cells set up in the target cities, but Kevin immediately became involved once he found out about it. He became responsible for acquiring key parts and distributing the uranium to the two cities. He was so trusted, he was even allowed to transfer the devices from place to place to avoid their being discovered. He might just as well have initiated the plan."

"So trusted he was going to turn over the names of the members of the cell to save his neck."

"It was necessary. He had to be free to have a new start. That bastard, Fred Juskow, in the counterterrorist team promised him that they'd set him up somewhere with money and a new identity if he'd talk to them." His voice hardened. "And then they let Tarther hire Zander to kill him just because he'd killed his little girl. They told me General Tarther was disobeying Homeland Security orders. But Kevin was dead, my boy was dead. What difference did that make?"

"Then the Pakistan disk had nothing to do with the deal you made with Venable, did it?"

"It was a good, acceptable substitution. Everyone wanted to get Bin Laden, and Pakistan was far away. It would have been another matter if it had gotten out that the counterterrorist guys had botched a job that concerned the deaths of millions of Americans on home turf."

"And did they botch it? It never happened."

"They botched it. When Kevin was murdered, the Iranians thought their operation had been discovered. The cell members in the two cities scattered to the four winds."

"Then how did they botch it?"

"They never found the nuclear devices. Kevin flew in from the Middle East and moved them to a hidden location before he went back to Pakistan. He made sure no one but him knew where they were hidden. That was going to be part of the deal he made with Homeland Security."

"But then Zander killed Kevin." She paused, trying to piece it together. "And you took over the negotiations. You wouldn't tell them where the devices were located, but as long as Venable had his hands on you, they thought that you wouldn't reveal where the devices were to the terrorists."

"I had Venable fooled. I had all of them fooled. They got careless."

"How do you know those nuclear devices are still operational? It's been five years. Wouldn't they disintegrate or something?"

"Kevin wouldn't allow that to happen."

"Look, why not let the Iranians ship in another bomb or two. Why set these antiques off?"

"You're blind. Can't you see the value of those devices of Kevin's? I assure you that when I contacted Cartland after we arrived here that he knew what a treasure I was offering."

"And what is the value? It's five years old and outdated technology."

"It's in place." He repeated, "In place. Do you know how incredibly difficult it would be to smuggle two nukes into two different cities? It was hard back when Kevin and the cell managed to do it. Homeland Security is a thousand times more sophisticated and well connected than they were five years ago. These devices are in place and only waiting for someone to press the switch."

"If they still work. If your Kevin didn't screw up."

"You're making me angry. If Kevin had lived, everyone would have known how brilliant he was. They'll still know it when those devices go off. Everyone will fear him and respect him."

"Bullshit. They'll know him as the monster he is and probably laugh when the bombs fizzle out."

"Bitch." She could feel the waves of rage he was emitting. "I'll show you what—" He stopped, then said, "That's right, I will show you. You and Zander. It's the perfect ending for you, Eve. I think we'll pay a visit to one of the cities where Kevin hid a device. I'll use you to draw Zander there, too. You'll probably be dead before it goes off, but you'll never know, will you? The suspense could be excruciating."

"You'll never draw Zander anywhere by using me."

"He came to the ghost town. I was very encouraged when he showed up."

She was silent. "Which city?"

"Does it matter?"

She had been afraid to pry into the names of the cities, but this question had seemed personal and natural. She tried to make her answer offhand. "I guess not."

"Let's see. Maybe somewhere close to Vancouver. We wouldn't want Zander to travel too far. I wouldn't want to discourage him." He thought for a moment. "Seattle. Yes, I think that would be just right. Have you ever been to Seattle?"

"No, and you'll forgive me if I'm not looking forward to it."

"I forgive you nothing. You've given Kevin and me a hellish time. But I'll always remember you, Eve."

"And I'll forget you as soon as you go join your beast of a son."

"I'm not going anytime soon. Kevin says that we're stronger because I'm on this side."

"Maybe he just wants to try to take you

over. I'm not saying I believe that Kevin is the spirit you say he is. But if that's true, he's a demon who cares nothing about you except to use you."

"He loves me. You have no idea how close we are. And we're getting closer every minute."

"Because you're losing your soul to make room for him to come back. It's all for nothing, Doane."

"Liar." He didn't speak for a moment, then whispered, "But that wouldn't be terrible, would it? The son is supposed to be better than the father. All the books say so. And Kevin was always special. He's so much more brilliant than I ever could be. He has such power. I wonder what it would be like to have that power."

Eve felt a chill. It was the first time she realized that Doane actually wanted to be his son. Not like Kevin, **be** Kevin. Kevin was evil incarnate; therefore, that was Doane's ambition. "I'm sick of talking to you. I'm going to sleep. Your son is dead. He has no power."

"You'll see," Doane whispered. "Seattle, Eve. Seattle . . ."

Seattle.

She had learned a great deal tonight. She might learn more later, but she had to concentrate on what she had already gleaned from this talk with Doane. Not about Kevin and his gradual merging with Doane. That was something that was drifting phantomlike in the darkness.

The two cities.

Cartland, the cell member Doane had mentioned.

Seattle, one of the cities that were to be targeted.

And the city that Doane had chosen as the place Eve was to die.

How could she make use of it?

They would be leaving tomorrow as soon as she put the final touches on Kevin's reconstruction.

She could only hope that Joe and Venable were tracking them and would show up soon. She couldn't believe that Joe's efforts of the last few days would be limited to that memorial service. Venable was an unknown quantity at present. Doane had thought he might be betraying him, but Venable had not been either truthful or open during these last five years.

But she had to have faith that they were

moving forward, and that somehow Venable had been forced to reveal the same story to Joe as Doane had told her.

And find a way to let them know where Doane was taking her. Not an easy task when Doane watched her every move whenever she was in the same room.

The bathroom?

Some way of writing on the mirror?

Steam? She had no lipstick.

No, that was strictly B-movie stuff.

Besides, Doane would undoubtedly check the bathroom before they left.

Think about it. Figure out a way.

Because now it wasn't only her and Zander's lives that were at stake.

Millions, Doane had said. Men, women, children caught in a deadly web through no fault of their own.

Innocents.

Find a way to save the innocents.

Lake Cottage
Atlanta, Georgia

Venable saw Catherine coming toward him, and he must have read the expression on her face. He smiled at the man to whom he'd been talking. "Excuse me. Business." He took Catherine's arm and started across the grounds toward the parking area. "Though he probably doesn't believe me. You're not a woman to bring to mind the thought of business."

"Oh, it's business all right," she said grimly. "Believe me, I'm not in the mood for social conversation. Where are we going?"

"My car. It's private. You're practically sending out sparks, and you'll attract too much attention."

"You're right, I don't give a damn how much attention I attract at the moment. You've been dodging me since I arrived here, and I decided to put an end to it."

"You've been more patient than I imagined you'd be." He opened the passenger door of the Lexus for her. "You've probably been talking to people and assessing the situation." He got in the driver's seat. "And now you're ready to pounce."

"Why didn't you tell me when Eve was taken? You know I would have wanted to be there for her."

"You were on a mission. Which you completed very successfully, by the way."

"Screw it. I could have arranged to leave Colombia. You could have sent someone else to replace me."

"But not as efficiently. You're remarkable, Catherine."

"Eve helped me when I needed her. She deserved the same from me."

He was silent for a long moment. "I know she did. But I couldn't let that matter. Not this time, Catherine. I couldn't bring you home."

"Why the hell not?"

"For the same reason I didn't want to send anyone to replace you in Colombia. You're remarkable." His lips twisted. "A little too remarkable. You would have dug deep. Turned the world upside down searching for Doane and Eve. I couldn't afford to have you do that."

She stiffened. "Dirty business, Venable?"

"Needful business, Catherine."

"Kendra said that she didn't trust the way you behaved at that ghost town. She wasn't sure it was in Eve's best interests."

"She was probably right. Kendra's very smart. I guess you found that out."

"Why the hell would you do something

that wasn't in Eve's best interest? Did you want to get her killed?"

"God, no. That's the last thing I wanted to happen. I like Eve. I did everything within the boundaries that I was permitted to save her."

"What boundaries?"

"I had to make my first priority to kill or capture James Doane. I had no choice."

"There's always a choice."

"You see? That's why I didn't bring you back to hunt for Eve. I wouldn't have been able to control you."

"Not if it meant letting her die because you wanted Doane's scalp. Company business isn't that important to me." She added grimly, "I should have known that it would be to you. You've spent most of your life playing their games."

"Yes, I have. Because it's worth doing. You believe that yourself, or you wouldn't have become an agent or stayed with it this long. Does it get dirty? Hell, yes. But we're lily-white compared to the other side." He paused. "And this time it was so nasty that I had to make decisions I didn't want to make."

"Eve's life for Doane's head?"

He didn't answer for a moment. "If necessary."

"You son of a bitch."

"Yes."

"Why? What was so important about getting Doane?"

"I had to shut him down. One way or the other."

"It was that urgent? It was worth Eve's life?"

"One life, Catherine. I had to put it in the balance. There wasn't any choice when I did that."

"What are you telling me, Venable?"

"Two cities, two nuclear devices, Doane with the knowledge of where they are and how to activate them. Is that clear enough? I had to take him out one way or the other. I had a chance at that ghost town in Colorado. I didn't do it. He got away and took Eve with him. The crazy bastard's out there somewhere, probably trying to make contacts to destroy those cities."

"Which cities?"

"Homeland Security wasn't able to find out both the target cities. They determined that one was Chicago, but we have no idea about the other one."

Chicago was a huge population center, Catherine thought. If the second city was equally populated, it could hardly be worse. "How bad is this device?"

"Powerful enough to take down a quarter of the city. And dirty. Our information isn't good enough to judge how dirty. They were planted over five years ago."

"And Homeland Security hasn't been able to locate them in all that time?"

"No. Doane's son supposedly hid them before he was murdered and evidently did a stellar job. But now we're sure that Doane knows where those bombs were placed. All he has to do is get in touch with Kevin's old al-Qaeda buddies who were in the cell in charge of setting those devices off and tell them where they are."

"Do we have any leads about who was in that cell?"

"We have a few names. The investigation was going pretty well until the general hired Zander to kill Doane's son. Then the panic started, and they all went underground. There was a Paul Berlitz, a George

Cartland, who appeared to be in charge, and a Mohammed Nali. We were gathering other names, but—"

"You haven't been able to find any of those men you ID'd?"

He shook his head. "Believe me, we've tried. For a while, we thought that they'd returned to Tehran. They might have done that, but we can't take a chance. The minute Doane took off from the safe house where we placed him, the game changed."

"New jobs, new identity papers? I suppose you checked out the usual sources in Chicago?" He gave her a sour look, and she shrugged. "I had to ask. I understand you haven't been following your usual modus operandi. Where do you go from here?"

"Locate Doane. Hopefully, capture him and make him tell us where those damn devices are located. Otherwise, kill him and hope he hasn't already told Cartland where Kevin hid the nukes."

"Either way, Eve could get caught in the cross fire."

Venable made no reply.

Catherine's eyes narrowed on his face. "Why are you being this open with me? You didn't even make me dig. Yet you've evidently been deceptive as hell with Joe Quinn and Jane MacGuire."

"I hoped I was going to be able to get rid of Doane without everything toxic coming bubbling to the surface. There are a few Homeland Security people whose jobs are on the line if that happens. And if you think I was reckless when we cornered Doane with Eve in the ghost town, you'd be stunned to know what those antiterrorist guys from Homeland Security would have done. Did you know there are drone bases on standby at the border? I got a call the next day from Major Eroldon asking why I hadn't called him to initiate a drone strike." He added grimly, "He was partially pacified when the word came out that Doane and Eve were dead. But he was still pissed off that I hadn't kept him in the loop."

"A drone strike," Catherine repeated. "He would have authorized a strike that would have killed Eve without even trying to get her out?"

"National security," Venable said sourly. "And also job security. A dangerous combination in the hands of bureaucrats."

"And if Doane was dead, how were they to make sure that no one had access to those bombs?"

"They prefer to think positive and get rid of the initial problem. Haven't you noticed that's been the standard operating procedure for the drone program?"

"You didn't keep them in the loop." Her gaze was searching his face. "Would you now?"

He didn't answer.

"Dammit, would you do it?"

"What do you want me to say? The problem still exists. My first reaction is to handle it myself to the best of my ability. Too many cooks in the kitchen are not good. Particularly when the head chef is an arrogant bastard like Eroldon." He met her gaze. "But if it comes down to needing extra firepower, you can bet I'll call for help."

"Great. Just great."

"Just as I'm asking help from you, Catherine. I kept you out of it before because I needed the chance to keep everything confidential, but I can't do that any longer. I need all the help I can get. We have to get Doane and get him fast."

"Screw Doane. We need to get Eve."

"Catherine."

"Okay, we have to stop Doane. But I **will** get Eve away from him before you turn loose those damn drones. What are you doing to track him?"

"Kendra identified the tire prints of the truck Doane used after he landed on the bank of the stream after leaving the cavern. They're commonly used on off-road vehicles. SSR series."

"Yes, she told me about it."

"We've begun checking all the cameras in the nearby areas to see if we can spot a vehicle that generally uses that type of tires."

"Any luck?"

"A sighting on the night of the fire of a tan Toyota 4-Runner with a dented left fender at the Wyoming border. It appeared that the driver was alone, but if Eve was unconscious, she would have been slumped down anyway. We're checking the cameras in both Colorado and Wyoming."

"No other reports?"

"No, the Toyota disappeared. We zeroed in on the state borders, but that came up zilch. But we're still searching."

"The smart thing would have been for him to get off the road and hole up."

Venable nodded. "We're checking every hotel, motel, and bed-and-breakfast in every town in both states. The state troopers have been cooperative."

"Good. We need them. It's a pretty flimsy lead to go on." Catherine opened the door and jumped out. "You can count on me to help find that bastard as long as you don't close me out on any information you get concerning him or those devices. One might lead to another."

"I'd be stupid to not let you have ammunition when I want you to take Doane down."

"Really?" She said gently, "I think you're already holding back on Quinn. But I want answers, Venable."

"You've had answers."

"No, you were playing footsie with Lee Zander for five years when you stuck Doane in a damn safe house. Everyone thinks Zander disappeared into the sunset after he was told Doane and Eve were still alive. But it would be unreasonable for you not to have tried to keep him in your pocket when you knew he could be a key player. I think you probably told him everything you told me, then arranged to stay in contact with him. I'd bet you're sharing information with him about what you're learning about the search. And Zander might have been lost to everyone else, but not to you. You can pick up your phone and contact him, and I'll bet you know where he is right now."

He was silent, then he said, "I can pick up my phone, but that's no guarantee he'll answer. Though he might since I've been feeding him what little information I have about the movement of any vehicles I've been able to find that use those tires. He's probably not been equally open with me, but I take what I can get."

"And you told him about that tan Toyota? I don't think so."

"Well, I was going to tell him . . . if I couldn't locate the car on my own." He chuckled. "And that's why I had to keep you a thousand miles distant when Eve disappeared. You're too sharp, Catherine."

"I know you. I watched you grow and change from the time you hired me when I was a kid on the streets of Hong Kong. Some of the changes I liked, some made me wary."

"I feel the same about you." He smiled. "But you're always interesting, Catherine."

"I want you to e-mail me the Zander info.

Where he is, what he's working on." She started to turn away. "And the file on the cell members who might be contacted by Doane."

"Okay. No problem. Though there's not much on record and most of it is undoubtedly phony."

"Whatever you've got."

"Catherine."

She looked over her shoulder.

"I believe Kendra found something in Doane's house in Goldfork. She doesn't trust me, but she might trust you. Did she say anything about it to you before she left?"

"That mysterious disk that you told everyone Doane was holding?"

"Did she say anything?"

"You're right, she said she didn't trust you."

"Did she find anything?"

"It wouldn't surprise me. But after the way you practically served Eve up as a sacrifice, I don't think you'll get it from her unless you can convince her that you'd never do it again." She looked him directly in the eye. "And, since you haven't convinced me, I doubt if you could convince her." She turned away. "Of course, you could come clean about what you expect to find on that 'disk,' and you might have a breakthrough. Think about it, Venable."

CHAPTER

6

Hyatt Airport Hotel
Atlanta, Georgia

"Nice hotel," Margaret said as she took her room key from Jane. "This will be a great change. I've traveled a lot during my life, but I'm more used to Motel 6." She entered the elevator and punched the button for the fourth floor. "I think we should go over the journal tonight. Suppose I meet you guys in twenty minutes. I've got to change out of this dress and high heels and get comfortable." She smiled. "Your room, Jane?"

"Fine," Jane said dryly. "I suppose I should be happy you asked since you seem to have taken charge." She glanced at Trevor and Caleb. "Yes?"

Trevor nodded.

"By all means," Caleb said. He got out of the elevator as the doors opened and turned left. "Margaret's viewpoints are always interesting. Twenty minutes."

Trevor got out of the elevator and took Jane's bag. "I'll see you to your room."

She shook her head. "I don't need—" He was already going down the corridor, and she had to rush to catch up.

He took her key and opened the door. "I know you don't need me. But I need to do everything I can for you." He smiled down at her as he handed her back her key. "I told you that I'd discovered my calling." He put her bag inside the door. He brushed his lips across her forehead and started down the hall. "Twenty minutes."

She stood looking after him for a moment, feeling a warm melting inside her. It wasn't passion though that was present also. It was a feeling that was different from anything she had felt in the time she was with him. It was like a wonderful, golden net that was holding her safe and secure away from all loneliness. She wanted to call him back and have him smile like that at her again.

He stopped as if he had heard her call him and looked back at her. "I meant it," he said softly. "It's going to be different for us from now on. I've never been a believer in fate, but I am now. I feel as if it's our time, and I have to reach out and take it before it goes away. Trust me." He turned and went down the hall.

"Trust me."

Only two words, but a concept so difficult for her to accept.

Because trust meant commitment, and that was even more difficult for her.

She shook her head to clear it and went into the room and closed the door. She couldn't think right now about Trevor and the promise that he offered. She had only one commitment, and it was to Eve.

She took the journal out of her bag and put it on the coffee table in the sitting room. Just looking at it jarred her out of the beauty of the moments before. Ugliness and horror and malice beyond imagination.

And, like Margaret, she wanted to get as comfortable as possible to mentally gird her loins at what was soon to be faced. She took her suitcase to the adjoining bedroom to wash and change. Then she'd order coffee from room service.

Twenty minutes.

"Coffee, good." Margaret plopped down on the couch in Jane's sitting room. "I grabbed one of those little sandwiches on the buffet at the service, but I need some caffeine." She had changed to jeans, tunic, and her usual flip-flops and looked even younger than her nineteen years. "You need a cup, too, Jane. You look more tired than I do."

"Yes, she does," Caleb murmured. He poured coffee into a cup and handed it to Jane. "But she'll be fine . . . for tonight."

"I'll be fine. Period," Jane said firmly as she took a sip of coffee. "It's been a rough day."

"Yes, it has." Trevor's thoughtful gaze was on her face. "You've had a lot of rough days since that blowup in the ghost town. I've been worried." His gaze shifted to Caleb. "So worried that I'm even glad of reassurance from you."

"You should be glad," Caleb said. "No one can know her physical condition better than I do." Before Jane or Trevor could reply, he turned to Margaret. "But we'd be wise to get this little meeting over with so that she can get to bed." He glanced down at the journal on the coffee table. "Jane said that when you read that piece of filth, you might have found something that will give us a lead."

"Maybe. It's a hodgepodge of grandiose bragging, porn, and poetic quotations." Margaret picked up the journal and flicked it open to one of the earlier pages. "As you say, it's all pretty much filth, particularly during these passages when he's describing his victims." She shivered. "Those poor little girls. It made me cry."

"The lead," Caleb prompted.

"Every now and then, during those obscene meanderings, he'd drop in a line that could be lost because of the sheer disgust you're feeling." Her gaze ran down the page. "Like this one. "Smooth skin, child skin, as satin soft as mother's." She flipped through more pages. "Blue eyes, staring at me, scared eyes, hating what was happening to her. Beautiful, beautiful eyes, almost as beautiful as mother's eyes." She looked up as she closed the journal. "There are several more comparisons like that one." She added deliberately, "Kevin's mother. All we've heard about is Doane, Kevin's father. But when he was committing these atrocities, he was thinking about his mother. And from the sampling I've read, there's nothing vengeful about those thoughts. If you weave them together, you get a picture of a son almost besotted by his mother."

Jane frowned. "But from what I've heard from Joe, most serial killers are driven by hatred for their mothers if the relationship enters into motivation at all."

"And it may not be a motivation," Margaret said. "I don't know. I just thought that since we have no clue about where to find Doane, we should try another avenue. She evidently had a powerful influence on Kevin." She paused. "If she's still alive. I don't even know that."

"Venable didn't mention Kevin's mother when he was talking about Doane?" Trevor asked.

"No," Jane said. "But evidently Venable left out a lot that we should have known." She reached for her phone. "And I can find out if she's still alive. Catherine Ling." She accessed her directory and dialed. Catherine picked up in three rings. "I need help. Venable's never mentioned Kevin's mother. Is she still alive? What do you know about her?"

"Nothing. Why do you want to know?"

"It's a question of exploring every avenue at the moment. Can you find out about her from Venable?"

"Probably. He's trying to keep me from rocking his boat, so he's being very cooperative. If not, I'll access CIA records. Give me twenty minutes." She hung up.

"Twenty minutes," Jane repeated as she hung up her phone. "Catherine is nothing if not efficient."

Catherine called back in fifteen minutes and Jane put her on speaker. "Harriet Relling is still alive. She divorced her husband when Kevin was only fifteen. Then she changed her name and moved to Muncie, Indiana. She teaches English Literature at Ferry Road High School."

"Any contact with Doane since the divorce?"

"No. The divorce papers said irreconcilable differences, but according to Venable's reports, she's very bitter. He did a thorough investigation on her five years ago when he put Doane under protective custody. As

of that time, she'd never had another relationship after the divorce and was reputed
to be something of a man-hater. Has a few
friends but is pretty much a loner. She's
an advocate for better schools and gives
talks around the state. She has a doctor-
ate in English Literature and has been offered positions at several universities but
has always refused. She organized the local autism walk three years ago. And, as
I said, she changed her name. She's now
Harriet Weber and told everyone in Muncie that she was a widow." Catherine
paused. "Venable says that she was not
put under the same surveillance as Doane
because the chances seemed miniscule
that she had anything to do with either of
them since the divorce."

"And Doane's surveillance was not as
tight as it should have been," Jane said. "Or
he'd have never been able to take Eve."

"I'm not arguing. Venable's judgment is
usually fairly good, but he's failed misera-
bly in this. Do you think it's worthwhile going to question Doane's wife?"

"From what you say, probably not," Jane
said slowly. "But I think I'm going to do it
anyway. There was something in the journal

that was very curious. It won't hurt to go check her out."

"Then I'll forward you the file that Venable sent me on her," Catherine said. "If you need anything else, call me."

"I will. What are you working on?"

"Zander. Who else? He seems to be the center of the storm."

"You're going to Vancouver?"

She was silent. "No, I'm taking another route. I'm leaving right away. I'll let you know if I come up with anything." She paused. "Good luck with Kevin's mother. I can't imagine what kind of woman could give birth to a monster. Yet there are quite a few monsters in the world, and they all had to come from someplace. Personally, I don't believe in heredity. I believe everyone is born with a soul, and that dictates his character. It was one philosophy upon which Eve and I agreed."

"What about Doane? It appears that he's also a monster. You're saying he didn't pass those traits on to his son?"

"Maybe Doane's soul was always tarnished, and it just became visible when his son revealed his own malignance." Catherine added impatiently, "I don't know. I don't sit around thinking about theories about good and evil. Everyone has gut instincts, and that's what I go by. My gut instinct tells me that Doane is a terrible man and growing worse with every passing day. I'll let God decide how Doane got that way . . . after I kill him." She hung up.

Caleb was chuckling. "I do like her." He got to his feet. "I, too, believe in gut instinct. But I don't entirely agree about heredity not having a part in what we are. I'm the living proof that certain traits are passed down through generations."

"Physical traits," Jane said. "Not necessarily souls. You told me that your ancestors back in medieval times were said by the villagers to be offspring of the devil. You don't have to be what your ancestors were." She added deliberately, "That's all bullshit."

Caleb glanced at Trevor. "What do you think, Trevor?" he asked mockingly. "Do I have a devil's soul?"

Trevor didn't speak for a moment. "I think that you're strong enough to be whatever you want to be," he said quietly. "And I believe that souls can change if the desire is there."

Caleb's eyes widened with surprise. "I wasn't expecting that. You continue to astonish me. I give you the opportunity to condemn, and you return it with generosity. It's really very clever since you come across in a very favorable light."

"It wasn't calculated, Caleb."

He smiled wryly. "I know." He turned to Jane. "I take it we're heading for Muncie, Indiana? When?"

"In a few hours." She checked her watch. "We don't want to roust Kevin's mother from her bed. We should arrive in Muncie about eight or nine if we can do it."

"Then we should all try to get a few hours' sleep." Margaret jumped to her feet and headed for the door. "Call me when you're ready to leave, and I'll meet you in the lobby."

"Margaret," Jane said. "I appreciate your—"

"Stop arguing, Jane. It takes too much energy." She smiled. "You can't just use me and throw me away."

"I'm not doing—"

"I'm going with you, or I'm going alone. That's your only decision." She opened the door. She glanced at Trevor and Caleb. "And you get out of here, too, and let her rest. All this talk about souls and devils and monsters. Too deep and too gloomy." She gestured in front of her at the open door. "Out."

Trevor's smile was faintly bemused as he allowed himself to be ushered into the hall. "Heaven forbid that we express any gloom and doom. However, I have to point out it was you, Margaret, who delved into the ugliest concept of all."

"Necessary." She pushed Caleb out the door, then stuck her head back in the room to repeat to Jane. "Call me."

Jane turned and headed for the bedroom. She was suddenly dragging in every limb, totally exhausted. She could use that few hours' sleep Margaret had suggested, no, demanded. The effects of the brief rest she'd had earlier in the afternoon had dissipated.

She didn't bother to undress as she curled up on the bed and closed her eyes.

Sleep.

Relax.

She wasn't at all sure that this journey would prove helpful, but if it didn't, they could fly on to Vancouver immediately.

They were at least no longer standing still. They were going to be on the move in a few hours.

She remembered Margaret's words as she burrowed her head into the pillow.

Close out the gloom and doom. Cling to hope and send all the devils and monsters packing . . .

Penthouse
Drake Hotel
Denver, Colorado
8:40 A.M.

Catherine hesitated for a moment before the door of the hotel room.

What the hell. Go for it.

She knocked firmly and waited for an answer.

An eye appeared in the security peep-hole. "Yes."

"I need to talk to Zander."

"Wrong room."

"You must be Stang. Let me in."

"Wrong room."

"Look, you clearly don't want to draw attention to Zander's being here. Let me in, or

I'll start pounding on the door and scream-ing that now that I've had your baby, you won't give me child support. You have no idea what kind of publicity and outrage that can spark. I'll give you one minute."

"I believe I'll have to call security."

"And that will cause even more of an uproar."

"Let her in, Stang." A deep voice and completely without expression. "I'll attend to it."

The door swung open. "I'm Howard Stang." Stang was a tall, thirtyish man in a beige sweater. "And you are?"

"Catherine Ling." The white-haired man who had spoken strolled forward from the balcony to confront her. He was dressed in black slacks and a white shirt whose sleeves were rolled up to reveal that there was a cast on his right forearm. He ap-peared ageless, but her immediate impres-sion was of power, elegance, and leashed violence. "If I'm not mistaken?"

She nodded curtly. "But I'm curious to know how you guessed. I didn't tell Ven-able I was coming to see you."

"Really? He didn't send you?"

"Hell, no. The two of you are dancing

around each other like Olympic fencers. He'd be afraid of sending you underground where he couldn't get his hands on you."

Zander smiled faintly. "I don't have to go underground to be sure that he can't get his hands on me. But Venable is proving moderately helpful, and I don't mind giving him limited access." His smile faded. "But I'm not pleased he was less than discreet about taking you or anyone else into his confidence."

"He didn't think that I'd go knocking on your door."

"Then he has bad judgment, and I'm even less pleased."

She changed the subject. "How did you know who I was?"

"A matter of elimination." He turned to Stang. "Why don't we get the lady a cup of coffee?" He looked at Catherine. "Or do you prefer tea? Since you grew up in Hong Kong, I'm sure that's your preference."

"Either will do." She shut the door behind her as Stang went to the phone. "Elimination?"

"You're bold, smart, and you have a certain dash. You had to have a CIA connection, or you would never have been able to locate me. Eve mentioned her friend, Catherine Ling, who was with the CIA." He waved his hand. "Elimination."

"Joe mentioned that you'd talked to Eve in the mountains. I didn't think I'd be the topic of conversation."

"You weren't, actually; she didn't bring you up until right before she took off into the woods. That's why I felt I had to check you out while I had nothing better to do here in Denver."

"And that's how you knew I grew up in Hong Kong?"

"Yes. And that you'd have been the first to try to find Eve if you'd known what had happened to her. No one told you, did they? Venable kept you in the dark."

Sharp. Very sharp.

She studied Zander. Ice-cold. Completely in control. Dangerous.

And challenging.

"And Venable heard about it from me," she said grimly. "I just found out when I got back to Miami yesterday morning."

"And you were angry, and you wanted to kill him."

"Yes, but I didn't. Because he thinks he was right, and he can help me find Eve." She looked him in the eye. "And he told me where you were even though he didn't know that I might blow your cozy little relationship."

He chuckled. "You make us sound like lovers. I assure you that I'm not of the gay persuasion, and there's nothing cozy about anything between Venable and me. We're both very wary of what the other might do." He gestured to a chair. "Won't you sit down? I'm finding your visit very entertaining. I've been extremely bored lately."

"I've not been bored," she said bluntly as she sat down in the chair. "I've been scared and sick and angry. I wanted to kill Doane. I wanted to strangle Venable." She looked up at him. "And I wasn't sure what I wanted to do to you, but it wasn't going to be pretty. I was told you had a chance to help Eve when she was free in those mountains, and you didn't do it. Why?"

"Doane was my target. Eve would have been in the way."

"They told me that Eve's your daughter. That had no impact on your decision?"

He shook his head. "Does that put me beyond the pale in your eyes?"

"No, my father was an American soldier who deserted my mother before I was born. My mother was a whore, who was hooked on drugs and let me fend for myself on the streets. I don't have any faith in family or obligation. But some people do. I hoped that you might be one of them. Because that would mean Eve has a better chance of surviving."

He nodded mockingly. "My regrets."

"Not accepted. Because even if you don't give a damn that Eve is your daughter, if you talked to her for any time at all, you know what kind of person she is. She deserves to live." She met his eyes. "And you seem to be in the best position to keep her alive. That's why I'm here."

"Really? Interesting." He sat down opposite her. "And what is your purpose, Agent Ling? Do you intend to try to intimidate me into doing as you wish?"

"Catherine. I'm not CIA right now, I'm Eve's friend," she said. "And if you can't act like a father, you should try to be her friend, too." She added, "And stop being sarcastic. You can't be intimidated. I don't even know if you'd care if you lived or died." She tilted her head. "I'm curious. Would you?"

"Sometimes. It depends on the moment. How about you?"

"Most of my moments are pretty damn good now. I have my son back."

His brows rose. "If you're not here to force me to your will, why did you come here, Catherine?"

"Venable said that you might be able to locate Doane by hacking security and traffic cameras and that he might still be in the area. I wanted to be on the spot if that happened." She paused. "And Doane wants you dead, and that gives me another reason to be here."

"And why is that?"

"I'm going to be your bodyguard."

She heard Stang give a strangled gasp across the room.

Zander's eyes widened. "I beg your pardon?"

"I'm going to take care of you," she said simply. "I can't let Doane kill you. You told Venable that Doane said he wanted to kill Eve in front of you. To keep Eve alive, I have to keep you alive."

"Did it occur to you that I might be able to take care of myself?"

"Yes, but I can't take the risk." Her jaw set

with determination. "I won't let Eve die because I left her fate up to a man I'm not sure gives a damn. So suck it up, Zander. You're stuck with me."

He gazed at her for a long moment, and she had no idea what he was thinking. "The hell I am," he said softly. "Do you realize how easily I could dispose of you?"

"I realize you're an expert. But it wouldn't be easy, Zander."

He didn't speak for another minute. "No, I don't think it would." He leaned back in the chair. "Tell me, do you wear a knife in a holster on your calf?"

"What?" she asked in surprise. "Sometimes."

"Now?"

"Yes, I didn't know what to expect. Why?"

"Just something Eve told me about you. I was trying to fasten a knife on her calf and she said that she wasn't like you and that you'd be more prepared."

"You gave her a knife?"

"It seemed to be the thing to do at the time. Of course, then I sent her off to face her fate with Doane. So don't think I was being particularly generous to her."

"I won't." She paused. "But maybe you

were, considering what a cold bastard you seem to be." She got to her feet. "May I go to the bathroom and freshen up? I just flew in from Atlanta and came straight here."

"By all means." He nodded at a door leading off the sitting room. "Make yourself at home."

"Oh, I intend to do that." She headed for the door he'd indicated. "And you might call housekeeping and get me a cot. Of course, I can always sleep on that sofa."

"You really meant it." He was gazing at her quizzically. "You're moving in."

"It's the most practical thing to do. I have to be near you." She tensed, waiting for the response.

"You're being absurd, you know. And you could be very annoying. You have that potential."

"Yes, I do. But I'm competent, reasonably intelligent, and I'm possibly the most stubborn person you've ever met. So unless you intend to drop me off that balcony over there, you're not going to get rid of me."

"Tempting," he murmured.

"I'm sure it is." She paused at the door. "So make up your mind."

He gazed at her without expression. "I object to destroying lovely pieces of art unless necessary. I'll keep you around until you annoy me too much." He added as he got to his feet, "But if I find that you're neither helpful nor as competent as you claim, that time will come sooner rather than later." He glanced at Stang. "Confrontation over, Stang. We'll keep her around." He turned and strolled back out on the balcony.

Catherine's gaze followed him. "Why do I feel like a stray puppy tossed over to you to watch, Stang?"

"You should be grateful," Stang said dryly. "And take into account that he meant what he said. You took a chance."

She had been aware of that threat the entire time she had been with Zander. "Life is full of chances. You just have to turn them into opportunities." She opened the bathroom door. "I'll be out in a few minutes, and you can show me the process of what you're doing to monitor those cameras. Do you know you're looking for a Toyota 4-Runner with a dented left fender?"

"Yes."

"But you didn't hear it from Venable."

He shook his head. "Zander never trusts one source, particularly if it's government connected."

"Very intelligent." She added, "And, after we go over the cameras, then I want you to go over the security measures in place here."

"Security?" He looked at her in amazement. "You really meant what you said about protecting Zander?"

"I don't usually say things I don't mean." She cast a glance at the door to the balcony. "He knew I meant it. That's why he was so pissed at me. That's the moment when it was touch-and-go."

"You're underestimating Zander. You may not have even reached that point yet," Stang said. "And I'm not looking forward to the time that you do. You seem sincere about wanting to help Eve Duncan."

"And are you sincere, Stang?"

"Oh, yes. And, like you, I've run a few risks because I wanted Zander to be more involved." He turned at a knock on the door and moved to answer it. "That must be your tea. I'm sure that you can spare time to drink it before you go about saving Zander . . ."

CHAPTER 7

Starlite Motel
Casper, Wyoming

"When are you going to finish?" Doane asked impatiently as he watched Eve's hands carefully smoothing the clay down one cheek of Kevin's reconstruction. "I thought you'd be done by noon today. Are you stalling?"

"Why should I be stalling? Do you think that I'm particularly fond of this tiny room? The sooner we get on the road, the better." She glanced at him. "If somebody recognizes you, I'll at least have a chance of getting away from you."

"But I'm a dead man." He smiled. "No one is looking for me . . . or you."

"That's right." She looked back at the reconstruction. "How could I forget? Hope springs eternal."

"He looks almost done. I'm tired of waiting." He was gazing at the skull in discontent. "I'll get the eyeballs. I have them safely tucked in a handkerchief in my suitcase."

"Forty more minutes." She met his eyes. "Do you believe I enjoy working on him? This is the third time I've had to make repairs on your Kevin's skull. And this time you didn't even salvage enough clay for me to do the job right. That makes it twice as hard to fill in and smooth." She had to turn his impatience into anger, so that he'd seek a release. It was the only way she could to think to get him out of the room. "Did it ever occur to you that it's a bad omen, and your son's skull should just be tossed in the nearest garbage can?"

"Bitch." His hand dug into her hair and he jerked her head back.

Pain.

"No?" she asked. "Well, he'll be just as much a piece of garbage if you don't let me finish him properly." She glared up at him. "But what do I care? You want trash, I'll give you trash."

He cursed and gave her hair one more vicious twist before he released it. "It's your fault you had to keep doing him over. You showed him no respect. You could have done him permanent damage by tossing that skull off the cliff while we were in the mountains."

"I can but try," she murmured.

He took a step toward her, then stopped. "Finish him. I'll give you thirty minutes." He handcuffed her right wrist to the chair. "I've got to get gas for the car at the motel gas station. I can keep an eye on the door of this unit from there. When I come back, you'd better be finished, or I'll beat you unconscious."

She looked down at the handcuffs. "This will be awkward working."

"Finish him." The door slammed behind him.

She drew a deep, relieved breath.

Okay, get to work.

She took some of the clay from the skull's reconstruction, not too much or Doane would know it was missing. She'd been telling the truth about the scarcity of materials. Then she flattened the clay out on the table. She took her spatula and started to write on the clay.

Not too deep or it would break apart.

A capital **S,** small **e,** and then **WA**. No room for anything else.

Seattle, Washington. Would it be clear to anyone looking for a direction? It was as close as she could come.

The **S** looked more like an eight. She'd have to do it over.

It broke apart when she tried to alter it.

Keep calm.

Only ten minutes had passed.

She still had time.

She carefully meshed the clay together and started over again.

Stang rushed into the sitting room.

"We've got another hit." He threw a map of Wyoming down on the desk in front of Zander. "Casper, Wyoming."

"Where?" Catherine jumped up from her chair and was across the room in three strides. "What part of the city?"

"Outskirts." Stang was looking at the computer 3-D map of the city. "Weiner says the camera was across the road at a tire store." He pointed at the building. "But it still photographed the motel gas station across the way." He pointed at four pumps. "There."

"Has Weiner verified?" Zander asked.

"Yes, he says it's the same vehicle he saw at the Colorado border. But we only got a visual for about ten minutes. Then it moved on and out of camera range."

"On the road?"

"No." He smiled. "It moved to the north in the parking lot and seemed to be going around a corner."

Catherine tensed as she gazed down at the map. "The motel," she said. "He's at the motel."

"That's my bet."

Zander was on his feet and heading for the door. "And mine. Stang, tell the helicopter pilot I'll be up on the roof in three minutes and to set a course for Casper, Wyoming."

Catherine was right behind him. "How long will it take?"

"Probably thirty minutes."

Excitement was tingling through her. Thirty minutes, and they had a chance of getting to Eve. But anything could happen in thirty minutes, and she'd seen victory turned to defeat too many times to take it for granted. "I'm calling Venable and telling him to have the state police start surveillance of the motel."

"Your choice," Zander said. "But one mistake, and we've lost him again. Are you willing to put Eve's life on the line if one of those troopers isn't as sharp as you'd want him to be?"

"No." She looked him in the eye. "Okay, but I'm going with you in that helicopter, Zander. What you know, I'm going to know."

He gazed at her for a moment. "Have it your own way. You're not stupid, and you impress me as being fairly lethal. I can see why Eve trusted you." He added softly, "But don't get in my way, Catherine."

"I won't get in your way." She passed him in the hall and punched the button for the elevator. "As long as you don't get in mine, Zander."

Casper, Wyoming

A sound at the door of the motel.
   Doane!

Panic iced through Eve.

No! It was too soon. She wasn't ready.

She jerked her hand from beneath the table where she'd been painstakingly sticking the clay to the underside. Carefully enough? What if it tore loose and fell to the floor?

It would have to do.

She quickly moved the spatula across the face of the reconstruction, smoothing, filling. She deliberately jabbed the spatula into the lower mid-therum area beneath the nose as the door opened.

"Damn!" She turned to glare at Doane as he came into the room. "I told you these cuffs would make me clumsy." She jerked her head at the indentation she'd made. "Now let me go, and I'll try to smooth the clay."

He unlocked the cuffs. "You really chopped up that clay."

"What do you expect?" She worked quickly, skillfully, to smooth over the place where she'd stolen the clay. "I only had one hand, and I couldn't—"

That was good enough. Doane would have to examine it under a magnifying glass to tell the difference from the time he'd walked out of the motel room. She sat back and gazed at the skull. "He's almost as good as new." Her lips twisted. "Though there are two words in that sentence that are completely bizarre when applied to your Kevin. He was never good nor new. He's as old as sin."

Doane took out his handkerchief and carefully unwrapped it. "I washed his eyes very carefully." He held up the glittering blue orbs. "He's going to be handsome again. In spite of all the harm you've done him, he can't be made anything but magnificent."

She looked down at the blue eyeballs shining up at her. This was the part of the reconstruction she dreaded. When she had first placed those eyes in the orbital cavities in the ghost town, it had come as almost a physical shock.

It wouldn't be so bad this time. She'd be prepared for it. She quickly inserted the blue eyes.

It was just as bad. Worse.

It seemed as if Kevin was glaring at her with supreme malice.

A wave of nausea swept over her.

"He always frightens you, doesn't he?"

Doane said softly. "You act so bold, but in the end he makes you want to go and hide."

"This skull doesn't frighten me. Neither does the thought of your son." She forced herself to look into those glass eyes. "He's dead. He has no power. He can't hurt anyone any longer."

"Tell that to the people in those cities that are going to be blown into the stratosphere. Tell them that Kevin has no power. Tell that to Zander at the moment that I kill him." He gazed lovingly at the reconstruction. "She brought you back again, Kevin. I made her do it, just as you said I should."

"Excuse me, your raving is making me ill." She got to her feet. "And I have to go to the bathroom and wash this clay off my hands." She picked up the hand towel she'd been using to wipe her hands and carried it toward the bathroom. Just as she opened the bathroom door, she deliberately dropped the towel and knelt to pick it up. From her position, she could see underneath the table to where she'd stuck the clay.

Damn, it was hanging precariously by one end of the piece of clay.

Maybe it would hold.

She snatched the towel up and slammed the bathroom door behind her. She quickly washed her hands of the clay, and then washed her face.

"Hurry up. You're wasting time. We're leaving."

She opened the door.

Doane was at the table, almost directly in front of the place where she'd stuck the clay. He seemed to be cleaning the surface of clay traces and all her work debris.

She stiffened in panic, then tried to hide the reaction. "What are you doing? I've never noticed you being particularly fussy about housekeeping before, Doane."

"You're messy as hell, and you leave very distinctive evidences of your occupation that are peculiarly your own."

"Only if you're on the lookout for a forensic sculptor. Let's face it, it's not the most popular profession in the world. And you keep bragging that everyone thinks I'm dead."

"And that's the way I want to keep it. I don't want any questions popping up that might lead anyone to study that explosion at the ghost town more closely. This is what my Kevin would do." He carefully placed the reconstruction in its leather container, which was much worse for wear from water damage. He glanced at her impatiently. "What are you doing just standing there looking at me?"

I'm hoping you won't try to pick up any debris that might have fallen on the floor.

I'm hoping that the clay piece under the table will stay fixed.

"What am I supposed to be doing? You tell me that you give the orders."

"Throw the clothes I bought you into that cloth grocery bag." He looked at her critically. "And put on a clean shirt. It's all stained by that clay, and I don't want you to attract attention."

"As you command. I promise I'll do you proud, Doane." She grabbed one of the cheap white tunic shirts Doane had bought at Walmart and ducked back into the bathroom.

Quick.

Don't give him a chance to spend more time cleaning that table.

And the soiled shirt? Use it.

She changed the shirt in a matter of seconds and came back into the room. She carried the stained shirt to her bed and packed it into the cloth grocery bag, making sure that a few scraps of dried clay dropped from the shirt onto the bed. She casually pulled the sheet over the clay as she put the grocery bag on the floor. "Anything else?"

His gaze narrowed on her face. "You're being very accommodating."

"I want out of here. I'm sick of being so close to you." She smiled. "And I want my chance to get away from you. Once we're on the road, I'll have that chance. I did it once. I can do it again."

"The hell you can. Do you think that I didn't make plans to make sure you didn't slip away from me? The only way you'll get away is when you're dead." He grabbed the reconstruction container, took her arm, and pushed her toward the door. "And then Kevin will have you. He's been waiting for you. He doesn't like it that you've been keeping him from the little girl."

It wasn't the first time that Doane had mentioned that ugliness about Kevin trying to get to Bonnie and that Eve's connection to her was preventing it. True or false, it struck terror in Eve. She might deny

Kevin's existence as an entity to Doane, but she had doubts. If there were special creatures of love like Bonnie on the other side, might there not also be demons? What did Eve know? All she knew was that by some special grace, she had been given the chance to keep her Bonnie with her even after she had passed on, and her daughter must be protected. "Your Kevin will wait a long time," she said. "Bonnie is stronger than he will ever be."

He muttered a curse as he slammed the door of the motel behind them. "Get in the car." He opened the passenger door and shoved her into the vehicle. He cuffed her right wrist to the seat belt. "No screams, or I'll gag you."

"That would look very weird to any by-stander."

"Not if I tie you up on the floorboard. You'd be very uncomfortable, I promise you." He started the Toyota. "Though the drive won't be as long as I'd like it to be."

She glanced at the door of the motel as the car pulled out on the road. Doane hadn't found the clay message.

Safe.

Not safe. That bit of clay could be found

by a maid cleaning up the room and tossed out.

It was the best she could do.

She could only trust that Joe and Jane might be close enough on her trail that they would find the motel.

And then they would have to find that message written in clay that she had so carefully hidden, she thought in discouragement. She wasn't expecting much, was she?

Not expecting, hoping, praying. It was a very slim chance but the only one she had.

"You're very quiet," Doane said. "I guess you don't want to be gagged. I'm glad you're being smart."

She would have to be smart, she thought. She could rely only on herself as she had done in the mountains. She glanced around, trying to see some avenue for escape.

They were on the outskirts of Casper, and there were very few buildings around except the motel.

A tire shop directly across the road.

A strip mall a mile distant.

Police? State troopers?

No. None in sight.

Oh, for a Dunkin' Donuts.

Joe would not be pleased she'd had that thought. That old, stale joke always irritated him when he knew how hard policemen worked.

Forgive me, Joe.

Lord, she missed him.

She leaned back on the seat and closed her eyes for a moment. **I'm so tired of this, Joe. I want to see you, touch you. I want this to be over. Let it just be a bad dream**.

She opened her eyes to see Doane in the seat next to her, the passing stream of traffic and the knowledge that the nightmare continued. All exactly the same, she thought dully.

No, not quite.

She heard the throb of the rotors of a helicopter in the distance. Then saw the silver blur of metal on the horizon.

But that was the only thing that had changed in that brief moment of poignant wistfulness, and it had nothing to do with wishes coming true.

She had to make her own wishes come true and fight her own nightmares.

She straightened on the seat and turned to Doane. "So what's the next step? Where are we going now?"

"Casper is about five minutes away," Catherine said to Zander as she studied the map on her lap. "And that Starlite Motel should be right there." Her finger tapped a building. "Have the pilot land somewhere nearby but not obvious enough to cause too much attention. Maybe in those hills over there."

"It's difficult not having a helicopter landing cause attention," Zander said dryly.

"That's why I said to try those hills."

"Any other orders?" Zander asked silkily.

"No," she said quietly. "Because you're obviously the dominant type who objects to not being in charge. I know you're in charge. I just have a problem with it when I know I'm just as competent as you are." She took out her phone. "Now I'm going to call the desk at that motel and see if anyone of Doane's description is registered and in what room. You do whatever you like about the landing. But please remember we'll need a car to get to the motel once we land."

He stared at her for a moment and smiled faintly.

"I had Stang arrange for a rental car before we left Denver. The driver is on standby within ten miles of that motel. All I have to do is call and tell him where to pick us up."

"Very good." She started to dial.

"I'm glad you approve."

"I never doubted that you were an expert in practically every way," she said coolly. "You'd have to be to have survived all these years. I just question your judgment where daughters are concerned. It's completely—" She broke off as the desk clerk at the motel answered. She immediately got down to business. During the call, she was aware of Zander's gazing at her curiously, as if she were some strange, rare species. She didn't care. She was curious about him, too, and he was stranger than she had ever dreamed of being.

"There's a man of Doane's description registered in Room 7A," she said a few minutes later as she hung up. "He's easy to describe." She made a face. "All you have to do is say he looks like your best friend or your favorite brother. I couldn't believe it when I saw the photos of him. Anyone would trust that face."

"A number of children whom Kevin wanted lured into his web trusted his father enough to let him bring them to him."

"So I've heard. There's something completely corrupt about deceiving and harming children." Her lips thinned. "May they both burn in hell." She glanced challengingly at him. "Or don't you agree?"

"Oh, I agree. Just because I expect to be sent to the nether regions myself is no reason to group myself with those beasts. There should be some sort of pecking order." He leaned forward, and told the pilot, "Put down in those hills while I call for the car." He glanced slyly at Catherine. "That appears to be the best place."

She nodded. "And it's very clever of you to realize—" She stopped as Zander's phone rang.

"Stang," he said as he accessed. "We're in Casper, Stang, is there—" He stopped, listening. "No, don't double-check. Call Venable and tell him to get the state patrol to be on the alert. No action, just surveillance." He hung up, and said grimly, "The cameras at the tire shop showed a vehicle of that description leaving the motel parking lot and turning north."

"Damn." Catherine's hands clenched. "How long ago?"

"Ten minutes."

Ten minutes, and they would have been able to catch them at the motel, she thought in frustration. "Can we turn north and try to locate them in the helicopter?"

"We can do it." He gazed at her coolly. "But the chances are that Doane would notice that kind of search and surveillance. A helicopter zooming down is difficult to mask or hide. Would you want to risk having Doane panic and kill Eve?"

"You know I wouldn't," she said between set teeth. "Okay, let the state troopers try to locate them and hope they don't blow it. What next?"

"There's the possibility that camera at the tire company didn't identify the correct car," he said, as the helicopter started its descent. "We go to the motel, check and see if that room is still occupied." He smiled faintly. "In which case, I'll kill Doane, and we'll avoid a good deal of bother."

"You can't kill Doane until we determine if he's told anyone about where Kevin placed those nuclear devices."

"Can't?" His brows rose. "You're sounding amazingly like Venable. I can and will do anything I please. It's Venable's job, and now evidently yours, to take care of saving the free world. Doane has been very troublesome to me since the day I killed his son." He added, "And very troublesome to your friend, Eve, as well. I'd think you'd want me to get rid of him."

"You're being simplistic. That's what I do want, but do you think Eve would want him killed at that cost?"

He didn't speak for a moment. "No, but when have I ever exhibited any interest in what she feels or thinks? You're not being reasonable."

"The hell I'm not. I'm just not being callous." Her eyes were glaring into his. "And I'm not being hypocritical. I think you're lying about not caring about Eve. Why don't you take a long look at yourself and see what you find?"

"And I think you might just be as idealistic and unrealistic as Eve." He opened the copter door and jumped to the ground the instant it landed. "We'll have to see who is right, won't we?" He strode toward the car that was waiting several yards away. "Stop talking, and let's get moving."

"Stand back." Zander was pressed on one side of the motel door. He took out his gun and fired a bullet to blow the lock. He waited a moment, then kicked the door open with his foot.

"Empty." Catherine entered the room and glanced around. She had not had great hopes, but she still felt terribly disappointed. No sign of any occupants except those two unmade beds. Eve was not overly neat but she never left an unmade bed. Even if the circumstances were totally bizarre, Catherine could not see her doing it.

"Come on," Zander said impatiently. "We need to get on the road."

"You wanted to be sure it was Eve and Doane in that Toyota." She went over to the beds and jerked the covers off first one bed, then the other. Nothing on the surface of the bottom sheet on the first bed.

On the second bed she thought the condition was the same.

No, not quite the same.

She reached down and picked up a few tiny crumbs from the sheet. "Clay. It was Eve. She was here. And she was trying to tell us she was here." She headed for the door. "Now we can go. Zander, contact those state troopers and see if they've seen them on the road."

Venable called Catherine when they'd been on the road just five minutes. "I've had a notification from a state trooper on Highway 25 that they saw a vehicle answering the description pull off the main road onto a side road."

"What's on that side road?"

"I'm checking it on the map now. Houses, a trailer camp, a small convenience store . . . Shit! A small private airport. Get the hell out there!"

"An airport," Catherine said to Zander as she hung up. "They're not heading for the state border. They're heading for an airport. We've just got to hope that Doane hasn't already arranged for his flight and that there will be a delay."

"You hope. I always operate on the worst-case scenario." Zander's foot pressed on the accelerator and the car leaped forward. "And that scenario is that Doane has made contact with Kevin's old friends, and they sent a plane to pick him up. Tell Venable to scramble some airpower and be ready to try to bring them down."

She reached for her cell, then stopped. "No."

"What?"

"I'm not sure **how** they'd bring them down, dammit. Venable said that Homeland Security was a little too eager about using the drones."

"He didn't mention that to me. But that's no surprise. Venable and I are not always entirely honest with each other." He increased speed again. He was going close to a hundred miles an hour now. "Then I believe we'd better forget about airpower and get to them before they take off."

Fast.

Faster.

The hills on either side of them became a green blur.

They'd be lucky if those state troopers they'd put on alert didn't try to pull them over, Catherine thought.

She glanced at Zander's face. It was

completely intent and resolute. He would not stop regardless of who tried to get in his way. She felt a sudden chill as she realized she was seeing the Zander who had earned a reputation that was feared in every corner of the world.

He was handling the Mercedes like a race car driver. He suddenly made a turn to the left that caused the tires to screech, but he never lost control. "How far?" he bit out.

"Three miles. On your left."

Dirt bumping and spraying beneath the tires.

Rocky Mountain Airport.

"Just ahead," she said. "I see a few hangars . . ." Her excitement was growing. "There's a Toyota parked before that little terminal building." She was getting a glimpse of the runway. "And there's a plane going down the runway!"

Zander was screeching to a stop in front of a chain-link fence. He drew his gun as he jumped out of the car. "Get the numbers on the side of the plane."

"You're going to shoot? You don't even know if it's them," Catherine said as she memorized the number.

"I don't know that it's not. It won't hurt to shoot the tires out before they—" He stopped as the Gulfstream left the runway. "Too late." He put his gun away. "Now we can go inside and see if they were on that Gulfstream or if they're in that terminal waiting for us." His lips twisted. "As usual, I'm subscribing to the worst-case scenario."

And the worst-case scenario proved to be accurate.

Five minutes later, Catherine was on the phone giving the registration numbers that were on the Gulfstream to Venable as they strode out of the terminal building and over to the Toyota Doane had abandoned.

She hung up the phone as Zander bent over the lock of the car. "Venable said that he'll make every attempt to locate the plane." She made a face. "And that the chances aren't even fifty-fifty if they continue to use out-of-the-way airports like this one."

"It's a weapon in the arsenal," he said as he picked the lock and swung open the door of the driver's seat. "Now let's see if we can find any other weapons he might have left in here."

"I'm surprised you picked the lock. I would have thought you'd shoot the damn thing off. You seem to be so fond of using your gun."

"Only if I'm in a hurry. We have more time now." He was rifling through the glove box. "We can start using more mundane methods."

She raised her eyes to the sky.

The disappointment was hitting home with wrenching force as she realized how close they'd come to Eve only to lose her.

Zander said they had more time now, but she wasn't so sure.

Doane was moving fast, and it appeared he had help.

How much time did Eve have left?

CHAPTER

8

Muncie, Indiana
Muncie Airport Terminal

"Ms. Weber?" Jane said when Harriet Weber answered her call. "This is Jane MacGuire. You don't know me, but it's essential that I talk to you. If I come to the school where you're teaching, could you spare a few minutes?"

"I'm very busy Ms. MacGuire." Harriet's voice was crisp. "I have students who need me. Perhaps we could make an appointment for next week."

"I need to talk to you right away. I don't want to disturb you in any way, but I have to ask you a few questions." She paused. "It concerns your ex-husband and your son."

Silence. "You've got the wrong person. I'm a widow."

"Your ex-husband's name was James Relling. When he was placed under federal protection, his name was changed to James Doane."

Another silence. "Are you a reporter?"

"No." She paused. "I wonder if you've been informed that your ex-husband was recently killed in an explosion?"

She didn't answer for a moment. "Yes, that CIA agent Venable called me and told me that James and some woman were blown up in a town in Colorado. I told him I didn't care, that I'd put all that behind me."

"I do care," Jane said. "I couldn't care more. That woman was Eve Duncan, who adopted me when I was ten years old, and he was responsible for her death. Perhaps you saw the media coverage?"

"No, I don't know anything about her or what happened. I didn't want to know. I told Venable that James was a stranger to me now, and I didn't want to hear anything about what kind of terrible things he was doing." She added harshly, "Is that why you came? You want to heap blame on me because of what he did to that Eve Duncan? Well, it's not my fault. Venable was supposed to watch him and keep him from doing anything bad. I've had nothing to do with James for years."

"I have no intention of blaming you for anything. I don't want to cause you any trouble. Just answer a few questions, and I promise I'll go away and not bother you again."

"Why won't you leave me alone?" she said angrily. "I told you, that was another life."

And Jane was feeling guilty at insisting. But not guilty enough to stop. Every avenue had to be explored with Eve in danger. "Just a few questions."

Harriet Weber was silent, and Jane could sense the waves of resentment in that silence. "Very well," she said shortly. "I'll meet you in the stands at the athletic field behind the school. One hour." She hung up.

Jane made a face. "She's not pleased." She turned to Trevor and Caleb, who had been listening on speaker. "And who can blame her? She worked hard to have a second chance, and she thinks I might blow it for her. I'll be as glad as she is when this is over."

Caleb smiled. "But not if you can squeeze something of value out of her. I take it that we're not invited to go along?"

She shook her head. "All she'd need to send her running for the hills is to see more than one person heading toward her. You're both high-impact. I sent Margaret to rent a car, and she can drive me, but I'm not letting her come to the meeting either." She got to her feet and started for the car-rental area. "I have to go down and sign for the car. Margaret's not old enough. I'll be back as soon as I can."

"And you're leaving us to our own devices?" Trevor asked. "Boredom can be dangerous."

"That sounds more like Caleb than you."

"I have my moments." He smiled. "Remember?"

Yes, she remembered all of those moments that had been charged with adventure and sex and a thousand other emotions that had made life full of zest. Gazing at him, she could feel a wave of nostalgia sweep over her, warm, sweet . . . She shook her head. "That was the past, Trevor. I'm living only in the present."

"Not true. But I'll settle for the present." He waved his hand dismissingly. "Have a good chat with Satan's mother."

"I will." Jane felt both their eyes upon her as she headed for the rental-car booth.

She saw Margaret step forward as she approached. "Everything is fine," she said. "Just sign and show him your ID. I gave him your credit card, so we're all set."

"My credit card? How did you get my credit card?"

"I took one of them out of the bedside table drawer in your hospital room a couple weeks ago. I needed it to get to Colorado to find Eve." She smiled. "I meant to give it back to you, but I kept forgetting."

Jane stared at her in disbelief. "Don't you think it would have been a little more honest to have told me . . . or even asked?"

"Yes, but you were all upset about imposing on me and might not have wanted to have anything to do with sending me after that bastard, Doane." She smiled with satisfaction. "So I took care of it. I didn't have enough money for a plane ticket, so I borrowed your credit card. I'll pay you back later. You can trust me."

"I'm sure I can." She signed the rental contract. "In the basics, but not to have everything clear and up front. Don't do that again, Margaret."

She nodded. "Whatever." She headed for the door. "Our car is in the pickup outside. You decided not to intimidate Harriet Weber by bringing along Trevor and Caleb?" She didn't wait for an answer. "That's smart. She'll be much more comfortable with just us."

"You're staying in the car."

"But I'm not intimidating."

"Margaret," Jane said dryly as she opened the terminal door, "in your own way, you're far more intimidating than either Caleb or Trevor."

"You did a very good job of reviving the embers of 'Auld Lang Syne,' Trevor," Caleb said as he watched Jane and Margaret go out into the parking lot. "But it was the wrong time for Jane. You should have waited until she could concentrate fully on you."

"There's never a wrong time, Caleb. Not

if the emotion is honest, and the memories are good." He smiled. "And I can understand how you'd feel a trifle annoyed by the fact that Jane and I have a history."

"I'm not annoyed. I was at first, but it's just something I have to deal with. In Jane's eyes, you're the knight in shining armor, and I'm Merlin the evil magician." He tilted his head. "You're a very good knight in shining armor. Not phony. Only interested in Jane's good. I don't think that I've ever met anyone as genuine as you are. There are even moments when I actually like you, Trevor."

Trevor burst out laughing. "God, how it must have hurt you to say that."

"I have my honest moments," he said. "And I won't ask you to lie and tell me that liking is returned." He was no longer smiling. "Because I'm not interested in Jane's good. I'm too selfish, and I've never felt about anyone as I do Jane. White-hot and pure unadulterated lust. And I **will** have her, Trevor. It's just a matter of time."

Trevor shook his head. "She needs something more and you can't give it to her. But I'm lucky enough to be able to do it. You're too intense, you'd burn her up."

He paused. "And I do like you in some weird, twisted way, Caleb. I just have to protect Jane from you."

"Oh, no, that won't happen." Caleb was smiling again. "But I'm glad that we have everything straight. Though I believe we both knew what we were up against from the beginning. Now we can concentrate on finding Eve, so that Jane will be free to think of other things." He met Trevor's eyes. "I agree with what you told Jane, boredom can be dangerous . . . but interesting. I think we should keep ourselves busy until she finishes with Harriet Weber."

Trevor's eyes narrowed. "How?"

"I have a few ideas." He started across the terminal toward the rental-car booth. "But they require wheels. Let's go get a car."

When Jane arrived at the athletic field, it was vacant except for a young boy in navy blue gym shorts who was running the track.

The only person sitting on the benches in the stands was a tall, well-built woman wearing a herringbone tweed coat that picked up the silver in her short, dark hair. She stood up as Jane approached her.

She was even taller than she'd first appeared, Jane noticed. She was perhaps in her fifties though she looked younger. The skin of her face was olive and appeared satin soft and almost entirely without any sign of age. She had magnificent dark eyes that were staring coldly at Jane.

"Hello, I'm Jane MacGuire. Thank you for agreeing to meet with me."

"I didn't have a choice. I wasn't sure how ruthless you'd be about revealing facts I don't wish revealed." She glanced at her wristwatch. "And I don't have much time. I have to get back to my classes. What do you want to know?"

"Did you keep in contact with your ex-husband?"

"I did not. I haven't seen him since the divorce." She asked a question of her own, "Who are you? Are you with the CIA?"

"No, why would you think that? I told you that I have a personal interest in what happened in Colorado."

"That doesn't mean you don't have a connection with the CIA. After my son was killed, that Venable from the CIA came to visit me and asked all kinds of questions. And he was the one who called me a few days ago and told me that my ex-husband, James, was dead. Do you work for him?"

"No, I'm an artist, but I do know Venable."

"Then he must have told you that I know nothing about James or Kevin. I left home when Kevin was fifteen, and I never saw either of them after that time."

"He said you were not involved, but I have to be sure. Things have changed since then. The stakes are higher." Her lips tightened. "And what happened to Eve was crazy. She meant everything to me. I'm trying to make some kind of sense out of it. I have to know why it happened."

"The disk? Venable told me about that disk. I know nothing about it."

"No, it seems that there was something else other than the disk that your ex-husband was holding as a blackmail tool. Did you know anything about Kevin's journal?"

She stiffened. "Journal? My boy had a journal?" She shook her head emphatically. "How could I know? When Kevin was a little boy, he liked to write stories, but that's all I remember." Her eyes were suddenly glittering with tears. "I thought he was going to be a writer or maybe a reporter when he grew up. But then I started to read his stories . . ." She shook her head as if to clear it. "And I knew—" She had to stop to steady her voice. "That no one would ever want to read those stories but someone— like him. But there wasn't anyone like him. No one could be that—sick." She lifted her gaze to Jane's face. "But you know what he was, don't you? That's why you're here."

"I know what he was." She moistened her lips. "And I know that your husband protected and helped him do unspeakable things. I don't blame you for leaving them. But I need to know if you know anything about his activities before or after your son's death. Your husband was involved in a plan that might have tragic consequences. It might save lives if you could recall something, anything."

"Leave me alone," Harriet Weber said with sudden violence. "I'm only a woman who tried to do her best, and yet you expect me to change what can't be changed. Why do you think I can save anyone? I wasn't able to do it before. I tried, but I couldn't stop him. I couldn't do it. They were both against me and I—" The tears had overflowed and were running down her cheeks. "Please—go away."

Jane reached out in sympathy to touch her shoulder, but the woman jerked away. Jane was tempted to get up and leave her as she was begging her to do. She was unbearably touched by the thought of the helpless battle the woman must have waged to save her son from his demons.

Then a thought occurred to her. "In the journal, your son made certain references to you. They were admiring, affectionate. Evidently, his attitude toward you didn't change when you left your husband and Kevin."

"Why shouldn't he love me?" she said hoarsely. "I was his mother. I loved and protected him all the days of his life. And when I found out that what he was writing in his stories was real, true, I protected him then, too. I didn't go to the police. I turned my back and hoped it wouldn't happen again."

"But it did happen again," Jane whispered.

She nodded jerkily. "And then I knew I couldn't stay with them any longer. I had to get away."

"Without telling anyone what a monster Kevin was?"

"He wasn't a monster; he was sick." She closed her eyes. "And I loved him as much the day I left him as I did when I cradled him as a baby. It doesn't change. I had to let fate punish him. Judge me if you wish, but don't do it until you walk in my shoes." Her eyes opened. "I cut all ties with James and Kevin, but I couldn't cut Kevin out of my heart. If I'd betrayed him to the police, it would have destroyed me."

"So you left him free to destroy others." Jane was silent a moment. "I understand your hurt, but I believe I would have found some way to stop him instead of just turning my back."

"You don't understand anything," she said fiercely. "You couldn't. No one could unless they knew Kevin. He could be so loving . . ." She swallowed. "That's why it was impossible to grasp that he would do those terrible—But he did do them, and he wouldn't listen to me. So I had to leave him."

"And your husband."

"By that time, James didn't pay any attention to me anyway. It was all Kevin. He didn't care what Kevin did as long as it was what he wanted. The most terrible things were right if Kevin told him they were." Her lips twisted. "I'd lost James long before I lost Kevin." She got to her feet. "I've had enough of this. I can't take any-more. You can do whatever you like. Tell the school administrators, tell everyone that I'm just as much a monster as Kevin because I ran away instead of trying to stop him." She drew a shaky breath. "Some-times, when I wake from a nightmare in the middle of the night, I believe that's true. So punish me any way you please." She turned and walked away.

"Wait."

Harriet Weber didn't turn around or stop. The next moment, she disappeared off the field.

It was just as well. Jane didn't know what she had wanted to say to Harriet We-ber, but she hadn't wanted the woman to leave like that. The pain and torment were too obvious. She wanted to somehow heal it. But how could she heal it when she had no empathy at all for the woman's deci-sion? She had chosen that her Kevin survive and risked countless others so that he would.

Jane moved slowly down the steps toward the exit. What had she accomplished by this meeting except disturbing Harriet Weber?

She had become so involved with the intensity of the woman's emotional response that it had been difficult to sort out what else had been said. She would have to analyze these minutes and consider if she had learned anything that could be helpful. Was Kevin's mother victim or, by her silence, accomplice? Perhaps both. Jane knew how she felt but, as the woman said, she hadn't walked in her shoes.

All that was clear now was that the dark ugliness that had been Doane and Kevin had also pulled Harriet Weber down into those stagnant depths.

Trevor and Caleb were not at the airport terminal when Jane and Margaret arrived back over an hour later.

Jane checked her phone. No message.

She called Trevor. No answer. Just voice mail.

Caleb? Same.

"Where the hell are they?" she said as she hung up.

"Somewhere interesting, I'm sure." Margaret was gazing at her. "Stop frowning. Do you know how absurd it is for you to even think about being worried about them? I can't imagine any men who would be better able to take care of themselves."

"I'm not worried." But she had to admit that she was wary. The mere fact that Trevor and Caleb were probably together made her uneasy. They struck sparks off each other. "I'm just . . . curious."

"Well, let's be curious about lunch." Margaret was nudging her toward the airport restaurant. "We'll leave them to starve as punishment for being incommunicado."

Trevor and Caleb didn't appear for another hour, and she and Margaret were almost finished with their meal when they strode into the restaurant.

"Scoot." Caleb sat down in the booth beside Jane. "Is that ham sandwich any good? I'm starved."

"Fair."

He motioned for the waitress. "Trevor?"

"The same. Anything. Coffee."

"Not for me. I'm zinging." He gave the order to the waitress and leaned back. "We had a good morning. How about you, Jane?"

"Not very productive, but I'll have to decide if—" She stopped, gazing at him. "You are zinging." She had seen him like that before, and it was usually when he was on the hunt or in battle. The charge of emotion he emitted was electric. Her gaze shifted to Trevor. He didn't have the same animal intensity as Caleb, but he was also wired. His eyes glittered, and he was smiling. She asked, "What have you been doing? I called you and got voice mail."

"It would have been inconvenient to answer the phone." He exchanged a glance with Caleb. "We were busy."

Jane gazed at them, annoyance mixed with bewilderment. What the hell was happening? They were like two little boys in a neighborhood club who were brimming with secrets and mischief. She had never expected that response from two men who were fully mature, sophisticated, and slightly antagonistic. "Is someone going to explain?"

Caleb smiled. "You left us with nothing

to do and twiddling our thumbs. We decided to do our own investigation on Harriet Weber."

"What?"

"We had her address, so we decided to go to her place and look around while you were conducting your interview."

"Look around? Are you saying that you burgled her apartment?"

"Burgled sounds as if we were thieves," Trevor said. "We had no intention of stealing anything . . . but information. We did, however, break into her apartment to do that, and breaking and entering is a crime." He grinned. "So I let Caleb pick the lock. He was amazingly good at it."

Caleb nodded in mocking acceptance of the praise. "I thought that was your plan. But you did the photography, and I'm sure that's not precisely legal."

"I couldn't trust you to do it," Trevor said. "It requires a steady hand and a certain selectivity. You wanted to whirl through the place like a hurricane."

"I can see Caleb's doing that." Margaret was staring curiously at them both. "But I believe you were both enjoying it, weren't you? You're not at all alike, and yet you found common ground. Interesting."

"In breaking into a woman's house." Jane stared at them. "Why did you do it?"

"We both thought whatever Harriet Weber told you should be verified," Trevor said. "It sounded as if it was going to prove to be an emotional, defensive interview on her part. Was it?"

"Yes. It couldn't be anything else. She was talking about her son, whom she'd left when he was fifteen, and a husband who had mentally left her years before in favor of Kevin."

"And never seen or heard from either one after that time?" Caleb asked. "What a tragedy."

She studied his expression. "What are you saying?"

"I'm saying that she had communication with her son, Kevin, until at least the year before his death. Mostly letters. I found several from him in a sleek, black cardboard box that contained a lockbox. It was beneath her bed." He shot a glance at Trevor. "Which I expertly burgled so that you could photograph the contents of those letters. There was no selectivity there. You photographed all of them."

Jane gazed at them in shock. "You're telling me that she was writing to him?"

"And he was writing to her. Very affectionate letters." Caleb paused. "And confiding, very confiding. The ones from Pakistan told her about his link with al-Qaeda. Every now and then, he would tell her about his latest kill."

Jane felt as if she'd been kicked in the stomach. "No."

"Yes," Trevor said. "And some of the details were worse than the ones in his journal. Oh, he said something about how he knew she wouldn't approve, that she'd told him how dangerous killing the little girls was for him. But he still told her about them. Let her know that the pleasure he got from the kill was nothing compared to his happiness being with her."

"Dear God."

"He loved her, Jane. If a sicko like him could love."

"And she loved him," Caleb said. "It didn't matter what he did. It was clear from his letters that she was giving him support and affection all through those years."

"But why would she divorce Doane and leave them both?"

"Perhaps she thought she could resist her love for the boy and was fighting it," Trevor said.

Caleb shook his head. "Except that in one of the letters, Kevin was complaining about the necessity for her living apart from him." He repeated, "Necessity."

Jane's head was whirling. "Okay." She was trying to get it straight. "Everything she told me today and Venable five years ago were lies. Except that she loved her son and couldn't bear to turn him over to the authorities. But there was more than that . . ." She lifted her hand to rub her temple. "Lord, was there more than that. If her supposed new life was all a fraud . . . Why? And was she also lying about Doane? Was there anything in the letters about Doane?"

Caleb shook his head. "We didn't run across anything in the letters, but we were practically speed-reading. You'll have to go over them again. We didn't find any other letters or documents with his name on them in the apartment." He grimaced. "Except the divorce decree. She didn't lie about that."

"What else did you find?"

Caleb shrugged. "Damn if I know. We were moving so fast that we were pulling and photographing everything in sight. We'll have to go through the camera roll later and see if we got anything important. Oh, one thing, she told you that she saw none of the media coverage of Doane's death. Not true. The first thing I did when I arrived at the apartment was to check her TIVO, and she had set that memorial service to record. She knew exactly what had happened to Doane and Eve. She probably knew who you and Joe were, too. That set up red flags that we should go over everything in the apartment very carefully." He took a bite of the sandwich the waitress had placed before him. "I ran a disk on her computer for current entries to see if anything interesting showed up. That will take some time to scan."

"You were gone a long time. You just searched her apartment?"

"Just? We did a magnificent job of searching her apartment and putting everything back exactly the way we found it." He shrugged. "But when we found out that our Harriet was not what Venable thought she was, I took time to run out to the nearest mall and bought a few bugs to keep track of what she was up to." He gazed at her inquiringly. "Okay?"

"More than okay. You both did everything right. I'm the one who screwed up," Jane said bitterly. "If she lied about Kevin, she could have lied about Doane. Which means that she might know where he is now."

"You didn't let her know that Doane and Eve might still be alive?" Trevor asked.

"Of course not. I admit I felt a little sorry for her. She was faced with a terrible decision, and, in my opinion, she made the wrong one. But there's no way I'd trust her enough to confide in her." She added harshly, "Though it appeared that Kevin had no such problem." Her hands clenched into fists. "She works with children every day of her life. How could she stand to hear what he did to them?"

"Just because she works with them doesn't mean she holds them in particular affection," Margaret said. "I've heard that some people can only care about one or two people in their entire lifetime. Maybe her one love was her child, Kevin."

"Well, she married Doane, and they had

a child. Evidently, they both loved Kevin above anything else in the world. If they shared that passion, then Doane must mean something to her. She has to know something about him." She was trying to control her rage. "Let me out of this booth, Caleb."

"I was waiting for that." Caleb got to his feet and helped her out of the booth. "But, at least, I got my sandwich down." He smiled down at her. "You're going to go see Harriet Weber again?"

"You bet I am." She looked at her watch. "It's past time for school to be over. I'll go to her apartment and talk to her."

"I'll go with you." Margaret started to slide out of the booth.

"No. I'm going by myself." She grabbed her bag. "This is between the two of us. She **played** me."

"Let me go with you," Trevor said quietly. "Anyone who would welcome letters that were that sick could be off-kilter herself. She could not only be a liar, but something much more dangerous."

"Are you trying to protect me again? I can take care of myself, Trevor. Have you forgotten that I grew up on the streets until I was ten and that after Eve and Joe took me in, he taught me martial arts?"

"I haven't forgotten. You're tough. I just think that you lack the killer instinct. I don't know if Harriet Weber does or not. Let me go with you."

"Hell, no. I don't want to be protected from that barracuda. If I don't have the killer instinct, what I'm feeling is pretty damn close. I feel like an idiot. She had me feeling sorry for the poor mother who was forced to give up her child. I thought she was in agony. I was even fighting to understand how she could walk away without finding a way to safeguard those children who were threatened by Kevin." She could feel the fury surge through her. "Understand? I could never understand her. She didn't care about those victims. She was only worried that Kevin might get in trouble by killing them." She started across the terminal toward the exit. "Well, she's not going to play me again. I'll find out why she lied and cram it down her throat. If she knows anything about Doane, she's going to tell me."

Starlite Motel
Casper, Wyoming

"What do you expect to find?" Zander asked as he threw open the door of the room Eve and Doane had formerly occupied. "We already know it was Eve who was here with Doane."

"Eve is smart." Catherine went into the room. "If you'd spent more time with her, you'd realize that, Zander. She left those clay bits on the bed as ID, but she'd try to tell us more than that."

"Where she was going," Zander said. "She'd find out from Doane where he was going to take her and try to let us know." He gave Catherine a level glance. "And I didn't have to spend much time with her to know that she's clever. She fought Doane on his own terms up in those mountains, and she would have won if she hadn't gone soft."

She frowned. "Gone soft?"

He shrugged. "I was in somewhat of a quandary, and Eve decided that she had to distract Doane from me. I could have handled it. I told her I didn't need her. She did it anyway."

"And Doane recaptured her." Catherine

shook her head in wonder. She repeated, "Gone soft. Is that what you call it? Why, you son of a bitch."

"Yes. I've never denied it. Just as I've never denied that I don't think the same way that other people do." He smiled. "Like you, Catherine. You have a great deal of trouble with my not being sentimental about Eve's deplorable lack of instinct for self-preservation."

"I may just test your self-preservation instinct," she said through her teeth. "I wonder how you'd—" She stopped. "You're **laughing,** dammit. Stop it."

He nodded. "I'm just amused by how easily you're aroused to anger in defense of Eve. She must be a very good friend to you. I admit that I yielded to temptation to see how you'd respond. It's my eternal curiosity."

"Screw your curiosity." She stared at him. "And I don't think you're as detached as you'd like everyone to believe about Eve. I've been watching you today, and you've been . . . intense."

"I'm on the hunt for Doane."

She gazed at him for a long moment and slowly shook her head. "Have it your way. But there were moments when you might have had Doane, but it would have put Eve in danger. You're not quite as ruthless as you pretend."

"I never pretend."

"Then you may be a split personality. I don't have time to psychoanalyze you." She headed for the bathroom. "I'll check out the cabinets and the shower for anything Eve might have left. You search this room."

"If I find something, do I get a prize?"

She gave him a glance and started looking through the lower cabinets. He was deliberately trying to annoy her. He didn't like orders, and she was probably lucky that his response had been verbal.

Nothing in the cabinets.

She went into the shower.

Nothing written on walls or soap.

Not good.

Nothing on the washcloths.

"Catherine," Zander called from the other room. "I won the prize."

She ran out of the bathroom. "What did—" He was kneeling beside the table and peering underneath it. "What is it?"

"I noticed the surface of the table was faintly discolored and it would have been natural to use it as a worktable." He had taken out a small penlight and was shining it underneath. "There's a small piece of clay stuck to the underside of the table. Can you think of any reason why anyone would do that?"

"Only one." She held her breath as he started to pry the clay from the table. "Be careful . . ."

"I'll not answer that useless bit of—" He stopped. "Part of it is hanging loose. I have to take my time, or it will break in two when I take it down."

"If you'll move, I could try—"

"I've got it."

"I meant my hands are smaller."

"I didn't think you meant I was inadequate to the task." Zander's fingers were moving with exquisite delicacy on the clay, working it away from the table. "I'm sure you'd never be so rude." The next moment, he'd extracted the clay and brought it from beneath the table. "There we are. Now let's see what we've got here . . ."

She opened the drapes to let more light into the room and hurried back to the table. "What is it?"

"Your extraordinary Eve," he murmured. "Four letters . . ."

"The last two are a **W** and an **A** preceding a period. The second one is an **e**. The first one is . . ." She frowned. "What? It's messed up."

"The clay is ultrathin at that edge," Zander said. "And it appears that she had to rework it. But the indentation should be clear." His index finger moved along the indentation. "It's difficult as hell . . ." He closed his eyes. "Give me a minute."

"You look like a safecracker."

"Only when necessary to my profession." His finger continued to move on the indentation. "It's an **S**." He opened his eyes. "And a dot following the **e**."

"You're certain?"

"Stop questioning me." He was gazing in concentration down at the clay. "You just don't want to admit I found the treasure. Only this time it may be the grand prize." He pointed to the **WA**. "She tried to make it easy for us. **WA**. The state of Washington." His index finger once more caressed the misshapen curve. "**Se.** What large city would be a likely target in Washington?"

"Seattle," Catherine said tensely. "The second city is Seattle."

"And that's where Doane is taking her." He got a tissue from the bathroom and carefully wrapped the piece of clay. "So why don't you get on the phone to Venable. Tell him to put everyone on alert for a possible landing in that area of the plane with the registration number we gave him."

"I will." She gazed in bewilderment at the tissue-wrapped clay. "What are you doing with that clay? Do you think we'll need it again? I thought you were sure that you were right about the destination."

"It's exceptionally rare that I'm wrong." He put the tissue in his jacket pocket. "But it's obvious that it took a great effort on Eve's part to get that message to us. She might like to have it for a souvenir."

"I doubt it." Her gaze narrowed on his face. "And I'm wondering if perhaps you might be the one who wants a souvenir." She held up her hand as he opened his lips to speak. "You're right, what am I thinking? Forget I said that. Not you. Not Lee Zander." She took out her phone and started dialing Venable. "That would speak of a trace of sentimentality, and that would be totally absurd."

He smiled and nodded slowly. "Totally."

Muncie, Indiana

Harriet Weber's apartment building was only a two-story brick structure, and her apartment, 1B, was on the first floor.

And Jane noticed there was a Jeep Cherokee parked directly in front of the entrance that was packed with dozens of boxes, clothes, and even a small TV.

Not a good sign, Jane thought, stiffening. If that was Harriet's car, then she was trying to escape to keep Jane or anyone else from asking any more awkward questions. Perhaps it wasn't Harriet's vehicle.

But that question was soon settled. As Jane hurried down the hall, a door opened, and Harriet came out carrying a suitcase.

She stopped short as she saw Jane. Her expression became suddenly wary. "What are you doing here? I told you that I was through talking to you. I don't care what you do."

"But I care what you do," Jane said grimly. "I'm not satisfied with your answers. I want to ask a few more questions." She glanced at the suitcases. "For instance, where are you going?"

"None of your business. I'm upset, and I

felt the need of a few days off work to recover." Her eyes filled with tears. "It wasn't easy reliving those horrible years. I would think you'd be more sympathetic."

Crocodile tears, Jane thought, intended to make Jane feel guilt. So clever.

Not this time, Harriet.

"I'm finding it hard to believe that you didn't see either your ex-husband or Kevin after the divorce," Jane said coldly. "From what you said, it was clear that you had great love for your son. How could you resist remaining in contact with him?"

"I have a conscience."

"You'll forgive me if I doubt that. Letting that monster have free rein to attack and kill children hardly gives credence to your code of conduct."

"Think what you like." She tried to step past her, but Jane moved sideways to intercept. "Get out of my way. Venable has nothing with which to charge me. You're interfering with a private citizen."

"I told you, I don't care about Venable. I want to know what you know about the movements of your ex-husband during the past years." She took a step closer to her. "And you will tell me. You bet I'm interfering with you," she said fiercely. "If you'd have interfered with what Doane and your son were doing, you could have saved lives. You could have prevented Doane from kidnapping Eve. Now tell me what you know."

Harriet's cheeks were suddenly flushed with rage. "If you don't get out of my way, I'll make you sorry you were ever born," she said harshly. "I know how to defend myself. My boy you call a monster taught me what he learned in the military. I could kill a soft little thing like you without any problem at all."

"But how could Kevin do that if you left him when he was only fifteen before he went into the Army? Remember, you never saw him again."

"I'd deny that I said that, and everyone would believe me. People do believe me. I've had a good deal of practice." She tried to push past Jane. "You're the one they'd think was lying."

Jane wasn't moving, and she stretched out her arm to block her.

Harriet finally lost the last vestige of control.

"Bitch!"

The edge of her hand shot out in a karate chop to Jane's arm blocking her way.

Jane blocked it and grabbed Harriet's arm and twisted it behind the woman's back. "Talk to me."

Harriet's heel shot back and struck Jane's knee.

Pain.

Her grip loosened, and Harriet tore away from her. She whirled, and her fist punched into Jane's abdomen.

Jane's breath left her, but she recovered and delivered a karate chop to the side of Harriet's neck.

Harriet staggered back, her eyes glazing over.

Not good enough, Jane thought. If she'd done it the way Joe had taught her, it would have put the woman out.

But it was enough to stop her for a moment. Jane dove forward, brought her down, and straddled her. Harriet struggled with ferocious strength, and Jane had all she could do to fight off several vicious blows to the head and body. "Give up," she said through her teeth. "Admit that this 'soft little thing' was enough to beat anything your Kevin taught you."

"The hell I will." Harriet's fist shot up and connected with Jane's lip. Then she rolled to the side and jumped to her feet. She snatched up her suitcase and started running down the hall.

Jane was only a few yards behind her as she ran out the front entrance to the Jeep Cherokee parked in front of the building.

"Stay away from me," Harriet hissed as she jumped into the Jeep. "Or so help me God I'll kill you."

"I won't stay away. I'll follow you to hell and back." Jane ran around to the passenger side. "Lock the door, and I'll break the damn windows."

"No, you won't." Harriet was fumbling in the glove box.

Jane caught a glimpse of metal. A gun.

The glass of the passenger side window shattered.

Jane felt the heat of a bullet whistle past her cheek.

She dodged to the side and fell to her knees.

Another bullet sparked the concrete beside her as Harriet pulled away from the building and raced toward the street.

Close. Both bullets had come very, very close, Jane realized.

And Harriet Weber had not only tried to kill her, but she was getting away!

She jumped to her feet and ran toward her car.

And was almost run over by Caleb and Trevor as they drove into the apartment parking lot.

"For God's sake." Trevor screeched to a halt. "You look like you've been through a train wreck." He jumped out and ran over to her. "Are you hurt?"

"I'm fine, but she's getting away. I have to—" She stopped and drew a deep breath. Get control. The violence and heat of the last minutes were still with her, and she had to think. "It's too late. She was driving fast, and I won't be able to catch her."

"Harriet Weber?" Caleb asked as he got out of the car. His gaze was raking over Jane, taking in the bruises and cuts. "She did that to you?"

"I'm fine." She ran her hand through her hair. "She wanted to leave, and I didn't want her to. I came off better than she did until she decided to grab a gun out of the glove box and try to shoot me."

"I'd say that would qualify as an unfair advantage," Caleb said. He gently touched her lip with his index finger, and it came away bloody. "I saw photos of her in the apartment, and she looked pretty tough. The fact that she was taller and stronger than you might be considered—"

"No excuses. She was good," Jane said curtly. "Why not? She told me her dear son had taught her self-defense. He must have also taught her to shoot if she couldn't talk her way out of a jam." She added, "But I'm good, too. I almost had her. That gun was not—" She stopped. "Okay, she's gone. Forget everything but the fact that she as much as admitted to me that she'd seen and interacted with Kevin during those years. It wasn't only letters."

"And she decided to take it on the lam when you confronted her with the possibility that she might be under suspicion."

Jane nodded. "She was already on her way out when I came over. Why? She could have tried to bluff it out. She impressed me as being very confident of her powers of persuasion. But for some reason, it wasn't worth it to her to go to the trouble to fight that battle." She added thoughtfully, "Maybe because she had another battle that was more important to her . . . and to Doane."

"No evidence of a connection with Doane," Caleb said. "Wishful thinking?"

"Shall I tell you what her connection with Doane is?" Jane said. "Violence. I had a taste of it today. Harriet Weber is full of venom, and she'd go to any lengths to get what she wants. Does she want Doane? Does she want revenge? I don't know. But she's a lead we have to follow. It may take us to Eve." She turned to Trevor. "I noticed Harriet Weber's Jeep was packed to the gills before I went in to see her. You said that you had planted some bugs in the apartment." She asked tensely, "Please tell me you managed to plant a few among her possessions."

He nodded. "But they were all audio bugs for eavesdropping."

"Shit."

He smiled. "Except for one device Caleb insisted on including."

"What device?"

"A micro GPS device," Caleb said. "I thought it might come in handy."

"But would she have taken it with her?"

"Oh, yes. She would definitely have taken it with her. And she'll keep it with her."

"Why?"

"It's inserted on the inner lining of the box where she keeps her son's letters." He held up his phone. "And I can monitor it from my cell."

Jane breathed a sigh of relief. There was no doubt that Harriet would keep those hideous letters with her. "Then let's get on the road and see if we can find out where she's going."

"I'll drive." Trevor opened the passenger door for Jane. "Caleb, you can concentrate on tracking."

"Margaret." Jane suddenly realized Margaret wasn't with them. "None of you were supposed to be here, but I can't believe Margaret stayed behind."

"Caleb suggested that she call Kendra and fill her in on the letters Kevin sent to his mother and see if Kendra could find something else in the journal that could have a connection with Harriet Weber." Trevor raised his brows. "I was surprised that she did it."

"I'm not," Jane said. "She didn't want Kendra to feel left out."

Trevor nodded. "We left while she was involved with Kendra."

"Margaret will punish you both," Jane said. "I don't know how. But it will happen."

"I figured the two of us could take care of any emergency you might run across. Though you managed pretty well on your own." He smiled at Jane. "But now you can sit back and concentrate on resting and recovering from what looks like the battle of the century."

"Trevor, I told you not to try to—" She broke off. She had fought that battle before, and he wasn't going to listen. She leaned back in the seat. "No comment from you, Caleb?"

"I don't have to tell you that you need to rest," he said quietly. "You've probably done damage. Your shoulder is going to start throbbing if it's not already."

"No serious damage." But she didn't tell him that he was right, and the healing wound in her shoulder was throbbing. She would be all right, she told herself. But now that the adrenaline was ebbing away, she was suddenly limp and exhausted. She didn't want to argue with anyone at the moment.

Except Harriet Weber.

If Harriet were back on the scene, Jane knew that she would be ready and able to take her on. The woman was corrupt in a way that was different from Doane but might be even more evil. She was feeling a rush of strength and rage at the thought of her.

But not now. As Trevor said, she needed to conserve her energy.

"Okay?" Trevor asked softly.

She nodded. "Tired." She smiled wearily. "But I found out one thing from my little dustup with Harriet Weber."

"What's that?"

"You were wrong, Trevor." She leaned back and closed her eyes. "So wrong. I definitely have the killer instinct."

CHAPTER

9

Denver International Airport

"It's time for you to leave me now," Zander said as he got out of the helicopter. "It's been delightful, but I'm getting a bit bored with you, Catherine."

"Liar." She smiled as she jumped to the ground. "You may be feeling a bit claustrophobic, but you're not bored. You just want to clear the decks while you go after Eve and Doane." She looked around the private hangar facilities. "What did you tell Stang when you called him? Where is he? Which plane did you lease to take us to Seattle?"

"Stang went on ahead and is meeting me in Seattle. I'm not going into the city blind. I have a few contacts who can help me find Doane, and Stang will start the ball rolling." He smiled. "And he arranged for that Gulfstream over there to take **me** to Seattle."

"It's a nice-size plane." She started across the tarmac. "I don't take up much space."

"I mean it, Catherine."

"I know." She looked over her shoulder. "And you're intimidating me a little. You have that ability in abundance, Zander. But I'm betting that I have an ace in the hole."

"And what is that?"

"I'm Eve's friend, and I care about her. She cares about me, too. I don't think that you'd harm me when you know I'm fighting for her."

"Of course, you could be wrong," he said softly.

She nodded. "I've been wrong before."

She held her breath as he stared at her without speaking for what seemed like a long time.

"I suppose I can tolerate you for a little longer." He turned and strode toward the Gulfstream.

She let the breath she'd been holding escape. First blood. She ran to catch up with him. "You'll have to do more than tolerate me," she said. "I've been thinking on the way from Casper, and I'm going to have to start moving on all fronts."

"You mean I'm not to receive your exclusive attention?" He wasn't looking at her as he reached the steps of the Gulfstream. "Thank God."

"Oh, you're the primary item on the agenda. I still have to make sure you're still alive at the end of the game." She climbed the steps and entered the plane. "But the situation is becoming tense, and I can't let you dominate it. Venable told you about those nuclear devices, right?" He didn't answer, and she continued. "I know he did. He might keep certain things from you as a power play, but he's scared shitless about those ramifications. He'd hope that you'd be willing to give at least minimal assistance."

He sat down in a leather seat and fastened his seat belt.

"I'm not that optimistic. So I'll probably have to take care of it myself." She sat down across from him, fastened her belt, and took out her phone. "But since I have to stick to you, I might need help. We have all kinds of information spread all over, and it's time to tidy up."

"Tidy up?" Zander repeated. "I hope you don't mean what I think you do. I won't have anyone get in my way."

"They're more likely to get in your way if they don't know where you're going to be at a given time." She paused to gaze at him before dialing. "Look, last time Eve was found in those mountains against all odds because the people who cared about her worked together to make it happen. Personally, I wish we had an army, but I'll take the same people with the same motivation. Am I going to tell them that Eve is possibly in Seattle? Yes, but I'm also going to tell them that Chicago is also a target, and there could also be leads to her there. For all we know, Doane might be trying to trick Eve."

"Eve didn't think that she was being tricked," Zander said. "I don't either."

"No, but we have to look at all possibilities." She added, "And I believe that Jane hasn't been telling me about something that Kendra and Margaret found in Doane's safe house. Kendra would never discuss it with Venable because she didn't trust him. She didn't talk to me about it either. I'm CIA, and she was probably a little nervous about my connection with Venable." She started dialing. "So I'm going to come clean with Jane and ask her to come clean with me."

"You'll excuse me if I go up to the cockpit and talk to the pilot," Zander said as he got to his feet. "I'm finding all this new broom and cleaning jargon slightly nauseating."

"By all means. I'm more at ease if I don't have you glaring at me." Catherine spoke into the phone as Jane answered. "Jane, Catherine Ling, I'm in Denver and there are things that you should know . . ."

The Gulfstream had taken off and been in the air for over forty-five minutes when Zander came out of the cockpit.

"Finished?" He sat down in the seat across from her. "Is everyone on the same page?"

"We're getting there." She frowned. "What do you know about Doane's ex-wife?"

"Not much. Except that after investigating her, the percentages were good that she wouldn't cause me any trouble."

"Your percentages may have been crap,"

Catherine said bluntly. "She changed her name to Harriet Weber and moved to Muncie, Indiana, but she evidently didn't change her affections when it came to her son, Kevin. She kept in contact with him by letter and possibly saw him on occasion. All in secret. Very ugly letters . . ."

"And Doane?"

"No sign of contact with him yet. Harriet Weber flew the coop when Jane confronted her, and Jane, Caleb, and Trevor are following Harriet in hopes she'll lead them to Doane."

Zander's lips twisted. "Don't we all have that same hope?"

"It's a lead," Catherine said firmly. "And we wouldn't have it without Kendra and Jane and everyone else who are working to find Eve. You can sit on your mountaintop alone, but I'll be slogging along and getting things done."

"'Slogging'? What an ugly word. And you're not an ugly person, Catherine. It doesn't suit you at all."

"It suits my attitude."

"But how are you going to 'slog' if you have to protect me on my mountaintop?"

Was there a hint of humor in those words?
It was hard to tell. But she found herself
smiling anyway. "I'm good at multitasking."

"I imagine you are," he murmured. "I'd
like to relax. Are we through with all this
cleaning and bonding and such?"

"Not quite." She took out her phone again.
"I asked Jane to phone Joe Quinn and fill
him in, but I have one more person I have
to call."

"And who is that?"

"John Gallo." She gazed searchingly at
him. "Did Eve tell you anything about Gallo?"

He shook his head. "Not really. She mentioned his name as Bonnie's father but
wouldn't say anything more about him. I
was made to understand that anything that
personal was going to remain personal.
She had the same attitude toward Joe
Quinn, but I had dossiers on him, so it didn't
matter. Just the length of her relationship
with Quinn spoke for itself." He paused.
"What does Gallo have to do with this? Why
do you have to call him?"

"Because he's wasting his time, and he's
too valuable to waste. Right now he's in Vancouver tracking you and probably scaring

all your contacts so badly they'll be scurrying for cover. I have to tell him I'm with you and that he should pull back." She made a face. "Easier said than done. Gallo is . . . not controllable. He goes his own way."

"Then why are you trying if he won't listen to you?"

"Sometimes he listens to me."

"Really?" His eyes narrowed on her face. "Tell me, do you share something besides friendship with Eve? Is Gallo your lover?"

"No, but if he was, it would be no betrayal of Eve. What was between them ended almost before it began, and all they shared was Bonnie."

"That's a big thing to share, possibly the biggest in Eve's life."

"Yes, and Gallo tells me that because they share it, Eve will always be his friend." She met his gaze. "And that's why he's trying to track you down. He's trying to save his friend, and you're the only path we've been able to find that might lead to her."

"How wonderful to be so popular. Lucky me." He leaned back in his seat. "How good is Gallo?"

"Very, very good. Brilliant. He was in the

Army Special Forces and they sent him on suicide missions." She smiled faintly. "But he always came back. Is that good enough for you, Zander?"

"It appears to be good enough for you, Catherine." He tilted his head. "Go ahead, make your call. We must tell Gallo that he'll have to wait to make my acquaintance. I know he'll be disappointed."

"No, he'll just make a decision whether he'll track me along with you, Zander. Since I'm sure you won't let me tell him where we are."

"Correct. You have me all to yourself." His tone took on a steely edge. "All the rest of your little group can stay out of my way."

"No promises." She started to dial. "They're all individuals and have minds of their own. I'm going to fill Gallo in on everything that's happened. I'm sure it will bore you. So why don't you go back up to the cockpit?"

"Oh, this call won't bore me," he drawled. "Because you obviously want to get rid of me. That opens all kinds of interesting questions to sift through."

She had been afraid that would be his

reaction. She would always have to be on guard against Zander's razor-sharp intellect and boundless curiosity, and her vulnerability to Gallo made her wary of exposing that possible weakness. She shrugged. "Suit yourself."

"Oh, I will."

"I didn't have the—" She broke off as Gallo answered. "Hello, Gallo. I need to fill you in on a few things that I've learned that may come into play."

"I haven't found Zander yet. He and Stang seem to have disappeared. Though I think I have a line on an electronics expert he uses on occasion. His name is Weiner, and I should be able to—"

"Weiner? No, leave him alone. The man's been practically having a nervous breakdown because he's afraid Zander will think he's betrayed him."

Silence. "Now I'm curious to know how you happen to have that information."

She braced herself. "Because I found Zander. I'm with him now."

"The hell you are."

"And he's not in Vancouver and won't return there until we find Eve."

He said softly, "And, dammit, how can we find Eve if we can't use him to do it?"

She glanced at Zander. "I don't believe he'd like to be used. But he may come around to being of minimal help."

"He's in the room with you, isn't he?"

"A plane, actually. And, yes, he's listening."

"And is he a threat to you?"

"Not at the moment. It's my choice to be here. If I behave myself, I may escape being thrown out over the Rockies."

"I want to talk to him."

"That wouldn't be a good idea. I was joking about being thrown out over the mountains."

"More likely the Pacific," Zander murmured. "I could talk to him, Catherine."

And that mocking tongue would probably stir Gallo into a fury. "Zander wasn't the only reason I called you. I wanted to make sure you weren't wasting your time looking for him, but there are other things I needed to tell you." She briefly told him all she had learned in her conversation with Jane, then their chase after Eve to the airport in Wyoming. "Seattle, not Vancouver, Gallo. He's going to try some way to get Eve with Zander in Seattle. At least, that's what Eve guessed when she wrote those letters on the clay."

"And Jane thinks that Doane's ex-wife may know something about Doane?"

"I don't know what Jane thinks. Harriet Weber is one big question mark right now. But she thinks it's worth pursuing. Kendra is working on the journal and seeing what connections she can make with the new info about Harriet." She paused. "There you have it, Gallo. It's all I can give you to work with."

"You're going to Seattle, aren't you?"

"Yes, but if you're thinking about teaming with me and Zander, forget it. Zander won't have it. He's barely tolerating me. You're on your own." She hesitated. "But there's a way that you could help Eve if you'll do it."

"Of course I'll do it," he said roughly. "Don't be ridiculous. What is it?"

"Joe Quinn is somewhere up there in Vancouver. Jane called and told him that Seattle was going to be the hot spot."

"I don't like where this is going."

"Joe is nearly crazy, he's so afraid about Eve. He's not going to be either cautious or safe. He may even give away the edge that Doane believes he's safe from pursuit. Joe will tear down to Seattle and go for broke." She paused. "Having someone around to balance that desperation would be very desirable."

"For God's sake, he's Eve's lover. I'm the father of her child. Don't you see a few difficulties in having me chum up with him? I assure you that Quinn will."

"You specialize in overcoming difficulties. I've watched you do it. It's a matter of whether you'll exert the effort. I can't persuade you. Only you can decide whether it's worth it to save Eve. I'll keep you in the loop with any information that comes up. I'm going to hang up now."

Gallo muttered a curse. "I need to be with you there. Why the hell didn't you bring me into the picture when you tapped Venable? Why face Zander alone?"

"Why not?" She looked at Zander. "We're making real progress in getting to know each other. He assured me that he wouldn't throw me out of the plane in the mountains.

It would definitely be the Pacific. Now that would extend our relationship over I don't know how many more miles. He obviously wants to keep me with him."

"That's not amusing."

"Actually, sometimes Zander is amusing." She added, "I don't have a choice. I have to work it this way, Gallo. I'll call you when I can." She hung up.

"He's very protective," Zander said. "He didn't like it that I have you in my clutches."

"I thought it was the other way around," Catherine said. "And some men are naturally protective."

"Of you." He chuckled. "But not of Joe Quinn. I found it clever how you manipulated him to do what you wished."

"I didn't manipulate him. It will be his decision. I just made a decision that would help find Eve."

"And you now have all your ducks in a row to move forward. It was fascinating watching you create an army out of a band of revolutionaries."

"They're brilliant, competent people. I did the best I could. But I'm handicapped from now on. As I said, they're on their own." She met his gaze. "It's you and me, Zander."

"That remains to be seen. But until I make a decision, you do have amusement value."

"I don't believe anyone has ever listed that as one of my primary assets."

"Doesn't your son think you're amusing?"

"We won't talk about Luke if you don't mind. You appear to be curious about everything and everyone around you, but I'm aware that knowledge can give one weapons. You must already realize I'm vulnerable where my son is concerned. I can't hide it now. But I can keep you from knowing any more about my relationship with Luke."

"As you like." His gaze shifted to the window next to him. "You're afraid I'll target your son to hurt you. It's very intelligent of you to consider the possibility, but I don't hurt children. It's one of my idiosyncrasies."

"We'll still not discuss him."

"You're wise not to trust me. You should hold tight to anyone you value." His gaze shifted back to her. "In many ways you remind me of Eve."

"I don't know why. Eve and I share a few philosophies, but we're not at all alike."

He smiled faintly. "Then why do I feel that if you were the one missing, I'd be sitting here talking to Eve? She'd be looking for you with the same passion you're show-ing trying to save her."

"I don't know why you'd think that." She tilted her head. "Perhaps you know her better than I do." She added slyly, "Or it could be fatherly instinct."

He looked disconcerted. Then he chuck-led and rose to his feet. "As I said, you do have amusement value." He headed for the cockpit. "Buckle up. I think we're on the way down."

She watched him disappear into the cockpit. The tension was easing, they had struck a balance, but she knew that he could turn and strike with lightning force if he decided to do so.

She glanced out the window and saw that they were going through wispy clouds. Zander was right, they should be landing in Seattle within minutes.

If they were right about Doane and Eve's being on the plane that had taken off from that airport in Wyoming, they should have landed in the Seattle area hours ago.

If Doane hadn't pulled a fast one and fooled Eve about the destination.

She felt her muscles stiffen at the thought

that they might be in the wrong city with little time to spare before Doane ignited those nukes.

No, she had to trust that Eve had given them the right information or go crazy.

She closed her eyes.

Be here, Eve.
Please, be here.

Driftwood Cottage

"We're home," Doane said as he took the blindfold off Eve's eyes. "And it's a very special home. Kevin loved this place."

"It took you long enough to drive here," Eve said as she looked up the hill at the cottage. "I thought you were taking me to Canada." Where was she? The area appeared completely deserted, and the drive from the small airport where they'd landed had seemed to be as long as she'd said.

Dark hills loomed in contrast with the beach where the car was parked. Sand, pale driftwood gleaming in the moonlight, a weather-beaten cottage on the hill.

Surf crashing against the rocky shore.

"Not as placid and beautiful as your cottage on the lake," Doane said as he pulled Eve out of the rental car and pushed her up the path. "This is Kevin's house. He bought it when he was in Seattle trying to find a suitable location for the device. He got a good deal of pleasure out of this place. He said it suited him."

"I can see how it might. Totally bizarre and theatrical." And chilling. The cottage was small and rustic, half-hidden by rocks but what she could see was like a scene from a horror film. In front of the cottage were scores of individual pieces of white driftwood whose twisted branches were oddly shaped like gleaming headstones. They appeared to be entreating mercy from the darkness of the sky above. The thought of Kevin's standing here and looking at those twisted branches was frightening. She could almost feel him beside her.

No, behind her. If she looked over her shoulder, would she see Doane . . . or Kevin?

"And I liked the thought of nature unchained," Doane said. "I believed it might increase your feeling of helplessness."

"It doesn't," she lied. She would not look over her shoulder at him. Instead, she glanced around the deserted beach and hills. "But it's not what I expected. You're not going to have much impact with your dirty bomb out here in the boonies. I was expecting a big-city locale."

"You'll get it." He pushed her inside. "This is what you might call a holding tank. I have to get everything ready before I throw you and Zander together for the finale."

"What do you have to get ready? I thought you told me everything was set to go, that all it would take would be pressing a button. Was that a lie?"

"I don't have to lie to you. I don't have to tell you anything."

"But you like to tell me all your plans. It gives you some kind of cheap thrill." She wrinkled her nose as she looked around the small room. It was dusty and smelled of mildew. The only furniture was a wooden table and simple kitchen chairs, a faded couch, an easy chair, and coffee table in front of a stone fireplace. "Your choice of prisons isn't improving. This isn't any better than that motel. How long do we have to be here?"

"Until I make arrangements." He pushed her down in a chair at the table and tied her. "And I'm going to have to leave you for a while to do it." He chuckled. "I see your eyes light up. Don't be too eager. You'll still have my full attention. But now that you've finished the reconstruction, you're not going to be occupied. I'll have to take care of that problem."

"I can't wait to learn how."

"You won't have to wait long." He put the case containing Kevin's skull on the table beside her. "And I'll leave Kevin here to keep you company." He opened the case and gently pulled the reconstruction from the box. "I know how much you like him to be close to you, to watch you."

She didn't look at the reconstruction. She knew every line, every curve of that face she'd rebuilt from the burned horror of the skull Doane had given her to re-create. It was a handsome face, but all she could see was the twisted soul beneath it. "If I get loose, the first thing I'll do will be to light a fire in that fireplace and throw him into it. It's where you should have left him instead of trying to resurrect him."

Doane's lips tightened. "And I'd throw you into the fire after him."

"Would you? But then your plans to make Zander suffer by killing me would be ruined. Not that he would suffer anyway." She looked at him. Questions. Find out as much as she could. "Where are you going?"

"I have to make sure that everything is ready and in place."

"In place? Where is this nuke?"

"It's safe." He looked away from her as he straightened the reconstruction on the table. "I don't have to worry about it. It's quite safe."

He was being evasive. Why? "Safe from what? Where is it?" Her gaze narrowed on his face. "If you're not afraid I'm going to escape from you, why won't you tell me?"

"You don't need to know. You'll find out soon enough."

A sudden, bizarre thought occurred to her. "Why, you don't know, do you?" she asked softly. "Your wonderful Kevin didn't trust you enough to tell you. All this time, you've been stringing Venable along and making him think he'd eventually be able to get that info from you, and you never had it."

"That's not true," he said harshly. "My Kevin did trust me. He just died before he could tell me where he stashed those nuclear devices. But I'll still be able to do it. I just have to talk to a few of Kevin's contacts here, and we'll be able to find it."

She laughed. "Who? His al-Qaeda buddies evidently weren't able to find those bombs in the last five years. Why should they be able to tell you now? Maybe no one knows where they are."

"Someone knows," he said curtly. "Kevin knew. And Kevin wanted me to know. He told me he put it all in his journal. But the message was so well hidden that I couldn't understand it. I went through the journal a dozen times, but I still couldn't see what Kevin wanted me to see. So I hid it away until I could spend more time on it." He added harshly, "Last week, I told Blick to go back to the house to get it and bring it to me when I was afraid things weren't going so well. But the fool had the journal taken away from him by your friend, Kendra Michaels."

"Good for Kendra," Eve said. "And now no journal and no nukes. You'd better take me to Vancouver and go back to plan one, Doane. Two deaths instead of millions."

"The bombs are still where Kevin put them. Your Kendra won't be able to figure out their location from the journal any more than I could." He added sourly, "But there's another way I can find out where they are."

"How? By communing with Kevin? I don't think so."

"There's another way," he repeated.

"I think Kevin lied to you and just wanted to soothe your ego. He didn't trust you, and he didn't want to give up the chance to go down in demonic history if you failed him."

"I haven't failed him. Everyone else has failed him, but I've stood strong and steady." He looked at the skull on the table. "Even Blick failed you, Kevin. But we took care that he didn't get a second chance." He reached in his pocket. "And I'm not going to give you a second chance either, Eve." He pulled out a hypodermic. "I have to be gone a few hours, and I'm not going to have you becoming troublesome. I think you need a nice long sleep after our trip."

He rolled up her sleeve. "And there will be no opportunity of throwing my Kevin into the fire even if you managed to get free."

"You appear to like to use drugs." Eve felt the prick of the needle on her arm. "You must have become used to them to lure Kevin's victims into his web."

He shook his head. "He didn't like them drugged. That's why I had to use all my skill and persuasion to get them to come with me. I told you, I can be very persuasive."

And Eve knew that to be true. At first, his kind, trustworthy face and gentle manner had made even Eve believe they mirrored an equally trustworthy soul. "I still find it hard to understand how you could do that just because Kevin—" She broke off. "You must not have any conscience at all, Doane."

"Kevin says conscience is overrated. He needed release. I gave it to him. Everyone who knew Kevin ended up giving him whatever he wanted. He was special. That's how it should be." He bent to look into her eyes. "You're getting drowsy, aren't you? I'll be able to leave you soon."

She was getting drowsy. The room was swimming around her. "Leave me now. I don't want to—have to look at you any— longer."

"Not yet. I want to be quite sure." He leaned back against the table. "You'll give Kevin what he wants, too, Eve." He reached out and touched her cheek. "Your blood, your life . . . your Bonnie."

"He can have two—out of three. He'll never have . . . Bonnie."

"You say that, but it means nothing. He already has her, all that's left is to break her connection with this world. That's you, Eve. When you die, he takes you both."

"Then he can't have me either." The darkness was weaving in and out around her. "Go away, Doane. Or if you want to stick pins . . . in me, use the real thing. Your words . . . are useless. You and Kevin . . . bluff . . . only bluff."

"Are we?" He was suddenly snarling. He jerked her closer to the table and set Kevin's skull directly in front of her. "Then why are you afraid to look at him? You may not be afraid of me, but you're afraid of Kevin. And soon you'll fear both of us."

He meant when they merged, she thought hazily. When Kevin crossed back and became—

Blue eyes staring at her from the skull only inches away from her.

Cold.

Nausea.

And then the panic.

They were only glass eyeballs, nothing else.

No.

Kevin's eyes, reaching out for her.

And for Bonnie.

Her chest was tight. She couldn't breathe. She could feel the perspiration bead her face as she fought the fear.

"Yes, that's what I wanted," Doane said softly, his gaze on her face. "I couldn't do it to you, but Kevin managed, didn't he? I keep telling you he's special." He straightened away from the table. "And now I'll leave you to him. He'll be sorry I gave you the shot. He always enjoyed the delicious sharpness of the response to whatever he did." He paused at the door. "But perhaps you'll be so afraid that the narcotic won't take effect, and you'll have him with you all the time I'm gone. Or maybe he'll follow you down and bring the nightmare with him. All kinds of interesting possibilities . . ."

Doane was gone.

But Kevin was here. Eve had carefully mended the ugliness of the burned and blackened skull, but the sight of it was abruptly before her.

Only a memory, she told herself. A memory heightened by the effect of the narcotic Doane had given her. For all she knew, Doane could have given her a hallucinogenic to mentally torture her.

It wasn't the drug.

It was Kevin.

Hate you. Take you. Take her.

"The hell you will." Her voice was slurred. "You're only bone and clay and glass."

Blue eyes staring . . .

She closed her own eyes, which were unbearably heavy. "And now I'm going to go to sleep and you . . . may go back to hell . . . where you belong."

Take you.

"No way . . ."

She could no longer see him, but she could still feel him there.

Frustrated? Good. She was tired of dealing with monsters and filthy perverts who were incomprehensible to ordinary human beings. She just wanted to go away . . .

• • •

"You have gone away. No one can touch you now, Mama."

Bonnie?

She opened her eyes, but Kevin's skull was no longer on the table before her.

Bonnie was sitting in the chair at the end of the table, her right leg tucked beneath her. Same Bugs Bunny T-shirt and jeans, same curly red hair, same beloved, radiant smile.

Oh, God, how Eve had missed that smile.

"And just where have I gone, baby?" she asked shakily.

"You're still in the cottage, but the drug Doane gave you took you deep enough so that I could break through the barriers Kevin put up. I was able to reach you. I told you that was the only way I'd found to come to you."

"I'm surprised you were able to get through. This was Kevin's place, and it's full of him. It's as if he's still here." She grimaced. "Even that hideous grave-yard of driftwood out front. It's kind of fitting that Doane gave me a drug to knock me out. It's like that sleeping-beauty tale, only instead of a garden of thorns keeping everyone out, there's that graveyard of driftwood."

"I had to work hard on it. This is a bad place." She suddenly grinned impishly. "But I was even able to get rid of that nasty Kevin's skull from your mind. I knew you'd be happier if he was gone. And Kevin was perfectly furious at both of us. Isn't that wonderful?"

"Wonderful. But he's still there?"

"Not as long as you're asleep. Everything is fine as long as you're deep under the influence of that narcotic. Doane did us a favor when he gave it to you."

"I don't believe that was how it was meant." Her gaze was running hungrily over her daughter. "But I don't care. May I say how glad I am to see you. It's been too long, Bonnie."

"I did the best I could. Kevin is very strong. But you know that, Mama, he makes you afraid." She tilted her head. "I didn't think I'd ever see you afraid."

"Only for you, Bonnie."

She nodded gravely. "I know that. Everything for me. That's how it's been since I came into your life."

"That's how all parents feel, baby. It goes with the territory."

"But now you should think about yourself, Mama. Let me fight for myself."

Eve went still. "And is it a fight with Kevin? Not some kind of spiritual suppression or—"

"Of course, it's a fight," Bonnie said bluntly. "Forget all those big, fancy religious or psychological ideas. There's nothing but evil about Kevin. He's . . . full of silences. I don't know what a demon is like, but he may show us if he's allowed to survive. He somehow managed to slip over the line, and now he won't go back." She paused. "He wants to cross another line."

"I know," Eve whispered.

Bonnie nodded. "I thought you did. So you have to fight him, too." She added, "But we can beat him. We have to do it."

She remembered something Bonnie had said. "Full of silences," Eve repeated slowly. "What do you mean?"

"He . . . smothers . . . everything. I don't know how he does it. Maybe it's something he brought with him." She bit down on her lower lip. "But it's . . . bad. Terrible. Final."

"Final . . . I don't understand."

"The soul goes on. Most of the time there's a chance for redemption, a new start. But with Kevin, I sense only silence from his victims. Nothing beyond. No second chance."

"Those children he killed?"

"Silence."

"Dear God."

"But if Kevin is destroyed, perhaps the silence would be lifted." She shook her head. "I don't know. We can only hope and pray. But we can't let him silence anyone else. He mustn't kill again. For him, silence is the ultimate power, far above the act of murder."

Millions dead in a nuclear holocaust.

"We have to stop it." Bonnie's gaze was on her face, reading her thoughts. "Not only the deaths but what might come after."

"You worry about the afterward.

Saving lives is enough for me to be concerned about at the moment."

Bonnie smiled. "You'll worry about everything. Present, future, afterward. I know you, Mama."

"One crisis at a time. Doane is my primary crisis." She made a face. "Or maybe it's Kevin. I get confused when I think about them these days."

"It will get clearer," Bonnie said soberly. "Because they're getting closer to each other all the time. Can't you feel that?"

"Yes."

"Kevin hates you. He wants to silence you."

"Silence." Eve had never realized how chilling that word could be. The ultimate power, Bonnie had said. "I'm sure he has a similar desire where you're concerned."

"It's different with me. He blames you. You're standing in his way. You have to be very careful."

Eve suddenly chuckled. "Bonnie, I'm tied up, captive of a homicidal maniac who's threatening to blow me up along with half of Seattle. And you're telling me to be careful?"

"Sorry." Bonnie giggled. "Sometimes I forget the present when I get absorbed in what's going to happen." A smile was still lingering. "But I'm glad that I made you laugh. I love to hear you laugh, and you don't do enough of it. I wish you were always smiling."

"I'm not the type. The people who know me would think I was having a breakdown if I went around grinning." Eve's smile faded. "But you make me smile. You always did. From the moment you were born, you filled every day with love and laughter. When you were gone, I couldn't find it again. I just like you to be here near me."

"I'm always near you," Bonnie said gently.

"I know, but I want to see you, dammit." She shook her head. "It's okay. I swore I wouldn't complain. You're busy saving the afterworld." She grimaced. "That makes you sound like a super-hero. Now that is funny when I look at you in that Bugs Bunny T-shirt."

"You like me in this T-shirt. It makes you remember me the way I was before I left you."

"Yes, it does." Bonnie had told Eve that after she had passed over that she could not remain the child she had been. The way she spoke, the wisdom, the maturity, had at first shocked Eve. No longer. Bonnie's soul was the same, and that was all that was important to her. She asked curiously, "Could you change how you look to me?"

"I don't know. I think so. But it's not important if you're happy with me like this." Her smile was loving. "It's all about you, Mama."

"No, it's not. You just want to keep me from joining you too soon. I'm trying, Bonnie. I know that Joe would feel as lost as I did when you were taken. I don't want him to hurt like that." She added wearily, "But I'm so tired of being without you, baby. Sometimes I think I'd be forgiven if I just let it happen."

"I know you do. That's why Doane is so dangerous to you. You wouldn't take your own life, you'd just not fight and let him strike you down." She shook her head. "You can't do that. The circle around you is widening all the time. Everyone you touch would feel the loss. All your friends, Zander . . ."

"Zander." She stiffened. "That's the first time you mentioned him. What do you know about—" She broke off. "He's not one of the people touched by me. Zander wouldn't be affected one way or the other."

"He would feel the loss," she said. "Doane is right about your death hurting him." She frowned. "You don't want me talking about him. You don't want Zander that near me. He can't hurt me, Mama."

"You're right, I don't want to talk about him."

"Then we won't do it. There are enough people who care about you without mentioning Zander."

She was silent a moment. "Is he . . . your grandfather, Bonnie?"

"Ask him. You don't want to hear about him from me."

Eve didn't know why she had asked that question. It had come tumbling out with irresistible force. "There are a number of questions I have to ask him when Doane brings us together." She added wryly, "Providing he allows us enough time before he presses the magic button." She held up her hand as Bonnie opened her lips to speak. "I know. I know. That sounded much too resigned. I'll work on it. I just didn't understand why you mentioned Zander instead of someone who does care whether I live or die."

"Like Jane?"

"Yes."

"I didn't mention Jane because you didn't, Mama. You talked about Joe's being hurt, but you didn't say anything about Jane."

"Of course I meant Jane, too."

"But you didn't say her name. Only Joe's."

Eve stiffened. "What are you saying? I love Jane, and I know she loves me. I wasn't trying to leave her out in any way."

"You do love her, but not in the same way you love me. It may even be a better way because she's your best friend. We never got the chance to become friends. That comes later between a mother and daughter."

"Then what difference does it make that I—Are you saying that I made some Freudian slip?"

"Maybe. I believe that I was always in the way of your relationship with Jane. You were searching for me, thinking about me for years and years."

"Jane always said that she never resented it."

"And that proves that she loves you. She wanted whatever would make you happy." She paused. "Just as I do. I feel very close to Jane, Mama. But she shuts me out. I can't . . . reach her. It didn't bother me before . . . well, a little. I understood that she'd put up barriers to keep from being hurt. But I can't let her be alone when she—you may have to do it for me."

"You're scaring me. What are you talking about?"

"I just want you to know that she's willing to do anything for you. Would she miss you as Joe would?" She hesitated, then said quietly, "She'd die for you, Mama."

She inhaled sharply. "Bonnie."

"I just want you to know that it's not only your life you're fighting for. Fight for Jane. She's going to need you."

"Don't you dare be all mysterious and enigmatic, young lady. Explain."

Bonnie shook her head. "Just love her and try to take care of her." She smiled with an obvious effort. "When you manage to get out of those ropes and start moving in the right direction. Did it occur to you that you wouldn't be in this situation if you'd taken your chance to get away instead of saving Zander? That makes it even stranger that you still resent him."

"Of course it occurred to me. It also occurred to me that you're trying to change the subject." And, knowing Bonnie, she realized that she was not going to yield any more information no matter how frustrated it was going to make Eve. Frustrated and scared. "If you're so worried about Jane, you take care of her. Ghosts should have some kind of special powers, shouldn't they? Well, if you do, don't use them for me. Use them for Jane."

"It doesn't work that way, Mama."

"I'm tired of hearing that. If I were there with you, then maybe I'd understand about—" She stopped. "I don't want to argue. These moments with you are too precious. I'll do my job. I'll help my Jane."

"I know you will," Bonnie said. "And we aren't arguing. I had to warn you, and I made you worry. If I could make it stop, I would. But now it's out of the way and I can just be with you."

"The last time you were able to come to me was when I inhaled that gas at the cabin. You disappeared when I started to come out of it. How much time do we have?"

"A long time," she said gravely. "A few hours, I think."

"What?"

"He gave you a very strong dose." She looked her in the eye. "A little more, and we would have been together."

Together. Death. "That potent?"

"He's angry with you all the time now. You hurl those barbed remarks at him, and they sting. He's beginning to get reckless."

Eve was feeling a little reckless herself. "At least it brought you to me."

"Mama . . ." She shook her head. "Yes, it brought me to you. Now, we'll sit here and take what's been given."

"And you'll tell me how you erased Kevin's reconstruction from my mind. I know he's right in front of me. Why can't I see him?"

"He doesn't exist right now. I can hold him at bay as long as we're joined together. I can feel his anger, but he can't do anything."

"You said you were getting stronger fighting him."

"I am. Because of you," she said. "And these hours with you are going to make me even stronger. As I said, Doane may have done us a favor."

"And Kevin will be angry with him. What a pity."

Bonnie threw back her head and laughed. Her red curls were gleaming, and her face glowed with vitality that seemed to light up the room.

Eve gazed at her and felt a surge of pure love. Spirit or not, this was her little girl, who had been born with a very special soul. She had been able to reach out and touch, gather, and inspire love in everyone who met her. Eve had been lucky to have been able to keep her for those seven years, and she had given up bitterness long ago.

"I love you, Bonnie." She was suddenly afraid. "And don't let that bastard get too close to you. I like you just fine unsilenced."

"Is that a correct word? You always used to correct me if I didn't use correct English."

"That was then, this is now. I don't care. You know what I mean."

"I'll keep Kevin away. You go after Doane." She smiled. "Don't be afraid, can't you feel the strength flowing between us? It will get stronger and stronger all the time we're together. It's like a deep river, and it will keep everything afloat. Can't you feel it?"

"No." Was love strength? If it was,

then she knew the river Bonnie was talking about. "It doesn't matter. We'll get through it." She gazed at Bonnie, and the warmth filled the world. "And I'm not afraid any longer."

CHAPTER

10

Stanley, Illinois

"She's heading for Chicago," Trevor said as he glanced at the GPS. They picked up Harriet's signal almost immediately after they had gotten on the road, and had been traveling at a safe distance behind her for the past hours. "Now why would she be heading for the big city . . . ?"

"A good place to get lost . . ." Jane said as she accessed the dossier that Catherine Ling had e-mailed to her. "But there's no indication that she has friends or a connection here. I'm going to check with Catherine and see if there's something I'm missing."

"Good idea," Caleb said. "Of course, she could be going to the airport. Chicago has connections to everywhere in the world. It would be logical for her to leave Muncie and go to an airline hub. We should have gone back to Muncie Airport and picked up my plane."

"But we don't know that she wants to leave Chicago," Trevor said. "Maybe there's something she wants to do there."

"The nuke," Jane said. "You believe she knows where it is?"

"I don't believe anything," Trevor said. "Except that Harriet Weber has displayed a discipline and strength in these last years that makes Doane's appear weak in comparison. Yet there is a similarity if you look for it. Doane pretended to be a heartbroken but innocent father for the last five years. She was evidently in masquerade mode for far longer and was so good that Venable didn't even bother to have her watched. But both were controlled by their son, Kevin."

"The question is whether Harriet was so influenced by Kevin that she became involved in the hiding of the nuclear devices," Jane said. "Muncie is fairly close to Chicago, and it would have been convenient for Kevin to have brought his mother into his scheme to destroy that city."

"Now that's true corruption," Caleb said. "She'd have to know how dangerous mass murder would be for him. Perhaps she tried to talk him out of doing it as she did the child killings."

"Or tried to make it safer for him by making sure he wouldn't be caught," Jane said grimly.

Trevor's brows rose. "You're leaning toward thinking that she would go that far?"

"You should have seen her face. She was proud that he'd taught her to defend herself. She liked the idea that the two of them were banded together against the world. I think she would have done anything for him." She frowned. "But I'll still check with Catherine to see if there's any other reason for her going to Chicago." She was dialing her phone. "Caleb, I want you to send those copies of Kevin's letters to my cell. Did Margaret have you send them to Kendra?"

"That's goes without saying. She wanted Kendra to have material with which to work." He paused. "The turnoff for O'Hare Airport is five miles ahead. We should have an idea which way Harriet is going to jump soon."

"Then while I'm talking to Catherine, call Margaret and tell her where we are." Jane smiled slyly. "I'm sure she'll be glad to hear from you."

"I think Trevor should call her. He's much more diplomatic."

"I'm driving," Trevor said. "It wouldn't be safe."

Caleb grimaced. "Okay. I'm stuck with it." He took out his phone. "How bad can it get?"

"You must tell us when you finish the call," Jane murmured. "Personally, I'd hesitate to—" She broke off as Catherine answered the phone. "Catherine, we're heading for Chicago. We're following Harriet Weber, and she proved to be a hell of a lot more dangerous than Venable thought her to be. I need to know more about her."

"I told you everything that was on the Venable file," Catherine said. "What do you mean 'dangerous'?"

Jane filled her in on her meeting with Harriet and the discovery of Kevin's letters. She ended with, "Why should she be going to Chicago?"

"The nuke," Catherine said bluntly. "I'd

guess she was knee deep in Kevin's plot from what you've told me."

"That was my first thought," Jane said. "Either she was a member of the sleeper cell, or she worked alone with him. She seemed very independent, very smart, and aggressive. Even though she seems to have been firmly controlled emotionally by him, she'd need to be an active part of whatever she chose to do. She wouldn't trust even Kevin's judgment over her own. She was his mother, and mother knows best. Even in their correspondence, she was evidently telling him gently what to do about his damn murders."

Catherine was silent. "You seem to have a handle on her."

"I learned by a huge mistake, but I think I know her now." She hadn't realized until actually voicing that knowledge how clearly she was seeing Harriet Weber's character. As they had been driving, she had been mentally going over what she had been told about Harriet's background in Muncie, then the actual contact. "First, you have to realize that she has an ego to match Kevin's and that she also lacks any hint of conscience."

"A sociopath?"

"Perhaps. I don't know. Maybe. But she did love Kevin."

"And you're excited."

"Yes, because I believe there may be a way to reach Doane through Harriet. I've got to try. You're in Seattle?"

"Yes, we just arrived. Stang picked us up, and we're heading toward downtown. Zander's not wasting any time. He has a rather unsavory contact named Slater who has his ear to the ground and may be able to help. I'll call Langley and see if they have any other info on Harriet Weber and let you know."

"Thanks. I'll be out there as soon as I can. I just have to check out Harriet's connection in—"

"Stop sounding so agonized. You can't be everywhere. You said yourself that Doane's ex-wife may be a strong lead. That's more than I have right now. We have a target city and a hope that we interpreted Eve's message correctly." She paused. "Seattle. Chicago. Both target cities. We're in Seattle, and I expect Joe and Gallo will show up soon. You're in Chicago. We should be able to control the situation if we—" She chuckled. "Zander is frowning at me. He doesn't appreciate my trying to run the show. I'll talk to you later." She hung up.

"Not very helpful." Jane pressed the disconnect.

"I disagree," Caleb said. "I think talking it out with Catherine was exceptionally helpful to you. You're seeing everything with crystal clarity now. You were a little confused after your brawl with Harriet. Every instinct was screaming, but you had to put it together." He smiled faintly. "You're not like me, who is content to let instinct rule and to hell with everything else. That's the difference between the primitive and the civilized." He glanced at Trevor. "Where are you on the scale?"

"I have my moments on both levels."

Caleb shook his head. "Never on mine, Trevor. We've managed to work together, but we're not on the same wavelength."

"You never know." He looked at Jane. "But one thing was decided while you were on the phone." He nodded out the windshield. "Harriet passed the turnoff for the airport five minutes ago. She's not trying to fly out of town." He glanced down at the GPS. "And she's exiting at one of the lakefront exits."

Jane tensed. "Don't lose her."

"I won't." Trevor shifted lanes. "You trusted me to be your driver. I wouldn't fail you."

Caleb made a face. "Not when it meant you didn't have to take the heat from Margaret."

"True. How did she take the news that we'd left her in Muncie?"

"No curses or threats, just cool acceptance and a comment that neither of us had behaved honorably. She said she'd be on her way to Chicago within the next hour and would tell us where to pick her up. If it was inconvenient, she'd get to Jane on her own."

"How is she getting here?" Jane was already dialing Margaret. "I doubt if she has airfare, and she gave me back my credit card. Maybe I can prepay her ticket or something."

No answer.

Voice mail.

"She gave you back your credit card?" Trevor asked. "Why did she have your credit card?"

"Don't ask," Caleb said. "But I think I can guess. Stop worrying, Jane. Margaret will find a way. She always does."

"But it might not be a safe way." She knew that Margaret had been left behind for the girl's own safety, but she wished now that she was with them. "I'll keep trying."

"Harriet's car has stopped." Trevor was looking at the GPS. "Her Jeep Cherokee just pulled off the street somewhere."

"Where?"

"I don't know. It could be a gas station or a grocery store." He was activating the map detail. He added softly, "Or a hotel. She's pulled into a Marriott Hotel parking lot." He exited the freeway. "Let's see if she checks in and sets up housekeeping."

"We don't want Jane to check into the same hotel." Caleb was accessing the hotel feature on his phone. "She's the only one Harriet would recognize. Even if she was registered under an assumed name, there's a chance she might run into Harriet." He found what he was looking for. "Here's a Radisson Inn a block away but within viewing distance of the Marriott. You check Jane into the Radisson and get her settled, Trevor. I'll register at the Marriott, find out what room Harriet is in, then take it from there."

"Take it where?" Jane asked. "And I don't like being relegated to anywhere that's not close to Harriet."

"I didn't think you would. But I need to be free to install a few electronic bugs in Harriet's room, then do some listening without worrying about you interfering."

"Me interfering?" Jane said. "I wouldn't do that. I'm more interested than either one of you in finding out if Harriet is in contact with Doane."

"You'd interfere because I'd be thinking about you instead of Harriet," Caleb said quietly. "I need this hunt for Eve to be over. That means I have to focus on giving you Doane and Eve."

"I've never seen you have trouble focusing," Jane said. On the contrary, his intense concentration had often made her uneasy. "Is this some kind of excuse?"

"No, it's different right now." He met her gaze. "You're ill and hurting, and I could make you feel better. You won't let me do it, and I'm frustrated. I'd probably do something that would blow everything for me.

It's better that I get away from you and do something else that I'm good at."

"And what is that?" Trevor asked with narrowed eyes. "You were exceptionally good planting those listening devices in Harriet Weber's apartment. Is there more to you than an expert Peeping Tom?"

"Fathoms," Caleb said. "I spent years chasing down the killer of my sister. I'm good at the hunt, I'm fantastic at the kill." He glanced out the window. "There's the Marriott. Let me out here, then go on to the Radisson. I'll grab a taxi, have the driver take me to the closest place where I can buy a few devices, and check in at the hotel. I'll call and report as soon as I find out anything."

Trevor pulled over to the curb. "I could go with you, Caleb."

"I don't need you." He glanced at Jane as he got out of the car. "She does. Look at her. For the last thirty miles, she's been fading."

"I have not," Jane said. "I'm just tired."

"Liar. I've been watching you. And I can **feel** you. You're almost as bad as you were before they let you out of that hospital." His lips tightened. "And you won't let me do anything for you." He turned back to Trevor. "Take care of her." His smile was suddenly reckless. "Or I'll come after you. I'm no caretaker like you. Do you know how difficult this is for me?"

"I have a good idea."

"No, you can't even come close." He turned and strode down the street toward the Marriott.

"This is all wrong," Jane said as she watched him go. "Caleb's being overcareful. We should have stayed together."

"If he'd been overcareful, you'd have taken him down and done what you wanted," Trevor said quietly as he drove into the Radisson parking lot. "It speaks volumes that you let him control the situation with only a token protest."

"I won't deny that I'm not well. I have to pick my battles, and there's a certain logic to Caleb's handling the first stages of Harriet's reconnaissance. He's very effective." And she was exhausted, she realized. She was bruised and tired and strained to the maximum degree. "But you don't have to stay with me. That's ridiculous."

"It appears that I do." He smiled faintly as he came around to her door and opened it.

"Caleb was bitter that he had to leave such a major opening for me. He meant it when he said that he'd come after me." He took her hand and helped her from the car. "You wouldn't want that to happen, would you?"

His hand was warm and strong on her own, and she felt a rush of feeling that was like a deep, swirling river of sensation. The exhaustion was suddenly eased, and she only wanted to stand here and look at him.

"Hey, that's not fair." His smile faded. "You're vulnerable, and I'm trying to remember. In spite of Caleb's claim not to have any caretaking instincts, even he actually showed signs of doing that for once." He made a face. "Oh, what the hell." He grabbed their bags, but his hand still held her own as he pulled her toward the front entrance. "Caleb probably only did it to tie my hands. Why should I let him get away with it?"

"Harriet Weber booked for two nights and she's in Room 1630," Caleb said when Jane answered two hours later. "I'm in a room directly above her on the seventh floor. She left her Cherokee packed except for an overnight case and the box of letters from Kevin."

"Yes, she wouldn't want to let those sentimental messages from her dear boy far away from her," Jane said bitterly. "Let's hope she doesn't examine the box too carefully."

"She'd have to be looking for that GPS bug. It's tiny, and I placed it very carefully. But it won't help us unless she's on the road. But I picked up a few very sensitive motion and listening devices that should do the trick. It shouldn't be too difficult to plant a few bugs."

"From the floor above her?" Jane asked.

"I told you, I'm in the suite directly above hers. She has a balcony, and so do I. There are sliding glass doors, and I've checked, and they're not sealed the way some hotels keep them. I'll have to wait until the hotel quiets for the night, but then I should be able to climb down."

"Like Spider-Man?"

"Piece of cake."

Jane believed him. Margaret called Caleb one of the wild ones. She was probably referring to the dark recklessness she sensed within him. But Caleb's years of hunting and stalking his sister's killer had developed and honed those abilities to the extreme. Jane had seen him move like a jungle cat through the forest after human prey and seen the wildness in him after he had brought that prey down. "And what if she has the doors locked?"

"I'll be prepared to jimmy them, but not many people feel threatened of anyone creeping in from that direction. As you say, Spider-Man is usually not a possibility. There's a chance she'll leave them unlocked if she strolls out there." He paused. "Stop worrying, Jane. I'll get the job done."

"Without falling and breaking your neck?"

"I'm touched. And I thought that you were only concerned about my getting your information."

"Don't be sarcastic. Of course I'm concerned about you."

"Yes, but you guard yourself so well that you don't let me see it very often. And I'm sarcastic because I'm very pissed off about the situation." He paused. "Do you know that we don't have to go through all this surveillance crap? I could go to her and make her tell anything she knows. It would take less than fifteen minutes. People fear pain and are terrified of death. When the evidence that's happening comes from their own bodies, it's doubly frightening. I've only showed you that blood can be a friend, but when I make it the enemy, it can be excruciating."

She moistened her lips. "You'd do that to her?"

"You think I'd hold my hand because she's a woman? No, that's something Trevor would do. I target anyone who is capable of being a threat. I take it on a case-by-case basis. I always have a few problems with the fairness question when it comes to women. I think it's ingrained in the genes, and has something do with the preservation of the species. But in my experience, women can be more savage and deadly than men if they're motivated. Harriet Weber shows the signs of being a very ugly customer and would fight with every weapon she has. If you like, I'll go after her and get your answers."

"And torture her?"

"It would probably come down to that. I wouldn't mind this time." He was silent. "She hurt you."

"And I hurt her, too." The brutal simplicity of his answer shocked her. "I fight my own battles, Caleb."

"I know. And I also knew that my offer would probably turn you off. I had to take the chance. It could save time."

Time. How much time did Eve have left? For an instant, Jane was actually tempted. "And if Harriet didn't talk, we'd have no chance of finding out if she has a connection with Doane. Or she could lie and send us down the wrong path."

"Not likely."

"It could happen."

"Yes, it could happen. If she has mental problems; and judging from her actions and the tone of those letters from Kevin, she might. Then she'd feel anger and not fear, and she'd die before she'd tell the truth." He added impatiently, "Okay, it could go either way. Forget it. You're obviously not going to let me run the risk. I just had to put the offer out there. Is Trevor there?"

She glanced at Trevor, sitting in the chair across the hotel room. "Yes, he's been listening. Do you want to talk to him?"

"No, I've said what I wanted to say to him. I just wanted to make sure he hadn't let you send him away. Trevor has a tendency to try to give you everything you want. I'm sure that makes him even more desirable in your eyes, but you need someone with you right now." He didn't wait for her to answer. "I'm hanging up now. I'll call you when I know something more." He hung up.

"You heard him," she said to Trevor. "He seems to have everything under control." She punched the disconnect on her cell. "And so we're delegated to sitting here twiddling our thumbs. I hope Caleb is pleased. I hate being here. I'm not going to be able to take it."

Trevor smiled. "Yes, you will. And Caleb is not pleased though he hopes all we're doing is thumb twiddling." He gestured to the bed. "Why don't you lie down and rest while I call room service and get us something to eat?"

"I don't want to lie down." She wearily brushed the hair back from her face. "Do you know, I was thinking about letting him hurt her? What kind of person am I becoming, Trevor?"

"Just an ordinary human under superhuman stress," Trevor said. "And the choices are few, and all with consequences."

"I think I would have done it," she whispered. "If he'd told me that he was absolutely sure that he could get those answers.

Eve's life against the pain of a woman who would condone the death of children. I would have said save Eve. There would have been no real question."

"Could Caleb really have done what he promised? Are you sure?"

"Eve was sure. She saw it happen. That was why she was uneasy whenever I was with him. But neither Eve nor I have ever known him to hurt anyone who didn't deserve it."

"You're defending him."

"I'm telling you the truth as I know it. Caleb is an enigma, and I won't say that I can read him. He bewilders me." Her lips twisted. "You know me, Trevor. The quintessential realist. I don't like to admit that there are people who have weird gifts. Yet how the hell can I deny that Caleb appears to be in a class by himself? He can hurt, he can kill, he can even heal. Anything connected with blood flow."

"Extraordinary. Anything else?"

She shrugged. "A few years ago, I thought that blood flow was capable of affecting the mind, too. Hallucinations. Mind games. But I can't be sure." She added impatiently, "I don't want to talk about Caleb."

"Neither do I. But it's always intelligent to gauge the strength of the opposition. He's beginning to come out of the shadows and make his presence known."

"He was never in the shadows. He doesn't pretend. I always know exactly where I am with him."

"And he offers to give you Harriet's head on a platter. If you'd said yes, would you have felt a kind of unholy alliance with him?"

"I didn't say yes."

"No, but you might still have to say it," he said soberly. "I'd like to take that burden away, but you wouldn't thank me for it."

"No, and I wouldn't tell Caleb to do something I wouldn't do myself." She met his eyes. "Any more than I would ask you."

"You wouldn't have to ask." He smiled. "I think when the time comes, I'll know. We're getting closer all the time. Can't you feel it?"

She did feel it. Just looking at him, she was experiencing a surge of warm intimacy that was banishing the fear and uncertainty. "We'll never be that close."

"Don't be defensive. I'm aware of where this is going. Your own battles and all of that fine rhetoric. Now stop trying to establish something we both realize is firmly in place. I know who you are. I know your mind and body. We were lovers." He held out his hand to her. "We are lovers. Come over here and let me hold you."

And how she wanted to go to him.

Trevor had been a part of her life for so long. He had been her first passion. Hell, she had learned passion from him. Did she love him? Sometimes, she had thought she loved him. She admired him and liked him and had desperately wanted to be with him. And it was that desire that had frightened her. She had felt herself being drawn closer and closer, and, if it had continued, she hadn't known if she would be able to remain her own person. Trevor's effect on her had always been too powerful.

Standing there looking at him, memories were flowing back to her . . . She was remembering the first time she'd seen him at the lake cottage when she was only seventeen. Even then, she'd been stunned by his charisma and sheer good looks. Trevor had swept her away and made her dizzy. She remembered the time when she had followed him to the airport in Herculaneum after he had pushed her away and tried to end the growing attraction between them. She had felt rejected and been angry and indignant and wanting to strike out.

"I'm only seventeen." She had looked him directly in the eye. "No matter what you think, that's a plus. I'm going to go home and live every minute of every day. I'm going to grow and learn and experience. I'm going to see if I can find a man who makes you look boring in comparison. It shouldn't be so difficult, and, God knows, I don't want to have to deal with you and your antiquated sense of what's proper and not proper. Someday, you're going to regret turning away from me."

He nodded. "Oh, I already do."

And that moment several years later in Scotland, after she had thought that Trevor had been killed. She'd had to fight desperately to keep from panicking.

"I believe I'm getting tired of being irresponsible," he had said. "Don't you think we'd make a great match?"

She felt a surge of happiness, followed immediately by wariness. "What are you saying?"

"You know what I'm saying. You're

scared to admit it. Well, I'm way past that point. You'll have to catch up. How did you feel when you thought I was blown to bits?"

She said slowly, "Terrible. Frightened. Empty."

"Good. That's progress." He took her hand and kissed the palm. "I know I'm rushing. I can't help it. I've got years of experience on you, and I know what I want. You're having to work your way through this. You don't know whether you can trust what we have." He smiled. "And it's my job to show you that this feeling isn't ever going to go away. Not for me, and, I hope to God, not for you."

And in the years that followed he had done his best to show her that she could trust that the passion between them was only the foundation for something deeper, stronger. It had not been his fault that her wariness was too intense for him to overcome.

As it was right now, she thought as she looked at him.

"Come to me, Jane," Trevor said again.

She didn't move.

"I'm not going to make love to you," he

said softly. "It's not the time. I just want to hold you and share whatever you're feeling. Does that sound so bad?"

It sounded wonderful. Too wonderful. She stiffened. "I'm not that weak. I don't need anyone to—Oh, dammit." She ran across the room and the next moment he'd pulled her into his arms and on his lap.

She burrowed her face in his shoulder. "Just for a minute. Okay?"

"Whatever you say." His arms tightened around her. "Personally, I prefer forever, but I realize you have limits. I'll work on the rest."

"I don't want to talk."

"You never did. Not about anything important." His lips brushed her temple. "I didn't care at the time. I knew you weren't ready for commitment. I thought we had all the time in the world. But lately I've realized that even a day is too precious to waste." He leaned back in the chair. "Shh, okay, no more talk."

Minutes passed in silence. She could feel the beating of his heart beneath her ear. How often had he held her like this when they were together? She had missed this closeness, missed **him.** "You're being very good to me," she said haltingly. "Why?"

"Caleb gave me orders." He chuckled. "I have to keep an eye on you."

"Stop joking. I mean why did you come to help me when you heard about Eve? We weren't together any longer. There were never any promises between us. You didn't owe me anything."

"I made a promise to myself. I told you what it was." His hand gently brushed the hair at his temple. "Part of the way I feel about you is all mixed up with making sure all goes well with you in the little things as well as the big ones. That's why you'll never have to worry that I'll ever try to dominate or crush your spirit. I want you to be happy. I **need** that for you. You can't be happy without Eve, so I have to give you Eve."

"She has to live, Trevor," she whispered. "We have to find her."

"We will." He got to his feet and carried her toward the bed. "And now you're going to take a nap, then have something to eat." He lay down beside her, holding her close. "Damn, you look fragile." His lips tightened. "Why not? You are fragile, or you'd never have let me cuddle you like this."

"I wanted you to hold me. It was . . . good."

His arms tightened. "Present tense. It is good. Future tense. It will always be good." He raised his head to look down at her. "You said I didn't owe you anything, but that wasn't true. I'm a cynical bastard, but you came into my life and taught me something that I never thought I'd learn." He kissed her gently. "I never loved anyone until you came along, Jane. You opened the gates."

Opened the gates . . .

Yes, she could see the gates swinging open, and beyond them, a treasure was glowing, beckoning.

Or was that Trevor?

"I want to . . ." She reached up and touched his lips with her finger. "I feel . . . I want you to be happy. I've always wanted that for you. But I don't know if I'll ever be ready for a commitment. You're probably better off without me."

"Hush." He took her palm and pressed it on his lips. "I'll never give up. I'm in this for the long haul." He smiled down at her. "And I have an idea that we're closer than you think. Someday soon, you're going to say that you can't live without me." He tucked her head into the hollow of his shoulder. "Hell, I'm halfway there, and that's—" He broke off and pushed her away. "You're warm." His hand touched her forehead. "How do you feel?"

"Okay." She moistened her lips. "I over-did it today. It's natural that I should run a little temperature." She closed her eyes. "Now let me take that nap." She could feel his gaze on her face. "One hour, then I'll eat something. Then I'll be fine."

Silence. She was afraid that he was going to argue with her. Please, don't do it. She didn't know how much of her strength remained.

"One hour," he finally repeated after a moment as he drew her back into his arms. "Then we'll assess the situation."

Driftwood Cottage

"Open your eyes, bitch. There's nothing wrong with you. Wake up."

Doane's hand stung Eve's cheek, and her head jerked back.

Bonnie was gone, Eve realized hazily. She'd been here only seconds ago, but now she was gone.

Her eyes slowly opened to see Doane's

face in front of her. His cheeks were flushed, and he was glaring at her with anger . . . and fear.

Fear? What was he afraid—

Doane struck her again. "Stop pretending. Talk to me."

"Why are you hitting me?" Her voice was a little slurred. She shook her head to clear it. "Unless it's just for sheer pleasure." Then she understood as she saw his relief. "You thought you'd killed me. You were scared that all your great plans were going to be destroyed by a little carelessness on your part." She grimaced. "Actually, a big carelessness. Evidently, you should monitor the quantity of drugs you give me if you want me alive for the grand finale. Kevin would never have been that clumsy."

"You seem to be recovering very quickly. You were probably just pretending as I said. I knew it." He was untying the ropes binding her. "And you appear to be cheerful enough."

"Not cheerful." But Eve realized she was more steady and serene than she had been for days. The hours with Bonnie had given her the joy and hope that she usually brought to Eve. "But judging from your expression, I probably had a more enjoyable experience tied up and unconscious than you did. No luck finding Kevin's nuke? What a pity he didn't trust you. How could he expect you to do his bidding if you were—"

"He did trust me," he said through set teeth. "I won't tolerate your sarcasm, Eve. I told you that he died before he could tell me what I needed to know. And I wasn't out looking for those nuclear devices. I had to see Cartland, one of Kevin's cell members, to make sure he'd be ready to send someone to activate them when I was ready."

"When you found out where they were," she corrected softly. "Aren't you afraid this Cartland will laugh at you when he finds out that you're just a puppet trying to be a big, bad terrorist?"

"All I have to do is make one phone call, and I'll know where they are."

"Then why didn't you make the call?"

"There are difficulties." He cuffed her left wrist to the arm of the chair. "But I'm going to make it right away. Kevin always meant me to have the information. I just have to convince—" He stopped. "But difficulties are meant to be overcome."

"And is Cartland ready to go when you give the nod?"

He nodded curtly. "I never doubted his eagerness. Just that he had a team still able to function quickly."

She was tempted to give him another verbal jab, but that would have only given her satisfaction. She had found Doane liked to talk about his plans and machinations to her because he regarded her as no threat. In his eyes, she was already a dead woman, but she was never sure when that information might possibly be a lifesaver. So keep him talking and store up facts and impressions. "Who do you have to call? Who did Kevin trust more than he did you?"

He didn't answer.

She tilted her head. "Someone he knew in the service? Maybe one of his al-Qaeda buddies?"

"Of course not," he said shortly. He turned and headed for the door. "I'm tired of listening to you. Damn you to hell. You're always clawing, biting at me. You're just like her. I'm going outside to make my call."

He slammed the door behind him.

Eve frowned speculatively at the door as she thought about both his response and his words. What had he meant?

You're just like **her** . . .

Lakeside Marriott
Chicago, Illinois

Perhaps she'd have to have plastic surgery after all, Harriet thought as she gazed regretfully into the bathroom mirror of her hotel room. Too bad. She liked her face. It had strength, and she could still see the fine features she had passed on to Kevin. She had considered the possibility before Kevin was killed and even investigated the safest place to have it done. She'd have to refresh that research, but it was still probably South America. She wouldn't trust anyone in the Middle East to do a good job even though she might count on them to hide her. They had no respect for the strength or rights of women, and they might be careless and expect her to meekly accept that philosophy.

She would **not** accept not being given her due. She'd always had doubts that Kevin might be making a mistake in dealing with Tehran, but she'd not been able to convince him. But he'd been full of dreams of power, and she'd given in to him and helped him as she'd done since the moment he was born. But she'd made preparations for disaster as well as triumph, and she'd known she might have to run and start a new life.

But Kevin's dreams had died, murdered by those bastards who had killed him and thrown him into the fires of that furnace.

No, his final dream had not died, she had not permitted it to be destroyed. It had just been put on hold until the time was right.

And that visit from Jane MacGuire had been the signal that the time was most certainly right.

Her cell phone rang, and she went back into the bedroom to pick it up from the bedside table. She grimaced as she checked the ID. James Doane. It was the second time he'd called in the last hour, and she'd ignored the first one. It was always best to keep the upper hand with him. She'd learned that during their first year of marriage and had kept the reins firm and taut.

But it was time to make sure he wasn't

doing anything that would jeopardize her own plans. She answered the call. "Do you have Zander yet? Thanks to you, everything is falling apart with the life I've built over the years. I won't have it be for nothing, James."

"Not yet. I've been busy." He added sourly, "It's your fault. I told you that we have to arrange to have those devices activated. I've been scrambling to set it up with Cartland." He added harshly, "And going at it blind. He keeps asking where Kevin hid those devices, and I have to put him off. When are you going to tell me?"

"Soon. Has Cartland arranged for my passport and line of credit at a bank in Samoa?"

"Yes." He added with barely contained anger, "You're treating me with no respect, Harriet. Kevin would not like that. He'd be angry with you."

"How would you know? You never really knew him. In any disagreement between us, Kevin always took my side. He thought I was right, and you were wrong." She said coldly, "And the only reason he tolerated you at all was that you helped him with those disgusting episodes with the little girls. It was so dangerous for Kevin, and yet you encouraged him. I've never forgiven you for that, James. I knew that someday they'd find out about him and that he'd have to have somewhere to run. You forced me to leave him, so that I could prepare a hiding place and an escape route for him. Do you know how I hated to leave him?"

"You told Kevin often enough," he said bitterly. "How you were sacrificing yourself for him. How you'd always keep him safe."

"It was a sacrifice. And he loved me all the more for it. You may have given him what he wanted, but, in the end, he trusted me. He confided in me, let me help him, accepted my suggestions." She paused. "He even let me choose where those nukes were going to be hidden. You should have heard him laugh when I told him where I thought he should put each one. He said that it was just like me to choose—" She broke off. "But he never told you, did he?"

"He was going to do it."

"Maybe. If he thought you could help him."

"I was closer to Kevin than you ever were. I'm still close to him."

James was getting defiant, and she

should not have been this argumentative. It wasn't to her advantage to make him angry. She was just frustrated that Jane MacGuire had forced her to make a move so quickly. "I won't argue with you about who Kevin loved more. That's all in the past. What's important is making sure that Kevin is properly revenged. I want Zander dead."

"Zander's death isn't enough. I always told you that those cities should be Kevin's funeral pyre."

"Then give me what I want and need. And I'll give you what you want. Have you forgotten that's how your arrangements with me always have to go forward?"

"How can I be sure that you'll do it? You can say that safe in your little cave in Muncie."

"I'm not in Muncie any longer. I had to leave. I'm in Chicago. That's why I have to make sure that you arranged for me to get out of the country the minute we're finished with Zander." She paused. "You didn't tell me that Kevin had a journal. Why?"

Silence. "How did you find out about the journal?"

"I had a visit from Jane MacGuire. She was asking about it."

"What? Did she mention me?"

"Don't panic. She didn't say anything to indicate that she thought you or Eve Duncan were still alive. She was very emotional about Duncan's death, and I got the impression it was a personal mission to try to keep any more deaths from happening. She seemed focused on this journal and the damage it could do. At one point, I asked her if she worked for Venable. She said she didn't, and I believed her. But she was damned determined."

He muttered a curse. "Why would she come to you?"

"I have no idea. Obviously, Kevin didn't go into deep detail about the location of the nukes in this journal since you still have no idea where they are."

"No, but I know that he must have mentioned them somewhere in it. He told me that he had to make sure that his secrets were secure if the journal fell into the wrong hands. He gave me his journal before he went back to Pakistan because he knew I'd keep it safe. After he was killed, I read the journal cover to cover and couldn't find a hint." He said in frustration. "But they've got to be there."

"Keep it safe? And instead you let those bastards who killed him take the journal away from you." She barely managed to keep the contempt from her tone. "Perhaps you shouldn't worry too much. There was probably nothing of importance in that journal. He might just have wanted to make you feel happier and part of the operation. He knew that you were jealous of how much he let me be involved in his affairs." She added, "But perhaps you should let me read it to be sure. I assume you have a copy?"

"Of course."

"But you're not going to let me read it."

"No, Kevin gave me the journal. I won't share it with you."

"I believe you're lying to me. You don't have another copy." She suddenly laughed. "Or it could be that you won't let me read it because he said nice things about me."

"He barely mentioned you."

"But when he did, it was complimentary."

"He was always besotted with you."

"So were you at one time." Before Kevin had been born, and she had focused all her attention on her son. Why not? James had always been just someone to use. She had created this child, and he had seemed totally her own from the moment she had looked at him in the hospital. She had concentrated on charming and making him love her with his whole heart, closing out everyone else around her. And James had accepted the rejection because he, too, had fallen under Kevin's spell. "But I won't insist on seeing the journal if you assure me there's nothing in it that would appear suspicious."

"He talks a lot about the little girls."

James had only said that because he'd known it would annoy her. "That's nothing. It won't affect the current operation."

"Where are those nukes hidden, Harriet? I want the location and the code to set them off. Answer me, dammit."

"You'll not get an answer until I'm ready to give it. Tell Cartland I want him to fly here and meet me in front of the Lakeside Marriott at ten tomorrow morning. He's to have my documents and the bank line of credit. The moment I have them in my hands, I'll take him on a little trip downtown to show him why he should cooperate with me."

"Cooperate with us." He paused. "Is it the detonator? You've never told me if Kevin gave you the detonator."

"You didn't need to know. You still don't need to know."

"He should have given it to me. Do you have it, dammit?"

"I know where to get it."

"Is that what you're going to show Cartland tomorrow? Are you going to give him the detonator?"

"No, I'm going to offer him something he may find almost as persuasive. And when I do retrieve the detonator, I have no intention of turning it over to either you or Cartland. I won't give up control. Besides, I may require an act of good faith from him. I haven't decided yet." She paused. "You should be happy that I want everything to move quickly. I want this over within the next two days. I don't like the idea that Jane MacGuire had the nerve to confront me." She added harshly, "I won't let them destroy me as they did my Kevin. I've waited years for you to locate his killer and make all your fine plans. So far, I've seen nothing but failure. I'm not waiting any longer.

Zander is going to die. And I'm going to be there to see it happen. The minute Zander is dead, I'll give you the location and code to set off the bombs. Then I'm on the first plane out of the country, and you can set loose Cartland and all his al-Qaeda friends to claim responsibility. But first things first, James."

"And then you're taking the money and running. You're not even going to stay around and make sure that Kevin's work was completed."

"I'll be sure. I don't have to see it happen to know that those cities will blow. Kevin and I set it up so that he could know and enjoy it when it happened." She paused. "And I'm not entirely unsympathetic to what you're feeling. A magnificent funeral pyre for Kevin is going to be something to re-member always. But I intend to be alive to remember it. That's what Kevin would have wanted."

"Would he? I'd sacrifice my life to give him what he wanted. You're thinking only of yourself."

"And so did Kevin. We understood each other perfectly. Good-bye, James. When

you're ready to have me watch Zander's execution, call me again but not until that
time." She hung up.

James was such a fool. He thought he
was so clever, but Kevin had always been
able to manipulate him with no effort. So
had she when she had thought it was worth
the effort.

She turned and went out on the balcony. It was the middle of the night, and
she should go to bed and rest. She doubted
if she could sleep. She was wired because
her life was going to change again. In a few
days, she'd be in a foreign country and
would disappear until it was safe to emerge
from hiding. No problem. She'd made her
plans, and this new life would be much
more to her liking than the one she'd led in
Muncie.

"It's all going to happen, Kevin," she murmured. "Zander thought he could take my
boy from me? All those Washington bastards thought you could be stopped from
doing what we wanted to do? No way."

The lights of the city were spread out
before her. What would it feel like to press
a button and see those lights go out and

not come on again? Would she feel the same heady power that Kevin would have known?

Perhaps.

Soon she would know . . .

CHAPTER
11

Jane vaguely heard Trevor on the phone as she sluggishly opened her eyes.

He was sitting on the side of the bed, and the phone he was using was her own, she realized suddenly. She struggled to a sitting position. "What is—"

"It's okay." He held up his hand to silence her. "It's Caleb. You were sleeping so hard, you didn't hear the phone ring. I answered the call for you." He pushed the speaker. "Caleb recorded an interesting call that Harriet received." He handed her the phone. "From Doane."

"What?" She was suddenly jarred wide-awake. "Caleb, did he say anything to her about Eve?"

"No, it was all about the location of the nukes and killing Zander." He briefly sketched in the content of the phone call to her. "So it's clear that Harriet is in control of the situation. She seems to have been in the background holding the reins since the moment Kevin was born."

"But there was an obvious conflict between her and her husband." Jane was trying to think clearly. "And Doane has Eve. As long as he has her, he's in control as far as I'm concerned. He's the one who can pull the trigger."

"But he won't do it until Harriet's in a position to witness Zander's execution and gives him the location and code for the nukes," Trevor said. "He wants it all."

"Then we have to keep him from getting it," Jane said curtly. "And follow her when she goes to see him execute Zander. Because that's the only way we're going to find Eve." Panic was beginning to rise within her. They were closer to Doane than they'd been since that debacle in the ghost town, but Harriet was another deadly element they had to battle. One false step, and Eve would die, and so might millions of other innocents. "Nothing is going to happen until Zander is dead. That will give us a little time. And we're not really sure she has the detonator even if she said she did. She wasn't going to give it to Cartland."

"Then I'm wondering what bribe she's going to offer Cartland when she's sees him later this morning," Trevor murmured.

"Who knows? We have to hope we'll find out more after we see where she goes to get it."

"You're sure you don't want to reconsider my offer to have a little discussion with Harriet?" Caleb asked.

"And risk her dying without telling us where we can find Doane?" Jane asked. "She's given most of her life to doing what her son would want her to do. Right now, she's full of venom."

"But she also has a keen sense of self-preservation. It could balance out."

"I won't risk it. I won't risk Eve." She swung her feet to the floor. "We'll stick close as glue to her until we—" She broke off as a wave of dizziness washed over her. She shook her head to clear it. "Trevor and I are coming over to your hotel. I don't want to be a block away when all the action is probably going to be going on where Harriet is. It's the middle of the night, and she's not going to be strolling around the hotel and run into me. Once we're in your room, I'll stay out of sight when there's any danger of being seen."

"Whatever you want. I'll be glad of the company. It's boring sitting around monitoring this tech equipment. Particularly since Harriet is probably through communicating for the night." He hung up.

"Let's go." She slipped her feet into her shoes. She didn't remember taking her shoes off, she thought hazily. Trevor had probably done it after she had gone to sleep. She didn't recall anything but being held by him, the sound of his heart beneath her ear, the sensation of being safe and treasured. "I'm feeling kind of logy. I think I'll go wash my face."

"Good idea." Trevor got to his feet. "It might even keep you conscious until we get to out of this hotel and over to the Marriott." His expression was grim. "Or maybe not. You look like hell, and you were sleeping like the dead when Caleb called. That ring should have jarred you awake. It didn't."

"I'm logy," she repeated as she headed for the bathroom. "But I can function. I'm not going to argue that I'm in great shape. That would be stupid."

"No, you've got a fever, and you should probably be back in the hospital. You're damn right you're not in great shape." He paused. "Will you let me take you to the emergency room and have them check you?"

"No, we don't have the time." She reached the bathroom and held on to the jamb for a moment to steady herself. "Two days. Harriet wants it over in two days. That means Eve could be dead in two days. I can hold out until all this is over. Please don't argue with me, Trevor."

He muttered a curse and was across the room in seconds. "Argue with you?" He drew her into his arms, cradling her. "God, all I want to do is hold you, love you. Can't you see that? If that's what you want, then I'll make it work for us." He was rocking her gently. "There's never going to be a time that anything I do will hurt you.

I'll never leave you or lie to you. The only person you trust is Eve, and I can understand that. But give me a chance, and you'll find that I'm worth trusting, Jane." He drew a shaky breath and pushed her away from him. "You don't need this right now. Hell, I don't know if you're clearheaded enough to realize that I mean every single word." He opened the bathroom door and gave her a little push. "Wash your face. I'll do a video checkout and we'll be out of here."

She stood before the vanity for a moment, staring at her reflection before she turned on the water.

Trevor was wrong.

She was confused, and her emotions were in a tumult of panic and joy and fear. Yet it was as if she were seeing a brilliant sunrise breaking through darkness.

Because with all her heart, she did believe every word Trevor had said to her.

Woodstock, Illinois

"Kendra?" Margaret said when the other woman answered. "Hey, I'm on a bus heading for Chicago, and I thought I'd catch up on what you're doing. Talk to me."

"You do pick the most convenient times for conversation," Kendra said dryly. "It's after midnight here, Margaret."

"But you weren't asleep. I gave you a puzzle to solve and a gigantic challenge." Margaret chuckled. "I knew you'd be burning the midnight oil when I e-mailed you those letters. Have you found anything interesting?"

"Other than corruption, evil, sadism, and a hint of incest?"

"All of the above."

"No, there are a few references that might have some meaning. I'm going back to the journal to see if I can connect the dots."

"What references?"

"Harriet evidently installed a healthy respect in Kevin for both her and her profession as an expert on English Literature. There are a few mentions of places they've visited that seem innocent but may not be. I'm working on it."

"You may not have much time."

"I've been working on that assumption since Quinn first called me. Now you throw these letters at me and make that ticking clock go into overdrive. It's not as if—" She suddenly broke off. She was silent a moment. "Maybe . . ."

"Kendra?"

"I've just thought of something. I'm going to hang up now, Margaret."

"How rude. You're just going to leave me hanging?"

"That's right, until I figure out if what I'm thinking has any potential." Her tone was still abstracted. "And what are you doing on a bus headed for Chicago anyway?"

"Now you ask me. Doane's wife is on the lam, and I was left to make my way there on my own. Well, actually, Jane would probably have found a way to bring me to Ground Zero, but I chose to do it my way."

"You and Sinatra. Why?"

"I wanted Jane to be a little worried about me and take it out on Trevor and Caleb. They deserve it."

"Wicked, Margaret."

"Justice, Kendra. I'll let you go now. I can tell you're only half listening to me. That mind of yours is going into high gear now that you've managed to make a leap."

"Not a leap. Not yet. Just a baby step."

"But you think you're onto something. You're excited."

"Cautiously excited."

"I don't think that's a concept I understand." She chuckled. "But I don't understand a hell of a lot of what makes you tick, Kendra. I just accept and enjoy." She paused. "Will you call me when the caution is gone, and you're just plain excited?"

"Of course. Don't be silly," she said. "But I wish I was there. I hate being out of the action."

"You may be initiating action on a grand scale if you've found the key to that journal. So get to work." She added mischievously, "And I'd dearly love to be the one to hand Jane a clue that Caleb and Trevor couldn't give her. It would prove just how wrong they were to leave me behind."

"As I said, wicked." Kendra was laughing as she hung up.

Perhaps a little wicked, Margaret thought, as she leaned back in the seat. But all actions had consequences, and Caleb and Trevor had to realize that any action taken against her would be paid in full. She owed a debt to Jane, and that meant she had to give her what she wanted most in the world.

Eve.

She looked out into the darkness at the countryside passing outside the window. She had never met Eve, but she had caught a glimpse of her strength and endurance at that horrible explosion at the ghost town in Colorado. She deserved to live, dammit. Margaret was feeling a strange closeness to her, as well as to Jane.

It's going to be okay, Eve. Things are happening. We're all working to get you back. And we're not going at this blind any longer. Kendra is onto something . . .

Lakeside Marriott

"You look terrible," Caleb said bluntly to Jane when he opened the door of his hotel room. His glance switched to Trevor. "Couldn't you get her to rest? What good are you?"

"Shut up, Caleb." Jane came into the room. "I did rest. And you should be concentrating on Harriet and not on me. Did she have any other calls?"

"No. By the sound of her breathing I think she's asleep." He watched Jane as she dropped into a chair by the table across the room. "She was out on her balcony for a while, then went inside to bed. I'm still monitoring her." He nodded at the two machines on the table. "One is a motion machine that allows me to be certain she's still in the room, and the other will record any phone calls."

She looked at the two machines on the table beside her. "So small. Snooping is definitely hi-tech these days. Are they difficult to operate?"

"No, in this day and age, everyone spies on everyone else. They have to make it simple. Piece of cake."

"Good." Trevor closed the door and moved across the room. "Then I'll take over the monitoring. You have something else to do."

"What?" Caleb's eyes were narrowed on Trevor's face. "You're very . . . tense. What are you up to?"

"I am tense." He met Caleb's gaze. "You have no idea."

Caleb stiffened. "No, but I can sense a certain animosity. What did I do?"

"Nothing." Jane was suddenly noticing that same crackling animosity Trevor was emitting. She had been so hazy that she had been oblivious to it before Caleb's question. "Absolutely nothing. Back off, Trevor. I can't cope with this right now."

"I know," Trevor said harshly. "You can't cope with a damn thing at the moment, and that's what's driving me crazy." He turned back to Caleb. "You're right, she looks like hell, and I think she has a fever again. She won't go to the emergency room. Not with that two-day deadline Harriet gave Doane. But she's sick and getting sicker. I can't take that." His hands clenched into fists. "I can't watch that happening to her."

"So you're blaming me?" Caleb said. "I was able to use touch to cause the blood flow in her body to have a temporary healing effect on that wound. But I told her at the time that what I did to her wouldn't last if she didn't get rest. She knew that, Trevor."

"I know you did." He was silent, then said through his teeth, "So do it again."

Caleb's eyes widened. "Did I hear you right?"

Jane gazed at Trevor in total shock. It was the last thing that she had expected.

"Oh, yes," Trevor said. "This blood thing you did with her worked on the wound before. You told her it would work again. Were you lying?"

"No, it will do the job. Because she also has my blood due to the transfusion, I could probably do it several times before it proves without value."

"**Not** several times. Once. Just once."

"This isn't your business, Trevor," Jane said. "And certainly not your choice."

"No, it's your choice," Trevor said curtly. "Now make it. You know it has to be done if you won't go to the hospital. It's either get better or collapse, and you won't let that happen. Two days. You can't afford to lose any time if it means it might take Eve from you." He jerked his head to the door leading to the bedroom. "Get in there and get it done."

She sat there, staring at him before she said coldly, "I beg your pardon?"

He was beside her in seconds, grabbing her by the wrist and pulling her to her feet. "I have to do this quick. I can't take it otherwise." He pulled her across the room and threw open the bedroom door. "Forget that I seem to be giving you orders.

Just do what you need to do. I know you're a little afraid of what Caleb makes you feel, and you're fighting letting him touch—" He cradled her face in his hands. His expression was tormented but his eyes held nothing but tenderness. Jane felt caught, held, swept away by that tenderness. It seemed to fill the entire world. She couldn't look away from him. "I wish I could fight him, too," he whispered. "But I promised I'd always take care of you. At this moment, this is the only way I can do it." He gave her a quick, hard kiss before turning away. "What are you doing just standing there, Caleb? I'll sit here and monitor those damn units. You're not needed here. Take care of her."

"I don't believe I like the way this is going," Caleb said slowly. "You're entirely too much in control."

"I don't feel in control," Trevor said roughly. "I feel like I'm going through hell." He strode across the room away from Jane. "And if you do anything to her that she doesn't want done, then I'll hunt you down and kill you. Are we clear on that point?"

"Perfectly." He looked at Jane and smiled. "But it's always up to the lady what she wants or doesn't want. Jane?"

She stared at Caleb. Darkness. Power. Electricity. Everything about him drawing her toward him. She glanced at Trevor, but his back was turned to her.

Rejection.

No, release.

Eve. Two days. Only two days.

She drew a shaky breath. "Yes." She turned on her heel and strode into the bedroom. "Yes, dammit."

She heard the door close behind her a moment later and turned to face Caleb. He was leaning back against the door, and his expression was unexpectedly sober. "Well, what next?"

"You know what's next." He frowned. "But I don't like it this way. How the hell can I fight someone who would be that disgustingly noble? No matter what I do, he's going to be with you. I don't want him in that bed with us."

"This isn't a ménage à trois," she said coolly. "It's you and me and a job to be done. Let's get it over with." She slipped out of her shoes and sat down on the bed. "You're sure this is going to work?"

"It worked before, didn't it?" He was walking toward her. "I didn't lie then, I won't lie now. It's all a question of the blood flow to the wound. I'm no healer, but I can control the process that heals and masks symptoms very well indeed. As I told you, there are medical laser experiments going on right now to determine the effectiveness of blood flow."

She smiled crookedly. "But you're an expert."

"And it scares you."

"I don't like feeling . . ." She inhaled sharply as he began to unbutton her blouse. His knuckles were brushing against the flesh of her breasts, and she could feel the blood leap, sing, as he touched her. "You're not objective."

He chuckled. "Hell, no. Pure lust. But that helps the process, too. The blood zings, and so do I." He slipped her blouse and bra off her shoulders. "And so do you." He rubbed his cheek against her breast. "I can feel your heart pounding." He pushed her down on the bed. "Remember how it goes . . . Close your eyes and just let the blood take you away."

She closed her eyes.

Heat.

Tingling.

Every nerve was alive, every muscle tense.

Blood pounding in her wrists, in the hollow of her throat, rushing to the tips of her nipples.

The muscles of her stomach convulsed.

"That's right," Caleb murmured as he slipped onto the bed beside her. "Just a little more, and you'll be on your way." He rubbed against her, and she could feel the soft wiriness of his chest hair against her breasts. His hand was cupping the wound on her shoulder. "Feel that tingle? It's healing, Jane." His tongue was licking at the edge of the wound. "I'll take all the poison away." He was over her, rubbing against her.

She slowly opened her eyes. "You're . . . naked. It wasn't like that before."

"No." He smiled recklessly down at her. "We were in a hospital room, and I was being careful of your sensibilities. I don't feel like being careful tonight. If Trevor is out there pulling the strings, I like the idea of indulging myself a little." He was straddling her, his hands on her body. Everywhere he touched, the flesh warmed, tingled. She was panting, gasping.

The room was whirling around her.

The blood . . . pounding, peaking, pounding again.

It went on forever.

His hands on her, his mouth moving, his teeth!

She arched up from the bed with a low cry.

"I can keep it going. I can make it fantastic for you." His dark eyes were gleaming down at her. "Let me come in, and I'll make you scream so loud that Trevor will be out there grinding his teeth."

Trevor.

And Caleb above her, fierce, sensual, wicked.

Trevor . . .

"No," she whispered. She closed her eyes, shutting him out. "No, Caleb."

He froze above her. Then he muttered a curse. "I shouldn't have mentioned him. Okay, I'll have to pay for that mistake." He started to move again. "But you may have to pay a little, too. Suppose I give you something to remember before you go back to him." His tongue traced the curve of her lip. "You need at least another few hours before the healing is complete. Let's just lie here and let the blood do its work." He lay down and drew her into his arms. "I'll just hold you, no physical seduction . . . Why, I'm almost as noble as Trevor. Just relax . . ."

How was she supposed to relax in this feverish state to which he'd brought her? Not likely.

Yet in a few minutes she found, incredibly, that she was relaxing, growing sleepier by the minute . . .

No, she was wide-awake.

She was naked, lying on the grass in a garden. She could smell the roses and the scent of spices on the warm breeze. The sun was on her skin. Her breasts were taut, heavy.

And she was aching, tingling, throbbing.

But Caleb was here, Caleb would make it stop.

"Of course, I will," he whispered. "I wouldn't leave you like this."

And then he was over her, in her, going deep, deeper.

She arched, her nails digging into his shoulders.

Deep. Deeper.

She was on fire. With his every move, the throbbing increased, the ache became insatiable.

"Like it?" he murmured. "Want it?"

"Yes," she gasped. "Give me—"

"Oh, I will. Hold on."

A moment later, she felt her throat tighten as she smothered a scream.

"Again?" He was moving again. "You're not ready to stop. You still want it."

It seemed impossible but it was true. "I . . . still . . . want it."

"Of course, perfectly natural. It's because we've held it at bay for too long. Then we'll try it a little different this time." He pulled her over on top of him. "But it will be just as good, then I have a few other ideas . . ."

She climaxed again a few minutes later.

"Again?" he whispered. "You're such a delight, and I can tell how much I pleased you. Let me do it once more . . ."

It wasn't just once more. She didn't know how many times they came together in a sexual frenzy. It seemed to go on and on, and she couldn't get enough.

But, at last, Caleb moved away from her. She felt terribly alone and instinctively tried to pull him back.

"Shh, it's time to sleep now. It was all right to have your mind active while the rest of the blood in your body was in motion, but you need to go dormant for a while." He bent back over her and kissed her. "But wasn't that spectacular?"

She didn't know what he was talking about. Spectacular, yes . . . Everything else was beginning to blur. The garden, the scent of roses, the sun . . .

All had faded into nothingness.

And darkness.

"Enough." Caleb's voice was soft in her ear. "You should be ready now."

Ready? Ready for him to come over her and again begin that mad, sexual marathon that had driven her—

Wrong. Something was wrong. How could that have happened? How could she have let it happen?

And then she realized just how wrong it had been.

Her eyes flew open. "No!" She bolted upright in bed. "You son of a bitch." She glared at him. "Your damn tricks."

He chuckled as he rolled over and raised himself on one elbow. "You enjoyed those tricks enormously." His smile faded. "And so did I. I had no idea you were that responsive. I had to force myself to stop."

"Responsive? It wasn't real. It was a hallucination. You were playing mind games with me."

"And what games they were . . ." His eyes wandered slowly from her breasts down her body. "You're beautiful, you know. Even more beautiful than you were in that garden. That's one of the disadvantages of having to concentrate on maintaining a fantasy. I have to build the entire picture when I'd prefer to enjoy the reality of you."

"Bastard." She was jerking on her clothes. "It was **all** fantasy. I had nothing to do with it."

He shook his head. "I'm sure that would be comforting, but it's not true. All I did was lull you into a responsive state and give you a pleasant setting. Every one of those emotional reactions were your own. That's the way it works, Jane."

"Then it was a physical response to what you were doing to the flow of my blood."

"Perhaps a little. Most of it was—"

"I'm not going to listen to this." She glared at him as she finished buttoning her blouse. "It was deceit. I'm not going to forgive this, Caleb."

"Someday. Just another hurdle to overcome."

"The hell it is." She got to her feet and strode toward the bathroom. "That was an . . . invasion."

"Only mentally. Just imagine what it would have been like if I'd actually been in you."

"You imagine. You're so damn good at it." She splashed water in her face. "And my mind is as important as my body. You make me—"

"Forget your outrage for a moment. I did nothing to hurt you physically. I was careful and didn't let it interfere with getting you well. Do you realize how strong you're feeling? Stop a minute and gauge the difference from when you walked into this room. I don't want you to leave me until I'm certain that I've done my job."

"Done your job?" She wiped her face on the hand towel and threw it on the vanity. "Oh, you've done more than your job, Caleb." She strode back into the bedroom. "I want to strangle you."

"No pain? No exhaustion?" He was ignoring her rage. "You feel entirely normal? Think. That's why you came here. Let's get that right."

She drew a deep breath. It was hard to think through this emotional turmoil. "I feel normal physically. I believe that part came out okay. Other than that I feel . . . used."

"Really? Then that makes two of us." He sat up and leaned back against the headboard. He was still naked, and he looked arrogant, beautifully indolent, and an entirely sexual being. Yet she was suddenly aware that that indolence was false, beneath it a storm was brewing. He was angry. "So don't expect me to feel too badly about returning the favor." He smiled. "It's not my nature."

"You're angry." Caleb had disguised it behind his usual enigmatic, cynical facade, but Jane was now realizing something else. "And you've been angry since the moment I walked into this room."

"Why not? Trevor gave me orders, and you graciously but reluctantly agreed to do what he wanted. No one asked me to help you. It was all between the two of you. I was merely the go-between, a tool." His smile vanished entirely. "I didn't like the role I was assigned to play. I've been an outsider all my life, but I've never felt it quite this deeply. I made it clear to you that all you had to do was come to me, and I'd help you. If you'd just come to me, it could have gone differently. Who knows? I might have even been able to go against nature and shown you a little of Trevor's magnificent selflessness."

"You're saying it's my fault?"

"I'm saying that there's blame enough for everyone." He shrugged. "And that I could have been far worse than I was tonight."

"If you were that resentful, why didn't you refuse? Why didn't you turn your back and walk away from me?"

He didn't speak for a moment. "I find I'm not capable of doing that." He shrugged. "So I made the best of it. You got what you wanted. I didn't entirely get what I wanted, but you're not going to be able to forget that little preview of what's to come. We'll be even more fantastic when we finally come together."

"We're not ever going to come together. I hate to be weak, and you took advantage of that weakness. Do you think I'd ever trust you again?" She drew a long, shaky breath. "You're right, Trevor and I did use you. It was wrong. I should have shown you gratitude and not taken anything for granted."

"Screw your gratitude," Caleb said roughly. "And I never expected trust from you. You've been wary of me from the moment we met. I accept that since the fringe benefits will be extraordinary. As for being weak, you're not weak. You're strong, and I love that strength. You just wanted what I gave you. If you feel a little overwhelmed, you'll rally and find a way to control anything I do to you."

She shook her head adamantly. "No, Caleb."

"Yes, Jane," he said softly. "Now go on out to Trevor and tell him all is well and that I've done as ordered. He's probably ready to have a breakdown by now. Not that I'd mind. But you'd be all teary and emotional, and it would be another step back for me."

"Not just a step. Trevor is miles ahead of you," she said quietly. "What happened tonight proved that to me."

"But the game's not over. It's scarcely begun."

"It's over, Caleb." She opened the door and saw Trevor standing at the door of the balcony gazing out at the city. She felt a sudden rush of relief and joy. "You just can't see it. It couldn't be more clear to me."

Trevor must have heard her because he turned to look at her as she shut the door behind her. "You were a long time."

"Yes."

"Three hours and thirty-five minutes."

"You kept track?"

"Oh, yes. Every minute. Every second. Are you okay?" He gazed at her searchingly. "It did what it was supposed to do?"

She nodded. "I feel the same way that I did after Caleb did his voodoo the last time. It should last me long enough. I only need a few days."

"Yes." He was silent a moment. "And was everything else about it the same?"

"Yes . . . and no." She came into his arms and laid her head on his shoulder. "Hold me, Trevor."

He stiffened, then his arms slid around her. "Why do you need me to hold you? Should I go kill Caleb?"

"No, I don't need protection. Caleb and I understand our positions. He told me to tell you that he'd done what you ordered."

"You said yes and no. What was the no?"

"He was angry."

His grip tightened. "Did he hurt you?"

"You want to know details?"

"Not if you don't want to tell me."

"I want you to know everything you want to know. I don't want to close you out of what happened. I know sending me to him wasn't easy for you."

"It was hell." He paused. "Did he rape you?"

"No." She added, "And no, I didn't really have sex with him."

"Really? That's a little too tentative."

"Mind games. I told you that Caleb had that capability." She paused. "And the touching was more intimate than the first time. That's all that was different."

"I still think I should kill him." He tilted back her head and looked into her eyes. "Because I'm sensing something else about you. There's a difference. You're more . . ." He searched for a word. "Open."

He was right, she had never felt more open, more free. All the boundaries were gone. She smiled. "But that's a good thing. Can't you understand that?"

"No, why don't you tell me?"

"I will. Because I realized something when you sent me to Caleb tonight. Not at first, I was too confused and hazy to be able to think clearly during those first moments, then Caleb was dominating every—"

"I don't want to hear that."

"But I have to be honest with you. I want you to know everything that I'm feeling. It's important. You were right when you said that I have an erotic response to Caleb. I can't seem to help that response. It may have something to do with that damn blood thing. I don't know. But I don't have to act on it. And it's just sex, Trevor."

"Just? That's damn important."

"But not most important." She took his face in her hands and looked him in the eye. "Love is more important. Love and trust." This was harder than she'd thought it would be. "I . . . love you, Trevor."

"Love," he repeated. "That's the first time you've said that to me." He paused. "Have we had a breakthrough?"

"I do love you." She moistened her lips. "And I trust you. You said I didn't trust anyone but Eve, but I do trust you. You'd never lie or do anything that wasn't honest or good."

"I'm no angel, Jane. You should know that better than anyone."

"I trust you." She kissed him. "Now will you stop trying to talk me out of this? It's all new to me, and I'm having a tough time adjusting. You wanted trust and commitment? You've got it. Unless you've changed your mind."

"Changed my mind? After all these years of trying to get you to admit that we were born to be together?" A brilliant smile broke the gravity of his expression. He picked her up and whirled her in a circle. "And all

I had to do was throw you into bed with another man." He kissed her long, hard. "But that's not going to happen again."

"It would if you thought it would help me," she whispered. "Because that's what your love is about, Trevor. It's giving and caring and not taking." She nestled closer. "And I thank God for it. I do love you, Trevor. You said I seemed open. That's the way I feel. Everything is flowing out to you. I want to give you my thoughts and feelings and dreams . . ." She suddenly broke away from him. "Let's go bring Caleb out here to monitor those machines. I want to go somewhere and be alone with you."

"My, how aggressive." He smiled. "I'm not sure that Caleb will welcome that call to duty."

"He said we'd used him, and I realized how callous I'd been. We shouldn't have done it. It was wrong," she said. "But this time I don't care. We don't have much time, and I'm going to steal a little." She headed for the bedroom door. "You call down and get us a room on this floor, and I'll go get Caleb."

And hope that he was not still naked, she

thought dryly. She wouldn't put it past him to open the door nude for sheer devilment.

But when Caleb opened the door to her knock he was no longer naked but wearing jeans and a turtleneck sweater. He smiled. "You need me?"

"To monitor the machines." She added deliberately, "Trevor and I are getting a room. Unless you've decided that you're going to opt out of finding Eve."

She couldn't read his expression, but she could see the tension of the muscles in his shoulders and abdomen. "That would be very foolish of me. I told you it wasn't over." He strolled out into the sitting room. "By all means, run along. Comparisons are always interesting." He dropped down in the chair by the table. "I'll let you know if you should drop everything and come running." He glanced at Trevor. "But you should thank me for the gift I gave you."

"No way." Trevor took Jane's hand and led her toward the door to the corridor. "I'd be a fool to do that when this is how it was meant to be. You didn't give me anything, it was all Jane. And I'll take it and never let go." He looked down at her as he whisked her out of the room. "Now and forever, so help me God."

"That sounds like a wedding vow." Her voice was uneven. Love, trust, devotion, commitment. So many emotions she had been afraid to feel were brimming within her in this moment. "I like it. Now and forever . . ."

CHAPTER

12

Bayside, Washington

"Joe, just think about it," Catherine urged. "Gallo is damn good. He can help you. Two can sometimes accomplish more than one."

"Okay, I'll think about it."

"That's all I ask. Stubborn. You're both so damn stubborn. I got the same response from Gallo." She hung up.

Two can sometimes accomplish more than one.

Catherine's words might have rung true to Joe, but it all depended on what two you were talking about, he thought as he hung up. Gallo might have been a top-notch Special Forces guy, but Joe did **not** want to have to deal with him. Gallo would want to go his own way and try to control everything and everyone around him.

Like Joe did, himself.

That was different.

Or, if it wasn't, it was irrelevant that they had similar philosophies if they didn't have to work together. He didn't need Gallo. The minute he got into Seattle, he would make contact with Detective Brewer in Seattle Homicide and see what the word was out on the streets about any new cell movement. Then he would hit the bars and try to pick up—

His cell phone rang.

He stiffened when he read the ID.

Ben Hudson.

He hadn't thought of the boy since he had left the hospital after Jane had drawn Doane's sketch from the description Ben had given her of Eve's kidnapper. He should have thought more about the kid, dammit. The reason Ben had ended up in that hospital was that he was trying to protect Eve. "Ben? Are you okay? What can I do for you?"

"You should have taken me with you," Ben said reproachfully. "I told you that Bonnie wanted me to keep Eve safe. I let her down when I let that man take her away from the cottage. I have to get Eve back."

"I told you that was my job, Ben. You can't—" Be patient, Joe told himself. He had to remind himself that Ben might still have the mind of a child, but that spirit and heart he possessed were special in more ways than one. In their search for Bonnie, they had come upon Ben, who had been having dreams of Eve's daughter. Eve believed that Bonnie's ghost actually visited Ben because they were kindred souls. Joe had to acknowledge there was some kind of mystical connection when Ben had ended up in the hospital because one of his Bonnie dreams had sent him to try to protect Eve from Doane. Joe owed him. He could have been killed instead of just injured. "You were wounded and in the hospital. I didn't have time to wait for you to get well. Are you still in the hospital, Ben?"

"No, they let me leave yesterday. That man, Venable, told the people at the hospital that they could release me into his care. He must be a good guy."

"Venable?" Joe repeated warily. He wasn't sure that he liked this. "Yeah, sometimes."

"I told him I wanted to call you and tell you that I have to come and help right away." Ben's voice was desperate. "He thought that was a good idea. Where are you, Joe? Mr. Venable didn't know."

And Joe would just as soon he didn't know anything more than Joe wanted to tell him. He had learned his lesson in Colorado, when Venable could have gotten Eve killed when he'd tried to control the situation to suit himself. It was clear Venable was trying to manipulate Ben to get what he wanted, he thought grimly. "Is Venable there with you, Ben?"

"No, we're at a motel. He's in the next room. He said that he'd help me come to you if you'll tell me where you are."

"Look, I know you want to help, but by the time you get here, we'll already have Eve safe." God, he hoped he was telling the truth. "We're close, Ben. She's going to be okay. Stay where you are, and I'll have Eve call you as soon as she can."

"No, why are you telling me that? Bonnie says she's not safe. She says he gets angry with Eve, and she almost died last night."

Joe couldn't breathe. He felt as if he'd been kicked in the stomach. "What are you talking about, Ben?" Keep calm, fight through the fear. "Talk slowly and clearly. You had another dream about Bonnie? When?"

"A little while ago. That's why I have to get to you. Bonnie said you have to get her away from him right away."

"I know that, dammit. What do you think I'm—" He tried to temper the harshness of his voice. "What else did she tell you? Eve hasn't been hurt yet?"

"I don't think so. Sometimes I think Bonnie doesn't tell me everything she knows. But Eve is still alive, Joe. She was asleep, not dead. Like that princess in the fairy tale. Bonnie said Eve even joked about it to her. A sleeping princess in a cottage not a castle and not a garden of thorn-bushes but a graveyard of driftwood."

He frowned. "What is all this nonsense? You're not making sense."

"I think Bonnie was trying to tell me where Eve is now. She didn't know exactly. She could only see what Eve was seeing, what Eve knew about the place."

"A graveyard of driftwood to keep every-one away from sleeping beauty?"

"He gave Eve something to keep her

asleep," Ben said simply. "Bonnie was afraid she'd never wake up."

Joe muttered a curse. "Anything else? Did Bonnie tell you anything else, Ben?"

"You're scared, aren't you, Joe? I'm scared, too."

Joe closed his eyes. God, yes, he was scared. "Yeah, I'm afraid for her. You've got to think hard and tell me everything about your dream."

"It wasn't very long. Bonnie said that she had to fight to get through, that someone . . ." He thought for a moment. "Kevin was keeping her from reaching anyone close to Eve. I'm the only one . . ."

"Anything else?"

He was silent, thinking. "Only that it was Kevin's castle, I mean cottage, where Eve is now. Is that enough? I repeated everything she told me just like she wanted. Can we find her now?"

Garden of thorns, graveyard of driftwood, a cottage belonging to a man dead for the last five years. Pitifully slim clues given to a special boy from a spirit from beyond. He should be in hopeless despair.

He was not in despair. He would not let

that happen. He was desperate, but he was reaching out to grasp this fragile straw that Ben was handing him. "We'll find her. I just have to think and put all this together. You did good, Ben."

"Then let me come to help you find her. I won't get in the way."

"I'm on my way to Seattle. That's a long way from you. I can't wait for you to get here. Bonnie wouldn't want me to wait, would she? She was worried, or she wouldn't have come to you. She'd want me to find Eve as soon as I can."

Ben's silence was troubled. "No, you can't wait. Eve almost died. I'll find my own way. Maybe Bonnie will help me."

"Ben, stay where you are. I don't want you to—" It was no use arguing with the boy. He would do what he thought was right. "Take care, Ben. Keep in touch." He hung up.

His stomach was tied up in knots.

Eve almost died.

Stop thinking about Ben's words. Move forward.

But one thing to do first.

He dialed Venable. "I assume you bugged Ben's phone?"

"Would I do that to a fine boy like Ben Hudson?" He paused. "What do you expect. You've all shut me out. Even Catherine offers me only crumbs about what she's up to. I have to take what I can get." He added dryly, "Though that hogwash Ben was spewing wasn't worth the planting of a very fine piece of electronic equipment." His tone roughened. "I won't have roadblocks put in my way, Quinn. The risk is too great. This isn't only about Eve. I want Zander. He may be the only bargaining chip I have to get Doane and the location of those nukes."

"I'll get your damn bombs. And I'll throw Doane's body at your feet as soon as I get my hands on him. But I won't have you dangling Ben on your string to force me to play the game your way. He's a good kid, and he's trying to help."

"Yeah, dreams and ghosts and all that crap," Venable said. "I can offer you a hell of a lot more help. I sent a team from Homeland Security into Seattle as soon as Catherine told me she was heading there. I also sent a team to Chicago to back any play there. Just keep me informed, dammit."

"If I can do it without risking Eve. Otherwise, I'll handle it myself." He listened to Venable curse. "And I don't care if you think Ben's words were crap or not. Pretend you believe him and see if you can unearth any records about a cottage outside Seattle that Kevin may have purchased five years ago."

"The information is probably buried, and it could be a waste of my time." He paused. "We could make a deal."

"I've told you how it's going to be. You'll do it because you're scrambling for any clue to lead you to Doane." He changed the subject. "Now, Ben is going to try to get up here. That's okay as long as someone is looking out for him. That means you, Venable. You'll be heading up here anyway now that you know Catherine and Zander are in this area. You take good care of Ben, or I'll make you pay, Venable."

Silence. "Threats? We used to be on the same side."

"Not if your side considers Eve expendable." He didn't wait for an answer. He hung up.

He drew a deep breath. Don't think, don't feel, just move forward efficiently and at top speed. He dialed Gallo's cell.

Gallo answered on the second ring. He said warily, "I take it that Catherine contacted you, too? I assure you that I don't like the idea of our working together any more than you do."

"I agree, but I'll accept it because I may need you."

"What?"

"It depends if you can swallow what Venable calls Ben's hogwash," Joe said curtly. "If you can't, I don't want you."

Gallo was silent as moment. "Ben Hudson? What hogwash?"

"He dreamed of Bonnie, and she told him a few things. She was scared for Eve, but she couldn't reach the people closest to her. She said Kevin was keeping her away." He paused. "Well, simpleminded hogwash, Gallo?"

"Because he dreamed of Bonnie?" he asked quietly. "Then call me simpleminded, too, Quinn. I was in a North Korean prison for years, and I dreamed of Bonnie. I didn't even know she was my child. I had no idea Eve was even pregnant when I left to go into the Army. All I know was that when I was on the point of death from starvation and torture, a little girl with red hair came down into that darkness and kept me alive. Yes, I believe that Bonnie could come to Ben. Do you?"

"Yes, I didn't for a long time, years. I had to learn to suspend disbelief." He cleared his throat. "And Bonnie's let me keep Eve through all these years, so I have no trouble believing she wants us to find her. Though as far as clues go, she didn't give us a hell of a lot." He tried to think of Ben's exact words. "Bonnie said Eve was joking about her being sleeping beauty but instead of a castle it was a cottage, and instead of a garden of thornbushes, it was a graveyard of driftwood."

"That's all?"

"Something about its being Kevin's place."

"A cottage and driftwood and a connection with Doane's son," Gallo said. "It was more than we had before."

"That's what I thought." He paused. "But we have to move fast to find it. Doane gave Eve an overdose and almost killed her. That's why I called you. As Catherine said, two can cover more ground than one. And I'm calling Kendra and telling her to check those letters and the journal for any reference that might lead to answers."

"Good move. Spread the word. I'll call Catherine and let her know to call Jane or Margaret. I'm at a Starbucks in Everton, Washington. How close are you?"

"About twenty minutes."

"I'll stay here. But be quicker than twenty minutes if you can do it." He hung up.

Those last sentences had sounded remarkably like orders, Joe thought with annoyance. Gallo was instinctively trying to take control. It was just what Joe had been wary about.

Screw it.

He'd take any chance he had to take to bring this nightmare to a close as quickly as possible.

Eve almost died.

Keep her alive for me, Bonnie.

And while you're at it, I'd appreciate it you'd keep a rein on your father. God knows, I don't need trouble from Gallo.

Seattle, Washington

"Eve's definitely here in Seattle?" Catherine's voice was tense. "It sounds like it from that driftwood description. I thought the chances were excellent, but there was always the possibility Doane had laid a false trail, Gallo. It's good to have confirmation."

"Venable wasn't so accepting," Gallo said dryly. "He thought the source was suspect." He paused. "Do you?"

Catherine hesitated. "Bonnie? Let's just say that I may not have met your little ghost-girl, Gallo, but Eve believes in her, you and Joe believe in her. I grew up in Hong Kong, where spirits are a part of the culture. I'm willing to take your word that I should take a chance on her." She quickly changed the subject. "A graveyard of driftwood? Couldn't Ben pin her down to more than that?"

"Catherine, I haven't the faintest doubt that you would make the attempt to third-degree even a ghost, but Ben has the simplicity of a child, and he worships Bonnie." She could hear the amusement in his voice. "We'll have to work it out for ourselves. Quinn and I are both moving forward, and he's put Kendra on it." He was silent a moment. "I can't do anything else since you won't trust me enough to let me come to you. Has Zander been able to get a clue to where Doane might be hiding out?"

"No." She could feel his tension and impatience growing, and she didn't want to struggle against Gallo just then. "I have to go. I'll call you if I learn anything more." She turned off the speaker as she hung up. Stang was driving the car, and she turned to Zander, who was sitting beside her in the backseat. "You could trust Gallo. He could be helpful, Zander."

"My dear Catherine, I trust no one." He smiled. "Not even you. And I doubt if Gallo would prove as amusing to me as you've turned out to be." He tilted his head. "Of course, he might amuse you. I believe I caught a strong hint of electricity between you. But neither of you really have time to indulge yourselves at the present time."

"Cut the crap," she said impatiently. "You heard him. He called about Eve."

"And sleeping beauty and a graveyard of driftwood." His tone was objective. "And Bonnie. I was fascinated by your reply to Gallo's question about whether you believed in her. It was all quite interesting and reasonable, but Gallo wasn't here to see your expression."

She gazed at him warily.

"You were dancing around answering

him. Why? Were you lying or just not telling the entire truth?"

"I wasn't lying." Dammit, his gaze was fixed curiously on her, and she was already familiar with that curiosity. He wouldn't give up. "Okay, I'm hardheaded, and it's difficult for me to admit that I believe in Bonnie." She moistened her lips before she said reluctantly, "But I saw her."

"I beg your pardon?"

"You heard me, I saw her. We were in that canyon where she was buried. I came out of the forest, and I saw her with Eve."

"Imagination?"

"I **saw** her. She was there, then she was gone. I never mentioned it to Eve, but I think she knew." She lifted her gaze to Zander's face. "I don't go around hobnobbing with ghosts, but Bonnie was as real as you are to me."

"Indeed?"

"Don't give me that supercilious bullshit. According to you, you're Bonnie's grandfather. If anyone was able to see her, it should have been you." Her stare became challenging. "Have you seen Bonnie, Zander?"

His smile never wavered. "Perhaps."

She hadn't really expected an answer.

No one was more guarded than Zander. "Which means?"

"I had a hallucination when I was down in that mine shaft in Colorado. Of course, I was in shock from pain, and it was natural that I see a red-haired little girl telling me I had to save her mother. I'd had Eve and her daughter thoroughly researched, and if I was to have a hallucination, it was entirely logical."

"If it was a hallucination, why did you say 'perhaps'?"

"Because of my time with the monks in Tibet. They taught me that nothing was certain." He shrugged. "And this conversation is beginning to bore me. I'm sure that any granddaughter who has my genes would be exceptionally intelligent, but the idea of banking a search for Eve on those few words isn't reasonable. Nor is there time to pursue a thread that flimsy. I prefer to go in another direction."

"For instance?"

"I'll let you know when I do." He was no longer smiling. "Or maybe not. You just wander along on your path toward that mysterious driftwood graveyard. It's a little too whimsical for me."

"I'm not going to wander anywhere that's more than a shout away from you. I haven't changed my mind about your being the ace that could lead me to Doane." Her brows rose. "Are you still trying to get rid of me?"

He was silent a moment, staring at her. "I find myself oddly reluctant at the thought of your getting in my way when I have to take care of Doane. It would probably be fatal, and I'm not accustomed to not being able to ignore that aspect of the job."

"I'm touched," Catherine murmured. "You'd actually be sorry if you had to remove me if I got in your way? Don't worry, I'll try to keep myself alive to avoid causing you any serious mental distress." She suddenly chuckled. "And I won't flatter myself that I'm at the root of that distress. It's because I'm Eve's friend, isn't it?"

"Ridiculous."

"I don't think so. I'm not sure what you feel about Eve and how much it's affecting your actions, but there's some kind of cause and effect involved."

"You don't believe it's your charm and endearing personality?" he asked with silken menace. "I don't appreciate your thinking that I'm transparent enough for you to read me. It annoys me."

She smothered the sudden ripple of fear. Being with Zander was like walking a tightrope. Most of the time, she felt fairly confident, but then he'd show his teeth, and the chill would come. Don't let him see it. "I can't read you. But you and Eve came together while she was on the run from Doane in the mountains. You couldn't be with her for even the shortest time without realizing how special she is. She'd make her mark on you." She forced herself to look him directly in the eye. "And Doane may be your target, but he's not the reason you're on the hunt. It's Eve."

"Really?"

"Really. You've gone to extraordinary lengths to assure that Doane wouldn't kill her."

"Extraordinary? Not likely."

"Extraordinary," she repeated. "For you, Zander. You're probably in denial and perhaps don't realize your motivation, but you want Eve to live."

"Because she's my daughter?" he asked mockingly.

"I don't know. You'd have to tell me." Her lips twisted. "And I'm not about to force that issue. I'm already in enough trouble with you."

"And you're clearly terrified," he said sarcastically.

"I'm afraid of you," she said bluntly. "You're intimidating as hell, and I have to work my way through it. But that doesn't mean that I can't do it. You have to respect me, or you'd leave me behind in your dust." She paused. "And I believe you do have your own plan to get Doane. I don't want to be left out of it. I won't get in your way, and you can count on me to watch your back."

"And protect me?"

"I know that you didn't like that." She grinned. "Stang nearly had a heart attack." Her smile faded. "But it's what I have to do. You're the prize, Zander."

"I've no quarrel with that statement. It's quite true."

"And prizes have to be given a certain security."

"Only if it's a prize that's being distributed by someone else. No one has the power to control this particular prize." He tapped his chest. "Not you, not Quinn, not Venable. No one. I won't be traded, bartered, or held hostage. Don't try it, Catherine."

"Not if I can see any other way," Catherine said quietly. "Eve wouldn't thank me for it. That's why I was glad that Gallo called and gave us that info about the driftwood. I'm looking for any way out." She grimaced. "So stop threatening me, and let's see what we can do to find that son of a bitch that doesn't require me giving Doane your head on a platter."

"I really don't believe that's a possibility," he said coldly. "And if you persist in—" He broke off and suddenly chuckled. "And now you're trying to run me as you do the rest of Eve's little army of rescuers? This is my hunt, and I've allowed you to come along for the ride. We're not 'we,' and we have no common purpose."

But at least he was smiling again. "Not even the common purpose of keeping you from becoming beheaded?"

"By you."

"By me."

She shrugged. "Why not help me, Zander? Don't make me trail after you. As you said, there's not much time. I'm trying to gather every bit of information I can, and

we're all having to frantically piece it together."

"Yes, I've watched with fascination you
trying to pull all those strings. Don't try
that with me. I'm no puppet."

"Neither are Joe or Gallo. And Jane Mac-
Guire is a tough cookie. We're all just people trying to work together to keep Eve alive.
If I seem to be making the effort to coordi-
nate what's going on, it's because it's so
damn difficult to work through this web that
Doane and his son wove years ago." She
added soberly, "And according to what Jane
is telling me, Doane may not even be as
terrible as his ex-wife. I told you what Harriet Weber said to Doane about not giving
him the location of those nukes until he'd
set you up for execution."

"Yes, charming lady."

"A beast, like her son, like Doane."

"But with excellent taste in executions.
She chooses the very best."

"It's not funny." She shook her head. "I
care about this, Zander. I care about Eve.
I care about those millions of people who
may die if we can't stop Doane and that
bitch from pressing that switch. Help me,
dammit."

He was silent. "No, it's not funny. But I have problems with caring. I . . . think I may envy you. So much passion . . ."

"Help me."

"How?"

"I don't know." She moistened her lips. "Venable says you're a brilliant man. Figure some way out of this nightmare. Look, there are two objectives tied in a Gordian knot. It would be easier if we only had to worry about Eve. But there are those two nuclear devices." She held up her index finger. "Chicago. Jane, Trevor, and Caleb will have to find them and try to disarm them. Harriet Weber is in contact with Doane, and she may be the key to finding him. She's also the one who knows where those bombs are located and can ignite them."

"Kill her," Zander said coolly.

"And risk having Doane killing Eve because he would have no chance to give his son his grand funeral pyre?"

"Killing her would be Venable's decision."

"Not mine. I want it all. I want Eve alive." She held up another finger. "Seattle. Find the bomb stashed here. Find Doane and save Eve. Much less complicated than Chicago."

"You're being simplistic. It all relies on finding Doane."

"And it's all linked to Harriet Weber." She met his gaze. "That's why I can't pull any strings. I have to depend on other people who care about Eve." She paused. "Like you, Zander."

"I told you, I have problems in that area."

"I don't give a damn. Work your way through it. This is scary stuff, and I need a partner. You won't let me bring in Joe or Gallo. So you're stuck with me."

"Am I?"

"Are you?" she whispered. "Say yes, Zander."

His gaze held her own for a long moment. "What a Delilah you are, even when that's not your intention. Yet you're not really a Delilah, more like a woman from an Ayn Rand novel. I'm beginning to pity Gallo."

"Say yes."

He looked away from her. "Again, too simplistic. I'll consider your proposition and see if it suits my purpose." He leaned forward and told Stang. "Find a hotel. I need to have a meal and make a few phone calls."

Catherine was surprised. "So soon? You only contacted one person, that Monte Slater.

And you said he didn't know anything. Maybe you should try someone else."

"Slater has a pipeline to everything that goes on in Seattle. He's expert at information gathering. If he doesn't have a line on Doane, no one does. He'll call me if he hears anything."

"There may be someone better. You should go out on the streets and find them yourself," she said. "Or let me go. I don't know the city, but I know how to dig. Before I was recruited for the CIA, I made my living in Hong Kong selling information."

"So I heard," Zander said. "I'm sure you were extraordinary."

She shrugged. "I was hungry. That's who we need now. Someone who is hungry. Tell Stang to pull over and let me out. Give me my chance to find Doane."

"Zander?" Stang asked, his gaze on the rearview mirror.

"I think not," Zander said. "We'll do it my way. The hotel, Stang. I wouldn't dream of throwing Catherine out in the streets to face who knows what criminal elements." He smiled faintly. "She might offer to act as their bodyguard." He glanced at Catherine. "Besides, our guest needs to rest, but she won't do it. She'll probably spend her time investigating the area's driftwood. Right, Catherine?"

She didn't answer the question but looked away from him and out the window. "Say yes, Zander."

Chicago

The first pale streaks of dawn were creeping over the horizon when Margaret's bus entered the city. Time to announce her arrival and find out where in this huge city she could find Jane, Margaret thought. She pulled out her phone and started to call Jane. Then she stopped as she glanced at the sunrise. Why wake Jane at this hour? She needed all the rest she could get. No, she could get the information from Caleb or Trevor, and she didn't give a damn at the moment if she woke either one of them. They were both definitely in her bad graces.

She dialed Seth Caleb. "I've reached Chicago. Would you like to tell me where to find Jane, or do you still want to play games?"

"You're the one who extended the play

by becoming incommunicado. You know Jane would have made sure that you'd be brought here safely."

"I had to make a point so that you wouldn't be so stupid again."

"Point taken," he said dryly. "Why are you calling me instead of Jane?"

"She's not well. I didn't want to disturb her."

Silence. "She's much better now. And I, for one, wouldn't mind if you disturbed her."

The words were spoken without expression. Yet Margaret could sense the darkness. "I don't go by what you mind or don't mind, Caleb." She paused. "But if Jane is having problems with you, I'd better know about it. Where are you?"

"Lakeside Marriott. Room 1730."

"And Jane?"

"I didn't ask her. Somewhere on this floor. You'll have to find her yourself."

Something was definitely not right. "I told you, I don't want to wake her. I'll come to your room." She hung up.

She stared thoughtfully out the window. Storm clouds and an explosion on the brink. What had been happening in these last hours? Well, she would know soon. At least, he had said that Jane was better. Which might be the cause of those storm clouds. It was just as well Margaret was on the scene to act as buffer.

Lakeside Marriott. She got to her feet and weaved her way down the aisle to talk to the bus driver. His name was Harry Milton and after hours of casual conversation he probably liked her well enough to do her a favor. If she handled it right.

"Hi, Harry." She beamed at him. "Do you know where the Lakeside Marriott is? Do you suppose it's too far out of your way?"

CHAPTER
13

Twenty minutes later, Margaret was knocking on the door of Room 1730.

Caleb opened the door. "That was quick."

"The bus driver dropped me off." She strolled into the room. "I didn't want to waste time getting transportation from the bus station. You have to catch me up with what's been happening since you arrived here." She dropped down in a chair by the balcony doors. "First, Harriet Weber. Anything?"

"A telephone call from Doane."

She stiffened. "What?"

"I thought that would make you sit up and take notice." He sat down opposite her.

"And it was something of a role reversal from what Venable thought."

"Tell me."

She listened closely as he described in detail the conversation between Doane and his ex-wife.

"Holy shit." She shook her head. "Yeah, I can see the role reversal. She's seems very dangerous. Sort of a black widow devouring her mates."

"Trust you to compare her to one of your nature friends," Caleb said. "Personally, I see Harriet as very human, with abundant Borgia qualities."

"I don't have any black widow friends," she said absently. "I've tried but I can't communicate with insects. And I wouldn't choose a black widow anyway. It may be natural, but I can't bear the thought that they eat their mates." She was still thinking about Harriet. "If she's in control, it opens an entire new view of what we might—Have you called Kendra?"

"Yes, I was designated official town crier. I called both Catherine and Kendra. Catherine was a good deal more receptive than Kendra. Oh, and she gave me some more info about where Doane might be keeping

Eve. Something about a graveyard of drift-wood . . ." He briefly filled her in on those details from Ben Hudson. "She'd already told Kendra, and Kendra was interested but impatient. She said that she was being bombarded, and she didn't need that right now. She said between Kevin's journal and the letters, she was going crazy."

Margaret nodded. "She'll be better soon. Puzzles drive her crazy. Her mind works double time until she sees the connections. But I think she's beginning to do it."

"How do you know?"

"I talked to her a few hours ago when I was on the road. Something suddenly occurred to her, and she brushed me off and sent me on my way. I made her promise to call me."

"Will she do it?"

She looked at him in surprise. "Of course. She promised me. She's like Jane. Honor and fair play mean everything to her. I'm expecting a call from her at any time." She shrugged. "And besides, it's the only way Kendra can participate without being on the spot. She'll probably try to use me as her stand-in."

"And you don't object?"

"Not unless it interferes with my helping Jane. Kendra is very clever and won't let that happen. She knows that's why I'm with Jane."

"You've made that crystal clear."

She leaned back and studied him.

Darkness again, and the storm was closer. "No one can say I'm not honest." She paused. "For instance, I don't care about all this lust and emotional fireworks you and Trevor are obviously experiencing around Jane. I've never gone through it, so I can't see what all the shouting is about. I've never been able to read you, but I'd guess on your part it's probably purely animalistic, and that's part of nature. Trevor is on a higher plane, and I think he genuinely cares about her."

"I'm really not interested in your opinion, Margaret."

She nodded. "Because you screwed up."

He didn't answer.

"You told me Jane was better. That means you probably did that blood thing that you did to her before. Right?"

He slowly nodded.

"And that you didn't mind if I disturbed Jane. I had to think about that for a minute."

"But I'm sure you came up with an answer."

"You wanted her to be disturbed because she was with Trevor." She tilted her head. "And at this time of night it's logical to assume that they're sleeping together."

"Very logical."

"So you did something she didn't like."

"Wrong." He smiled recklessly. "I did something she did like . . . too much."

She shook her head. "If Jane went to Trevor, it's probably because you did something pretty bad. You might not even recognize that it would seem that bad to her. You're two different species." She thought about it. "No, you probably did know. But you're one of the wild ones, and you didn't care at that particular moment."

"None of this is your business, Margaret. You're annoying me."

"I know. But Jane is my business. Mating is natural. I don't give a damn what you and Trevor do to her as long as it's okay with her. Maybe this time it wasn't." She frowned. "So, I thought I'd warn you that if you sent her running to Trevor, I'm going to help her to stay there."

"The **hell** you are."

The storm was no longer hovering but there before her. Dark eyes glittering with intensity. Lips drawn back from white teeth.

"I told you that honor and fair play mean a lot to Jane. I think that Trevor understands that. She'll be safer with him."

"Stay out of this, Margaret."

"Can't," she said simply. "She took that bullet for me. I owe her. It's not over until it's over." She smiled cheerfully. "But now that you understand my position, we can forget about it unless there's a problem. I do find you very interesting, Caleb. Sometimes, the most unpredictable animals are the most fascinating."

He shook his head in disbelief. "You're incredible." He added harshly, "And I don't even know why I'm even listening to a half-baked kid like you."

"Half-baked?" She thought about it. "I do have a lack of experience in some areas, but in others I'm ahead of the game. So I don't think you can call me that. Maybe three-quarters baked?" She got to her feet. "And now I have to go to the bathroom and get a drink of water. Will you order me breakfast? Orange juice, roll, and coffee."

"Haven't you heard you shouldn't eat in

the hall of the enemy?" he asked sarcastically.

"Don't be melodramatic. You're not my enemy." She moved across the room. "Unless you—" She stopped as her phone rang. "Kendra. I told you she'd keep her word." She answered, "I'm already in Chicago, Kendra. You took long enough. I'm with Seth Caleb. I'm putting you on speaker."

"Whatever," Kendra said impatiently. "I think I've got it, Margaret. It was easy once I connected the dots."

"I've seen you connect dots before, and there's nothing easy about it," Margaret said. "I don't see the same paths that you do."

"You have to come back to the prime realization that Harriet has always had a passion for English literature and move forward from there. She even infected her son, Kevin, with the same passion. He wanted to please her, and he knew that was the best way of doing it. It was clearly something they shared from the time he was a child."

"Where are we going with this?"

"The setting of those explosives was the biggest thing in Kevin's life at the time that he became involved with that al-Qaeda cell. He wanted to make Harriet a part of it."

"Why?"

"From the comparisons Kevin made to Harriet about those poor little girls he raped and murdered, I'd guess he was trying to make up to her for the one crime for which she flatly condemned him."

"She only disapproved because she thought it was dangerous for him."

"But it caused her to leave him so that he'd have a safe haven if he needed it. I doubt if Kevin could be made to feel guilt, but he couldn't stand the thought of not being perfect in her eyes. He needed to have her approval. In the case of the nuclear project, he needed to give Harriet the idea that they were on the same team. A sort of dark, macabre camaraderie."

"Those who blow up a city together, stay together?"

"Or two cities. Yes, that's the idea. That's also the reason why Kevin made the journal too complicated for Doane to decipher. I believe Kevin was always playing his father off against his mother. But it was Harriet who he couldn't bear to lose. He really meant the journal to go to Harriet, but he died before he could take it from Doane and give it to her."

"And how did Kevin involve Harriet in setting up the explosion?"

"Why, he let her plan it. He made it an intimate game between the two of them. Harriet loved control, and he knew it. So he used the passion they both shared and let her choose how and where to pull off the explosion."

"And it's in that journal?"

"Nothing blatant. He wouldn't want to give anything away to Doane. This was a precious secret between Harriet and him. Kevin teased her with it. Oblique references. There were also the same type references in the letters he wrote to her about that same time."

"Dammit, what references, Kendra?"

"I'm getting to it. Don't be impatient."

"Why shouldn't I be impatient? You've given me nothing but psychological mumbo jumbo about two sickos."

"It's not mumbo jumbo. It's an analysis that is based on hours of—I can hear you seething, Margaret."

"That's impossible. But you know me well enough to realize that's exactly what

I'd do. More analysis. Now what is this intimate little charade Kevin and his mother were practicing? And what did it have to do with Harriet's obsession with English Literature?"

"Everything." Kendra's voice was tense. "I think I've found what we're looking for. Look, the journal was written to be read by Harriet, not Doane. We saw Doane's house, and the man isn't a reader. But Harriet could pick up on some fairly obscure literary references."

"So we're back to those literary references again. Give me an example."

Margaret heard a rustling of papers on Kendra's end of the phone. "Late in the journal, he gets on a rant about wanting the world to pay for its hatred against him. At one point, he says he'll 'see the brave day sunk in hideous night.'"

"I don't recognize that. But, then, I'm more into Dr. Seuss than obscure English quotations."

"I didn't recognize it either, but I knew it didn't seem like his own words based on everything else he'd written. It's from a Shakespeare sonnet. Then, a bit later in the journal, Kevin writes that 'quiet minds cannot be perplexed or frightened but go on in fortune or misfortune at their own private pace—'"

"'. . . like a clock during a thunderstorm,'" Margaret finished.

Silence. "You know that line?"

"Maybe I know a few things other than Dr. Seuss. I've read **The Strange Case of Dr. Jekyll and Mr. Hyde.**"

"And you remember that quote? You never cease to amaze me, Margaret."

"What about the letters? Did they help?"

"The content didn't give me much yet. Maybe later. But the envelopes do."

"How is that?"

"The postmarks. The dates line up with his journal entries. The postmark on one envelope tells us that he mailed a letter from Seattle on June 4, and it was stamped at a postal facility just a few blocks from the King Street Station. It's the biggest clock tower in Seattle. And, the day that he referred to that Shakespeare sonnet rant in his journal, he mailed another letter from downtown Chicago. It was in the vicinity of two fairly notable clocks. It's interesting what he left out in both quotes. The full Shakespeare line is '**When I do count**

the clock that tells the time, and set the brave day sunk in hideous night.' And the Stevenson line is 'Quiet minds cannot be perplexed or frightened but go on in fortune or misfortune at their own private pace, **like a clock during a thunderstorm.**'"

Margaret inhaled sharply as the concept hit home. "Clocks . . ."

"Yes, the first quote was in a Kevin journal entry from Seattle. And there's another reference here, from Osbert Sitwell. That one is from another of the letters from Kevin to Harriet, and the envelope is also stamped Chicago and dated a little before Kevin's death." Kendra flipped more pages. "It says, 'Killing time is only the name for another of the multifarious ways by which Time kills us.'"

"Time **kills** us?"

"I think Kevin is telling us something here. No, I'm almost sure of it. You need to check the clocks in those cities."

"Easy to say. There must be hundreds of clocks and clock towers in Chicago and Seattle."

"But both Kevin and his mother have

gigantic egos. They wouldn't play around with small stuff. It would amuse them to go after a place that would garner headlines."

"I assume you have a few ideas?"

"I'm e-mailing you a list of possibles. I just sent you pictures and map data for several of the most-high-profile clocks in Chicago and Seattle." She paused. "I don't want to influence you, but I'd zero in on the Wrigley Building downtown, next to the Chicago River. There's a huge clock tower atop the building, but there's also a clock at the nearby baseball field. They might have chosen either one. Or neither one."

"And Seattle?"

"I'd go first to the King Street Station. Besides the postmark on the letter, that clock tower is one of the most recognizable structures in the entire city." She was silent again. "All of this is just my opinion, Margaret. No proof. I'm still working on alternate—"

"Stop trying to punch holes in it," Margaret said. "You did great work, and you know it. Try to get some sleep. We'll take it from here."

"Not entirely," Kendra said dryly. "Every time I turn around, someone is throwing something else at me. I've got to double-check my findings on the journal, then dive into Pacific Coast driftwood."

"I'm not going to try to talk you out of it," Margaret said quietly. "It's too important. All of this talk about clock towers and terrorist plots. It's all world-shaking and horrible, but the nightmare for Jane may be what's behind that driftwood you have to locate."

"Or her salvation," Kendra said. "I'll keep on it, Margaret." She hung up.

"She's astonishing," Caleb said slowly as he watched Margaret thrust her phone back into her pocket. "Jane told me about her, but I guess she's something you have to experience."

"You could say that," Margaret said. "And thank God when she's for you instead of against you. Kendra doesn't suffer fools gladly."

"I got that impression."

"You were going to order me breakfast." She checked her watch. "But that's okay. I'll wait until after I call Jane, and we'll all have it together."

"Of course, there's the issue of disturbing Jane," he murmured. "You've changed your mind about that?"

"It's not important right now." She looked at him impatiently. "I told you all that sex stuff doesn't mean diddly-squat to me when you put it in the balance. Kendra worked her butt off to give us a chance to put a roadblock in the way of Harriet Weber's plans. I've got to tell Jane." She frowned. "And you said Harriet was going to pick up the detonator this morning. Maybe that will give us a clue about where they planted the device."

"Perhaps. 'Diddly-squat' . . . what an unusual term . . . But, then, there's nothing usual about you." Caleb got to his feet. "I'll call Jane for you and invite her to breakfast."

She shook her head. "I'll give her another fifteen minutes, then do it myself." She went headed for the bathroom. "You'd enjoy it entirely too much."

The sun was almost over the horizon, the amber gold streaks soft against the dark clouds. Beautiful, Jane thought drowsily, as she turned away from the window and cuddled closer to Trevor.

And **he** was beautiful. Strong and full of light and warmth like that sunlight.

"Awake?" he whispered in her ear. "I thought you were dozing."

"Maybe. I don't know. I tried not to sleep. I didn't want to let go." Her lips moved across his cheek. "I didn't want to let **you** go."

"I'm not going anywhere," he said softly. "I've got you, and I'm going to keep you." His hand gently stroked her hair back from her face. "That's what I've been trying to tell you since I came back. You haven't been listening, you stubborn woman."

"I'm listening now." She nestled closer. "I am stubborn . . . and scared. I think I must have loved you since the moment I saw you all those years ago. You took my breath away. All that charm and charisma and you were so damn Greek-god beautiful."

"Beautiful?" He made a face. "Your artistic tendencies must have blinded you. I'm no Greek god."

"No, maybe not. According to the myths, Greek gods weren't always very kind or sane or unselfish. Not like you."

"I'm not unselfish. Not where you're concerned. I want to reach out and grab and hold. I hope I'm sane, but it's easy to be kind to you, Jane."

"Is it? You're wrong, you know. I'm hard to love. No one ever loved me before Eve came into my life. A few of my foster parents pretended for a while, but something always happened, and they sent me away."

"Stupid bastards." He cleared his throat. "You were better off without them."

"I think so, too. Because then Eve came." She raised herself on one arm and looked down at him. "Look, I don't feel sorry for myself. I didn't mean that, Trevor. I'm a very good artist, and a good person, and I'll make damn sure that we have a great life together. I just wanted you to know that I don't have any illusions about being the easiest person in the world to live with."

"Just so you do live with me and don't walk away again." His lips brushed the tip of her nose. "I'll take care of the rest."

"Never again, Trevor," she whispered. She lowered her cheek to the hollow of his shoulder. "I was lying here thinking. Do you know what I want most in the world, no, the universe?"

"Whatever it is, I'll get it for you."

"We'll get it together. I want to be back at the lake cottage. I want to sit in the porch swing with Eve and watch Joe making barbecue down by the lake. I want to see you strolling down to talk to him and look back at me and smile." Her lips brushed his collarbone. "Family. And you part of it."

"I think we can manage that. Though Joe will have to teach me to barbecue. Anything else?"

"We watch the sun go down. And then we say good night to Eve and Joe and we go home together." She could feel a tightness in her throat. "And we talk the way we did tonight, not holding anything back."

"Do we make love?"

She laughed huskily. "Of course, that goes without saying."

"Oh, I think that should definitely be said. We do it so well."

Yes, they did, she thought dreamily. They knew each other's bodies and how to make them respond. Their passion tonight had been slow, hot, sweet, heady. Completely satisfying. "I agree. I didn't mean to make such an important omission."

"Understandable. It wasn't the focus tonight."

She had a sudden thought and raised herself to look down at him again. "Why wasn't it the focus? Was it because of Caleb? Did what he did tonight interfere with—"

"Hush." He kissed her and shut off the words. "It was necessary. Did I like it? Hell, no. But nothing you and Caleb could do together would interfere with what I feel for you." She opened her lips to speak, and he put two fingers on her lips. "And the reason that sex wasn't the focus was that it's always there for us, and it's always magic. The focus tonight was on the miracle."

"What miracle?"

"Commitment. Barbecues and porch swings and family." He kissed her gently. "Dreams. Love ever after."

Love ever after.

Oh, yes, she did love him so much. Yesterday. Today. Tomorrow.

And Ever After.

If she was to keep from crying, she had to make a joke of it. "Ever After? It sounds like something from a Disney movie. That's schmaltzy, Trevor," she said huskily. "Nice, though."

"I like the idea of Ever After. It means that all the things that have gone before are just the beginning, that all the mistakes and the happy times we've gone through are only building blocks." He kissed the tip of her nose. "And I find I'm developing a tendency toward schmaltz, on occasion." He pulled her down into his arms again. "But strictly sincere schmaltz. Did I embarrass you? You'll have to get used to it."

"I think that's possible." The rays of the sun coming into the room were stronger. Life was invading, she realized reluctantly. "It's almost seven. I suppose we should get up."

"In a little while." He smiled. "I believe my focus is beginning to shift toward—"

Her phone on the bedside table rang.

She stiffened. Caleb?

No, Margaret.

She accessed the call. "Margaret, where are you?"

"In Caleb's room. I've ordered coffee and breakfast for everyone. Thirty minutes?"

Jane looked at Trevor. "Maybe a little longer."

"It's important, Jane," Margaret said quietly. "Things are breaking."

"What—"

"Thirty minutes." Margaret hung up.

"She said it was important," Jane said as she pressed the disconnect. She lay there, gazing at him. Dear God, she loved him. She didn't want to leave the cocoon that they'd built together in the past hours. "I guess we have to go."

"You know we do." He got up and scooped her up in his arms and turned in a circle. "And important can be good." He kissed her before setting her on her feet. "There will be other miracles. They'll be that much better if we go out and earn them."

That's right, they were just starting out. It was hard to remember that when she had just found out that all the paths they had traveled had come to this wonderful crossroad.

It was hard to remember and harder to believe.

No, she would not be negative. She didn't even know from where that crazy thought had come. She would reach out and grasp that gold ring, and everything would be fine. She would find Eve. She would keep this love. There would be dreams and love and miracles.

"You take the first shower." Trevor patted

her behind as he nudged her toward the bathroom. "Then you can run down and talk to Margaret. I know you're going to be on edge once you start thinking."

He knew so much about her, she thought as she closed the bathroom door. That knowledge was a miracle in itself. She was already eager to find out what Margaret considered important. She moved quickly to the shower and turned on the spray.

Trevor said it could be good news. Please, let it be good news, Margaret.

"Eat your breakfast, Jane," Caleb said mockingly as he poured more coffee in her cup. "You have to keep up your strength. I'd hate to waste all my efforts."

"Be quiet, Caleb." Jane turned back to Margaret. "Clocks?" Excitement was sweeping through her. At least one answer in this hellish puzzle. "Bless Kendra. If we can locate those nuclear devices, then no matter what Harriet does, we'll be in control. We could go forward with finding Eve without that hanging over us."

"Not true," Trevor said. "We have to do more than locate them—have them disarmed. Or at least prevent them from being detonated."

"And you said Harriet denied she was going after the detonator this morning," Margaret said. "But she'll have to go get it sometime. Could you steal it, take it away from her?"

"We don't even know if the detonator is here or in Seattle. And once she has it in her hands, the danger increases. If she panics, she might set it off before anyone could get near enough to her to take it away from her. It would have to be handled with extreme delicacy."

"I can't see her in a panic," Jane said dryly. "I think she has a keen appreciation of her own value and a well-developed sense of self-preservation." She added thoughtfully, "But Harriet wouldn't like to risk defeat. She might set off those explosions from sheer bitchery. She's supposed to meet with this Cartland. Perhaps we can work something through him."

"Or call in Venable," Margaret said quietly. She held up her hand at Jane's expression. "I know that you're afraid that he'll sacrifice Eve to national security. It's

a legitimate concern after the way he almost got her killed in Colorado. But you
have to consider that you may have to do
it. You can't let Harriet even get close to
setting off those bombs."

"I know that I can't," Jane said curtly. "But
I'm not going to run that risk while there's
still a chance that we can take care of it
ourselves. We still have some time. She's
not going to set off those explosions until
after Zander is executed." She moistened
her lips. "And Zander isn't going to be killed
until Doane kills Eve. He wants him to see
Eve die. It's all connected."

"Yeah, let's see, we find out where the
nukes are stashed here in Chicago and
have them disabled," Caleb's lips twisted.
"Then we follow Harriet when she heads
for Seattle and joins Doane. We rescue
Eve, kill the bad guys, then have the nukes
in Seattle disabled. Piece of cake."

"I know it's a nightmare." And his listing
of those nightmare elements was causing
her desperation to soar. "You can opt out,
Caleb," Jane said. "I've told you that before."

"Same answer," he said shortly. "But
somebody had to outline the problems.
Trevor is ready to leap tall buildings with a

single bound for you. Well, I'm not Superman, but I'm damn good, and I have a few talents he lacks. There's a job to be done, and I'll do it." He smiled recklessly as he glanced at Trevor. "I'll even work with you to do it." He looked down at the photos on Margaret's phone. "Two very famous clocks here in Chicago. Which one do we try first?"

"Neither one," Margaret said. "I'm heading for Wrigley Field right after breakfast to check out that clock at the stadium. You tend to Harriet Weber and let me do the advance work."

"Advance work?" Trevor's brows rose. "And that is?"

"Rats," Margaret said flatly. "I took a look at that clock. It's in the scoreboard and maintenance has to be done on the scoreboard and the clock. That means that there are places inside where a device could be placed. I don't think it would take that much space."

"Rats," Trevor prompted.

"There are rats everywhere," Margaret said. "Particularly around the rivers and lakes. Rats are always hungry and looking for food. They don't care what it is and will try anything."

"Even a nuclear cocktail?" Caleb asked.

"Anything," Margaret repeated. "And they may remember the taste, or the death of another rat from ingesting, or location. If there were human food scraps in the area where the device was planted, it would be particularly memorable."

"You mean if Kevin dropped a few bites of a McDonald's Big Mac when he was planting the bomb, it might be a giveaway?" Jane asked. "That was over five years ago, Margaret. How long do rats live?"

"Wild rats can live from five to seven years." She shrugged. "I'm not hoping for that kind of contact. But you can never tell. Rats tend to breed in the same area if food is readily available, and a baseball stadium and an office complex have that advantage. There might be places in either that they use as a pathway or—"

"And you expect to be able to pin those rats down to a location?" Trevor said skeptically.

"Possibly. It's worth a shot. At least, I won't attract much attention the way you would. Both you and Caleb are very memorable. People generally sort of take me for granted." She made a face. "As for the rest, no promises. Rats aren't really reliable."

"Pity," Caleb murmured. "If they were, I think you might pull it off."

"Really?" Margaret tilted her head. "You mean it?"

"You're remarkable," Caleb said. "Annoying but definitely remarkable. And Jane told us about the way you charmed that wolf in the mountains."

"You don't charm wolves; you accept them and hope they accept—"

The machine on the table by the balcony doors pinged softly.

"Our Harriet's moving." Caleb rose swiftly to his feet. "It may take her a while to shower and dress, but I'm not going to take a chance. I'll go down and watch the suite until she takes off to meet Cartland." He glanced at Jane. "Stay here. The last thing we want is for Harriet to see you. I'll call you when she's left the hotel."

The next moment the door closed behind him.

Stay here?

Jane got to her feet. She did not want to stay here. She wanted to be on the move, part of the action. But there was no doubt it was the sensible thing to do. At least, she was here in the same hotel as Harriet, close to the action and not parked "safely" a block away.

"Jane," Trevor said.

"I know, I know. I'll do what's smart and discreet." She turned to Margaret. "Okay. But I'll go with you to Wrigley Field. Maybe I can do something to—"

"Perhaps we'd do better to stay here and explore that driftwood thread that Ben Hudson—" He stopped as he saw her expression. "Problem?"

"I'm not going to stay cooped up in a hotel room doing computer research on driftwood. I'll leave that to Catherine and Joe. I spent all those days in the hospital doing the same kind of research to find that place in Colorado where Doane was keeping Eve."

"And you found it," Trevor said softly.

"I only did it because I wasn't strong enough to go after Doane myself. I had to rely on others to do my job." She met his eyes. "I won't do that again. I'm strong, Trevor. Thanks to Caleb, I've never felt stronger." She grimaced. "Damn him."

"But that isn't all, is it?" Margaret was studying Jane's expression. "You don't believe Ben Hudson?"

"Of course I believe he's telling the truth as he knows it. Who wouldn't? When I was drawing that sketch of Doane from Ben's description, it was like looking into a crystal-clear pool. He'd never intentionally lie."

"Intentionally seems to be the key word," Margaret said quietly. "You're saying that his dreams are hallucinations? Yet you've evidently had some very strange dreams yourself. Were your dreams of Cira and her Anthony hallucinations?"

"Maybe. I've never ruled that possibility out."

"Because you have problems accepting anything that's not strictly black-and-white." Trevor smiled. "But I believe that Cira managed to suspend your disbelief on occasion."

She was silent a moment. "But I never claimed that she was a ghost who talked to me and told me how to run my life."

"Ah, there we have it," Trevor said. "The crux of the issue is Bonnie. I had a few reservations myself when I heard the story, but I was willing to go along since Quinn appeared to be taking it seriously. He's a cop, and I thought there might be minimal substance." He tilted his head. "He believes in ghosts?"

"I don't discuss it with him." She saw him gazing quizzically at her. She would not lie to him even by omission. "I don't know about ghosts in general. I think he believes in Bonnie. I **know** that Eve believes in her."

"But you can't bring yourself to do it?" Margaret asked.

"It doesn't have anything to do with me. If they want to cling to Bonnie even beyond the grave, if it brings them peace or happiness, why should I mind? All I want is for Eve to be happy." She tried to steady her voice. "And safe. I want her to be safe. And I can't go chasing off on a wild-goose chase that could waste time and kill her."

Margaret nodded. "Then you shouldn't do it. Let Kendra and Catherine work on it." She chuckled. "That's actually funny. There aren't two more hardheaded women that I know and I'm tossing a ghost at them." She got to her feet and gave Jane a hug. "Personally, I don't know if you're right or wrong. But it doesn't matter. I'm here for you no matter how you want to handle this. By all means come along to Wrigley Field and we'll play hickory dickory dock. Only substitute rat for mouse." She glanced at Trevor. "You can come, too."

"Thank you," he said dryly.

"You're welcome. You can keep an eye on Jane while I'm busy up behind the clock." She smiled. "You'll like doing that. You can hardly stop staring at her anyway."

Trevor's gaze shifted to Jane. "Yes, I will like that very much, Margaret."

Jane was caught, held. She could not look away from him.

Today. Tomorrow. Ever After.

"We'll leave right after we get the call from Caleb that Harriet has left the hotel," Margaret said. "In the meantime, I'll call Kendra and see if she's come up with anything else." She pulled out her phone. "I'm feeling a little **de trop** at the moment. You're practically glowing, and Trevor is . . . I don't know what." She waved her hand as she started to dial. "But go ahead, continue. It's interesting, and I think I like it. It's kind of . . . warm."

"A bank, Harriet?" Cartland gazed at the BANK OF AMERICA gold lettering as he opened the glass door for her. "It's not what I expected."

"Why not? A bank is where treasures are stored." Harriet smiled. "And Kevin and I decided that Bank of America, the king of capitalism, should be where we kept the key to our kingdom. Don't you find it amusing?"

"No, there was nothing amusing about Kevin's shifting those nukes without telling me or anyone in the cell," Cartland said bitterly. "It wasn't a one-man operation. We had a right to know where they were." He scowled as he followed her through the plush marble halls. "And it caused the entire project to go down the drain when he was killed."

"But now it's resurrected," Harriet said. "And Tehran will be more pleased than if you had been able to set off those bombs five years ago. The political climate is much tenser now. Every victory is shouted from Tehran. You do agree that virtually destroying this fine city and Seattle will be a great victory?"

"Don't be stupid," he said shortly. "Of course it will. Why do you think I'm here? I didn't want to deal with you. Kevin wouldn't listen to anyone else after he brought you into the project. I knew it was going to cause trouble. Now it's happening again. Doane came to me and offered us the nukes. Then, all of a sudden, he said that you had to be bought off. Well, I've done it. You have what you want. Now prove that you'll give us what we want."

"I'm not stupid, Cartland," she said coldly. "You've obviously been associating too closely with your Middle Eastern cohorts who think that 'woman' is a synonym for 'feeblemindedness.' And you've not bought me off, you've only made the first install-ment." She was heading for the safe-deposit-box section. "I've decided that I have job for you to do that will make my depar-ture from these shores a little safer. Now be quiet until we get this business over with. Then we'll talk, and you'll find out the price for being touted as the next Bin Laden."

"She took him to the Bank of America on State Street," Caleb said when Jane picked up the phone. "I'm e-mailing you a photo of Cartland. He's in his forties, well dressed,

dark hair. Very much the American busi-
nessman."

"You didn't expect him to look like he just
stepped off the plane from Tehran," Jane
said. "Did you hear anything? Could you
plant any listening bugs?"

"No time. And it would take a hell of a lot
more sophisticated mobile equipment than
I could pick up at a mall or on the street."
He added dryly, "So even if I could get close
enough, the only way I could get anything
would be to read their lips. Maybe your
friend, Margaret, might have that kind of
skill, I don't. I'm outside the bank, and I'll
wait until they come out and follow them."
He paused. "It may come down to me protecting that bitch if Cartland decides to try
to take her down."

"She's into power. I can't see her not being able to manipulate him."

"He's a terrorist."

"Same answer. Be careful, Caleb. We're
on our way to Wrigley Field. Call me as
soon as they leave the bank."

"Yeah, I'll do that." He hung up and leaned
back against the door of the bakery across
the street from the bank. This wasn't the
kind of stalking of which he was fond. He

had done it before during the years when he was hunting down his sister's murderer, and he had learned all the tricks. But it was more detective work than seeking out prey.

It would have been so simple if Jane had permitted him to go after Harriet and make her talk to him. Simple and completely efficient.

Don't think about it. Do what Jane wanted him to do. Keep the flame burning low.

His time would come.

Cartland frowned as he gazed down at the sheaf of papers in the open safe-deposit box. "What the hell is this crap? I thought you might be going to give me the detonator."

"I never said that. I just said you'd find it valuable." She picked up the papers and handed them to him. "And interesting. Kevin wasn't sure that you wouldn't cause him trouble with Tehran when he moved those nukes. He set about getting insurance." She watched his face as he scanned the documents. "You weren't always hard-line al-Qaeda. You made deals that Iran would find not only disloyal but offensive to their religious creed." She listened to him cursing for a moment. "If they knew about those transactions, you'd be on their hit list. And you know how deadly it can be for those on that hit list."

His angry gaze swooped up to her face. "Blackmail, you bitch."

"Yes," she said. "I had to be certain that you understood that I'm not anyone you can discount or try to manipulate. We can work together, or you can go on the run and hope you have a week before they butcher you." She stared him in the eye. "Until this is over, I'm in charge. Do we understand each other?"

He didn't speak for a moment, and she could read the struggle in his expression. "Maybe," he muttered.

No maybe, she thought triumphantly. He had caved. He might try to save his pride, but she had him. "Then I'm willing to show you this." She lifted the black cloth in the bottom of the box on which she'd placed the documents. "Since we're going to be such good partners in the battle for Islam."

Cartland's brow furrowed as he looked down into the box. "A cell phone? What the hell?"

"Why are you surprised?" Harriet said. "You set off bombs all the time using a cell phone as a detonator."

"But this is an antique." He gazed skeptically at the large, clumsy-looking cell phone. He took out his own sleek, thin iPhone. "Technology has left it in the dust."

"It was the last thing in technology five years ago," Harriet said. "And once the phone is charged it will still work beautifully. I consulted with an electronics expert just six months ago." She looked him in the eye. "Believe me, all I'll have to do is put in the code. Boom. There goes Chicago and Seattle."

"Both cities?"

"My Kevin was brilliant. You never appreciated him. We were going to get on a plane to Samoa, and as the door closed, he was going to press in the code."

"That's still your plan?"

"With certain modifications."

His voice was suddenly eager. "You said you weren't going to give me the detonator."

"Do you see me handing it over to you?" She took the cell phone out of the box and slipped it into her handbag. "But now that you understand who makes the rules, I don't object to proving that I have it."

"I want that cell phone, Harriet."

"Forget it. It would do you absolutely no good without the code. Surely you don't think I'd give that to you?"

"I believe you could be persuaded," he said softly.

"How nasty. Are you threatening me, Cartland? Remember those documents? On my death, my lawyer will FedEx a copy to Iran. And do you think I brought you here to flaunt this detonator in your face? I know you have no problems with torture. Kevin told me all about you and your friends. He said you were amateurs. That's why he took the devices away from you."

"He was a traitor." His cheeks flushed. "I was glad when I heard he'd been killed."

"And you all ran for cover." She smothered the rage she was feeling. Cartland still had his uses. "Think what you like. I know what my son could do." She took a deep breath. "You're thinking that you don't have to know where the nukes are located if you have that detonator. You're quite right. That's why you have to deal with me and not my ex-husband. I have the detonator, and I have the code. That gives me all the cards, Cartland. And it puts me in the driver's seat." She added, "You'll like the way I drive. I'm waiting for James to give me the death of the man who butchered my son. Then I'll personally set off those nukes. You won't have to do a thing but accept the responsibility. You'll have no risk. You and your little group can take credit and become big men in Tehran. And I'll have a red herring that will give me time to go underground. Interested?"

"Maybe," he said cautiously.

"You're very interested."

"You want more money."

"Yes, one more payment would make me happy. It should be sent to the same bank a week after the explosions take place. I'm taking a chance on you, of course. But I still will have those documents, and I'm sure that you won't want those politicians in Tehran to know that I'm the one who will be responsible for the explosions. It would be humiliating for you to have them know that you took credit for the work of a lowly woman. I'll just disappear into the sunset."

"That would be best," he said slowly.

"I thought so."

He was silent. "Just one more payment?"

"And perhaps a favor or two."

He stiffened. "Favor?"

"Kevin told me that you were a very clever man. You trained at a camp outside Berlin that specialized not only in bomb making but assassination. I'm sure you've just gotten better over the years."

"You want me to kill someone."

"It would make it safer for me to leave the country. Safer for me to disappear. Safer for you to maintain the reputation I'm going to hand you."

"Who?"

"No one who should cause you any problem. Just a woman who pushed in where she shouldn't be. James says that I shouldn't worry about her, but then James can sometimes be a fool." She smiled. "Her name is Jane MacGuire."

"Why do you want her dead?"

"She knows about my son's journal. That means that she may find out more than I'd like her to know about our project. I've no desire for her to suspect that I had anything to do with either your group or the explosions. She may have some kind of connection with a CIA agent, but she had a purely personal reason for hunting me down and harassing me." Her lips tightened. "And she won't give up. I saw it in her face, heard it in her voice. No matter where I go or how much time passes she'll be right behind me. I won't permit that to happen, Cartland. Take care of it for me."

"How do I get to her?"

"That's your problem. Her family lives in Atlanta. She's the adoptive daughter of Joe Quinn and Eve Duncan. I last saw her in Muncie, Indiana." She paused. "I want it done quickly. I don't want to have it hovering over me. Find her. Kill her."

"I'll find her." He smiled grimly. "It shouldn't take long. The advantage of living in a technical world is that no one can really get away from it. I'll have Samli run a check on her smartphone. Unless it's been specially blocked, it should be easy enough. He's located troubling people for me before. I can probably give you her location down to half a mile or so."

"You can really do that?"

"Anybody can do that, if they know the right person. A couple hundred bucks to an employee of one of the wireless carriers will tell you exactly which tower Jane MacGuire's phone is pinging at any given time. No muss, no fuss."

"And no warrant."

"Actually, the cops don't even need a warrant for that. The phone companies have a cozy relationship with most law-enforcement agencies. This isn't exactly legal, but it's also no big deal. Any private investigator in any fleabag strip center could do the same thing for you. There are thousands of underpaid telephone employees who are glad to supplement their incomes."

"But I don't want a private detective to do it. I want you. How long will it take?"

"I'll put Samli on it and he'll be able to narrow down her exact location within five or six hours. Once I have her zeroed in, it's all over."

"Excellent." She closed the safe-deposit box and locked it. "When you tell me that I no longer have to concern myself with her, I'll be able to concentrate on more important things."

"When?" Cartland asked bluntly. "How soon will you punch in that code?"

"Don't nag me. I don't like it. It's all coming together." She turned and headed for the door. "Within two days, you should be a very happy man." She glanced at him over her shoulder. "And if you take care of the Jane MacGuire matter, I'll be a very happy woman."

CHAPTER

14

Seattle

"The King Street Station tower," Catherine told Gallo. "Margaret said Kendra's bet was on that clock tower to be the one where Kevin placed one of his nukes."

"We'll check it out and see how we can get inside. Though there's a good chance it's being watched. We won't be able to move on it. The last thing we want is to goad Doane and Harriet into a panic."

"I'm just hoping that we'll be able to pull all these strings together at the last minute," she said wearily. "And praying that we won't be the one in a panic."

"Not you, Catherine."

"Don't count on it. I checked with Langley about any real estate purchased by Kevin here in Seattle, and they haven't come up with anything. Of course, he probably buried the paperwork under a dozen names or companies. It will take time." She paused. "But maybe Venable could get it faster. He has more clout. I may have to go that route."

"You'll do what you have to do." He changed the subject. "Joe and I have been to the Marine Museum, and we've been talking to the curator about driftwood. We tapped a lot of technical and historical background, but I doubt if it's going to prove valuable."

"I went at it from another angle. Tell me about the museum info."

"Driftwood is any wood that's been washed onto a shore or beach of a sea or river by the action of winds, tides, waves, or man. It's a form of marine debris."

"Anything about a connection between driftwood and graveyards . . . tombstone . . . death?"

"No, actually, it's usually considered beneficial to life. Driftwood provides shelter and food for birds. Fish and other aquatic species as it floats in the ocean. Gribbles, shipworms, and bacteria decompose the wood and gradually turn it into nutrients that are reintroduced into the food chain. The wood can also become the foundation for sand dunes when it comes ashore. On the surface, nothing sinister, Catherine."

"Eve saw something sinister. Where does the majority of the driftwood come from?"

"Hard to determine exactly because of wave erosion. Most of the driftwood comes from remains of trees washed into the water by storms, flooding, or other disasters. Other causes are logging, cargoes from ships, buildings, ships themselves. There was one hell of a flood of driftwood that came ashore from the Japanese tsunami."

Catherine recalled seeing the news stories about the tons of horrible ghostly debris that had washed ashore. She had never thought of those huge boats, tools, and fragments ripped from the farms and seaports of Japan as driftwood. Yet evidently they were. "I don't think that Kevin's driftwood was from that disaster. The time frame isn't right. Is there anything else that you found unusual?"

"I told you, interesting but probably not of value. Let me think . . . Okay, you're not supposed to burn driftwood. It produces dioxins which are carcinogenic. Very unhealthy because of the chlorine of the seawater."

"I didn't even know there was chlorine in seawater. But burning driftwood isn't an immediate killer?"

"No."

"And that's all?"

"You've pumped me dry, Catherine." He added solemnly, "No, how could I have forgotten. One more thing. According to Norse mythology, the first humans, Ask and Embla, were formed out of two pieces of driftwood, an ash and an elm by the god Odin and his brothers. Do you think it's of any importance?"

"Very funny."

"No, but I had to strike a light note. For the most part, the visit was very boring. And I only gave you the highlights. I would have invited you to come along if you hadn't been tied up. Though I hope not literally." He paused. "How is Zander?"

"Stubborn." Her gaze shifted to Zander, across the sitting room. "But I'm working on him. He's not stupid, he must see I'm right about letting you and Joe help us."

Zander smiled and silently shook his head.

"Stubborn," she said again. "As I said, I've been doing some research about driftwood, too. I've been looking in the local newspapers to find any stories about unusual driftwood or collectors. There were a few articles about artists who use driftwood as a medium of expression."

"None who created graveyards with it?"

"Not any who gave interviews about doing it. I've also been gently nudging Kendra."

"Gently?"

"I've been as gentle as I could," she said curtly. "I know she's doing the best she can. I just need it faster." She swallowed. "I have a feeling that we're running out of time, Gallo. We're all working so hard for Eve. But it's like treading water in a whirlpool. Any minute, she could be pulled down and never come up."

"Then we'll tread faster and stronger," Gallo said. "And you'd better get Zander to do something positive. He's still the best hope Eve has to survive." He added. "If the bastard even cares."

"Oh, he cares." Catherine met Zander's gaze. "I know that he does."

"I'm not that certain," Gallo said. "If I learn anything more about the driftwood, I'll call you. Take care of yourself." He hung up.

"I'm touched by your faith in me," Zander said with a faint smile. "Though not by your ability to read either my emotional capability or my character. Gallo was much closer in his assessment."

"Gallo doesn't know anything about you."

"Neither do you, lovely Catherine."

"Enough," she said. She hoped she was telling the truth. He was an enigma, but perhaps he had given her the tiniest glimpse. "Gallo wants some positive action from you."

"I heard. I really don't care what Gallo wants. Though I'm sure that you do."

"It would be positive if you'd let Gallo and Joe join us here."

He shook his head.

She gazed at him in frustration. "What are we doing at this damn hotel anyway? We've been here for hours. Did you finish your calls?"

"Yes."

"And you told me that the one person

that you contacted hasn't been able to tell you anything about where Doane might be. Shouldn't we be out asking more questions, trying more of your contacts?"

"No, one is enough."

"Then let's **do** something."

"You are doing something. You're acting as my bodyguard. Isn't that what you said was going to be your mission?"

"It's no challenge when we're holed up in this hotel." She paused. "You know that Gallo could probably find us if he made the attempt. He was one of the best under-cover Special Forces guys either one of us has ever run across."

"But he won't make the attempt because it would upset you, and he wants you to trust him. I considered the possibility of his intrusion but discarded it."

"He may change his mind if Joe gets desperate."

"You're the one who is getting desper-ate. I was detecting a hint of tension while you were speaking to Gallo."

"More than a hint."

"Yes." His smile faded. "And it was justi-fied. Because you're right. Time is running out, Catherine." He got to his feet and headed for the door that led to the bedroom. "So I'd advise that you gather all your friends and cohorts who are so earnestly trying to find Eve and make magic happen." His voice was grim. "Because she's going to need it."

"You're restless," Stang said quietly. "That's unusual for you, Zander. Well, actually not an unusual state, just unusual for you to show it."

"You regard it as a form of weakness?" Zander asked. "A break in the armor?"

Stang was immediately wary. There was something seething beneath that surface that he didn't wish to explore. "I didn't say that. It was just an observation. You know as well as I do that you're careful not to let anyone see too deeply." He smiled. "I've worked for you for years, and you're still a mystery to me."

"But you always said that you liked it like that. You prefer it," Zander said mockingly. "It's safer for you not to get involved. Isn't that right?"

"That's right." Stang's gaze narrowed on Zander's face. "But you've wanted me to be involved since Eve Duncan was taken.

I still don't know why, but here I am. I thought for a while it was that you wanted me to be Eve's advocate. You're a hard man, Zander, and you won't let yourself bend. You might have wanted me to strike a balance and give Eve her chance."

"Oh, another sign of weakness?"

"No," he said quietly. "Humanity."

"An even worse insult. I'm not fond of the human race, Stang."

"I know."

"You know too much about me. Perhaps it's time I rid myself of you."

"Go ahead. There was always that risk when I came to work for you. But it's been interesting when I wasn't terrified of you." He grimaced. "Which wasn't very often. Most people are frightened of you, Zander." He nodded toward the door of the sitting room. "Even Catherine. I think she fights it every moment, but the fear is there. She just doesn't let it stop her from trying to manipulate you. It's quite fascinating." He paused, then asked the question that he'd wanted to ask for days. "Was **she** frightened of you, Zander?"

Zander didn't pretend not to understand. "Eve? No, she wasn't afraid. She wasn't afraid of me or Doane or anyone in the whole damn world. We sat together in front of that campfire for hours, and there was wariness but no fear. And she's not afraid now. No matter what he's done to her, she wouldn't let fear enter into it." He stopped, thinking about it. "I've always used fear as just another weapon, but lately I've not— it's a weapon that isolates and she wouldn't let me be isolated."

"A very special person?"

"You're acting as her advocate again, Stang."

"Yes. As you wish me to do." He tilted his head. "But I'm not sure it's necessary any longer. Is it?"

"You'll have to decide that for yourself." He turned away from the window. "You seem to be doing a lot of that lately."

"May I ask a question?"

"Why not?"

"What are we doing in this hotel room when you're restless, foul-tempered, and obviously wanting to strike out?"

"That's what Catherine asked. However, without the personal insults."

"Did she get an answer?"

"Not really. But since you ran the risk, I'll

give one to you." He shrugged. "We're doing something I totally detest." He turned back to the window. "Waiting. We're waiting, Stang."

Wrigley Field

"There's a ball game going on. The Cubs are playing," Trevor said as he saw the people streaming into the stadium. "That may mean problems, Margaret."

"No, it's better. Crowds are always better. Buy tickets. Enjoy the game." She turned to Jane. "Look, you and Trevor meet me at the car in the parking lot in two hours." She grinned. "Or if you hear a ruckus, you come running and keep them from throwing me into jail. Okay?"

"What?" Jane was frowning. "No, it's not okay. I'm going with you." She looked at the huge clock on the scoreboard. "Though how the hell are we supposed to get inside?"

"I'm going to look for the maintenance man and have him take me. Did you think I was going to climb it and break in?"

"Maybe," Trevor said. "I wouldn't put it past you."

"Forget it," Margaret said. "It's easier to rely on persuasion than force." She turned to Jane. "And it will also be easier for me if you aren't with me. You're beautiful. You attract attention. I need to lull, not stir."

"How will you get maintenance to let you up there?" Trevor asked.

"Most people can be handled. I'll make up a story. I'm good at that."

"I'm sure you are," he murmured.

"So take her away." Margaret waved a hand at the ticket booths. "And buy her a hot dog. She didn't eat much breakfast." She started to turn away. "I'll see you in two hours."

"Margaret, dammit," Jane said in frustration. "Let me go."

"No, this is my job," Margaret said quietly. "It's what I do. You'd be in the way." She moved quickly away and slipped into the crowd. She didn't look back. She knew what she would see. Jane worried and frustrated and Trevor, a rock, guarding her from every danger. What would it be like to have someone care that much about you, she wondered. She would probably never know. It was the Janes of the world who attracted love and romance and all that other stuff. They were like lightning rods.

Margaret chuckled. But she attracted a few lightning bolts of her own every now and then. But her strikes were confined to dogs and wolves and sundry other creatures. And now she had to explore the minds of the wild rats running around this stadium.

She sighed as she moved toward the tall security guard standing near the refreshment stand to ask where she could find the maintenance chief. She was not looking forward to dealing with rats. She would have preferred a dog or a cat, but you had to take what was available in the animal world. There might be a feral cat, but a rat was far more likely.

Worry about that later. Now her main concern was getting into that scoreboard clock. Take the first step and go from there. And the first step was this security guard, who was smiling politely at her. Change that politeness to sympathy or empathy.

"Hi." She beamed at the security guard, carefully noting his name on his badge. "I

wonder if you could help me, Officer War-
ren? I'm Margaret Simpson, and my daddy
is head of maintenance at Busch Stadium
in St. Louis. Well, actually, he was head of
it, but he was laid off a few weeks ago. I
thought I'd talk to the maintenance head
here and get an application for him to fill
out. Daddy's always been so impressed
with what a great team you all have up here
in Chicago." She gazed up at him plead-
ingly. "Do you suppose that would be possible, sir?"

"You can't stay here very long," Tom Foster,
the maintenance engineer, said testily as
he frowned at Margaret. "I don't know why
I let you talk me into bringing you up here.
I'm a busy man, and I don't have time for
this."

"You brought me here because you're a
kind man, and you know that we all have
to help each other," she said quietly. "I can't
tell you how grateful my daddy will be that
you took your valuable time and gave me
that application. Even if you all can't find it
in your heart to give him a job, I'll tell him
how nice you were to me. He's always
wanted to see the workings behind this

scoreboard. Wrigley is a part of history."
She held up her iPhone. "I'll just take a few
pictures and make a few notes to take home
to him. Will that be okay, Mr. Foster?"

"I guess it will have to be," he said sourly.
"We're up here now."

"Don't let me get in your way. I'm sure
you have things you have to check," Margaret said as she curled up on the floor
beside a huge metal support beam. The
area was cramped in this old, iconic scoreboard. "I'll just stay here and make my
notes."

He gazed at her uncertainly, then muttered something beneath his breath as he
turned and walked away.

She'd probably have fifteen or twenty
minutes tops, she thought. Foster impressed her as being hardworking and
conscientious, and he wouldn't waste the
opportunity to accomplish his work now
that he was here. He'd been hard to convince to bring her up to the scoreboard
clock, but he'd finally relented.

She closed her eyes, shutting out the
sounds of the crowd and the announcer,
the clicks of the scoreboard . . .

Open your mind.

Life. There was always so much life sur-rounding you if you let it into your con-sciousness.

Pigeons. Lots of pigeons.

Nothing there.

A feral cat. Maybe . . .

No, he was young and more accustomed to haunting the downtown restaurants than the stadium. A visitor, not a regular.

A raccoon? Unusual.

She spent five minutes on him before she gave up. Intense but not a decent mem-ory.

Okay, the rats.

And she didn't have much time. She'd have to throw open her mind and do a gen-eral scan. Not pleasant. With rats, it was like having your brain devoured.

She drew a deep breath and tried to ar-mor herself.

Then she opened her mind.

And was swept away by impressions.

Darkness.

Hunger.

Yellow teeth gnawing, biting. Some short, some long. Try to isolate the rats with the long teeth. They would be the oldest. Rat's teeth continued to grow until the day they died.

Savage, hunting, scavenging.

Where?

Dark hallways, a hole near the scoreboard. Across the field and behind the kitchens of the refreshment stands.

Where else?

By the river, plastic, death. But not any longer.

Why?

Doesn't matter. Only the cold. Only the cold . . .

Running.

Clock.

Wires. Eat the wires.

Run.

Eat.

Eat . . .

"You're pale," Trevor said as Margaret strolled across the parking lot toward their rental car. "Something go wrong?"

"Nah, I guess I'm a little tired." Margaret jumped into the backseat. "Was it a good game? Did the Cubs win?"

"We wouldn't know," Jane said. "Do you

really think that we'd be able to concentrate on a ball game? Not likely, Margaret."

"Did Caleb call? Anything on Harriet?"

"She went back to the hotel after she left the bank. No other calls or visitors," Trevor said as he started the car. "And why are you asking questions instead of answering them?"

"I'm trying to get my head together." She shrugged. "I'm a little . . . scattered. I feel . . ." She tried to find the right word. "Chewed."

"Pleasant," Trevor said.

"No, it wasn't. Believe me, it wasn't." She was silent a moment. "But it was productive. At least, I think it was." She added. "The nuke is not in that field scoreboard and clock or anywhere around it. I didn't think it could be when I saw the interior, but there's always a possibility. But the rats know that scoreboard and surrounding areas inside and out, and they're not familiar with anyplace that could house a device."

Trevor's brows lifted. "They told you so?"

"Trevor," Jane said. "She's having enough trouble with this."

Margaret smiled. "Thanks. I don't like rats

much. I have a hard time dealing with them. They . . . drain me."

"And it was all for nothing?"

"I didn't say that. I said the nuke wasn't at Wrigley Field." She paused. "But there's a good chance it might be at the other clock tower."

Jane stiffened. "What?"

"There are a couple of the older rats that evidently commute back and forth between the baseball field and the other clock tower. The pickings are richer here during the summer and fall. But when the stadium closes up, and it gets cold, the office complex is the place of choice for the winter."

"So?"

"There's a death memory in the lower level, near the river. Several rats were killed when they tried to gnaw through the wires surrounding a box that had been slid into a cavity in the walls."

"How long ago?"

She shook her head. "I only get impressions. It's lucky there's a memory at all. But rats don't necessarily always learn from their mistakes. Those old rats keep going back when they're hungry. There's plastic that they gnaw at . . . and some kind of circular-tube-type gadget."

"If they ate the wires, maybe they actually disconnected the bomb," Jane said.

"Or if they were outside the box, maybe the wires were meant to be an alarm system," Trevor said. "That seems more likely. Kevin would have wanted to protect his treasure. Could you tell what else was in the room, Margaret?"

"No." She thought about it. "But the circular tube had a WR—and the rest has been eaten. The only reason that made any impression on them was that it was on the wall."

"They're into wall art?" Trevor asked.

Margaret gave him a disgusted glance. "No, haven't you noticed that you seldom see a rat in the middle of the room? That's because they have terrible vision, and they feel uneasy unless they can hug the wall."

"It never occurred to me," Jane said. "But the nuke device is tucked away in the wall, and, therefore, it's rat fodder?"

"It's possible. I guess it could be some other box that's been hidden there," Margaret said. "But no one goes to that room.

It's deserted whenever the rats decide to raid."

"Then it's worth a shot," Trevor murmured. "Let's get back to the hotel and get a schematic of the Wrigley building and see if we can figure out where that room is located." He smiled at Margaret. "Of course, we could send you back and have the rat third degree continue."

"No, you couldn't," Margaret said flatly. "I'm done. It's up to you now." She leaned back on the seat. "Take me back to the hotel. I need a hot shower and a long nap." She closed her eyes. "Then I'll be fine. Too many rats . . . I just have to get away from them . . ."

"Here's the Wrigley floor plan." Caleb turned his iPad around on the room-service table. "It's a damn big building."

"We only want the lower floors." Margaret was scanning the floor plan. "And probably an area that's not usually frequented. Kevin wouldn't have wanted to risk stashing the device somewhere that it would have been easily discovered."

"And how do we find a room where no one would generally go?" Jane grimaced.

"Particularly in a high-rental place like that building. It's not reasonable that any space would be wasted."

"And we could spend all evening going over this map and still not be sure." Trevor was gazing down at the computer. "But there's one way we'd know for sure." He jabbed his finger at a cubicle on the plan. "Security."

"What?" Jane frowned. "Security's not even on the lower level."

"No, but their motion cameras are focused down there. They'd be all over the building." Caleb nodded. "And if we could get our hands on a set of the security tapes, we'd be able to run them and find the type of area that we're looking for. If there's no motion activity, then there's a good chance that we're close."

"And how are we to do that?" Jane asked.

Caleb exchanged glances with Trevor. "Distraction, then a discreet snatch. I can provide the distraction. In fact, such a good distraction that they won't even suspect that you were the one who made off with the tapes."

"So I'm the one who runs the risk of the snatch," Trevor said dryly. "And I have to rely on you to make sure that I don't get arrested."

"No," Jane said. "We'll think of something else, Trevor."

"No, it's a good plan." He smiled at Caleb. "He knew that's where I was headed when I mentioned security. And I even trust him to make an excellent distraction. It would be too obvious for him to do anything else."

"What kind of distraction?" Jane asked warily.

"One of the security guards will start worrying about the possibility that he's having a heart attack." Caleb held up his hand. "Not pain, I promise. Just a rapid beat. It will end when he's on his way up to the medical center. The other guard will probably stay with him until he's at the facility. If he's not, I'll have to think of something else." Caleb turned to Trevor. "I lure the guard away, and you get the tapes. And there would be no immediate discovery of anything wrong. You don't have to access anything recent. You can go back to past-date files and get a day that's already been filed away. That would be fine for our purpose."

"I don't like it," Jane said flatly.

"You'd like it less if Harriet flew the coop, and we didn't know where that nuke was located," Trevor said. "We may have to move fast, and knowledge is power."

He was right, Jane thought reluctantly. Harriet was on the move now, and all she was waiting for was Doane to tell her that he had Zander. Time was the enemy.

And time was running out.

Running out for Eve and for all those other innocent people whose lives would be taken if they took a wrong step.

The enormity of that responsibility was suddenly there before Jane.

Dear God, what right did they have to make that choice?

She felt the muscles of her stomach clench. They had been sitting here making plans, ignoring the fact that the situation had changed. Ignoring the fact that they had no idea what Harriet had given to Cartland when she went into the bank. They were working blind, and if there was any possibility that she'd shared information with him about the location of the detonator, it could change everything. She looked at Margaret. "We can't even be sure that nuke is in that building, can we? It's all guesswork."

Margaret nodded. "I never said anything else. I could be wrong."

And the consequences of guessing wrong were catastrophic. Jane had been struggling desperately to try to fight the battle alone for Eve's sake. Now she knew she couldn't take a chance even though it was tearing her apart. God, she felt sick. "We have to bring Venable into it. We don't have the right to do anything else."

Trevor reached over and covered her hand on the table. "I was wondering when you'd make that decision," he said quietly. "I could see it coming."

"I couldn't," she said. "Even Catherine doesn't trust Venable to put Eve first." She moistened her lips. "But Eve wouldn't want us to run that kind of massive risk for her sake. We have to tell Venable what we've found out about Harriet." Her hand clenched around Trevor's. "**Damn,** I don't want to do it."

"So we don't go after the security tapes?" Caleb asked.

Jane tried to think. "If we call Venable now, and he sends in a team to locate that nuke, then it could ruin any chance of our being able to track Harriet. If she hears about it, she might panic, and that's the last thing we want."

"We could verify it's there," Caleb suggested. "It will only take a couple hours to get those tapes. Then we could use the location as a bargaining chip with Venable to try to control his actions."

"He's not easily controlled," Jane said. But any way to force Venable to listen to their suggestions to use caution would be valuable. "Okay, we'll get the tapes, go through them, then call Venable." She looked at Trevor. "And I'll go with you to get them."

Both men instantly shook their heads.

"I'm tired of this. Don't tell me no," Jane said. "I won't stay here and send you out to do my job. That's happened too often." She gazed at Trevor. "I'm not going to get in the way. I won't step in unless I see that you're in trouble." She made a face. "You keep saying that it's your job to act as some kind of guardian for me. I don't agree with you. But if that's what you believe, then it should go two ways."

He shook his head.

"Yes," she said firmly. "I'll be your getaway driver or something. I'm going to be with you, Trevor."

He sighed, then slowly nodded. He glanced at the two machines on the table across the room. "Someone has to monitor those machines."

"Margaret can do that," Jane said. "And the only thing we've heard from Harriet this evening was her ordering room service." She looked at Margaret. "Will you do it?"

"Of course," Margaret said. "Though being a getaway driver would probably be much more interesting. On the other hand, I've no desire to chance running into any rats. I've had enough of them for today. Besides, I need to call Kendra. She needs to work on figuring out where Kevin and Harriet would have hidden the detonator and what kind of code would set it off. Not that she doesn't have enough to do. When do you leave?"

"It's seven now," Trevor said. "Another hour." He got to his feet and held out his hand to Jane. "Let's go to our room. I want to be with you."

He was not smiling. His expression was curiously grave.

"Trevor?"

Then he smiled. "Stop worrying. I just realized that I'm not going to be able to have my way with you all the time. I don't like that bit about taking care sometimes going two ways. I want it all."

"Tough." She slipped her hand into his grasp as she rose to her feet. She wanted to be alone with him, too. She wanted to hold him. She felt heavy and sad and desperately worried that she was making a terrible mistake that could be fatal for Eve.

And that moment of gravity of Trevor's had shaken her a little. She'd had the strange feeling that there was something . . . frightening beneath that flip answer. "But we have an hour for me to show you the error of your thinking." She didn't look at either Margaret or Caleb as she and Trevor headed for the door. "Call us if there's anything we should know, Margaret."

"Oh, we will," Caleb said. "Count on it."

10:05 P.M.

"It's about time you called me, Cartland," Harriet said curtly. "You said it would only take five or six hours to find MacGuire. I've been waiting and I—"

"Be quiet, Harriet," Cartland said. "I'm not talking to you until you come down to the lobby, and we're face-to-face."

She stiffened. "What do you mean? Are you giving me orders?"

"I'm trying to keep you from making a fool of yourself," he said roughly. "But it's probably too late. Meet me downstairs in the lobby in ten minutes, and we'll take a walk."

"The hell we will. I really would be a fool to go anywhere with you."

"Meet me in the lobby," he repeated.

"Why are you—"

But Cartland had hung up.

Harriet felt a mixture of impatience, anger, and panic as she hung up the phone.

How dare he call her a fool? Kevin was right to have broken with Cartland.

She drew a deep breath.

Think, don't feel. That's what she'd always told Kevin.

Calm down.

In spite of her precautions, Cartland could be trying to lure her out of the hotel to be taken by his men. They wouldn't like the idea of a woman's being in control of the operation.

Or it could be something else.

I won't talk to you until we're face-to-face.

She looked down at her phone.

Had she been the fool Cartland had called her?

It could be either one.

She had to know.

She got to her feet and grabbed her handbag. Leave the detonator in the suite or take it with her? If she left it, Cartland's men might break in and steal it. She would rather trust herself to protect it. She checked her gun, then put it in her handbag beside the detonator.

Now she was prepared to face the bastard and any tricks he might be planning.

She almost hoped Cartland was trying to pull a fast one.

The alternative was humiliating and unacceptable.

CHAPTER

15

Cartland was standing a few yards away when the elevator door slid open. His expression was grim.

"I'm here," she said coldly. "But I'm not going anywhere with you." She nodded at the bar across the lobby. "If you want to talk, we'll talk there."

"No. It's not safe." He took her arm. "Just walk with me around the lobby. Slowly. It's not going to take long, then I'm out of here."

"Take your hand off me."

He dropped his hand. "I'd like to break your neck," he said through his teeth. "I wouldn't even be here if I had my way. But

I talked to Tehran, and they're over the moon about the prospect of having the project reinstated. I wouldn't be forgiven if I had to tell them we'd failed again."

She stiffened. "So you're going to try to take the detonator from me. I won't let—"

"No, I'm trying to clear the path for you to make it happen. If it's still possible. If Jane MacGuire hasn't blown everything that we're trying to do."

"Jane MacGuire," Harriet repeated. "What's she got to—" She inhaled sharply. "Did you find her?"

"As I told you, no problem. Her phone wasn't protected, and Samli had her location within four hours."

"Good." Her gaze narrowed on his face. "Then did you have someone—Is that why you didn't call me sooner? Did you take care of her?"

"No, it would have taken longer to make a safe kill even if we hadn't discovered problems."

"Problems?"

"Do you know where Samli first located her?"

"I'm sure you're going to tell me."

"She was at a baseball game at Wrigley Field this afternoon."

Shock. "No, your Samli made a mistake."

"He doesn't make mistakes like that."

"You're saying she's here in Chicago."

"Samli was concerned, too, since I told him that she was probably in Atlanta or Muncie. So he called me and asked for instructions. I told him to stay with the signal. Do you know to where he followed it?" He gazed at the bank of elevators. "She's in a room on the floor above you. The room isn't registered in her name. She's staying with a Mark Trevor. CIA?"

Shock after shock. "I don't know. I've never heard of him. He could be, I guess."

"Or maybe not. One bed. They're evidently sleeping together."

"I told you, I don't know. I've never heard of him."

"And what the hell was she doing at that baseball game?"

Harriet was afraid that she knew. Wrigley Stadium. Five years ago, Harriet had considered that clock, then told Kevin it wasn't right.

The clock.

That bitch had the journal and was beginning to figure out the code of the game Harriet and Kevin had played. Panic and rage tore through her. "How do I know?" She tried to keep her voice from trembling. "Maybe she was meeting someone there."

"Maybe. And if she was at your hotel, you can bet that they've wired your place."

"Yes." It wasn't a sure thing but definitely a possibility. She tried to think back at everything she'd said to Doane. Incriminating. Terribly incriminating. But no information that could prevent them from going forward if care was taken. And screw that those calls were incriminating. If you weren't caught, there couldn't be any accusations or evidence, could there? Just change her tickets and transfer the line of credit. Disappear in entirely another direction.

God, but Cartland was right, she'd been a careless fool. And Jane MacGuire was close to taking her down.

No! She would not have it. She'd still have it all.

But she had to control the situation, control Cartland and control the way James was handling the disposal of Zander.

Cartland, first.

"So what are you going to do?" She gave

him a cool glance. "You said that Tehran still wants you to go forward. Does that mean that you'll still give me your cooperation?"

"You mean more money," Cartland said. He was silent a moment. "It's possible. If you can convince me that you can pull this disaster out of the fire. I've checked all my sources with the FBI and CIA, and there's no word on any surveillance of you or this hotel. MacGuire's phone wasn't protected, and that probably means she's not linked directly to the CIA. You said you were even sure she wasn't CIA."

"It's not quite a disaster." She added grudgingly, "Though I obviously underestimated MacGuire. However, she's obviously still floundering if she hasn't contacted Venable to close in for the kill. She can't know I've retrieved the detonator. I told James that wasn't going to happen. She's only an artist, and I told you that she had a personal vendetta going. She's an amateur, and we can run rings around her. We just have to move very fast." Her thoughtful gaze rose to the crystal chandelier casting a glittering ambience over the lobby. "I need to be out of here tonight and on my way to Seattle. Arrange it. A private jet." Her gaze shifted to his face. "And if you decide that you're going to take me to an undisclosed location for questioning, I'll blow the plane out of the sky. Not only that, but I'll set off the nukes without giving you warning or time to get out of the city. You and the other members of your group will become martyrs. You don't impress me as the type of terrorist who is eager for paradise."

"You're bluffing. You wouldn't sacrifice yourself."

"Yes, I would. I've waited for five years to get revenge for Kevin's death." She met his gaze. "And life isn't the same without my son. I won't let anything get in the way."

"And what do you intend to do once you're in Seattle?"

"What I meant to do in the beginning. Just a day earlier. Zander will die, and I'll type in the code," she said. "I'll give you an hour's notice to get out of the city. But I wouldn't wait if I were you. Kevin and I were never sure how powerful the blast would be. Get out the minute you put me on that jet." She wasn't sure he was convinced. "In eight hours at the latest it will happen. If I move fast, no one can stop me. No one can stop you. You'll be a hero to al-Qaeda.

Don't back away because of a little mistake that I can fix."

He stared at her for a moment, then shrugged. "I'll have a car for you within the hour to take you to the airport. It will take me that long to arrange a charter. Anything else?"

"A phone. I can't chance using mine in case it's been bugged."

He smiled. "I thought of that." He reached into his pocket and handed her a pay-by-the-minute phone. "This should do."

"Not quite." She handed it back to him. "I want your phone. I won't chance your giving me a phone you've bugged either."

He frowned, then handed her his phone. "It's an inconvenience."

"It's an insurance policy." She glanced around the lobby. Hell, she didn't know if she was being watched or not. It had to be safer than her hotel room. "Wait here." She dialed the phone as she strode over to the huge glass windows.

"This is Harriet. I've been waiting to hear from you, James," she said, when her ex-husband answered. "But now I'm not waiting any longer. Everything is falling apart.

I'm going to get on a plane and come to you. Do you have Zander?"

"Not yet. But I know he's in the city. I can—"

"I don't care what you know. I want Zander dead. It's time you made it happen. I don't give a damn about Eve Duncan. She's in the way. Kill her, then go after Zander."

"No, I've planned it all. I won't give it up because you're impatient."

"You fool. Listen to me. You let that journal be taken from you, and now Jane Mac-Guire and Venable and God knows who else are getting close to those nukes. If we don't act soon, we'll have to drop everything and go on the run. Then Zander will live, and I won't have that happen." Her voice hardened. "Get Zander. I don't care how you do it, but you have him by the time I get out there, or you'll ruin everything." She paused. "And Kevin would never forgive you. He never tolerated failure. You remember that, James."

"I never failed him."

"Then don't do it now. This is your last chance. Either do it your way, or step aside and let me go after Zander myself. Kevin would rather I do it anyway. He always knew he could trust me."

"Trust you? He only played with you, the way he played with those little girls. I'm the one who—" He broke off, and she could tell he was struggling with rage. "I'll have Zander by the time you get here. I told you I was close. Not because you want it, but because Kevin would hate to have you spoil everything I've planned."

"I'll call you when I get off the plane, and you can give me directions how to get to that cottage." She paused. "And tell me that you have Zander staked out and ready for the kill." She hung up.

She felt an instant of fierce satisfaction. If anything would move James, it would be the words she'd thrown at him. He always had a tendency to be too careful and stick to his precious plans, but she'd always been able to manipulate him and guide him the way she wanted him to go.

Now she'd had to crack the whip and make sure that he brought Zander under the gun.

We'll have you, Zander. Another few hours, and you'll be a dead man.

She turned on her heel and strode back toward Cartland.

"You look . . . satisfied," he said, his gaze on her face. "Maybe even triumphant. I hope that means something positive."

"I am satisfied." She headed for the elevator. "Where is Jane MacGuire now?"

He shrugged. "She left the hotel a few hours ago. Do you want me to check?"

"No." Harriet had no desire to have him trace the MacGuire woman's steps if they were leading anywhere near that nuke. Harriet had to remain in control. "It's not important now."

He lowered his voice. "I promised you I'd take care of her. Do you still want me to do it?"

Did she want that bitch dead? Oh, yes, with her whole heart. But not by anyone's hand but her own. She no longer wanted just to get rid of an inconvenience. Jane MacGuire had humiliated her and endangered her plans, and that had filled her with rage. Harriet wanted to pull the trigger, to see her die. "As I said, it's not important. You've told me what I needed to know about her. I'll take care of it." She punched the button for the elevator. "Just get me out of the city. I'm going upstairs to pack. Call me when you're ready to send the car."

Driftwood Cottage

"You didn't go outside to take that call, Doane," Eve said. "Were you caught by surprise?" She studied his face. "Yes, I believe that's probably it. Who is Harriet?"

"A bitch like you," he said through his teeth. "No, maybe worse than you. She thinks that she can tell me what to do. If I do what she wants, it's because I choose, and Kevin wants it. It has nothing to do with her."

"Who is Harriet?" Her gaze narrowed on his face, trying to put it together. "Kevin . . ." Then it came to her. "Kevin's mother?"

"A bitch. She thinks she rules the world." The words were spitting out. "She thinks that she was the only one Kevin loved. He didn't care for her. He only used her."

"It appears he only used everyone."

"Well, I'm going to be done with the bitch and done with you." He turned on his heel and went to the chest across the room.

"She didn't need to tell me to get Zander. He's already in my sights." He opened the top drawer. "I was going after him tonight anyway."

She stiffened. "You know where he is?"

"Why, where would a father be when his daughter is in trouble?" he asked mockingly. "It seems Zander wasn't fooled by that explosion in Colorado. He's here in town and asking questions about me."

"About you, not me."

"If he knows about me, then he knows that you're also alive." He shrugged. "And that could mean that Quinn and Jane Mac-Guire may have staged a very elaborate distraction while they hunted me down. Not that it matters now. It will all be over tonight." He took a large pistol out of the drawer and put it on the table. "And I'll be done with Zander and you." He added, "And maybe that other bitch, too."

"You're going to shoot him?" Her gaze was on the pistol.

"Eventually. Right now, I'm going hunting." He stroked the butt of the gun. "This was Kevin's tranquilizer gun. He used it occasionally when he did his own hunting. One shot, and they would be out."

She felt a chill. "Who would be . . . out?"

"Why not come and see." He yanked her to her feet and pushed her toward the front door. "Harriet said that Kevin and I had nothing in common, but he never shared this with her." He threw open the door and she felt a blast of cool air as he pulled her out on the porch. He gestured to the shimmering white driftwood. "You said it looked like a graveyard. That's how Kevin wanted it to look. It was his own little joke. He searched the entire coastline to find just the right-shaped driftwood." He whispered. "Why do you think that he did that, Eve?"

She was afraid she knew. "How many, Doane?" she asked hoarsely.

"Only two little girls. He took one from a suburb in Seattle and the other from a little town in Oregon. He was under pressure when he was here and needed release, but he didn't want to attract too much attention." He nodded at the driftwood closest to the house. "One is buried there if I remember correctly. The other I'm not sure . . ."

"Why bury them practically on his own doorstep?" she asked. "He must have been even more mad than I thought."

"He liked the idea of having them near

him. And the fact that no one knew what lay beneath that pile of driftwood amused him."

"His little joke," she repeated. She felt sick. A joke. And two little girls who had once been loved and cherished had died and never been brought home.

"We can go inside now," he said softly, his gaze on her face. "That's how I wanted you to look. You were too hard, too tough, like her. But I can hurt you if I go about it the right way."

He pushed her back into the cottage. "And I can hurt her. I just have to wait until all this is over." He pushed her down into the chair and began to bind her. "You'll be good when I'm gone, won't you? Just sit there and anticipate seeing your father. I may even let you have some time together before I kill you. He should appreciate what he's losing."

"He won't care if I live or die. How many times do I have to tell you that? We're strangers."

"Blood means everything. He killed my son. Blood for blood." He turned and picked up the tranquilizer gun. "And who knows? I may bury you both beneath that driftwood outside." He smiled as he headed for the door. "Kevin would like that . . ."

"I think you'd better come back to the hotel, Jane," Margaret said as soon as Jane picked up the phone. "Forget about those security tapes. Something strange is going on."

"We've already got the tapes. It didn't take us that long. We're already on our way back. What are you talking about?"

"I was monitoring those machines, and Cartland called Harriet. He wouldn't talk to her on the phone. She went down to the lobby to talk to him."

"What? Did she leave the hotel?"

"No, that was what I was afraid would happen. I followed her down to the lobby. She talked to Cartland, then made a phone call and went back to her room."

"Could you get close enough to hear the conversation?"

"No way. They were being supercareful." She paused. "And when Cartland called her, he didn't want her to talk on the phone. Does that suggest anything?"

"That Cartland might be afraid that her phone has been bugged," Jane said. "**Shit.**"

She turned to Trevor. "She may be on the run. She could take off at any time."

"But not yet." He stepped on the accelerator. "We should be back at the hotel in ten minutes."

Seattle

Catherine silently opened the door.

The sitting room was dark.

There was no sound.

But she knew Zander was in that room.

And Zander knew she was standing there.

"Really, Catherine, you're making me feel harassed," he said. "Though you're very good. I didn't even hear the door open."

"You're ready to make a move, aren't you?" she asked. "I've been **feeling** it all day. And you didn't want me to follow you. That means you found out something from that contact Slater you talked to last night. You know where Doane is."

"No, I have no idea . . . yet."

"But you **are** ready to move." Catherine turned toward the corner from where his voice was coming, but she couldn't make him out in the darkness. "You know something. I'm coming with you, Zander."

"You're not invited."

"Too bad." She glided forward. "Now let's stop playing hide-and-seek. Turn on the lights."

"But you have such a delightful voice coming out of the darkness. Very soft, very mysterious."

"If you don't take me with you, I'll follow you."

"I know you will." His tone was regretful. "And I can't allow you to do that."

His voice was issuing from about a foot right of the corner of the room, she judged.

"You won't kill me. Why should you? I'm on your side, on Eve's side."

"No one is on my side but me. I learned that a long time ago. And you would get in my way, Catherine. That could be a great danger."

She could feel her heart pounding. "Okay, but I'm on Eve's side. That means something to you."

"Does it?"

"Yes. That man Slater told you something. What?"

"Would I lie to you?"

"Yes."

He chuckled. "True, but in this case I'm not lying." He added, "And why are you trying to move closer to me? That's really not wise, Catherine."

"I want you to be able to see me, touch me. I want you to remember who I am, all our conversations. I believe it's much harder to strike down an antagonist you know."

"Not for me."

"Even you, Zander." She paused. "You were waiting for me, weren't you? Cat and mouse?"

"You're much more like a sleek, beautiful panther than a mouse. But yes, I was waiting for you. Since you're my bodyguard, I thought I should tell you something."

"I can hardly wait to know what. You haven't told me anything since I've been with you."

"Don't be sarcastic. Pay attention. Judging by your information from Jane MacGuire, once I'm taken, I figure that I'll probably have from five to eight hours before Harriet Weber shows up to witness my execution. After she shows up, I think that

Eve's survival will be very dicey. In case something goes wrong with my calculations, it might be wise if you find that driftwood cottage. Purely as a backup, you understand."

Shock jolted through her. "What the hell are you saying?"

"I've always intimidated Slater. He probably did know where to reach Doane, but he would never deal with me. But he'd put out the word that I was in town and where I could be found . . . for a price. By this time, Doane should have set up his ambush. I'd bet he's outside now waiting for me to appear."

"And you're going to walk into it?" she asked in disbelief. "No, that's a sure way to lose both Eve and you, dammit. I won't let you do—"

"I told you, I'm the one in control, Catherine."

"Not of Eve. You can commit suicide, but I won't let you take Eve with you." She gathered herself to leap. He'd be expecting it, but if she did a half—

"Find that cottage, Catherine. Just as a precaution . . ."

His voice was no longer coming from

the corner, she realized in panic just a second before the edge of his hand came down
on the back of her neck in a karate chop.
He was behind her.

How the hell . . . The bastard had been
throwing his voice and been behind her all
the time . . .

Darkness.

A cold, wet cloth on the back of her neck . . .

She slowly opened her eyes.

"You're going to be okay, Catherine."
Stang's voice was relieved. "I didn't think
that Zander would—But then I'm never
sure what he's going to do."

Anger shot through her as she struggled
to sit up. She threw the wet cloth on the
floor. "Neither do I, evidently." She glared at
him. "Did you know he'd set himself up?"

"No, he doesn't confide in me." Stang
took the wet cloth and put it on the coffee
table. "But I admit I suspected . . . something."

"How long have I been out?"

"About fifteen minutes. Zander phoned
me and told me to go into the sitting room,
then hung up." He made a face. "Considering what a bad temper Zander has been

in for most of the day, I was a little concerned when I saw you lying on the floor."

Fifteen minutes. There was no way that she would be able either to catch up or stop Zander. "I can see how you might be. I was an idiot." She rubbed the back of her neck. "I acted like a crass amateur. I wasn't expecting magician's tricks." She said in disgust, "He threw his voice, for God's sake. Did you know he could do that?"

"No, but it doesn't surprise me. He's an expert, and it would come in handy in his profession. Zander always takes time and effort to study ways to keep himself alive."

"Like walking into the lion's den?" she said. "That's a weird way to stay alive. Like risking Eve?" Her lips tightened. "He even gave me an estimate on the number of hours Doane would allow him to live if he couldn't manage to get away from him. Five to eight. That's all the time he would have, that Eve would have." She whispered, "Five to eight hours. How's that for a deadline."

Stang tilted his head. "Why would he tell you that? That doesn't sound like Zander."

"Just as a precaution, he said. He told me to find that driftwood cottage as backup."

Her hands clenched into fists. "He probably doesn't believe Kevin's cottage even exists. But he saddles me with setting up backup in case he screws up and Doane kills him. Or maybe he just wanted to keep me busy so that I wouldn't chase after him."

"Precaution," Stang repeated thoughtfully. "I've never known Zander to rely on anyone else for backup. He'd regard it as a mistake to trust anyone but himself." He smiled slightly. "You're to be complimented, Catherine."

"I don't give a damn about compliments. I care about Eve." She pulled out her phone and dialed Gallo. "Zander's gone. I think he's letting himself be taken by Doane. Or maybe not. What the hell do I know what the bastard will do? He's put Eve in a spot, and I—" She drew a deep breath. "We have to find that cottage, Gallo."

"Are you okay? You sound a little shaky."

"I have a sore neck from a karate chop, and I'm angry and scared that Zander has set off a chain of events that we won't be able to stop."

"Karate chop?" Gallo echoed. "Zander? I believe that I need to—"

"Stop it, Gallo. That's not important. Where are you and Joe? I'm at the Appleton Arms. I'll pack and come to you."

"No, we'll come to you. What room?"

"Two-forty."

"Stay where you are. Is anyone with you?"

"Stang."

"That's no protection. He's in Zander's pocket. We'll be right there."

"I don't need your protection," she said testily. "Though I was a fool about—"

Gallo had hung up.

Stang smiled. "I take it that Gallo doesn't accept me as a suitable guardian for you. Very perceptive. Now, if the roles were reversed . . ."

"You're employed by Zander. You have a certain loyalty to him." She dropped down in a chair. "You could be as tough as Rambo, and Gallo would still not trust you."

"Rambo. Rather dated but descriptive." He grinned. "And no one would recognize me with a machete between my teeth. I never wanted to be anything but what I am. An accountant with a talent for the stock market." He studied her. "Could I get you a glass of water, a cup of coffee? You still don't look so hot."

"I'm fine. I'm just angry with myself."

"I'll get you the water anyway." He disappeared into the bathroom and came out with a glass of water. "You shouldn't be upset." He handed her the glass. "It was a lost cause to begin with. Zander is a law unto himself."

"Bullshit." She took a sip of water. "He's a law until someone stops him. It will happen someday. It's only a matter of time." She met his eyes. "And then you'll be looking for another job."

"Yes."

"Would it be a relief? I've watched you with Zander, and I can't figure out your relationship. You're on edge with him, and yet . . ." She shrugged. "You'd be much more comfortable if you didn't have to deal with him."

"Without doubt. But he does make life interesting. Now, I'm not one to embrace challenges, but I got used to walking the tightrope." He added softly, "And you do love challenges, and being with Zander gave you a jolt of adrenaline, didn't it?"

"I don't need any jolts of adrenaline."

He gazed at her quizzically.

"All right, I admit that he's . . . unique."

She added, "But if you don't like challenges, why did you come to work for him?"

"It seemed the thing to do at the time."

"You're evading answering. Money?"

"No, money was never a problem for me. The stock market is usually my friend. Are you sure you don't want a cup of coffee?"

"No, I don't. I want you to answer me."

"Why are you so curious?"

"I'm not curious, I'm on the hunt," she said curtly. "Zander took me down, but he left me with you. You're all I've got right now. I may be able to use you in some way to get my own back and find Zander." She shook her head in despair. "If Doane doesn't already have him."

"The chances are Doane does have him. Because that's the way Zander wanted it." He added gently, "And that may not be as bad as you're thinking. Zander always has a plan."

"And will that plan include Eve? **Talk** to me. Help me. Tell me everything you know about Zander. I tried to convince myself that he wanted her to live, but how can I be sure, dammit?"

"You can't be sure." He was silent a moment, his gaze on her face before he finally said, "You want to know why I came to work for Zander? Didn't Venable tell you anything about me? I'm surprised he didn't share. I'm sure he dug deep and hard about everyone surrounding Zander to find something he could use to manipulate him." He grimaced. "But no one really regards me as being important in that area. No influence. I was probably just being watched to make sure I wouldn't kill Zander at an inconvenient time."

"**Kill** him?"

"My parents and my brother, Sean, ran a medical missionary in Africa. Good people. I loved them, but I didn't understand them. They didn't care about money or possessions and were perfectly satisfied working at that mission. On the other hand, I lived in New York, and I was fascinated by the game of acquiring money. I was very good at it."

"What has this to do with Zander?"

"Patience. A terrorist group overthrew the tribal leaders in the village, and the mission and everyone connected to it were murdered. My parents were lucky. They were killed almost immediately. My brother Sean was taken prisoner and held for four days.

He was not lucky. When they finally let me see him in the hospital, he was praying to die. After I saw him, I prayed with him. He died that night."

His tone was without expression but Catherine could feel his pain. "I'm sorry."

"So was I. Sorry and angry and wanting revenge. The government had rounded up the terrorists except for their leader, Abu Karr. He was in hiding in the jungle. No one could find him. The entire country was in an uproar about the massacre, and the president and his government were about to topple. The president was very dirty and involved with the pirates who raided the sea-lanes. He knew he had to give the people Abu Karr's head to save his own. The American ambassador told Sean and me there was a rumor the president had hired Zander to go after Abu Karr and kill him."

"And he did it?"

"Abu Karr was found shot in the head outside his cave. There was some controversy about whether Zander did it or not. The president claimed one of his generals found him and fired the shot. Zander was nowhere in the vicinity. A week later, the president was assassinated. So the question was did Zander kill the terrorist, then kill the president when he refused to pay? Or was the ambassador wrong, and Zander was not involved at all?"

"And what difference did it make?" Catherine said. "The beast was dead."

"It made a difference to my brother," he said quietly. "And that made a difference to me. Before he died, Sean made me promise that if Zander managed to kill Abu Karr, I would try to keep him safe, that I would never leave him until the day he died."

"But you said you didn't know if he killed him."

"I still don't. But I had to try to find out. I had money. I told you that was easy for me. I hired ballistic experts, and they studied the shot that killed Abu Karr. It was done at an extremely difficult angle, and the shooter would have had to be a magnificent shot. I hired local private detectives, and they found people who had seen a man of his description in two of the villages that bordered the jungle. It took a long time to get the report because Zander is like a shadow figure. I bribed people in the CIA, and they confirmed that Zander was in Africa at the time. They'd even had an agent report that Zander had something to do with the uprising." He shrugged. "No proof either way, and Zander would never admit to anything. So I was left with making the decision myself."

"And you went to work for him."

"I thought the chances were good that he'd killed Abu Karr, and I had to keep my promise. I figured that I might be able to find some more concrete evidence if I worked for him. So I changed my name and applied for the job of his accountant."

"And did you find any other evidence?"

"No." He made a face. "As Venable must have told you, Zander doesn't confide in anyone, and he certainly wouldn't leave records around concerning his 'business.'"

"You fooled him all these years?"

He shook his head. "I think he found out soon after he hired me, but he never mentioned it. I'm sure that he knew that the CIA had spread rumors of a report about his possible involvement in the terrorist uprising. I believe the situation intrigued him."

"I can see how it might," Catherine said. "Twisted bastard that he is." She smiled without mirth. "I told him that I was his body-guard. There's a certain black humor about the fact that you've been acting in that capacity all these years."

"I wouldn't have presumed to tell him that's why I stayed. You have more courage than I do." He paused. "You wanted to find out if you could use me in any way to manipulate Zander. You can see that the answer has to be not if it endangers Zander in any way."

"Is that why you told me about your brother?"

"Yes, along with the fact that you're desperate and in pain and I admire you. I didn't want you to waste your time." He held up his hand as she opened her lips to speak. "But that doesn't mean that I won't help you find Eve and Zander if we can find a way that is mutually acceptable."

"Why?"

"Because I want Eve Duncan to live. And because Zander wants me to help you. He didn't phone me just to send me to make sure you were all right after he took you down. He's an expert. He'd know exactly what he did to you and how long you'd be out."

She nodded slowly. "That's true. And how does he think you can help us?"

He shook his head. "I have no idea. I believe Zander may be a little desperate himself at this point. It's strange that I should think that . . . I'll do what I can. I'm not totally—" He stopped at a knock on the door. "That's probably Quinn and Gallo. I'll go let them in."

She jumped to her feet. "No, I'll do it." She ran across the room and threw open the door.

"Where's Stang?" Joe strode into the room. "Did you question him?"

"Are you okay?" Gallo asked her quietly.

"Yes, I questioned him," Catherine said. "He doesn't know anything. Take it easy on him." She turned to Gallo. "And yes, I'm fine. I told you that, Gallo." She tried to suppress the intense physical reaction that she always had to Gallo. She hadn't seen him for weeks, and the sexual tension was strong and heated. Ignore it.

"Then if you're fine, I'll tell you that you shouldn't have lowered your guard with Zander," he said coolly. "And that you were an idiot not to tell us where you were staying."

"I wasn't an idiot. I had a chance of manipulating the situation if I could keep control of Zander."

"But you didn't keep control." Joe's eyes never left Stang. "And now Eve's probably worse off because you didn't. And how do you know Stang doesn't know anything?"

"You've dealt with me before, Quinn," Stang said. "You know that Zander doesn't confide in me. He didn't tell me a word."

"And you didn't suspect anything?"

"Of course, I did. Zander was actually edgy. I even questioned him. He said he hated to wait."

"He was waiting for word to get to Doane so that he could set up himself as bait for Doane's ambush," Catherine said. "He knew that Doane wanted to kill Eve in front of him. He also knew that Doane's wife has to be there at the execution. Zander wanted time to kill Doane and get Eve away before Harriet arrived on the scene."

"How, dammit?" Joe asked.

She shook her head. "I don't know. Stang says he always has a plan."

Gallo muttered an oath. "That doesn't help us."

"It might help Eve," Stang said quietly. "He doesn't want her to die."

"But he risks her life because he won't trust anyone but himself," Quinn said. "Arrogant son of a bitch."

"Easy, Joe," Catherine said. She knew the words were futile. He was as desperate and afraid as she was of the impetus Zander's move might start in motion. "I may agree with you, but we just have to work around Zander." She added grimly, "That's what he was saying before he left. Backup. We have to find that cottage in case Zander and his wonder plan go down the tubes." She brushed her hair away from her face. "He said we'd more than likely have between five and eight hours after Doane got his hands on him. He had to be thinking about the time it would take Harriet to get out here. We've got to make them count."

"I haven't been twiddling my thumbs trying to find that cottage," Joe said. "When we were at the Marine Museum, I didn't get any solid answers, but the curator did remember seeing a book on artistry in driftwood that had some unusual designs."

"Headstones?"

"Not that he recalled, but he was fairly

vague. I've been searching every Web site and publishing house in Washington State to see if I could locate it. No luck." He frowned. "But I'm beginning to wonder if we're off base."

"What do you mean?"

"We've been assuming since the nukes are supposed to be in Seattle that the cottage is near Seattle. What if it isn't? You couldn't get any answer about land purchase from Langley. We can't find any mention of driftwood that fits the description. Not near Seattle. Not in Washington State. Why not look south, across the Oregon border? Kevin would have been safer if his hideout wasn't right on top of a target city. It couldn't hurt to take a look."

"Unless it's a waste of time. Then it could hurt Eve very badly."

"If you've got any other suggestion, I'm listening."

She didn't have any other suggestion. "We'll try Oregon." She moved back and sat down. "I'll call Langley and set them to exploring the possibility of Kevin's purchasing out of state. It might—" Her phone rang before she could dial. "It's Margaret." She accessed. "Margaret, may I call you back?

Things are crazy here now and we've got to find a way to salvage it before they get worse."

"That's not what I wanted to hear. This will only take a minute, Catherine. Jane asked me to call." She paused. "I think we may have big trouble."

CHAPTER
16

Chicago

"Has she made any phone calls?" Jane asked Margaret, when they burst into Caleb's suite twenty minutes later. "Is Harriet still in her suite?"

"As far as I can tell," Margaret said. "I heard her moving around the suite. She went to the bathroom. I heard water running. I didn't hear the corridor door open or close." She shrugged. "I'm glad you're here. I listened to every nuance of sound, but I'm not accustomed to interpreting those damn machines the way you are, Caleb."

"You interpreted what was going on

between Cartland and Harriet," Trevor said. "That's more important."

"Ever the kind diplomat," Caleb said as he strode across the room toward the machines. "But not necessarily truthful." He put an earphone to his ear and turned up the volume on the machine. He listened intently for a moment, then adjusted the sound again.

"Caleb?" Jane asked.

"Just a minute." He adjusted the other machine and listened again. "Son of a **bitch.**" He threw the earphone on the table and ran toward the door. "I heard conversation from some mother with her kid walking down the corridor. Harriet's door has got to be open!"

"How could—" Jane didn't finish the sentence as she and Trevor ran after Caleb.

"Use the exit stairs." Caleb was already running down them by the time Jane and Trevor reached the door. He burst out the door on Harriet's floor and ran down the corridor.

Jane could see the mother and little girl Caleb had spoken about at the end of the hall.

Harriet's door is open.

It wasn't open.

But Caleb was bending and carefully pulling out a small leather change purse that had been wedged between the door and the jamb, keeping it from closing.

"Quiet," Trevor said.

"Why?" Caleb threw open the door. "She's not here. We don't even know how long she's been gone."

"I heard her in the bathroom fifteen minutes ago," Margaret said as she joined them. "After that, it's anyone's guess." She watched Trevor going from room to room. "But did you hear that ping from the machine right before you ran out of your room?"

"Ping?" Jane repeated.

"Yeah, a ping," Margaret said. "I was the last one to leave your room, Caleb, and I thought maybe she was down here after all."

"Obviously, you were wrong," Trevor said. "No sign of her. All her luggage is gone."

"Ping," Caleb said as he pulled out his phone. "I synced those machines to my phone apps. It could have been a signal that the GPS was in motion." He stared at the phone. "Come on, baby," he said softly. "Give it to me."

"What?" Margaret asked.

"She took the box with Kevin's letters with her." Jane was holding her breath, her gaze on Caleb's phone. "The GPS may be able to follow her." Please let that happen, she prayed. Everything else had gone wrong. Let this one thing go right.

One minute passed.

Two minutes.

A soft ping, barely audible.

"**Yes.**" Hope flared. "Where, Caleb?"

"It's hard to pin down." He turned and headed for the door. "But it's the general direction of the airport. Let's not wait to be a hundred percent sure. She could be on a plane by that time. You drive, Trevor. I'll monitor the GPS."

She could be on a plane by that time.

The words echoed in Jane's mind as she rode down the elevator to the lobby.

While they played hunt and chase and dealt with Chicago traffic, Harriet might be lost to them.

She couldn't risk it.

She took out her phone as they got off the elevator. "We need help. I'm calling Venable. We can't let her get away."

•　　•　　•

Venable answered the phone on the second ring. "It's about time that someone decided to call to let me know what's going on. Where are you, Jane? And what the hell is—"

"I don't have time to give you chapter and verse," she interrupted as she got into the car in front of the hotel. "I need your help, and I need it fast, Venable. I didn't want to call you. I'm scared to death that you're going to do something rash, and Eve might die. I have no choice. So please shut up and listen. You're going to have to work fast. Catherine said that Homeland Security has teams in both Chicago and Seattle. Is there someone in that team in Chicago that you can trust to be discreet and not tip his hand?"

He was silent. "Yes, Paul Junot."

It was comforting that the name had come so definitely and quickly to his mind. "Then get in touch with him and get him out to O'Hare Airport right away. Harriet Weber is going to be leaving the city, and we have to know how and where she's going," she added grimly, "Though I think we know the where."

"Seattle?"

"You've got it. But once she's there, we can't lose track of her. That could be fatal. Tell Junot that he has to do his check without her being aware of it. The last thing we want is to have her panic." She was trying to think. "And you've got to have Junot set up a private jet rental for us. We'll probably need it as soon as we reach the airport."

"You don't ask much," Venable said dryly. "And why should I do it when I don't know what the hell is going on?"

"I'm only asking for what we have to have. We can't let her get away." She paused. "She's in control, Venable. We all thought it was Doane, but she's calling the shots, and she's calling them now." She heard him muttering an oath. "I'm going to hang up so that you can phone this Junot. I know you want answers, and I'll give them to you. But not now. Not until you get that done."

"I'll call you back," he said tersely.

She pressed the disconnect as he hung up. "God, I hope he can get his man out there fast." She looked at the GPS. "Is she still heading for the airport?"

Caleb nodded. "But she's not reached the exit yet. She could still change direction."

But Jane had the chilling feeling that Harriet was not going to change direction. Whatever had caused her to bolt from the hotel, she had a purpose and a focus.

"She just got off the airport exit," Caleb said. "She's committed."

Committed. It was a frightening word when applied to Harriet's plans. No longer a holding pattern. She was going forward."

"She's not heading for the main terminal." Trevor's eyes were on the GPS. "She's going to the private-and executive-plane area."

"Which means she could hop on a chartered flight and be off within minutes after she gets there," Jane said. "We could lose her."

"Easy," Trevor said. "This is Chicago. Things seldom happen that fast."

"Venable better be that fast," she said grimly. "I don't know what he can do about tracking her once she leaves, but he'll have to do it. " Her phone rang. "Venable, I was just going to call you. We just found out that she's heading for the private area at O'Hare. We'll be able to zero in on exactly what hangar within a few minutes. Do you have Junot out there yet?"

"No, but he has someone he trusts at the airport who can start the ball rolling until he gets out there. He e-mailed him a photo of Harriet Weber and told him to find her." She heard him relay the info she'd given him to someone in the background, and then he was back on the phone. "He's Don Breital. Paul says he's good."

"I hope he's very good. She can't know she's being followed."

"I know, you told me. No panic." His tone was hard. "Why are you so adamant about that?"

"I told you, she's in control." He wasn't going to be satisfied with that answer, and she didn't blame him. If she had to use him, then he shouldn't have to go at this blind. "And we can't be sure that she doesn't have the detonator for those nuclear devices."

"What?"

"She told Doane she knew where it was, and we can't be certain that she doesn't have it in her possession. She wouldn't necessarily tell Doane the truth. We weren't able to monitor every minute of her time since we've been following her. We don't know what happened when she went to a bank here in town." She added wearily,

"Hell, it's possible she stopped and picked it up tonight on the way to the airport. Though I don't believe that could have happened. We were on her tail almost immediately."

"You believe?" Venable said sarcastically. "You suspected all this, and you didn't call me?"

"Things were moving very fast, and we had to move with them. Most of it was guesswork, and we were trying to piece it together."

"And you didn't trust me."

"How could I trust you after Colorado? I only realized tonight that I had no choice. I just knew I had to find a way to keep you from moving too fast and cause Harriet and Doane to kill Eve." She added, "We think we know where those nukes are located. There's no question that we'll share that with you."

"Thank you," he said sourly.

"But we want something in return. Give us just two hours once we reach Seattle to follow her to where Doane is holding Eve. You can use your super-duper spy gimmicks to monitor her from a distance. Don't do anything fancy. Don't scramble F-18s

and try to take down her plane. Don't rush
her when she lands and surround her with
SWAT teams to do a precision kill and get
that detonator. If she has it, she **will** press
the button if she believes she's losing
control. And, if she finds out it's me following her, she's arrogant enough to not regard me as any real danger to her. It's
actually safer for you to let us shadow her."
She paused. "Please, Venable, I know
Harriet Weber. Everything I've told you is
the truth. I can understand where your loyalty lies, but just give me two hours."

He was silent.

"She's as fanatical as Doane about honoring her Kevin with this nuclear holocaust.
Don't make the mistake of not thinking
she'll do anything she has to do."

Venable was talking to someone in the
background again. "Breital says that a
Learjet was chartered late tonight and told
it had to be ready for an immediate depar-
ture."

"Harriet's parking," Caleb said. "Hangar
23."

"Hangar 23, Venable," Jane said. "Is that
the Learjet?"

He was gone for a moment. "That's it.

Gassed and ready to go. Breital is trying to find out what flight plan was filed."

"Providing the pilot follows the plan," Caleb said. "I've been known to fudge a bit."

"I can get a satellite and radar verification of the progress of any plane in the air once we get a fix on it," Venable said. "If I decide to let her get in the air."

"Well, bully for the CIA," Trevor murmured. "But you can't keep her from blowing up herself and two very fine cities if she chooses to do it."

"Yes, he could," Jane said. "His friends are all for the efficiency of drone strikes. But if she had even a hint that it was coming, she'd press the button."

"Breital just reported that a woman of Harriet Weber's description boarded the plane," Venable said.

"I thought as much," Caleb said. "The GPS indicates a move across the tarmac."

Relief flooded Jane at his words. It had been logical that Harriet would not leave Kevin's box of letters in the car after she'd taken it from the hotel, but it was good to have it confirmed.

The airport exit was just ahead, but they still had no confirmation from Venable.

"Two hours," Jane pleaded. "Give us a chance, Venable."

He was silent for a long moment. "Two hours," he said at last. "No more. And I'm making alternate plans in case there's a screwup. You wouldn't like my alternate plans. Junot's already made arrangements for the plane you requested. He commandeered an executive jet that was ready to fly to Las Vegas. That plane better be a hell of a lot faster than that Learjet because you'll have to arrive ten to fifteen minutes before Harriet Weber does."

Jane felt limp with relief. "Thank you, Venable."

"I won't say you're welcome. I'm still mad as hell with you. And I want those nuke locations." Someone was talking to him again. "Hangar 43. Get there and get there quick. It's a Gulfstream. Harriet's Learjet is requesting takeoff from the tower. You've got to hope she doesn't get it right away, or she might be too far ahead for you to make up the time."

"We're almost there," Trevor said.

But Venable was no longer on the line, and Jane could visualize him shaking and moving, cracking orders with whiplike effectiveness. She had no problem with that awesome efficiency as long as it wasn't leveled against them.

"I'll give Venable what he needs to know about the nukes as soon as we're on the plane," Margaret said quietly. "I'll have time to go through those security videos and see if I can zero in on a probable location."

Jane nodded. "Give the security tape to her, Trevor." She was glad not to have to concentrate on anything at the moment. Her mind was a jumble of fear and hope and desperation.

They pulled into the parking space by Hangar 43, and she jumped out of the car. She could see the Gulfstream, sleek and golden, like a crouching puma under the bright lights.

That plane has to be fast, Venable had said.

Everything was now dependent on their reaching Seattle before Harriet.

"We'll do it." Trevor took her hand as he came around the car. He smiled down at her. "Stop worrying. We'll send Caleb up to the cockpit to take over for the pilot. I'll bet he has a few tricks to cut some time off the trip."

"I'd already planned on it. I'll get us there on time." Caleb was striding across the tarmac toward the plane. "But you're not helping by standing around holding hands. Nauseating. Get on the damn plane."

Harriet gazed out the window of the plane and watched a plane take off from the next runway.

The pilot had told her they were fifth in line for takeoff, but she was not impatient. She was on her way. That was all that was important.

It was beginning.

She could feel excitement flush her cheeks.

She reached out and lovingly touched the box of Kevin's letters she'd set on the seat next to her. She felt as if she could feel that beloved energy tonight. Sitting in this plane, she was remembering the plan she and Kevin had made to go away. The minute the doors of the plane closed, he was going to press in the code to set off the nukes.

But he wasn't here to do that, she thought sadly.

I'm trying to make sure everything else

is all happening just the way you'd want it to happen, Kevin.

But that memory had made her recall something else she'd meant to do on this plane before it left the ground. Of course, she would call James later and tell him she was on her way.

But this other little task was something she had been anticipating.

She reached into her handbag and drew out the cell phone detonator. It was now fully charged and ready for business.

How do you know that old detonator would still work? Cartland had asked.

She felt a little thrill go through her as her forefinger gently rubbed the T key. So much power. Is this how you felt, Kevin?

That last quotation from Robert Service was echoing in her mind from the game she had played with her son, the final quote that would complete the sequence. He had not wanted to risk it in a letter but had called her on the phone. She could still remember the sound of his caressing voice.

You measure out my breath,
Each beat one nearer death . . .
Tick-tock. Tick-tock. Tick-tock.

Kevin was so clever. What was a more fitting detonation code for nukes hidden in a clock tower than the ticking of a clock? She slowly pressed in the code, letter by letter, every letter bringing the excitement higher.

TICK-TO

She was tempted to type in just more letter of the code to see if the thrill became more intense.

No, she wasn't entirely sure that the timing mechanism on the nuke might not grab the code before it was completed. Better to be safe. She reluctantly typed in the alternate code.

For a moment, nothing happened.

She frowned. What the hell was—

Then it came on the screen in bold gold letters.

TESTING. YOU HAVE ACTIVATED THE UNIT. DO YOU WISH TO CONTINUE WITH COUNTDOWN?

She smiled.

Oh, yes, Cartland. This old detonator definitely works.

Driftwood Cottage

Eve heard Doane's guttural cursing on the porch, followed by his heavy footsteps.

Then the door flew open, and he staggered into the cottage.

"Did you miss me?" Doane said. "As you can see, I brought you a present."

He was bent almost double with the weight of the man he was carrying on his back. She caught a glimpse of the sleek white hair and powerful body.

Zander. It had to be Zander.

She had been hoping against hope that Doane would fail. There had been a chance. Zander was incredibly skilled, and it had seemed impossible that Doane could take him down. But everyone had a nemesis. Evidently, Doane was Zander's. "Did you kill him?"

"No." He dumped Zander on the floor beside the couch. "That would have been a defeat. I told you how it was going to be." He buried his fingers in Zander's hair and jerked his head back. "He should be waking up anytime now. He was such a fool. All I had to do was wait in the parking lot of the hotel until he came to get in his car. He was out cold in five seconds. I gave the dart a little extra narcotic to make sure that he didn't cause me any trouble on the way here."

"Like you gave me a 'little extra'? Your judgment sucks. You'd better check to make sure that he's still alive."

"He's alive." He released Zander's hair and straightened. "I shouldn't have worried about having to deal with him after I got him in the car." He nodded at the cuffs on Zander's wrists and ankles. "He can't move. He's helpless." He added with soft venom, "Helpless. I love the sound of it. Can you hear me, Zander? You murdering son of a bitch, you're helpless. I've won."

"I hear you." Zander didn't open his eyes. "And it appears I'm at a disadvantage, but you've not won, Doane."

Doane reached down and slapped him across the mouth with a force brutal enough to break the skin. "Then fight back, show me." He slapped him again. "Show me."

"He doesn't have to show you anything," Eve said fiercely. "How brave you are, Doane. Always willing to strike out when it's only a child or a man who can't defend himself. Is that what you call winning? Maybe in your twisted—" Her head jerked back as Doane whirled and punched her in the face.

Pain.

"Really, Eve, I don't need you to defend me." Zander's eyes were open, and his gaze was on her face. His own face was without expression. "I wish you'd stop. I'm finding it a little humiliating. This situation is difficult enough for me." His stare shifted to Doane. "I never dreamed I'd be in this position. You're not good enough, Doane."

"Oh, but I am. I got you, didn't I?" He tilted his head. "And I don't think you liked it when I hurt our Eve." He drew back his hand and slapped her. "Perhaps I may entertain myself until it's time for our grand finale." He slapped her again. "There are so many ways . . . Kevin knew them all."

"By all means, if it amuses you." Zander's tone was bored. "But don't expect me to respond in the way you'd like. I don't know this woman. Even if I did, it wouldn't matter to me what you did to her. You keep thinking that because she's my daughter, it should make a difference. She's only the product of a one-night stand. I care nothing for her."

"It will make a difference," Doane said harshly. "I know the power of kinship. My love for Kevin ruled my life from the moment he was born. You may not think that it will make a difference, but when you see her die, you'll feel the loss, the emptiness. You killed my son, you bastard. I've waited five years, and tonight I'll kill your daughter."

"I don't know her," Zander repeated. "How can she mean anything to me? There's nothing you can do to her that would make me suffer."

Eve could see the mixture of torment and anger in Doane's expression. "It will matter when I—" He broke off in frustration. He wasn't sure, Eve realized; his grand revenge was disappearing before his eyes. "I think you're lying." He forced a smile. "But I'll assume there's some truth to what you're saying. You're such a cold bastard that maybe that part of you is frozen, too." He shrugged. "So let's let you get to know her. Everyone around her appears besotted by the bitch. Perhaps a few hours alone in her company will rouse all your fatherly feelings." He turned and headed for the door. "I have a few calls to make. One of them to my dear ex-wife to tell her that she's to come running if she wants to see you die, Zander." He looked back over his shoulder. "Don't think that I won't come back and check on you occasionally. You won't get away."

"How are we supposed to get away?" Eve asked sarcastically. "You have us both hog-tied, dammit."

"That's right. But one can't be too sure." He smiled. "However, I'll enjoy sitting out on the porch and looking out over Kevin's graveyard of driftwood. By the time I come back, I may have chosen the place to bury you. Side by side as is fitting for a father and daughter."

The door closed behind him.

"Did he hurt you?" Zander asked quietly.

"Of course he hurt me," Eve said. "What do you think? It's what Doane does."

"I know you can handle pain. I meant anything you can't get over quickly. Bleeding, broken teeth, concussion. Anything we'll have to deal with?"

She shook her head. "Bruises. One tooth

feels a little loose." She blinked her left eye. "And I'll probably have a black eye." She looked at him. "Your lip is bleeding."

"I expected worse. You distracted him and took the brunt."

"Not intentionally," she said curtly. "I just couldn't believe you'd been stupid enough to let him catch you. You're supposed to be so fantastic, and here you are trussed up like a Thanksgiving turkey."

"You're angry." He was suddenly smiling. "You mustn't let Doane hear you castigating me. He'll give up all hope of my coming to love you like a daughter."

"An impossibility. Love grows and builds with time and experiences. We don't have the time, and you never wanted the experiences."

He was silent, staring at her. "That's the first time that you actually sounded as if you believe I am your father. You always denied it before."

"I don't know what to believe." She added reluctantly, "But I think perhaps it might be possible. Doane says that I am. He's crazy and could be mistaken. But you say it, too, and you're not crazy. At least not in that way."

"I'm glad you qualified that." He tilted his head. "But since you don't trust either one of us, I believe that there may be another reason. Now who do you trust who has had access to you?" He studied her for a long moment. "Your Bonnie?"

She didn't answer.

He nodded. "Yes, I think Bonnie must have vouched for me."

"Don't joke."

"I know better. Did she say I was her grandfather?"

"No."

"Then what did she say?"

"She said . . . if I died, you would feel . . . loss."

"Oh, then she agreed with Doane. Angel and devil both coming to the same conclusion."

"Yes."

"Did she say anything else?"

"No, she knew I didn't want to talk about you."

"Why?"

She looked him in the eye. In this moment, when she didn't know how many moments were left, she would neither evade nor lie. "It hurt me. I shouldn't care, but I do. There were times when I was a little girl, that I'd see some other child with their father, and I'd feel . . . lonely. I wondered why I wasn't good enough, why I wasn't wanted. That was before I realized that the fault didn't lie with me but with the man who had walked away. My mother, Sandra, didn't really want me either, but she stayed with me, and we made it work." Her voice was suddenly fierce. "And I would have made it work with you, too, if you'd given me the chance. Family is important. You should have given me a chance."

"And you would have fought the world and the devil for my soul?"

"Don't laugh. Yes, I would have fought, and I would have won."

"I'm not laughing," he said gently. "And I believe every word you're saying. You know, I saw you once when you were about ten years old. You were tough and full of passion, and I could tell that either Sandra or life had created a very special person." He grimaced. "I couldn't claim to have anything to do with it."

Her eyes widened. "You saw me?"

"Only once. Then I turned my back and walked away." He smiled. "Like the selfish son of a bitch that I am."

"You were selfish." Her eyes were blazing. "You should have given me my chance."

"In my twisted psyche, I believe that I thought I might be doing that. Of course, it might have been ego and self-love raising its head."

"You walked away. Why?"

"By that time, I had risen very high in my present profession, and anyone near me could be a target of revenge from crime figures or foreign governments or any number of other individuals. You wouldn't have been safe."

"Bullshit. We could have worked it out."

"You keep saying that, but perhaps I didn't want to make the effort. Perhaps you would have been an inconvenience."

"Is that the way you felt?"

"Yes."

She studied him. "You're lying."

"I don't know how I felt all those years ago," he said wearily. "I was softer and not as honest with myself as I am now. Every year, I could feel myself getting harder and harder, and sometimes I thought that soon I'd feel completely numb."

"I don't care about your walking away from that ten-year-old girl. I never knew about it, and I'm not that little girl any longer. I want to know about now. I can see that hardness. Everyone can see the hardness. I want to see something else. You look me in the eye and tell me. Was Bonnie right? Do you feel anything for me? Loss. Would you feel loss?"

He didn't speak.

"You answer me, Zander."

"Difficult, Eve."

"I don't give a damn. You look deep and tell me the truth."

"I feel . . ." He stopped and when he spoke again his voice was uneven. "What do want me to say? Let's see, if Doane blew your brains out, would I feel a sense of loss?" He stared intently into her eyes, holding them. "I would feel such a sense of loss that he had robbed this ugly world of such a unique person that I would kill him in the most painful way possible."

She couldn't breathe. She couldn't look away from him. "Why? After all these years, why would it matter to you whether I lived or died?"

"God only knows. It could be that all during those years, I never permitted you close. It's only after Doane made me pay attention to you that I began to feel . . . something." His lips twisted. "And how I fought it. It was only the night of the fire at that ghost town in Colorado that I realized that you had become . . . necessary. It stunned me." He paused before he added hoarsely, "And it broke me."

"Nothing could break you."

"No?"

"And I don't want you to kill for me, Zander. I only wanted you to **care.**" She gestured with frustrated impatience. "Or for you, it could be the same thing. I don't know why it matters to me anyway. But it does. It **does.** Maybe there's a reason that we came together. I don't want anything here unresolved when I go to Bonnie."

"I've given you the only answer I can, Eve." The intensity suddenly left his face. "And don't be in too much of a hurry to tie up loose ends. I have no intention of letting you go to Bonnie anytime soon."

"You'd be more convincing if you weren't cuffed hand and foot, one arm in a cast, and with no weapons and—" She frowned. "I can't believe you let Doane catch you."

"I appreciate your faith in my prowess, but he counted on the fact that he'd catch me off guard."

"And he did it?"

"What do you think? No man is perfect. Though I do come close."

"You're better than Doane. You ran rings around him in that forest in Colorado." She paused, gazing at him in despair. And this Zander was the same man she had met in that forest. Even though he appeared helpless, as Doane had claimed, there was an aura of confidence and power that had been there when she was his prisoner. "I could wish that if you were going to get yourself caught, you'd choose a time when there wasn't so much in the balance."

"Your life? No, you're talking about those nukes that Doane wants to set off to honor his idiot son."

"You know about them?"

He sighed. "I've heard nothing but how irresponsible it is that I don't give my full cooperation and sacrifice personal will to the CIA, Homeland Security, and a zillion other bureaucrats. Catherine Ling is very vocal on the subject."

"Catherine? What does she have to do with this?"

"What doesn't she have to do with it?" he said dryly. "She barged into my life and announced I had to be kept alive so that I'd be a decent barter for you. She even had the nerve to appoint herself my body-guard. I had a hell of a time slipping away from her tonight."

"I can imagine you would." But she had trouble with the concept that even Catherine had been bold enough to confront Zander in his lair. It was both bizarre and humorous. "But she'd want more than me in that barter if she knew about those nukes."

"Yes, but you were the primary prize." He inclined his head toward her. "You're the primary prize for all of us, Eve. Except, perhaps, Venable."

"Then Venable is the one who is right," she said soberly. "And you should have paid attention to what Catherine was saying."

"I paid attention. But every one of those organizations would take me down if they could. I have problems working with any-one that I know will turn on me after they get what they want." He smiled faintly, "And it would happen, Eve. They would make promises, then find it convenient to forget. That's the world as I know it. It's the world you know, too."

"That doesn't matter."

"Then what does matter?"

"The children."

"Ah, but of course."

"And the parents who gave them life. I'm not important at all when you put those on the scale."

"I beg to differ. But, then, I'm far more callous than you'd ever dream of being. After decades, I've only managed to care about one individual, and you mustn't ex-pect me to suddenly throw open the gates to anyone else. It's not going to happen."

"I don't expect anything from you. You bewilder me." He had said he cared about her but she didn't know how she felt about him. He was completely out of her experi-ence. Perhaps he was out of everyone's experience.

But she wanted to know him, she realized suddenly. He had been an emptiness within her, and she had put that emptiness aside and tried to forget it existed. How long had she lived with that secret bitterness she would not admit even to herself?

Release it. It would only corrode and hurt her if she held it close. But she had to know one thing more than he had told her.

"Did you . . . love my mother?"

"Sandra?" He slowly shook his head. "Sex. Pure sex. And she cared nothing for me. We met in Florida when we were just teenagers. We were both wild and hungry for life. After high school, I'd gotten a job working on a freighter that was due to leave Daytona in four weeks for South Africa. Sandra's mother had brought her down there on vacation, and she was partying on the beach every night." He shrugged. "So was I. Booze and drugs and sex. Sandra liked them all. I wasn't the first or the last man that she took under that pier to screw." His gaze was on her face. "You don't like my saying that. You're protective of Sandra even though she wasn't a good mother to you."

"No, I don't like it. But I asked you, and

I'm not ignorant about Sandra's past." She paused. "And she was good to my Bonnie when she was alive. She loved her. Everyone loved her." And she vaguely remembered Sandra's telling her about that vacation in Florida and that Eve was conceived at that time. "If she was that promiscuous, how did you know I was your daughter?"

"I didn't." He grimaced. "The next week I took off for Johannesburg. Three months later, I received a letter from Sandra telling me that she was pregnant and that she was certain that the kid was mine. I didn't believe her."

"Why not?"

"Because my shipmate, George Royce, who had also spent a good amount of time beneath the pier with Sandra, received a letter stating that she was sure George was the father. I figured that she had just sent out letters to all of her partners, hoping that one of us would believe her. She wasn't too bright to send a letter to both George and me. She might have known we might talk to each other."

No, Sandra had never been bright. "Desperation?"

"Perhaps." He was silent. "But I preferred

to think she was victimizing me. It was more convenient. I wasn't a particularly good kid, but I still had a few ingrained scruples left at that period of my life. Enough to feel a twinge of guilt. I sent her some money and turned my back on her."

"But you came back later. Why did you come back?"

He shrugged. "Curiosity? That possibility always stayed with me. Maybe because those nights in Daytona were the last care-free time I had before my life changed." He corrected, "No, before I changed. I'm the one who joined a mercenary army in Johannesburg and discovered my true vocation. Any blame belongs solely to me, not fate. I learned to accept that truth with no excuses. That's probably why I wanted to make sure that I'd made the right decision about Sandra."

"And how did you do that?"

"DNA. It was difficult, but I managed to get your hairbrush and a blood sample."

She stiffened. "And what did the DNA show?"

"That for once Sandra had told me the truth," he said quietly. "You're my daughter, Eve."

She inhaled sharply. She had been expecting it, but his words still came as a shock. "I'm surprised you went to those lengths."

"I was curious."

It could be true but she didn't think that was the entire story. "And if I was a target because I was your daughter, then you had to know that someone else might find it out, too."

"Someone else did find out. Doane. I wasn't careful enough when I was checking that DNA. I left a trail. At the time, I had no idea that a man could be so obsessed that he would spend five years hunting down every single bit of my history. I should have known. You wouldn't be here now if I'd taken care of Doane five years ago."

"If," she repeated. "Who knows? Doane is crazy. We just have to take what we've been given and try to get out of this. Though we haven't been given a hell of a lot." Her brow wrinkled thoughtfully. "Doane mentioned Kevin's mother, Harriet, out of the blue. What do we know about her?"

"That she's in control, that her dainty little finger is on the detonator, and she's only waiting to set it off until she sees Doane blow my head off. And that she's probably going to be here very soon to take care of that little matter." His brows rose. "Is that enough information?"

"More than enough. How soon?"

"She's in Chicago, so we may have a little time."

"Doane hates her. We may be able to use that."

"Divide and conquer? Don't count on it. Where my imminent demise is concerned, they stand united. I killed their beloved Kevin." He added, "But all is not lost. Catherine will be scouring the coastline for a cottage with a graveyard of driftwood."

She stiffened. "What?"

"Providing there really is a macabre collection of driftwood outside? Since I was unconscious when Doane brought me here, I wasn't able to verify its existence."

"Yes, it's there. How did you know?"

"Bonnie evidently knew about it and passed the description along."

"Bonnie . . ." She felt a rush of warmth and love. "And you believe it, Zander?" For some reason, she desperately wanted him to believe that Bonnie's soul still lived.

"Don't be rid—" He stopped as he saw

her expression. "Perhaps. I shouldn't, of course. Ghosts are mere hallucinations, but I find myself wanting to believe what you believe. I'll have to see how accurate she is about that graveyard before I pass judgment." He glanced at the door. "I don't know how much more time Doane's going to give us. He's too erratic. Look, we can't wait until Harriet gets here. That would be cutting it too close. We have to make our move before that."

She stared pointedly down at her bound wrists. "And how are we supposed to do that?"

"Why, just follow my lead . . ." For an instant, she thought she saw a twinkle in his eye as he smiled mockingly. "Like a good and obedient daughter."

CHAPTER

17

Venable called Jane when they'd been in the air over thirty minutes. "Change course. We've just found out that Harriet's not heading for Sea-Tac Airport. Her pilot's flight plan calls for her to land at Sandhurst Airport. It's a small coastal airport southwest of Seattle."

"Tell me you won't have anyone there to meet her," Jane said. "You'll keep your word."

"Unless something happens to indicate that Harriet's plans are escalating. Then all bets are off." He changed the subject.

"You promised to tell me the location of those nukes. I need that info, Jane."

"But you won't act on the information while we still have a chance to get our hands on Harriet and Doane? That's first on the agenda, right?"

"I'll get a force together, and we'll be poised to move to defuse those nukes at the first sign that there's any immediate danger."

"In your opinion."

"In my opinion. Give me the locations."

"We can't be certain. According to Kendra, there's a good chance that the one in Seattle is somewhere in the King Street Station. You'll have to explore to find out exactly where."

"Got it. As long as we know the approximate location, I can arrange a flyover by a plane with terahertz spectroscopes. They can detect plutonium signatures at great distances," Venable said. "What about Chicago?"

"The Wrigley Building, where there's another clock tower. We think it's on the lowest floor, but we can't be—"

"I think I've found it," Margaret said from

across the aisle. She held up a security video.

"Wait a minute, Venable." Jane asked Margaret, "What did you find?"

"There's a small room down there where the Wrigley executives used to store boating equipment. I don't know if it was supposed to be emergency stuff since the complex is on the river or if the executives once did some public-relations gigs on the water. Anyway, there are black-and-white photos on the walls that show them standing at the rail of various craft and having a good old time."

"Where are you going with this?"

"That it must have been decades ago. Everything is covered with dust except for the oars and various pieces of equipment that are covered by plastic." She made a face. "Very well chewed plastic."

"What else?"

"Half of a life preserver. The rats really must have loved the material that was used to make that preserver. W and R were the only letters left of the original Wrigley." She paused. "It was leaning against the wall beneath a large wood panel that had ships carved on it. I couldn't tell if there were any burned-out wires in the area."

"If it was a room that had been deserted for decades, it would be a safe place to hide that device," Trevor said. "Maybe your rats are more reliable than you thought, Margaret."

"They're not my rats," she said flatly. "But they may have come through for us. Though I guarantee that wasn't their purpose. They only have one purpose."

"Talk to Venable. He'll want to know everything there is to know about that room." She handed Margaret her phone. "It might be a good idea to skip the bit about the rats."

"No, he has to take me the way he finds me," Margaret said. "He'll survive it. Venable has had to deal with me before." She started to speak into the phone.

"I have to go up to the cockpit and tell Caleb of our new destination," Jane told Trevor as she unbuckled her seat belt. "You heard me try to pin Venable down. He wasn't having it."

"I think he's trying." Trevor reached out and gently stroked her cheek. "He likes Eve. If he can, he'll give her every break."

"If he can," she repeated. For the briefest instant, she rested her cheek on his hand. He had strong hands, wonderful hands, she thought. Hands that brought pleasure and built that golden cocoon that shut out the world and made everything safe and good. As safe and good as Trevor was himself. She gave his palm a quick kiss and rose to her feet. "I can always count on you to make me see the bright side."

"That's what I want for you. The bright side all the way." He smiled. "So give Caleb his new marching orders and come back, and we'll work on it. We have a few hours we can steal before we have to hit the ground running. I'm going to use every one of them."

Jane's smile lingered as she headed for the cockpit. A few hours to steal. A few hours to be close to him and build a few more memories.

Loving memories. Bright memories.

Driftwood Cottage

"Harriet's on her way." Doane's face was flushed as he came back into the cottage.

"She should be here within a few hours. You're a dead man, Zander."

"You've been saying that for too long. Repetition is boring."

"You won't be bored when I blow her brains out." Doane took a step closer to Eve and touched her hair. "All that ugly brain matter tangled in this pretty hair . . ."

"Crude. Why do you persist in thinking that it will matter to me?"

"When it gets down to those final moments, it will matter." He smiled down at Eve. "Harriet wanted me to just kill you and get you out of the way. She just never understood how unsatisfying that would have been. She never admits she's wrong."

"When will she be here?"

"Beginning to be frightened? I'd say perhaps three hours. You have time to bond a little longer." He went to the cabinet. "And I have time to dig two graves out in Kevin's garden." He pulled out a shovel. "Those places I chose will do very well, Eve. I've never dug a grave for anyone but Kevin's little girls. Well, there was that agent who got in my way back at your lake cottage, but he didn't matter. There was no pleasure in it. This one will be different."

"Would you like help?" Zander asked. "If you'll undo these handcuffs, I'd be glad to volunteer."

"Do those cuffs bother you? Do you feel powerless? That must be maddening for you. You are powerless, Zander. Those are the finest military handcuffs, and they'll hold you until the bullet goes into your brain."

"Then I take it my offer is refused?"

Doane's smile lost a little of its malicious pleasure. "You arrogant bastard."

The front door slammed behind him.

"I thought for a minute that he'd take that shovel to your head," Eve said dryly.

"There was a possibility but not a very great one. It would have spoiled his precious finale. He's exceptionally single-minded."

"I've noticed that."

"And he won't complete the show until Harriet is here." He was staring thoughtfully at the door. "It would be much easier to take Doane out before she arrives on the scene."

"Oh, would it?"

"But, since she apparently may be more dangerous in your eyes, I'd have trouble convincing you to run the risk of her blowing up Seattle and Chicago if she became upset that we had shifted the balance."

"Yes, a good deal of trouble, Zander." She shook her head. "And I'm having trouble with believing this discussion. You're talking as if it's a done deal."

"No, there will be difficulties. It might be nice to have skilled assistance if it proves very dicey. We'll have to see if Catherine comes through."

"Catherine?"

"I told her that she had to redouble her efforts to find this lovely cottage."

"And what did she say?"

"Well, nothing really. That was about the time when I knocked her unconscious." He smiled. "But I'm sure that she'll do as I suggested."

"I'm not certain those circumstances would lend to compliance. Catherine doesn't appreciate force."

"But she does appreciate you. I think she probably weighed her anger at me and her affection for you, then got to work." His smile faded. "If you want to take down Harriet, too, we'll have to wait until she's almost here before we bid good-bye to Doane."

"She's almost here now according to Do-ane."

"But she's not on the doorstep. Timing is everything."

"And Catherine may appear and come to our rescue."

"Wouldn't that be delightful? Of course, it would ruin my image, but I might be able to bear that coming from Catherine." He thought about it. "No, I still couldn't stand it."

"Then there's no question she'll do it for sheer punishment's sake. You should not have knocked her out, Zander."

"I do many things I shouldn't do. I'm sure you've heard."

"Yes." It was bizarre sitting here in this equally bizarre and dangerous situation perfectly at ease with him, talking and even smiling. "You do have that reputation."

"And I'll do a few more before this night is over." He met her eyes. "And I won't re-gret one single act. After all, I am a lost soul, Eve."

"I don't know about that. Bonnie says there are second chances."

"And, of course, she's an expert."

"She wouldn't claim to be an expert. She

only tells me what she's learned since she left me."

He was silent a moment. "And since she's my granddaughter and therefore supremely intelligent, I'm inclined to believe her." His lips twisted. "But only inclined considering her ethereal state. Suppose we change the conversation to a subject on which we both agree."

Her brows rose. "And what is that?"

"Why, Catherine, of course. Tell me all about Catherine. She was a little too uptight to confide in me while she was my so-called bodyguard."

"And I won't break her confidence unless given permission." She added quietly, "But I will tell you that she has amazing perseverance. She'll find us, Zander."

"Oh, I'm sure she'll make every attempt. And there's no doubt she's pulled Joe Quinn into the search front and center by now."

"Joe's always front and center."

"You really do care about him?"

"With my whole heart."

"I can't say the same. Quinn and I were at odds most of the time we were on the search in Colorado."

"That doesn't surprise me. You're both alpha males." She added quietly, "Joe has a tendency to trample down opposition if it gets in his way. He wouldn't like the idea that he couldn't control you. And you probably felt the same way about him."

"Yes, but I was right."

"Right, perhaps. But I'd wager not particularly moral."

"And now we're back to the lost soul." He smiled. "And our joint wish that Catherine and your Joe are having a successful bonding to find Doane's graveyard. Hopefully before he manages to put us in it."

Seattle

"Dammit, Catherine, where the hell is that information on Oregon real-estate records?" Joe asked as he strode back into the sitting room. "You said that Langley promised it to you within the hour. I should have known those bureaucrats would drag their feet when they're most needed."

"They're not bureaucrats. I've worked with these agents, and they do their best. Sid is very sharp." She glared at him. "I hate bureaucrats as much as you do, but you can't condemn the entire world because you're hurting, Joe."

"I can if what they're doing is hurting Eve."

She dropped the argument because she was almost as impatient as Joe. "Did either of you find that online book about driftwood artistry?"

"I didn't," Gallo said. "Nothing in any of the libraries or sites in Washington State."

"You should have looked at Oregon," Joe said. "I found a reference to a self-published Portland University book that contained photos and descriptions by a Josiah Natlow. One of the descriptions was of several pieces that resembled head-stones."

Catherine inhaled sharply. "Where?"

"It didn't give a location. I've tracked down Natlow's telephone number, and I've been calling him for the last ten minutes. No answer," he said through set teeth. "Get that answer from Langley. We're running out of time. According to what Jane told us, Harriet Weber should be landing in three hours."

"You call Natlow back," Catherine said. "I'll get on the line to Langley."

"Good."

"May I suggest we get on the road," Gallo said quietly. "Quinn is right, every minute may count."

"Just wait until I get through to—" Her phone rang, and she glanced at the ID. "Langley." She punched the speaker and the access button. "It's about time. What have you got for me, Sid?"

"Success," Sid said. "And if you'd been asking the right questions, we would have gotten it for you sooner. Kevin Relling purchased a small acreage five and a half years ago. The paperwork was buried beneath four fake companies and one legitimate franchise, but I finally dug through all the shit."

"Near the beach?"

"On the hill above with beach access."

"What about the driftwood?"

"Give me a break. There's no way these records would mention driftwood."

"Where is it?"

"Right below Oregon's northern border with Washington."

"On the Oregon side?"

"That's what I said."

"Give me the address."

"Twelve Moonspinner Place."

"Sickeningly poetic for the domicile of a mass murderer."

"Yeah, anything else?"

"No. Thanks, Sid." She hung up and jumped to her feet. Excitement was zinging through her. "Come on, we've **got** it." She started for the door. "Gallo, do you know far it is to the Oregon border?"

"About 140 miles from here."

"Shit." Joe was jerking open the door. "God, it's going to be close."

"What about a helicopter?"

"By the time we get to the airport and rent it, we'll have lost too much time," Joe said. "And if Doane hears a plane overhead, it could trigger—" He broke off. "We'll just have to break every speed record and take the fastest highway. I'll drive, Gallo. You keep calling Natlow to verify. I'll Google the house and area and see what we're up against."

A few minutes later, they were in the car and heading through the city streets. Catherine knew they couldn't travel any faster until they got on the highway, but she was breathless, tense, and only wanted to **hurry.** Joe was right, it was going to be incredibly close. "What if Sid is wrong?" she asked jerkily. "Wrong address? Wrong Relling? We don't have time for mistakes."

"You're borrowing trouble," Gallo said quietly. "And I don't believe he's wrong. I just pulled up the Natlow photo that Quinn found in that Portland University site." He handed her his phone. "Pretty convincing."

Stark white branches curved in a wild, horribly macabre simile to a headstone. She felt sick as she stared at it. Death. Both Doane and Kevin had been totally absorbed with death as a means to power. This piece of driftwood was meant to fling that ugly power in the faces of anyone looking at it. She hadn't the slightest doubt that this photo was part of Doane's tapestry of evil.

She swallowed as she handed Gallo's phone back to him. "Very convincing. Now let's get to the damn place and find Eve."

Sandhurst Airport
Washington

The Gulfstream's engine was still whining as Jane, Trevor, Margaret, and Caleb ran down the steps and moved toward the blue-and-white hangar. The pilot immediately taxied into the hangar to get out of sight.

Caleb craned his neck, his gaze searing the sky. "If Venable is correct, Harriet could be arriving at any moment."

"We just have to hope that they didn't have a last-minute course change." Jane glanced around the small single-runway airport located southwest of Seattle. "I thought you'd arranged a car for us."

"I did." Caleb pointed to a black Range Rover parked next to the hangar. "Curb service."

A portly man in a gold shirt emblazoned with a rental-car-company logo climbed out and walked toward them with keys and contract. Caleb had barely finished signing the paperwork when Jane heard the sound of a jet in the distance. The next moment, Caleb's iPad made a pinging sound in his satchel.

"They're back in range," Jane said. She looked up at the approaching plane. "That has to be them. Let's move."

Trevor snatched the keys from Caleb's hand. "I'll drive."

"I gathered that," Caleb said dryly.

"Come on!" Margaret had already opened the Range Rover's rear door and was climbing into the car. "I think I see a car coming toward the airport. That may be Harriet's welcoming committee. We have to get out of sight."

Less than a minute later, they were idling in a small lot near the airport's exit. Two minutes after that, a Cadillac Escalade drove past and headed toward the Learjet that had just landed.

"Whew," Trevor said softly. "Entirely too close."

"Two men in the front seat," Caleb said. "That shouldn't be too much of a problem."

They watched as Harriet came down the steps of the Learjet carrying her overnight bag and the box of Kevin's letters. One of the two men who had met her politely tried to take the bag from her, but she waved him aside and got into the Cadillac.

A few minutes later, the Escalade drove past their Range Rover as it exited the airport.

"Okay, here we go," Caleb said as he looked at the iPad. "And we have a strong signal."

Trevor slowly turned the wheel and waited

until the Escalade had turned the corner before he started to follow it. Five minutes later, they had left the small town behind. Twenty minutes later, the scenery became sparse and barren, with tall grass lining the two-lane highway. The sky was over-cast with a damp blanket of marine layer and only an occasional sliver of moonlight as they drew closer to the coast.

"Faster, Trevor." Jane's hands were clenching with tension. "I think we're los-ing her."

Trevor shook his head. "If I get any closer, she'll see us. It's been five minutes since we've seen another car."

"No worries." In the backseat, Caleb raised the iPad screen. "I still have her right here. Strange, she's heading south, not north toward Seattle. But she can't make a move without my knowing it. She's mov-ing fast, but not—"

Margaret's phone rang. "It's Catherine. Should I—"

"Not now," Jane said, her gaze on the road ahead.

But after Margaret's call had gone to voice mail, Jane's phone rang. It had to be important if Catherine was going through her list trying to reach them. "Catherine, what is it?" Jane asked.

"Something good at last," Catherine said. "I think we've located Doane's cottage."

"What?" Jane's heart leaped. "That's fantastic. Where is it? Are you—"

"Harriet's stopped," Caleb said.

Trevor eased off the gas pedal. "You'd better be sure of that."

"Positive."

"I'll call you right back, Catherine." Jane hung up.

"Where?" Trevor asked Caleb.

"About half a mile ahead. Probably just around that bend."

Jane leaned back to glance at the iPad screen. "What's there?"

"Nothing as far as I can tell. Absolutely nothing." He waved his hand toward the tall grass along the road. "More of the same."

Trevor cursed under his breath. "They may have seen us."

"Unlikely, considering how careful you were," Caleb said. "For once, your conservativeness may have been an actual benefit, Trevor."

Trevor thought for a moment. "Okay,

everyone get down. I'm going to do a drive past."

"Now, that's not a conservative move," Caleb said.

"Do it," Trevor snapped.

Jane, Caleb, and Margaret slumped far down in their seats so that Trevor appeared to be the only one in the car. He stepped on the accelerator and roared around the bend.

"What do you see?" Jane asked.

"Her car's parked on the roadside. No one's inside. Caleb's right, there's nothing else around here."

Jane sat up and looked around. Just as Trevor said, there was the car but no trace of Harriet and the two men. "I was hoping when they stopped that it was at Doane's cottage." Had they changed cars? Jane felt the muscles of her stomach tighten. To come all this way and possibly lose her . . . "Stop the car. Now."

"I don't like this," Caleb said slowly.

"There's another curve up ahead," Trevor said. "We'll park on the other side and walk back. We'll find them, Jane. They couldn't have gone far."

"Unless they changed cars."

"If they did, they left Kevin's letters in that Cadillac. I'm still getting a ping," Caleb said. "And that's not likely."

Trevor rounded the bend and pulled over. He, Jane, and Caleb got out of the car. Margaret was about to follow them, and Jane shook her head. "No, you stay here."

"I go where you go," Margaret said quietly.

"Not this time. I'm not protecting you, Margaret. I'm just trying to be sensible. What if something goes wrong?"

She frowned. "Then I'd want to be there."

"No, we'd want someone to be able to sound an alarm, to call Venable or Catherine, anyone who could help. You're that person." Her voice became firm. "I'm not asking, I'm telling you. Stay here."

She finally nodded. "For a little while. Until I know if you're in trouble."

Jane hurried to join Trevor and Caleb as they moved through the tall grass at the roadside.

Caleb's eyes were narrowed, darting like those of an animal on the hunt. The sleek panther had returned. "Stay low. We want to see them before they see us."

They crouched and moved through the

grass. Only now did Jane realize just how close to the beach they were. She heard the crashing of waves and felt sand beneath her feet. She peered through the grass to see that a tall dune was all that separated her from the narrow beach. She started to move toward it when Caleb grabbed her arm. "Stop."

Jane pulled away. "Like hell. What if there's a boat beyond that dune? Or maybe Doane's cottage? If they're over there, I—"

"They could see you, and it would ruin everything. Let me run back to the road and come back from the other side of their car."

Trevor nodded. "Good idea. I'll circle around this dune and approach from the other side."

Jane looked between them with exasperation. "What am I supposed to do? Sit here and do nothing?"

Trevor smiled. "I wish I could talk you into that, but I know better."

"Damn right, I'll go straight up and over and see if I can spot them on the beach."

Caleb stepped toward her and handed her his revolver. "Stay low. There's a good stand of grass on this side of the dune.

Use it for cover. And if you see them, wait for us before you try to follow."

She looked at the weapon in her hand. "I can't take your gun, Caleb."

He pulled a seven-inch LHR combat knife from his ankle sheath. "I prefer this. Messy, but quieter. I've never been one to attract attention to myself."

"We both know that's not true."

"We'll discuss it later." He nodded to Trevor and sprinted back in the direction from which they'd come.

Jane put the gun in her waistband and turned back to Trevor. "Be careful," she whispered.

He hesitated. For an instant, she wasn't sure he would leave her. Then he gave her a quick kiss. "You, too."

She watched as he ran down the length of the long sand dune. She dropped to her hands and knees and started her climb to the top.

She suddenly cocked her head, listening. Had she heard a woman's voice?

Hard to tell over the sound of the pounding surf.

She continued slowly up the dune, an inch at a time.

She reached the top and drew a deep breath, listening.

No sound but the surf.

She raised her head to peer down at the beach.

A gun was leveled at her face from only a foot away!

"Welcome." The man crouching there was one of the men who had met Harriet at her plane. "She's been waiting for you. Now be very quiet, and you might live for another few minutes."

Shit. If she tried to jerk her gun out of her waistband, he'd pull the trigger.

"That's right, freeze." He rose unsteadily to his feet, slipping on the loose sand. He turned to signal someone below.

Use the distraction. Move.

She hurled herself over the dune and toppled the man who was already precariously balanced on its face. She heard him cursing as they both tumbled down the other side toward the beach.

Rolling, twisting, turning . . .

She was struggling to grasp the revolver in her waistband. She grabbed the handle just as she hit the beach and rolled over to her feet. She leveled the gun at the man who was still flat on his back but struggling to sit up. He'd lost his gun on the way down, and it was several feet away. Don't let him get near that gun again.

A shot rang out.

Pain seared the flesh of Jane's lower arm and her own gun dropped from her hand. What the hell? Jane spun around.

"In the end, a woman always has to take care of things herself if she wants them done well." Harriet was walking toward her. "Look what you've done to poor Craig. Of course, he deserved it for letting you take him by surprise."

"She didn't do anything. I . . . slipped." The man Harriet had called Craig was scowling.

"Shut up, Craig. I should have known Cartland would send me two bunglers." Harriet moved forward, her gun extended before her. "I'll take care of this from now on." She glanced at Jane's arm and smiled with satisfaction. "Good shot. Just a flesh wound, as I intended. Hardly bleeding at all. Kevin taught me, you know. I didn't want you to die before I could talk to you."

"So talk to me." The gun she'd dropped was only a few feet away. Could she reach it before Harriet pulled the trigger?

"I wanted to tell you that you've lost. That I had won." Harriet's face was full of triumphant malice. "And I wanted to see your face when you realized what a fool you were. You thought you were so clever. When Cartland told me that you'd followed me to my hotel, I had to wonder how you did it. When I got back to my room, I searched it very carefully and found all your little bugs. But that didn't tell me how you'd followed me from Muncie." Her lips twisted. "And then I thought about my Kevin's wonderful letters and how you must have committed the final desecration by going through them. And had even planted a GPS bug in the lid of the box. Can you imagine how angry that made me?"

"I don't really care."

"You'll care when I pull this trigger. Kevin and I beat you. We used your own trick to lure you out here. Kevin would have been proud of me."

"I don't doubt it. You're two of a kind. I don't know who is the more evil."

"You thought you were going to stop me?"

Harriet leveled the gun at her. "You've caused me so much trouble. I wish I could take more time with you. But I can't afford to indulge myself."

She was going to pull the trigger. Jane couldn't wait any longer. She gathered her muscles to leap for the gun she'd dropped.

"Harriet." Trevor's voice. "Don't touch her. Drop your gun."

Harriet whirled, startled, at this new attack. Her hand tightened on her weapon as she saw Trevor with a gun in hand. "Keep back. I'll kill you. I'll kill both of you." She was spitting venom. "You must be her lover, rushing to the rescue. How fitting that you'll die with the little whore."

"Get away from her, Harriet." Trevor moved a step closer. "We both have guns, but you'll be a dead woman the instant you pull that trigger. My gun is pointed at your heart, and you'll be dead in seconds. I don't think that's what you want. You have all those grand plans. Or maybe you're expecting help from that gorilla who was guarding the other side of the dune? He won't be coming. I took care of him before I moved on you." He glanced at Craig, who had made a motion toward his gun in the sand a few yards away and told him, "And there will be a bullet between your eyes if you're not very, very still."

Craig froze.

A flicker of uneasiness crossed Harriet's face. "I don't need him. I don't need either of them." She reached in her pocket and pulled out a large, clumsy-looking cell phone. "I don't need anything but this detonator. I was saving it for the grand finale after I kill Zander, but I'll set it off now if you don't put down that gun. And, if you shoot me, I'll activate it as I'm falling to the ground."

Jane inhaled sharply, her gaze on that antique phone. Millions of deaths, she thought. One touch, and millions of deaths.

"So it's a game of chicken? I won't put down my gun," Trevor said. "Don't be foolish. I couldn't be sure you wouldn't use your gun to shoot Jane. That's what this is all about. But I'll let you walk away from here. We'll be right behind you, but you'll have a little head start."

"You fool. Can't you see as long as I have this detonator that I'm the one who gives the orders?"

"No, all I see is a danger to Jane." He

met Harriet's eyes. "And I won't risk her life no matter what you threaten. Look at me. I don't care about anything else but Jane. Can't you see that? Now turn around and walk away."

She hesitated, staring at him. "You really mean it." Then she shrugged. "It's only a postponement. I swore on Kevin's soul that I'd kill the bitch." She moved away from Jane, toward the road. "And that's what I'll do. As quickly as I—" She suddenly whirled and the gun in her hand was belching fire.

Trevor flinched back as the bullets tore into his body.

Jane screamed.

Everything seemed to be moving in slow motion.

She jumped to her feet.

She had to get to Trevor.

Not fast enough.

Not fast enough.

He was falling . . .

The muzzle of Harriet's gun swung toward Jane.

"No!" Trevor was stumbling toward Jane. "Get down. Let me do—"

Then, suddenly, Caleb was there on the

scene, moving lightning fast. His knife sliced across the throat of Harriet's henchman, Craig, who was scrambling for his gun. An instant later, he was knocking Jane to the ground and covering her body with his own.

"Good . . . That's good . . . Caleb . . ." Trevor's knees buckled, and he fell, his gun firing at Harriet.

Blood blossomed on Harriet's shoulder. Then she was gone, running toward the road.

Jane didn't even look at her as she struggled to get from beneath Caleb's weight.

Trevor . . .

Agony tore through her.

Three shots. Three bullets.

She ran to him and fell to her knees.

Blood. Dear God, so much blood. Stomach. Chest.

So much blood.

"She's gone?" Trevor was looking up at her. He whispered, "You're safe?"

"She's gone." He was **alive.** She had to keep him alive. "I'll call 911 and get someone out here. Don't talk. I have to stop the blood, Trevor." She was so scared. The tears were running down her cheeks. "You hold on, okay? I have to find a way to stop the blood."

"I'll . . . hold on." He smiled at her. "It's not yet, Jane."

Not yet. Those two words scared her more than she had been before. "Not ever, Trevor."

"Ever . . . After," he said. "You shouldn't be afraid."

Today. Tomorrow. Ever After.

"Of course, I'm afraid." She started to unbutton his shirt. "I will be until I get you well. Be still. I don't want to hurt you." She pushed aside his shirt. "I **hate** that she did this. I want to—" She gasped as she saw his chest and abdomen. Three wounds and so much blood she couldn't see where one ended and the next began.

"Do you want me to try to help?" Caleb asked quietly. She hadn't known he'd come to kneel beside her. "I don't know how much of the blood flow I can stop, but I can try to direct it somewhere in his body."

"Yes, help him. Do something." She grabbed her phone and called 911 while she watched Caleb place his hands carefully on the wounds.

Was the flow slowing? Make it slow, she

prayed. Caleb knew so much about blood. He had said he was no healer, but just this once let him be able to heal Trevor.

She waited, holding her breath.

And her prayers seemed to be answered. "See, it does seem to be slowing," Jane said, relieved. "Thank you, Caleb."

"Don't thank me," he said harshly. "I couldn't stop—" He took his hands away from Trevor. "Don't thank me."

She looked at him in bewilderment.

"Then I'll thank you, Caleb," Trevor whispered. "You gave me a little time, didn't you? Precious gift . . ." His gaze was on Jane's face. "Listen . . . I have to go away now. I don't know much about this, but I don't think it's forever. But you have . . . to go on as if it is forever."

"Trevor?" She couldn't understand what he was saying. She wouldn't understand. Because if she did, it was the end of everything.

"Caleb stopped everything but the internal bleeding." His voice was unsteady. "He couldn't . . . stop that. She . . . did too much damage."

"No." She shook her head. The panic was rising. The darkness was moving closer.

"Stop talking like that. You're not going to die."

"I don't know what death . . . is, but I'm mad as hell I'm not going to be able to be with you and Joe and Eve at the barbecue on the lake. Maybe the . . . second time around." His voice seemed to be failing. "And I won't be there to take care of you and make sure that you're happy and safe and that everything—" He stopped. "That worries me."

This couldn't be happening, Jane thought dazedly. Where the hell was that ambulance? Surely someone could save him. He was so good, so special, someone had to save him. "I can take care of myself," she said brokenly. "But I want you here. You have to stay with me. Do you hear me?"

"Shh, love. You'll get through it. You're so strong." He reached up and touched her cheek. "My own love." His glance went past her to Caleb. "You know . . . what's necessary . . ."

Caleb stiffened. "No," he said emphatically. "I won't do it. You can't do this to me. I won't be used."

Trevor smiled. "Yes, you know . . ." He

turned back to Jane. "Now just hold my hand and tell . . . me you love me. Okay? I think that's all we have . . . time for."

"I do love you." She kissed him, the tears running down her cheeks. "And I'll love you forever. You gave me . . . so much. I just wish you'd stay so that I could start giving back. Please. Please do that."

"Not this . . . time. I want to give you . . . anything you want. I can't . . . do it, love . . ." His eyes were closing. "Maybe . . . Ever After . . ."

CHAPTER

18

"The medical examiner is here, Jane," Caleb said gently. "There are things to do. You have to let them take him."

She looked up at him dully. She'd been aware of the flashing lights and the techs, but it was as if they had been on another planet.

She didn't want to let go of Trevor's hand even though she knew he was no longer in that body. It would be the final parting, and she didn't think she could bear it.

"Jane," Caleb said. "Dammit, what can I do? I'll do anything you want me to do. Tell me."

He was angry. No, that wasn't it. His eyes were glittering with moisture. Strange . . .

"Jane."

They were all waiting, she realized. Waiting for her. She had to do what the world judged right and normal.

She had to let him go.

She closed her eyes. It's not really good-bye, Trevor. You said I was strong, and I'm not right now. But I have to be strong for you. They're right. It's not finished, not for you, not for me. She opened her eyes. She tried to steady her voice. "I heard you, Caleb." She put her lips for the briefest moment on Trevor's hand, then slowly, slowly released him. Stop the tears. They would only get in the way. "I'll see you later . . . Trevor."

Later, my love.

She got to her feet and turned away. She couldn't stand to see them take him away from her. "It's okay, Caleb." It was a lie. Nothing would ever be okay again. "Tell them to do their job."

She stood there, vaguely aware of Caleb's voice, the voices and movement of the ME ambulance techs, and the slamming of the ambulance doors.

"Jane." Margaret was standing beside her. Jane had been vaguely aware of her reaching out in silent sympathy from the moment she had run down to the beach when she had heard the shots. But she had been careful not to intrude on Jane's grief until now. "I'm not going to talk about Trevor right now. You're not ready. But there are things I have to tell you. I think Venable knows what happened here. You said he'd be monitoring what we were doing and would step in if he thought he should." She made a face. "I'd say death and Harriet on the loose would qualify. The police didn't bother you when they got here, but they started to question me and Caleb. Then the detective got a telephone call, and they suddenly backed off and just started the forensic stuff. I think Venable pulled strings to keep them off us until he could get here."

"You're probably right," she said dully. She had to concentrate on what Margaret was saying. "And that should be pretty soon."

"Yes."

"That's not good." She forced herself to turn and look at the flashing lights of the ambulance as the driver got back in the vehicle.

"They'll be gone in a minute," Caleb said quietly as he came back to her. "Hold on, Jane."

She **was** holding on. It's better now, Trevor. I can do it.

"Go with them, Caleb. You, too, Margaret."

He turned to face her. "We'll follow them in the car with you."

She shook her head. "I'm not going with him. Not right now."

He went still. "Why not?"

"I have something else to do." Keep your voice even. Don't break down. Every minute that passed, she was getting stronger. You were right, Trevor. I can get through this. I can do what has to be done. "You said you'd do anything. Well, I'm asking you to go with Trevor, take care of him, and do all those things that have to be done. I can't stand the thought of his being alone."

"He's dead, Jane. I know you can't think straight, but try, try." Caleb cursed beneath his breath as he saw her expression. "I know what you think you have to do. You want that bitch dead? You go with Trevor and let me do it."

She shook her head.

"My God, look at you, you're a basket case. Trevor wouldn't want you to do this. You know that, Jane."

"He would want me to be strong. She killed him, Caleb."

"Let me do it."

"I can't do that. Evil. She's so evil. She killed him to get to me. She didn't care that he was good and fine and everything that her monster of a son could never be. She just . . . destroyed him because he was in her way." She gazed at the ambulance. "She's never going to kill again. I'm going to send her to hell to join her son."

"I'm not going to be able to talk you out of this, am I?" His eyes were burning in his taut face. "I'm tempted just to knock you out until you're thinking clearer."

"Everything is very clear to me, Caleb. It couldn't be more clear."

"Look, if I get close to Harriet I can—"

"You said you'd do whatever I wanted you to do."

He stared at her in helpless fury. "Shit." Then he turned on his heel and strode toward the ambulance. "I'll take care of your dead lover. And then maybe I'll have to come back and bring your body back to the same morgue." He jumped into the passenger seat and motioned to the driver. "At least make a token effort to keep me from having to do that."

"He's right, Jane," Margaret said gently. "But it doesn't matter if he's right or wrong. You won't let me stay with you?"

She shook her head.

"I'm not going to force it. I want to do it, but I'd probably feel the same way if it was someone I loved." She gave her a quick hug. "Take care," she whispered. "And move very fast. Venable should be roaring up anytime now." She turned and moved toward the ambulance.

Jane watched the taillights of the ambulance until the vehicle disappeared around the curve in the road.

"I have to do it, Trevor," she whispered. "You'd understand. You always understood." But Caleb was right, Trevor wouldn't like it. He always wanted to keep her safe.

But her safety didn't matter any longer. Nothing mattered but Harriet's death. By

Caleb's last words, she knew he had known that, and it had added to his frustration.

Move.

If Margaret was right, Venable might be here and get in her way.

Harriet had at least an hour head start, but she would not be hiding. She would be going to Driftwood Cottage to accomplish her final act of revenge for Kevin's death. She had a destination.

And so did Jane.

As soon as she reached her car, she pulled out her phone and called Catherine.

"I've been trying to reach you," Catherine said. "We were worried. You hung up, then there was no answer when I called back later."

"Some things were happening. The last thing that I heard you say was that you thought you'd found that Driftwood Cottage. Did you find it?"

"Yes, we're on our way there now. We're about thirty minutes away at a powerboat-rental facility at a town near there. Joe Googled it, and the cottage is on the beach, surrounded by hills, but he says that there's too much danger of being spotted as you approach the cottage. It's better that we come in from the sea."

"The sea?"

"That's what he says. I trust him to know what he's doing."

"Then you'd better hurry. Harriet is on her way, too. And she's not going to care if Doane spots her coming toward the cottage."

"You're sure?"

"Yes, I'm sure. But she's wounded. She's bleeding. I don't think it's serious, but it could delay her if she has to stop the bleeding. I can only hope it does."

"Wounded?" Catherine was silent. "Jane, what the hell happened?"

If she told her, it would break the fragile balance. "I'll tell you later. Look, maybe I'm closer to the cottage than you. Give me the location." She typed in the location on the GPS. "I am closer. I'll get on the road right away."

"Wait for us. Don't do anything on your own."

"I won't be on my own."

Catherine was silent. "Jane, is everything all right with you? You sound . . ."

"Nothing is wrong." Except that her world

had ended. Except that Trevor was in the back of that ambulance and would never come back to her. "I'll call you when I reach Driftwood Cottage." She hung up and buried her head on the steering wheel.

Take just one minute.

Get control again.

One more call. She sat up and dialed Venable.

"You blew it, Jane," Venable said harshly as he picked up the call. "Stay where you are. I'm coming after you."

"I know you are. I don't care. Shut up a minute. I have to tell you something. Harriet has the detonator. I wasn't sure before, but I saw her with it. She has it, and she'll use it." She paused to steady her voice. "So do whatever you can to locate those devices and defuse them."

Silence. "We've already located them. They're in the clock towers as you said. Our flyovers picked up the plutonium signatures. I've already got a team headed inside. Very discreetly, as we agreed." His tone hardened. "But there's nothing discreet about what happened with you and Harriet Weber tonight."

"Forget being discreet. It's too late for that. By the time they get to those nukes, it will be settled one way or the other."

She hung up the phone as he started to fire questions.

She'd done what she could.

Now all that was left was getting that detonator away from Harriet and trying to save Eve.

Hurry.

Even if Harriet had been delayed by doing first aid on that wound Trevor had inflicted, she was probably close to the cottage now. When she got there, it could be only a matter of minutes until Harriet and Doane decided to make their kills.

Eve.

Panic shot through her, piercing the agony.

Eve could die.

They were so close to saving her, yet all that bitch, Harriet, had to do was to pull the trigger, and she would die.

As Trevor had died.

No, Harriet, not again. Never again.

Her foot stomped on the accelerator, and the car jumped forward.

Driftwood Cottage

"She's not here." Doane's eyes were glittering with anger as he stormed back into the cottage. "Harriet promised me that she'd be here by this time. The arrogant bitch is probably keeping me waiting on purpose. I wouldn't put it past her. She's always played games like that."

"You mean she's not eager to witness the grand execution," Zander said mockingly. "What an insult to me."

"And to you," Eve said to Doane. "Do I detect a lack of trust?"

"Shut up, both of you." He was dialing his phone. "I won't have her spoiling everything. I'm not going to let her—" He spoke harshly into the phone as she came on the line, "Where the hell are you? I'm not going to wait any longer. You can't do this to—" He broke off, listening. "I don't care what happened to you. I don't believe you anyway. Fifteen minutes. You'd better be here. I won't wait a minute longer." He punched his finger savagely down on the disconnect. "Excuses. She said that she'd been hurt and had stopped at an emergency clinic to get the blood stopped. Bullshit." He headed for the door. "She told me she was nearly here, that she'd just started over the hills. If she's telling the truth, I should be able to see her headlights from the beach." He glared at them over his shoulder. "If I don't see them in ten minutes, I'm coming back here." He smiled savagely. "And all the bitch will see when she gets here will be two corpses." The door slammed behind him.

"I believe it's time we got out of here," Zander said. "It appears that Doane isn't going to wait until Harriet darkens his door."

"I got that impression," Eve said. Her heart was pounding hard. She hadn't thought she'd be this frightened. She had known this moment was coming. "By all means, if you can pull a rabbit out of your hat and get us free, I'll be interested to see it."

"No rabbit. But you're in the right ballpark." His brow was furrowed with concentration. "I'm working on it. These handcuffs aren't easy with this broken arm."

Eve stared at him. "You really think you can pick the lock?"

"No. Not in a reasonable amount of time,

anyway." Zander shifted, and suddenly both hands popped up in front of him. His left hand was entirely free of the cuff.

Eve's eyes widened. "I thought you said—"

"I didn't pick it." He showed her his hand, which looked horribly malformed. "I dislocated my thumb and little finger. It's something I learned a while back from a very talented escape artist in Thailand who had aspirations to be Houdini."

"It looks painful."

"Not nearly as painful . . . as popping them back." He used his other hand to move his thumb and finger into their joints.

He winced. "Now for the other one. The right hand is a little more difficult because of the swelling due to the cast on my arm."

Eve watched in amazement as he did the dislocation on his other hand and slid off the remaining handcuff. He popped his thumb and finger back, then flexed both hands like a master pianist who had just finished a challenging concerto.

He grimaced. "Not pleasant. But in my profession, it comes in handy on occasion."

"I can imagine." She pointed down to his

leg cuffs. "But I doubt if you can dislocate your toes."

"Even if I could, it wouldn't help. But fortunately I can easily access these locks."

Zander reached behind him and yanked sharply on the carpet. It separated from the floor. He felt the underside of the edge and pulled up a single carpet staple, which he proceeded to bend in two places. He inserted it into the lock of his left leg cuff.

"These look daunting, but larger locks are often easier to pick than smaller ones. More room to work in." He frowned in concentration. The left cuff fell to the floor. He repeated the motion with the right leg cuff. It was off even faster.

"Now let's get you out of these ropes." He jumped to his feet and ran behind her chair. He worked at the complicated knots for a moment, then was quickly unwinding the ropes from her body. "Come on." He grabbed her hand and jerked her to her feet. She almost fell as the blood rushed back to her legs. He grabbed her by the waist and half carried her toward the door. "You'll be okay in a minute. We've got to **move.** We don't know how long we have before Doane decides to give up on Harriet."

He might have already done that, Eve thought. He had been angry and impatient and ready for the kill. The beach wasn't that far away from the cottage.

He might be on the other side of that door with a gun in his hand.

Oregon Coast

Joe cut the powerboat's engine and raised his high-powered binoculars toward the shore. "That's the cottage. We can't risk taking the boat any closer."

Gallo stood up, his gaze on the shore. "We're still miles away."

"If Eve is there, and Doane sees us coming, it's all over. We can't risk it."

Catherine took the binoculars and looked for herself. "Those objects on the beach . . . that's driftwood?"

Joe nodded. "Some of those pieces are probably ten, twelve feet tall. Amazing, aren't they?"

"Disturbing. They look like giant talons clawing up from the sand."

Joe pulled a package from a canvas bag and placed it over the side of the boat. He yanked the pull cord and a gray, six-foot raft inflated. He tied the raft to a cleat and started loading weapons into it.

Gallo studied the raft. "Quinn, I don't see how there's room in there for us and all that artillery."

"There isn't. We're swimming."

"Interesting. You're not joking?"

"No joke. We'd be too easy to spot in there anyway. I'll attach a towline to my belt and drag it in. You and Catherine can drag yourselves in."

"We weren't Navy Seals like you, Quinn."

Catherine unzipped her jacket to reveal a wet suit that accentuated her sleek, toned figure. "Stop giving him a hard time, Gallo. You swam nearly that far when we were trying to reach that sub off the coast of China."

He smiled. "But I had you standing by to aid and assist."

"If you think I'm towing you into shore, you're crazy."

"Too bad. It would have been fun. I suppose I can manage it by myself." Gallo turned toward Joe. "But I have to point out that one phone call from Catherine, and we could have an entire squadron down here backing us up. Providing you want to trust Venable again."

"I do **not**," Joe said curtly. "We've already been down that road. It almost got Eve killed. If you're not in, Gallo, just stay here. Catherine and I can handle it."

"I think you know better than that," Gallo said quietly. "I felt I had to state the options. It's too important to rush in because that's what we want to do. Do you think I don't feel the same way you do, Quinn?"

Joe met his eyes. "No, you don't feel the same. You couldn't. But I'll grant that you may feel something approaching it."

"I won't argue with you. I've told you how I feel about Eve. She's my friend and the mother of my child." Gallo pulled off his shirt and slid into a blue wet-suit top that matched the bottoms he was already wearing. "One way or another, we're getting her back today."

Joe nodded. "Damned right we are." He finished packing the raft and jumped into the water. He clipped the tether to the belt of his wet suit as Catherine and Gallo joined him. Joe started toward shore with long, powerful strokes. "Let's go get her."

"This way!" Zander pulled Eve left as they hurtled out the cottage's front door.

She pointed to a path that extended down the other direction. "That one runs parallel to the beach. I think Doane's car is—"

"No cover there. Hurry."

They ran up the hill and almost immediately found themselves in the midst of an area populated by tall rock formations. "Do you know where we're headed?" she whispered.

"No idea at all. How could I? But if he comes after us, I can take care of him."

"Without a weapon?"

"Hands and mind are weapons. Sometimes conventional weapons only get in the way."

"I still like to have them available," she said dryly.

"Okay, if you prefer." Zander moved toward a half-buried chunk of driftwood and tore off one of the branches. He held up the sharp, jagged end, about eighteen inches long, and looked at her questioningly.

Eve shook her head. "That's not going to do much good against his gun."

"Complaints. Complaints. It's all we have." He handed the branch to her. "This one's yours."

"Thanks a lot."

He broke off another sharp piece and hefted it. "Let's get moving."

They slid between the rock formations. With each twist and turn, Eve saw more spires of driftwood on the beach below them, looking like a series of insane modern-art sculptures created in a fever dream.

More like a nightmare.

She tensed.

Footsteps were pounding behind them.

Doane.

Zander's head lifted as he listened. "I believe our absence has been noticed," he murmured.

The footsteps stopped.

"Did you think you could get away?" Doane shouted. "I can track you even in the dark. I can feel you, smell you." More footsteps. "I can't risk waiting for that bitch, Harriet. It's time you paid the price. Both of you. Kevin wants his pound of flesh. Kevin's here, Eve. Can you feel him?"

She felt that familiar, icy chill run through her.

Fight it.

Fight it with everything she had.

Doane laughed maliciously. "Just like old times, Eve. Me chasing you through the wilderness . . . But this won't end as well for you. For either of you."

"Don't listen," Zander whispered, perhaps sensing how Doane's words were affecting her. "Keep moving."

They crouched low and snaked through the rocks.

Doane's voice called out. "You're going to watch each other die . . . Just as I planned, just the way it was meant to be."

What in hell was he doing with this taunting?

Of course. He was trying to provoke a response, any response, so that he could zero in on their location. Give him nothing.

She turned to Zander. "I can try to draw him toward me. If he's distracted, maybe you can make your way back to him."

Zander smiled. "You're willing to act as bait? Not this time, Eve. I'm not letting you out of my sight."

Her lips twisted. "Bad timing for a tender family moment."

"I haven't had that much experience." He grabbed her arm and pulled her forward. "So we stick together."

Blam!

A branch exploded next to her head.

She and Zander ducked as Doane rapidly fired four more shots in their direction.

They crouched lower and scrambled for a cluster of rocks ten feet ahead.

Shit. That was too damned close.

"The only way down is through me," Doane yelled. "You don't believe me?"

She and Zander continued through the rock formations, trying to stay close to the larger ones for cover.

"I promise you . . . it's a dead end. Your choice is a rock wall and a fifty-foot drop that will kill you quicker than I will."

Not likely, she thought. Doane had waited too long, and he was hungry.

She and Zander negotiated the twists and turns of the nature-built maze until she heard another sound ahead. More crashing waves, but these sounded . . . different. The rock formations abruptly ended, and Zander abruptly blocked her path.

They were standing on the edge of a sheer cliff. Waves crashed on the rocks below.

Doane was right. There was no place else to go.

"I told you so."

Eve and Zander whirled around. Doane stood fifteen feet away, with his gun trained on them.

He was smiling. "We're done now," he said softly.

"You have no choice now, Zander," Eve said in a low voice. "There's a cluster of rocks over there. Get to them and take him down when you can." She took a step forward so that she blocked Doane's view of Zander. Think. Use what she knew about Doane. She raised her voice. "Kevin doesn't want this, Doane. He told me. You're making a terrible mistake."

Doane's smile faded, his brow furrowing in puzzlement. "What?"

"You're right. You were right all along. He does live. He's with us right now."

"You're lying. Do you think I'm a fool? You've never believed me."

She'd caught him off guard. Keep his attention focused on her. She didn't sense any action from Zander behind her, but that meant nothing. He moved like a cat.

She took another step closer. "I didn't want to admit it. But how else was I able to reconstruct his face so well? Every blemish, every detail?"

Doane's pistol hand was starting to tremble. "It's what you do. His skull . . . and the pictures."

"Not like that. And I didn't see the photos until later. You saw what I did. I brought Kevin back. And the only way I was able to do that was for him to work through me. We bonded. We became one. Kevin lives and breathes through me. If you kill me, you'll be killing him all over again."

Doane was sweating. "You're lying. I was the one he wanted to join with."

"You weren't close enough. I was there, and he reached out and took. That's what Kevin always did, right? Think about that skull. Think about how much I made it look like Kevin. I'm good, but not that good. Kevin is the only one who could have done that."

Doane's eyes moistened. "Is it true? Kevin . . . ?"

"Yes. No one is that good." She raised

her hand and touched her chest. "Kevin is here."

"He should have waited for me." His hand tightened on the gun. "If you're lying, I'll—" Doane took a step toward her, then froze, his back arching.

His eyes widened, bulged. "No . . . you bitch."

He coughed. An instant later, blood dripped from his nose and mouth.

Eve started at him in bewilderment.

What was happening?

Doane fell to his knees, then tumbled face-forward onto the ground. Only then did Eve see the large knife protruding from his back.

And twenty feet behind him she saw Joe, still in his throwing stance.

Shock. Disbelief. Joy.

"Joe . . ."

"Stay there. He's not dead yet." He rushed up the trail and kicked the gun away from Doane's still-twitching hand. Then he turned to Eve, and his voice was shaking. "Are you okay?" He didn't wait for an answer but crushed her in his arms. "You don't have to answer. I heard you with Doane. You're very much okay." He kissed her. "And if you aren't, I'll make you that way. God, Eve . . ."

"I know . . ."

"It's not good form to indulge in public demonstrations of affection." Zander came out from behind the cluster of boulders. "Particularly in the presence of a botched assassination."

Joe's eyes narrowed. "Botched?"

"Well, he's not dead yet, is he? I was making my way around to do it right when you came on the scene."

"He'll be dead within a few minutes."

Zander nodded. "And it wasn't a bad throw. You were probably better when you were in the SEALs."

Joe muttered a curse and turned to Eve. "I'm not alone. I brought friends. Catherine and Gallo are on the other side of the house. We split up to search when we didn't find you in the house. Jane is on the way."

Zander was smiling at Eve. "You were truly ingenious, Eve. I'm very proud of you. I hope you had an equally inventive story ready to keep Doane from wanting to kill **me.** Just in case your little distraction didn't work."

"I would have had to be Scheherazade

to block him from that obsession." She shuddered. "From the very beginning, you were the real target." The tension and horror of the last moments were hitting home.

No, more than that. From the time Doane had taken her from the cottage and the people she loved and started her down this nightmare path of madness and terror, she had been the victim fighting for her life. It was incredibly difficult to believe that she was not still that victim.

"Eve." Joe's gaze was on her face. "It's over."

"Is it? I don't think so. Not quite yet." She walked over to Doane, who was still on the ground, gasping for breath. She looked down at him. All those days of torment and captivity, of trying to hold on to sanity, of fighting being the victim.

He had to realize that she had never been that victim, that she was the one who had won.

Eve knelt beside him. "Just so you know, Doane . . ."

He looked up at her with bloodshot eyes.

She bent lower and whispered, "I really **am** that good."

Doane looked incredulously at her, an

expression that froze forever, as one last breath escaped from his body.

Jane could feel her chest tightening with tension as she looked out at the moonlight gleaming on the sea. She had just entered the hills, and the cottage should be somewhere beyond them on this road.

Was Harriet ahead of her?

Or had she already reached the cottage?

Was Eve dead?

Jane wouldn't think of that possibility. She would just keep going and hope.

She rounded the curve and saw the cottage in the distance. It was brightly lit, but Jane could see only one car parked on the beach in front of it.

And it wasn't the Cadillac Escalade Harriet had been driving. Relief surged through her, taking her breath. Harriet hadn't reached the cottage. Not yet. Eve could still be safe.

But where was Harriet? She'd expected her to be delayed but not—

Her phone rang. Catherine.

"Eve's safe, Jane." Catherine's voice was shaking. "We got to her in time."

"Thank God. I can't believe—" Jane had

to stop as emotion overcame her. "How is she? He didn't hurt her?"

"Not physically. We'll have to see how much of the stuff he threw at her had any mental effect." She paused. "Joe killed Doane."

"Good," Jane said fiercely. "Harriet?"

"No, she's not here yet. Doane got a call from her that she'd had trouble halting the bleeding in her wound. She was supposedly approaching the hills at that time."

"I'm coming out of the hills now. I can see the cottage." She said slowly, "The only answer is that she's behind me."

"Stay where you are. We'll come up to—"

"No." She pulled off the road into the trees. "There's probably not time. And the last thing we want is for her to see you all coming after her and panic. She still has that detonator."

"All the more reason for—"

"No, Catherine." She hung up.

No, Catherine. I have to be the one to do it. She has to be mine.

She got out of the car and pulled out the revolver Caleb had given her at the sand dune. That seemed such a long time ago.

A lifetime ago. Trevor's life.

She moved away from the car, so she would have a clear view of the road.

Come on, Harriet. I'm waiting for you.

She listened.

No sound.

It would come.

She would come.

One minute.

Two minutes.

Three.

A sleek, powerful roar in the distance.

The Cadillac.

Closer. Closer.

Right around the bend.

She prepared herself and raised the gun.

Make it count, Joe had always said.

The Cadillac came around the bend.

Blam! Blam!

She blew out the two front tires.

The Cadillac went skittering across the road, and it was so close she could see Harriet's strained, angry face behind the steering wheel. Then the car was down in the ditch, and Harriet was scrambling out of it.

"You took a long time to get here," Jane called out. "That was Trevor's fault. When he shot you, he already had three bullets in him, but he still managed to pull that trigger." She heard Harriet cursing. "I hope he hurt you. Because I intend to hurt you, Harriet."

A bullet struck the metal fender of the car a foot from Jane's head.

"I told you that it was only a postponement," Harriet said viciously. "I'm glad that you showed up so that I can put an end to you. Then I'll go to that cottage and kill your precious Eve." She pulled out the cell-phone detonator. "And then I'll tend to Kevin's last bit of business."

Kevin's business. A million deaths . . .

Death.

Trevor . . .

Don't think of Trevor now. Her hand had to be steady.

She moved carefully into position.

Another bullet shattered the driver's mirror a few feet away.

"That was close, wasn't it? I told you I was a good shot."

"Yes, you did, didn't you?" Jane said. "And you are. But it won't do you any good. You won't kill me, and all your other plans are going to go down the tube. Doane screwed up, and Zander and Eve are free."

Silence. "You're lying. I talked to James not fifteen minutes ago."

"Doane is dead." She aimed carefully. "And so are you, Harriet."

"What are you talking about? You're the one who—" She screamed as her right hand exploded. The detonator dropped to the ground.

Jane quickly aimed again. She fired four shots in quick succession.

Harriet screamed again and bent double in the dirt.

Enough. It was done.

Jane got to her feet and slowly walked over to where Harriet lay on the ground.

Harriet was gazing dazedly up at her. "I'm going to get up in a minute. You . . . couldn't have hurt . . . me. Not you . . ."

"Oh, I hurt you. You were boasting how well Kevin taught you to shoot." She stared fiercely down at Harriet. "He taught you to kill. Joe taught me to shoot, too. I got pretty damn good. But it was to protect myself. Everyone thought that in the end I would never have the killer instinct. I didn't think so either until I met you."

"I'm not going to die," Harriet said as

she struggled desperately to sit up. "You're not strong enough to kill me. I'll find a way to survive. I always have, and I always will."

"You're already a dead woman. I aimed very carefully. One shot to blow your right hand off so that you wouldn't be able to press those buttons. One shot to the other hand to get rid of your gun." She added with cruel malice, "And three shots in your abdomen and chest, just like Trevor's wounds. He died very quickly. Since that stump of a hand is bleeding even heavier than his wounds, you should die even sooner. No one can save you. Not your Kevin. Not Doane."

"I'll save myself." A trickle of blood was running from the corner of her mouth. "Bitch. A weakling like you will never—" She trailed off as pain overcame her. "Why do you think you could ever—destroy me? You're like those silly children Kevin had to have. Weak. Worthless . . ."

"I have destroyed you."

"Liar." Her eyes were glazing over. "James told me he thinks Kevin . . . is becoming part of him. I . . . laughed at him. Kevin wouldn't want him. He's not strong enough. Not like me. I'm the one Kevin always . . ."

Her eyes were closing. "Kevin, help—me. I always—helped you. Sweet, sweet, beloved . . . Now you have to—help me." She roused herself, and her words came strong and biting with venom. "**Kill** her!"

For an instant, Jane felt an icy chill. And then it was gone.

And so was Harriet.

Her eyes were wide-open, staring blindly up at the night sky.

Jane stood there looking down at her for another moment. No regret. No guilt. She only wished Harriet were still alive so that she could do it again.

The true killer instinct.

Eve.

Jane picked up the detonator, turned, and slowly headed down the beach road toward the cottage on the hill. She could see the lights in the cottage casting a glare over the driftwood graveyard. Then the shadowy figures that she thought were Catherine and Gallo.

And standing on the hill beside the cottage she saw Eve, with Joe beside her.

She kept her gaze fixed on Eve as she started to climb the hill. The agony and numbness were still present, but the love and warmth of all their years together was suddenly there before her, within her. All the death and sorrow surrounded her, but Eve was alive, and that was enough for right now.

Eve stepped away from Joe and held out her arms. "Jane?"

And Jane went into her arms and laid her head on her shoulder.

Are you watching, Trevor? It's what you'd want for me.

Yesterday . . . Today . . . Tomorrow . . .

The sun was rising in a glorious, blinding burst of orange over the ocean, and Eve stood on the beach, lifting her face to the morning breeze.

Freedom.

It seemed so long since she had felt this sense of freedom from threat and ugliness. She had held that smothering fear at bay, but it had always been there in the background, waiting to pounce and take her down. Now she was almost afraid to lower her guard.

But if she didn't embrace freedom, then Doane would win.

She would not let him win.

She glanced back at the hillside, which was crawling with police and forensic teams digging up those driftwood graves. They had already found one poor little victim from the directions she'd given them. They were still searching for the other child.

"You don't have to stay here." Joe was walking down the beach toward her. "Let the police do their work." He slipped his arm about her waist. "I want to take you home."

"And I want to go home." She leaned back against him. "But I need to finish it, Joe. I can't walk away." She looked at Jane, who was sitting on a craggy rock down the beach. "But she shouldn't be here. She's hurting, Joe." She shook her head. "And she's changed."

"Yes." He brushed his lips against her temple. "And so have you."

"What? No, I haven't." She frowned. "How?"

"You're stronger. I can see it, feel it."

She was silent. "I thought maybe I was just getting harder. I hated Doane for having the power to do that to me."

"Not harder. It's just that everything that's not essentially you has been peeled away. What's left is strong . . . and beautiful."

She tried to laugh. "You're prejudiced, Joe."

"I've studied every nuance and quality that makes you who you are. No one is a better judge." He suddenly whirled her around in his arms and buried his face in her hair. "And I love every single bit of who you are." His voice was hoarse with feeling. "God, I'm glad to have you back. I was going crazy."

The pain and passion in his voice was thick with intensity, and it shook her to her core. "Me, too." Her arms tightened around him. "Doane and Harriet caused so much pain . . . and maybe the worst thing they did was giving birth to Kevin. All the evil in both of them seemed to be embodied in him. Even after he was killed, the evil seemed to grow. It reached out to me and you . . . and Jane. Oh, God, Jane."

"Give her time. She'll survive."

"No choice." She paused. "Trevor has no family. I offered to have him buried at the lake on that hill beyond the woods. Is that okay with you?"

"Of course it is. Is it okay with her?"

"I think so. She's hurting too much to

make many decisions. I'll broach it to her again after we get home."

"That's a good idea." He didn't speak for a moment. "Zander wants to speak to you. He asked me to tell you."

"He's still here? I thought he'd gone. He disappeared after all the police and CIA agents got here."

"That shouldn't surprise you. He's un-comfortable with law enforcement." His lips twisted. "And they're uncomfortable with him. Most of them would prefer he not be around for them to worry about."

"You included?" she asked quietly.

"I would have said yes several hours ago. The arrogant bastard runs his own show, and he took a big chance with you."

"And now?"

"He saved you. We might not have got-ten here in time, and he saved you. What the hell am I supposed to say? I'm still pissed off at the way he did it, but he did do it. So that means I have to be in his corner." He pushed her back away from him. "So go up and talk to him. He said to take the path that goes behind the cot-tage."

She nodded and turned away. "Why don't you go up to those rocks and sit with Jane? She won't want to talk, but she'll like it that you're there." She didn't wait for an answer but started across the beach toward the hills.

The path wound behind that driftwood graveyard down the hill and around to the next hill. It was only as she turned the last bend that she saw the smoke curling from a small fire.

Zander was sitting cross-legged in front of the fire, and he looked up as he saw her. "Does this remind you of that campfire we shared in Colorado?" He smiled. "That seems a long time ago, doesn't it?"

"Not really. Not to me." She sat down opposite him. "And I don't think you asked me to come here to reminisce. That's not your style, Zander."

"And why do you think I did want to see you?"

"I don't know. But I know why I wanted to see you." She paused. "You saved my life. I wanted to thank you."

"Don't be maudlin."

"Gratitude is not maudlin. And you're not accepting it at all graciously. But, then, I didn't expect anything else. It's too human and probably makes you feel uncomfortable."

"Very perceptive. You've gotten to know me entirely too well. It's time we parted company."

She stiffened. "By all means, don't stay around anyone who might make you feel something besides curiosity and boredom."

"My thought exactly. That could be very dangerous for me. Look what happened with you. I got a busted arm and almost ended up dead."

"I never asked anything of you."

"I know," he said softly. "That's the problem." He looked across the fire at her. "You make me ask it of myself. How much more dangerous that is, Eve."

She couldn't look away from him. He had become so close to her. How could that be when she still didn't understand him? He was an enigma that she wasn't sure she could ever solve. But she wanted to solve it, she realized with sudden desperation. She wanted to understand him. "So you're telling me that you're leaving? I didn't expect anything else. It's not as if you have anything to keep you here."

He nodded. "That's right. Nothing at all. Nothing has changed." He smiled. "And I didn't bring you here to bid you a fatherly farewell. As you said, not my style."

"Why did you bring me?"

"I have a good-bye gift for you."

"What? Now that's truly maudlin, Zander."

"No one would ever describe this gift as maudlin." He reached behind him into the tall grass and brought out a leather case. "I don't think you would either."

She stiffened. She knew that case too well. "Is this your idea of humor?"

"Would I be that cruel? Well, I would, but not to you, Eve." He unfastened the case. "No, this is a true gift. You're never going to forget these days with Doane, but you have a chance of its gradually blurring. But not if you know this is somewhere in the world." He drew out the reconstruction of Kevin and studied it. "You did a magnificent job on him. He's been with you every minute, in your mind, under your fingers. The stuff of nightmares . . ."

"Yes." She forced herself to look at the reconstruction. Is it over, Kevin? Has your power to silence vanished? Have you faded back to the hell from where you came?

No smothering sense of evil.

No reaching out to grasp and take.

Has he gone, Bonnie?

"He frightened you?" Zander's gaze was narrowed on her face. "Why?"

"You wouldn't understand." But the fear was gone, she realized. Bonnie's answer?

"No, I probably wouldn't. But I do understand about nightmares." He smiled. "I believe I'll take this one away from you."

"What do you mean?"

"If this skull exists somewhere, it will always haunt you. So it will no longer exist." He held out the reconstruction to her. "Do you wish to make sure of that? Or would you like me to do it? I thought I'd offer you the opportunity."

"What opportunity?"

"Can't you guess? Why do you think I built this fine fire? Five years ago, I sent Kevin's body to a crematorium to be burned. If Doane hadn't snatched his head from the blaze, you wouldn't have had to deal with putting his skull back together." He added mockingly, "Now I can correct that little error."

Her eyes widened. "You're going to burn this reconstruction?"

"I regret burning your wonderful work, but I prefer to think of it only as Kevin's skull. And I'm going to burn Kevin's skull to ashes. Then I'm going to toss those ashes into the most disgusting mire I can find. I thought about the ocean, but that would be too clean for him."

"Yes, it would."

"I won't ask if you approve. Your work is to save, not destroy. I just wanted you to know it was being done and that you could trust me to do it right."

She gazed at Kevin's handsome features, which reflected none of the evil that had corroded his soul. All the murders, all the innocent children . . . She felt suddenly sick. No one should ever look at him again and not know what he was. And she would not let Zander be responsible for doing what she thought was right. "I trust you." She took the reconstruction from him. "But I won't let you do it alone." She took a deep breath and threw the skull into the flames.

The fire leaped high and hungry as if in blazing welcome.

She stared at the skull as the fire began to consume it.

"It's time for you to go," Zander said quietly. "You've made your decision and acted on it. You don't need to see it happen. It will take a long time for it to burn down to ashes. In a furnace, the heat is more intense, but this fire will do what's necessary. I'll tend it all day and all night, longer if need be. Then I'll dispose of the ashes."

She got to her feet and moved toward the path. No, not like this. She wouldn't leave him like this. She turned and looked at him. "Thank you for my gift, Zander."

He grimaced. "I'm happy you're pleased. I thought you'd think it was a suitable good-bye present for a man of my profession and character."

"You never do anything that's suitable. But it's a gift that I'll remember you thought about, then gave to bring me peace. That's a very precious gift, Zander."

He looked a little taken aback. "Are you getting maudlin again?"

"No. I'm being sincere. I know it's hard for you to recognize the difference. I think I may have to teach it to you." She met his eyes. "Because if this is a good-bye present, you've wasted it. I'm not saying good-bye to you."

"You're not? You may not have a choice."

"Bullshit. I'm not intruding into your life, but I'm in it now, and I won't be thrown out. You did that when I was ten years old. It's not going to happen again."

He smiled faintly. "You're intimidating me, Eve. And your judgment is very, very faulty. Do you really want to have anything to do with a lost soul like me?"

"I don't know. It depends on you . . . and me. But it's not good-bye." She started up the path. "So we'll see how it goes."

He chuckled. "Because your Bonnie believes in second chances?"

"Because **your granddaughter** believes in second chances." She didn't look back. "And so do I, Zander."

Epilogue

Lake Cottage
Atlanta, Georgia
Four Days Later

"Déjà vu," Catherine said to Kendra as she gazed down from the porch at the guests milling on the grounds below her. "It reminds me of the day that I was here for that phony memorial service for Eve." No, not really, she thought. There were no public figures or media at Trevor's funeral. Only the people who had been on the hunt for Eve and a dozen or so friends of Trevor's who had flown in from Europe. They were all moving from group to group, talking soberly. Except for Seth Caleb, who was standing apart and alone, drinking a glass of wine. Her gaze rested on him for an instant before moving on. That fascinating face always made her pause, and particularly today, when she could sense the tension behind it. "I was so angry and bewildered when I showed up here that day . . ."

"And relieved when you found out she was still alive," Kendra said. "God, it's good to have her back. I only wish to hell that this was a celebration and not a genuine funeral." Her gaze was focused on Eve and Jane, who were standing together down by the lake. "Jane is managing to hold it together, but I don't know for how long."

"As long as she has to do it." Catherine had watched Jane all through Trevor's funeral and burial this morning, and her heart had ached for her. She had been pale, tragic, but there had also been strength and endurance. "And she has Eve. You can almost see Eve . . ." She tried to find the words to describe the bond between the two women. "She's kind of spreading invisible wings to enfold her Jane." She suddenly stiffened. "There's Venable. I wasn't sure he'd be here. He was pretty pissed off at Jane for not letting him know about Harriet sooner." She headed for the steps.

"I'm going to intercept him and make sure that he doesn't say anything to her."

"He wouldn't be that insensitive, would he?" Kendra asked.

"I don't think so, but I'm not taking any chances." Catherine glanced back over her shoulder. "And he should thank you for figuring out where those nukes were located. Who knows how long it would have taken him to find out where Kevin placed those devices? It could have been a threat for years."

"Stop it," she said testily. "I don't want thanks. I had my fill of it with Eve when I got here. She's free and back home, and that's all that matters." Her gaze returned to Eve and Jane. "And we can only hope that the healing begins soon."

Catherine silently seconded that wish as she ran down the steps. Healing for Eve, who had been tortured mentally and physically. Healing for Jane, who had lost even more than Eve.

Venable was gazing at her with a sardonic smile as she came toward him. "Catherine to the rescue?"

"It depends on how much of an asshole

you turn out to be," she said soberly. "You're not getting near Jane if you're here to give her even one word of condemnation. She's had enough."

"I agree," he said. "Though she was wrong, and I was right." He added, "And, by complicity, you were also wrong, Catherine."

She lifted her chin. "Then fire me, Venable. You could make a good case."

"I thought about it." He shrugged. "But I'd be cutting off my nose to spite my face. You're the best of the best. I'll need you next week when I send you to Guatemala City."

"I'm not going anywhere next week but home to my son. Find someone else."

"I could hold your disloyalty over your head and—" He broke off, then said wearily, "But I won't do it. I'm tired of being the bad guy. Someone's got to do it, but not me. Not right now. I've got to go over there and try to explain to Eve why I was willing to risk her life. I like Eve and Joe and Jane, and I let them all stay under the gun. They may never forgive me because I can't even say I'm sorry."

"Maybe," Catherine said. "You'll just have

to try. You might begin by expressing your condolences to Jane for losing the man she loved. It might establish a rapport that could carry you through."

"I was going to do that," Venable said. "I'm not that much of a bastard."

"No, you're a good guy when you're not trying to save democracy." But she was suddenly bone weary of dealing with Venable and his agendas. "But I don't care about jumping back on your bandwagon right now. Go do your duty and clear the way for me to say my good-byes. By midnight, I'm going to be on a jet to Hong Kong, and tomorrow I'll be with Luke and Hu Chang."

"Really?" His brows rose as his gaze wandered through the crowd to a table where Gallo stood talking to Margaret. "And what about him?"

Catherine's gaze followed his, and she felt the familiar jolt of pure sexuality as he lifted his eyes and saw her. He smiled faintly and inclined his head.

Heat.

Electricity.

Both of which interfered with what she had to do. He was a complication. She needed her son and her best friend in the world and not to be swept away by Gallo. She turned away. "I'm leaving for Hong Kong," she repeated.

"He'll follow you," Venable said softly.

"I can't stop him. He'll have to do what he has to do. He won't have an invitation."

"You could avoid him by going to Guatemala City."

She ruefully shook her head. Venable was as obstinate as a mule. "No way." She started to make her way through the crowd toward Joe, to say her good-byes to him. "Find someone else, Venable."

"You're exhausted, Jane," Eve said in a low voice. "Go on up to the cottage and go to bed. There are only a few people left, and they'll understand."

Jane shook her head. "I'll wait. I don't want to leave it up to you. Trevor was my—" For an instant she lost track of what she had been about to say. He was my heart. My life. My love. "All of this is my responsibility. It was kind of you to offer this service, but you shouldn't have to—"

"Oh, be quiet, Jane," Eve said. "This has nothing to do with kindness. This has to do with family, and if you weren't in shock, you'd realize that. Joe and I only want to get you through this. That's all that's important."

"No, what's important is that I have you and Joe beside me," she said unsteadily. "You've kept me from falling apart during these last few days. I know I've been behaving like a sleepwalker. It's not fair to you."

"You'd have gotten through it on your own. You're tough." Eve touched her arm affectionately. "It was our privilege to be with you. But now it's my privilege to send you to bed. Scoot." She gave Jane a quick kiss on the cheek. "If you won't go to bed until everyone has gone, I'll see that they take the hint." As she started to turn away, she stopped and glanced at Seth Caleb, who was standing alone a few yards away. He had a glass of wine in his hand and he lifted it to Eve as he met her gaze. "But I'm not sure that Caleb will take the hint. I may have to send Joe to reinforce it. He's been hovering over you like an eagle who's spied prey."

The last thing Jane wanted was a confrontation between Joe and Caleb. "Leave Joe out of it. It will be okay. Caleb has been very civilized ever since he got here today."

She tried to smile. "Even subdued. That's a first for him."

"You'd know better than I," Eve said. "He didn't look subdued to me. He looked like a hurricane waiting to happen. I won't have him upset you."

"He can't upset me." Not today. Everything that could be done to her had been done. "Stop worrying, Eve. He might just be waiting to offer his condolences."

"Yeah, maybe," Eve said doubtfully. "Just motion to me if he gives you grief." She moved toward the remaining pockets of guests. "I'll be there for you."

Eve was always there for her, Jane thought lovingly as she watched her. Ready to do battle. Ready to offer a shoulder to comfort.

"I'm surprised she left you alone." Caleb was at her elbow. "She's been guarding you all day." He lifted his wine to his lips. "We've all been in protective mode toward Eve, and now she's returning the favor."

"Hello, Caleb. Eve knows you're volatile, and she didn't want me to have to deal with you today. She wasn't sure if I could handle it."

"Can you?"

"I can handle it. I can handle you." She added wearily, "But I don't want to do it today."

"I know," he said curtly. "You're so fragile, a wind could blow you away. You're bleeding inside. I can see it. Feel it."

"Am I? I guess you're probably right. At least, figuratively. You know a lot about blood."

"Not enough to save your lover."

She stiffened. "No, you couldn't do that. Though you did try."

"You bet I did." His dark eyes were glittering in his taut face. "I tried everything I knew. I didn't want Trevor to die. I knew it would be like this. Now he's a damn martyr. How can I fight a martyr?"

"Do you mind if we don't talk about this right now?" she said unevenly. "I think perhaps it's time you left, Caleb."

"Yes, it is. But I can't go until I've said what I have to say. It's been seething inside me, and it has to come out." His grasp tightened on the delicate stem of his glass. "And all these fine people who love you and sympathize with your loss would tell me not to put you through this. But everyone knows what a selfish bastard I am."

"You weren't selfish when you tried to save me from being shot. You covered me with your body."

"Unusual circumstances. I didn't think, I just acted." He took a step closer to her, and said through his teeth, "I was **angry.** She was going to kill you. She'd already shot Trevor."

"You still did it."

"Don't make the mistake of thinking I'm all that's good and noble like Trevor. I'm not like him. I **won't** be like him."

"No, there's no one who could be like Trevor." She smiled faintly. "And he wouldn't like you calling him noble. I remember that when you did it before, he laughed at you."

"He laughed because we were so different. He had a code of honor, and I am what I am. We weren't even on the same page." His lips tightened. "And yet he said I could be anything I wanted to be."

"I remember that."

"But I won't be what **he** wants me to be." His voice was suddenly harsh. "I liked that son of a bitch. I didn't want to like him, but I did anyway. Even at the end, I was mad as hell because I couldn't save him."

His dark gaze was burning into her own. "And then he looked at me, and I knew what he was thinking, what he wanted of me. It was all about you."

She shook her head in bewilderment. "I don't know what you mean."

"He had an obsession about taking care of you, of making sure you were safe and well. He was crazy about you, so that shouldn't be surprising. But even as he was dying, he was worrying about you."

"I know." She tried to keep her voice from breaking. "That was Trevor."

"But he found a solution, didn't he? He looked at me, and I could see what he was thinking. What he was asking. You didn't even realize that, did you?"

"I still don't."

"He wants me to take care of you, to keep you from being unhappy, to guard you." His voice was harsh with exasperation and anger. "He wants me to be **him,** dammit."

"That's crazy."

"Do you think I don't know that? Even Trevor couldn't believe that I'd be able to change dark to light. But he wanted to tie my hands. And he was willing to let me stand in and take care of what he regarded as necessary."

She shook her head. "You have to be mistaken."

"Am I? Think about it."

"And, if you're not mistaken, then you're still not someone who would let your life be influenced by Trevor's irrational wish. He was dying, Caleb."

"A dying man's last wish," Caleb said. "You're right, a callous bastard like me shouldn't pay any attention to it. Because if I did, it would interfere with everything I intend to do to you and with you. I can overcome this setback. Given time, memories will fade, and I'll be ready."

She shook her head.

He smiled. "You don't think so now, but it will happen."

His voice was soft and silky, the passionate intensity nearly tangible. She could suddenly feel the force, the power, the fire of him. She instinctively took a step back. "My memories of Trevor won't fade."

"Then you won't be doing what Trevor wanted you to do. He didn't want you to look back. Remember what he said when he knew he was dying."

You have to think of it as forever.

"It doesn't matter. I can't let him go." She moistened her lips. "I'm going to go to bed now. Please leave, Caleb."

He nodded jerkily. "That's all I have to say. You won't see me for a while. I'm sure you'll be relieved."

She nodded. "You disturb me. I don't need that right now."

"It's the nature of the beast." He paused. "Aren't you curious why I'm so angry about what Trevor did?"

"He did nothing. He expressed a wish."

"He did more than that. He managed to delve deep and brought up feelings that I've kept buried and forgotten. I found my-self wanting to do what he wanted me to do. Why do you think I've been staying in the background for the last few days? I was taking care of you, dammit. Do you think I don't know I disturb you? I was be-ing sensitive."

"I'm sure it was only temporary. But you managed to forget all about sensitivity to-night."

"Because I was going away, and I had to let you know why. I wasn't about to fade into the sunset."

Darkness outlined in flames.

"I don't think that's possible for you."

"And my going away is because I want to give you a chance to heal. That damn sensitivity again. I want to move forward, not retreat."

"Then I'm glad you had second thoughts. There's nothing for you here."

He ignored her response. "And I don't think that instinct to take care of you was temporary. I've noticed the effect is still lingering. God knows, I hope it's temporary. The last thing I want is to be chained like that. I watched you suffering today, and it nearly killed me. But it was my pain and had nothing to do with Trevor or what he wanted from me. That's how it has to be. Oh, I'll let Trevor tie my hands for a while. I'll do what he wanted." He finished his wine with one swallow. "But I'll get over it." He put his glass on the table beside him, and she could sense the frustration and anger back in full force. "I'll fight it until I break free." He smiled recklessly. "Just thought I'd give you warning."

He turned and walked away from her.

She felt limp with emotion as she watched him. She'd thought she was numb, but he'd managed to make her come alive. He'd aroused her to bewilderment and ruthlessly inserted his presence in her mind.

And he'd brought back that agonizing memory of Trevor's dying and her not being able to help him. It was never far from her, but she'd forgotten some of the nuances that concerned Caleb. Caleb trying to save him. Caleb angry and rejecting being used by Trevor.

Trevor gentle and loving and trying to protect her even after he was gone.

She felt the sting of tears. Why Caleb, Trevor? You might as well have set a hungry tiger to guard a flock of sheep. I don't need him. I don't need anyone but you.

She was losing control. She had to get away from there to the safety of the cottage before she broke down. She moved quickly toward the porch steps.

"Jane."

She stopped at the steps as Margaret appeared beside her. She hadn't seen her for more than a few moments today, but she'd been aware of her always there, helping Eve, talking to Joe. "Hi, Margaret." She swallowed. "Thank you for being here. I meant to—"

"Stop being polite," Margaret said bluntly. "Are you okay? I saw Caleb with you. I was watching him today, and all the lightning was flashing around him."

"That's a strange term. The lightning didn't strike me. He wasn't gentle, and he jarred me. But I survived it." She smiled shakily. "But now I need some alone time. I was numb, and now I feel too much alive."

"Caleb generates that emotion. I think it's part of that wild DNA." She shrugged. "Most of the time, that's not such a bad thing. Maybe this is an exception. Maybe not. You've been a sleepwalker for the last few days." She made a face. "Completely understandable. I'll let you go up and get to bed. I just wanted to say good-bye."

"You're leaving?"

"You don't need me. You have Eve." She gave her a hug. "I envy you Eve and Joe. It must have been wonderful growing up with them."

"Yes, wonderful. Are you going back to Summer Island? Devon called and told me that my dog, Toby, is doing well, but she wants to keep him with the other dogs for a while. She says he's responding to the contact therapy and acting like a puppy. I'd like to know you're with him."

"I'm not going there right away. Kendra's invited me to come out to San Diego to her place for a visit. It should be interesting."

"And fairly explosive. You two seem to strike sparks wherever you are." She kissed her cheek. "Thank you, Margaret. Keep safe. I'll miss you."

"No, you won't. I'll be around. You can never tell when I'll come knocking on your door." She turned away. "Now go upstairs and rest. I'll help Eve shoo everyone else away and clean up."

Jane didn't argue. She started up the steps. The heaviness and sadness were becoming overwhelming. Another good-bye from someone who had become her good friend.

And the final good-bye to her love.

2:35 A.M.

"God, you're tense." Joe cuddled Eve closer in bed. "Jane?"

Eve nodded. "I just heard her go down

the hall toward the porch. She's not sleeping again."

"She always loved the porch. From the time we brought her home, the two of you would sit out there for hours."

"I want to help her, Joe. There ought to be something I can do, something I can say."

"You've said all the right things. You just have to wait for her to heal." He raised himself to rest on one arm and looked down at her. "I know that sounds lame. I don't know what else to tell you."

She gave him a quick kiss. "It doesn't sound lame. It sounds like you trying to give me comfort and love. There's nothing lame about that." Her arms slid around him, and she buried her face in his chest. He smelled of soap and lemon and the musky essence that was Joe himself. She remembered all the nights while she was with Doane that she had tried not to think of Joe's smell, the feel of him. It had hurt too much. "I was lying here thinking how lucky I am that I have you," she whispered. "And that I mustn't ever take you for granted. You close your eyes, and suddenly love and all the beautiful things it brings can slip away from you."

"Yeah." He cleared his throat. "Only I didn't have to find that out. I've known it from the moment I met you. I've never taken you for granted, Eve." His arms tightened around her. "I never will."

"We have so much, Joe." She could feel the tears sting her eyes. "What a rich life we've built together, the years, the experiences, so many memories."

"And you're thinking that Jane will never have that."

"I hope she will. Somehow. Sometime." She reached up and gently touched his cheek. It was hard with the faintest stubble. Everything about him was hard and warm and vibrantly alive. God, please keep him this way. Keep him strong and well and full of laughter and joy. Never take him away from me. "I love you, Joe."

"Thank God." He kissed her, long and deep. "I know that." He suddenly pulled her up in bed. "I also know that you're sad and want to help our Jane." He got to his feet and held her robe for her. "So go out there on the porch and work it out between you like you always do."

She hesitated, gazing at him. "But I don't want to leave you."

"I'll be here when you get back." He smiled. "Always, Eve."

She glanced back at him as she opened the door. There had been some deeper meaning in those last words. Joe could read her so well. Had he also read that silent prayer for God to care for him and keep him by her side?

"I'll be waiting. Never doubt it." He repeated softly, "Always . . ."

"What are you doing out here, Jane?" Eve asked as she stood in the doorway leading to the porch. She came over to the swing where Jane was sitting. "It's the middle of the night. I hoped you were sleeping, dammit."

"I tried. It didn't work. I didn't mean to wake you." Her gaze went to the lake. "It's beautiful, isn't it? Trevor and I spent a weekend on Lake Como once. But this is just as wonderful. I told him that I wanted to be here with him when Joe barbecued. He even mentioned it at the last . . ." She had to stop and steady her voice. "Sorry. I know you have to be tired of me not being able to—I should be stronger. You shouldn't have to put up with it. I've been thinking that maybe I should go back to London and start working."

"You'll do what you think is best for you. Work can be a salvation." She sat down beside her on the swing. "But not because you think you're being a bother to us. Give yourself a little time. It's not even been a week, Jane."

"It seems longer." She was silent for a moment, then whispered, "It hurts, Eve. He was so . . . God, I miss him. I keep remembering everything about him. The day I met him when I was only seventeen. Do you remember that day? He looked like a movie star and could charm the birds from the trees. You were worried I'd be dazzled by him."

"And you were," Eve said. "You were too young. I was grateful that he had some sense and walked away from you."

"I'm not. They were wasted years. Maybe if I'd followed him then, I'd not have become so set in my ways, and we'd have worked our relationship out earlier." She gestured. "I know. What-ifs are useless. He's gone, and I have to deal with it."

"Oh, Jane, it's natural to have regrets." She leaned back in the swing. "After I lost

Bonnie, I thought I'd go crazy thinking about all the things I should have done and didn't. She wanted a puppy, and I didn't get it for her. I was going to get one for her that Christmas. But that Christmas didn't come for her. There were so many things . . ."

"You gave me my puppy, Toby, after I came to you. Was that why?"

"Probably. I wanted desperately for you to be happy. I'd learned by then that you live for the day and not tomorrow."

"Because tomorrow might not come." She looked out at the lake again. "But you think tomorrow did come, don't you, Eve? You think Bonnie comes back to you."

"Yes," Eve said quietly. "I know she does. I've never kept it a secret." She paused. "But you have trouble believing it, so I didn't want to make you uncomfortable by mentioning it."

"You know me, hardheaded realist. But if it brought you peace, I wanted you to have it. I wanted you to have anything that would make you happy."

"Peace and happiness . . . Yes, she brings me both."

"I . . . like the idea of death not being the end. I never thought much about it. I was too busy living. Now all of a sudden . . ." She had to stop again. "Trevor said he didn't know anything about it either, but he thought there was something more . . ."

"He was right." She pulled Jane to her and nestled her head on her shoulder. "So much more, Jane. But no one can tell you. You have to find it for yourself."

"I guess so." She could feel Eve's heartbeat and smelled the clean smell of the soap she used. It brought comfort and healing to the aching void that seemed to span the world. "I can't believe what you say about Bonnie. I'm sorry. I want so badly to believe it, but I can't."

"Don't be sorry." Eve brushed a kiss on her forehead. "You don't have to accept anything that I say except when I tell you that I love you. Now hush and try to relax. I want you to be able to sleep."

They were silent for several moments, listening to the cool breeze rustle the branches of the pine trees. How often during the past years had they been out here together, Jane thought. Talking, laughing at Toby's antics, just unwinding from the day. She had never dreamed that one night she would be clinging to Eve and having a conversation that was this heartbreakingly painful. She should have known this day would come. Life was never perfect. She finally raised her head. "I'm keeping you up. You should be getting to sleep, too. Didn't I see the FedEx man deliver something day before yesterday? Are you starting to work?"

"Yes, providing you don't need me. I can put it off."

"No, don't let me get in the way. You've wasted enough time on me." She jumped to her feet and pulled Eve up. "I guess I wasn't thinking." She grimaced. "Only feeling. Life goes on."

"It wasn't a waste. It's strange that the terrible thing that happened to me had a domino effect on the people who care for both of us. Friendships became stronger, characters became defined, confusion became clear. And you found and lost something pretty damn wonderful. Good or tragic, it wasn't a waste. It made us stronger." She put her arm around Jane's waist as they walked toward the door. "And I needed the time to get my head together, too. Doing Kevin's reconstruction was like nothing I've ever experienced. It will be good to get back to doing reconstruction on children instead of monsters." She glanced at Jane as she opened the door. "Yes, life goes on. Bad, good, or indifferent. Whatever it is, we have to open our mind and heart to it." She smiled. "Now I'm done preaching." She gave a mock yawn. "Time I headed for bed before I get too disgustingly sanctimonious. Good night, Jane." Her voice trailed behind her as she moved down the hall. "If you need me, call . . ."

She wouldn't call, Jane thought as she followed Eve down the hall. Eve had already given her too much time when she had her own nightmares to lay to rest.

Jane's nightmares would come as they had every night since Trevor's death. She had carefully hidden that from Eve. Then, after the nightmares, she would wake, and the tears that wouldn't stop followed.

Maybe not tonight.

Maybe she could hold off the memories of that night of death that brought those nightmares. Trevor had said she was strong.

Let her be strong tonight.

The nightmare was the same. Jane woke from it with tears running down her cheeks.

She sat up in bed, breathing hard.

Don't let go.

Don't give in.

Take control.

Dear God, it was hard. The despair seemed to be deep and endless.

You shouldn't have died, Trevor. You had everything to live for. I would have made your life so good. If anyone had to die that night, it should have been me.

The pain wouldn't go away. It was starting to overwhelm her.

Don't cry.

Hold on.

Ever . . . After. You shouldn't be afraid.

Yes, that's what he had said. She could hear it as if he were in this room.

Today. Tomorrow. Ever After.

You should be here now. I should be able to touch you, tell you how much I love you.

I don't think it's forever. But you have . . . to go on as if it is forever.

I want to **see** you again. Maybe if I concentrate hard enough . . . Eve says she believes Bonnie comes to her. I don't care if it's just some hallucination. It brings her happiness . . . She lifted her hand to push her hair back from her face. I know, I'm acting crazy. You wouldn't be proud of me now.

Shh, love. You'll get through it. You're so strong. My own love . . .

Maybe if I concentrate, I can imagine—

"He doesn't want you to do that, Jane. You have to remember what he said to you."

She stiffened. Those weren't the words Trevor had spoken that night. Maybe she truly was beginning to hallucinate.

"Trevor?"

"No, he won't come to you. He said it wouldn't be good for you. You're so stubborn. You hold on with all your strength and won't let go. He has to protect you from hurting yourself."

Trevor always was trying to guard her, even in this weird hallucination, she thought with a bitter pang.

"It's not a hallucination. Eve told you that you had to open your mind and heart. You've done it, Jane. Can't you feel it?"

"I can feel that I'm talking to some figment of my imagination."

"And not the someone you want to be

there." **Soft laughter. "But I'll have to do. Trevor sent me to explain why you have to put the thought of him aside. Oh, you'll keep him in your memory and your heart, but he wants you to have your life. It hurts him that you're hurting."**

"I don't want to hear this."

"Because it means starting to give him up. It's what he wants, Jane."

"No, he loves me. He'd want—" He'd want her to have freedom and happiness and no chains. The gentle answer came drifting like a warm cloud out of nowhere.

"And he can't have chains either. He has so much to do there."

"There? Not here? You're not with him in the great beyond?" she asked mockingly. "This hallucination needs proofing."

"No, I'm not with him now. Close your eyes. Where am I, Jane?"

"Is this a game?" Jane closed her eyes. "I'll play along. Sort of hide-and—"

She stiffened.

A presence.

Gentle.

Knowing.

"Here."

Her eyes flew open. She swung her legs to the floor and jumped out of bed.

The next moment, she was out of the bedroom and running down the hall. Her heart was pounding. Open your mind and heart . . .

She threw open the porch door.

"Hello, Jane. I've been waiting for you a long time."

The little red-haired girl sitting cross-legged on the porch swing smiled at her. **"This will be much better. Now we can talk, and I can make you understand so many things."** She tilted her head, and her smile became luminous. **"You do know who I am?"**

Jane stared at her for an instant, as the shock and bewilderment faded away. "Yes, I know you." She started toward her. No dream. No hallucination. Proof of Forever. Proof of Ever After. "You're Bonnie."